This was lust, plain and simple, and that wasn't acceptable. So what if he looked at her with heat in his eyes? What man didn't? Of course he wanted her—her nature, her raison d'être, was to be an object of desire for males. But that didn't mean she had to fulfill those desires; not when another one of her girls would serve that purpose just fine.

"I *am* doing what I want, Mr. Rand," she said firmly. "Let's go find you another woman."

Surprise crossed his features, and she felt the thrill of a minor victory. Apparently he was a man used to getting what he asked for.

"I want you," he said, and she fought an unexpected rush of pleasure.

"And if I don't want you?"

He pressed a hand to his chest. "I think that would break my heart."

With her most seductive smile playing on her lips, she leaned forward and caressed his cheek. "I guess you'll have to learn to live with disappointment."

BOOKS BY J. K. BECK

When Blood Calls
When Pleasure Rules
When Wicked Craves

WHEN PLEASURE RULES

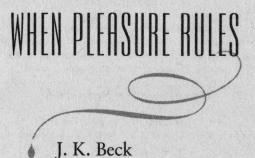

J. K. Beck

BANTAM BOOKS
NEW YORK

When Pleasure Rules is a work of fiction. Names, characters, places, and incidents are the products of the author's imagination or are used fictitiously. Any resemblance to actual events, locales, or persons, living or dead, is entirely coincidental.

A Bantam Books Mass Market Original

Copyright © 2010 by Julie Kenner
Excerpt from *When Wicked Craves* by J. K. Beck copyright © 2010 by Julie Kenner

Published in the United States by Bantam Books, an imprint of The Random House Publishing Group, a division of Random House, Inc., New York.

BANTAM BOOKS is a registered trademark of Random House, Inc., and the colophon is a trademark of Random House, Inc.

ISBN 978-0-440-24578-0

This book contains an excerpt from the forthcoming novel *When Wicked Craves* by J. K. Beck. This excerpt has been set for this edition only and may not reflect the final content of the forthcoming novel.

Cover art: Cliff Nielsen

Printed in the United States of America

www.bantamdell.com

2 4 6 8 9 7 5 3 1

Thanks to Aaron for the late-night IMs, Jess for the insane speed of her reads, Kathleen for the long, chatty phone calls, Catherine and Isabella for (mostly) respecting that Mommy's closed door means Mommy is working, and Don for a thousand and one games of Trouble to entertain the kids when Mommy needed to finish "just one more page."

WHEN PLEASURE RULES

CHAPTER 1

The shadowed moon hung low in the Parisian sky, thin fingers of dark clouds obscuring its feeble glow.

Only 72 percent waxing gibbous. Not enough to wrench the wolf within free, but more than sufficient to wake it.

A dozen years ago, Rand wouldn't have known a lunar phase from a lunatic fringe. Now those phases burned in his blood, his power and strength growing with the moon.

Within, the animal writhed, ready to hunt. Ready to end this thing.

He made no noise as he followed the Avenue des Peupliers toward the Avenue Neigre in the Cimetière du Père Lachaise. On either side of him, the houses of the dead rose in the moonlight, their smooth stone surfaces gleaming.

He slid into the shadows and closed his eyes, letting the sounds of the night surround him, the scents find him. He'd been a soldier before the change, first on the streets of Los Angeles, later in Saudi, in Bosnia, in the Middle East. A kid who'd protected his turf. A soldier who'd targeted enemies of the state.

He remained a hunter now. A wolf stalking its prey.

The change had intensified his senses and augmented his strength. He could see now regardless of the level of illum, with his own eyes instead of the night optics he'd trained with so many years ago. But this enemy could do the same, so the darkness gave him no advantage. But the moon remained his ally, and even at only 72 percent, he could hear the softest whisper, could catch the faintest scent. The brush of wind over wood. The scurrying of insects. The scent of rotting corpses.

There.

He opened his eyes, twisting his head as he caught the para-daemon's earthen scent, like decaying leaves mixed with shit. He followed it, the excitement of the hunt burning in his gut as he stole down the cobbled street and then onto the narrow gravel lane that was the Champs Bertolie.

His muscles were tight and ready to pound the bastard, but he'd brought weapons with him, too. The Ka-Bar sheathed at his thigh. The switchblade in his hand. The length of wire he'd habitually kept in his pocket since the week before his ninth birthday. They were as much a part of him as the wolf that writhed within.

He'd dressed in black, his dark skin smeared with camo paint and his shaved scalp covered by black knit, rendering him nothing more than a shadow in the darkness. He heard the sharp snap of a grate creaking open and realized his target had entered one of the tombs. Rand sniffed the air—he'd lost Zor's scent. In its place, he smelled only fear.

Fear?

A hint of foreboding twisted in his gut. Even if the para-daemon knew he was being tracked, he was too arrogant to fear Rand. Yet the scent was unmistakable. He tensed, realizing with sickening surety the source of the fear.

A female.

The fucker had abducted another female.

He hadn't heard that any more Parisian therians had gone missing, but that was the only explanation. Zor had taken another, and now the female werewolf was trapped and terrified and possibly dying.

A cold rage sliced through him, so intense it threatened to overcome reason. He pushed it back, calling up his training to use the fury rather than be used by it. The scent led him north, and he moved silently, curving around the monument until he stood, back pressed to the stone, near a wrought-iron gate that acted as a door to where the dead rested within.

Another step, along with a slight tilt of his head as he peered around the corner, and he could see inside, his hyped-up vision making it easy to see the kenneled woman. Her eyes were rimmed in red, her lips pressed tight together as if she refused to give Zor the satisfaction of seeing her cry.

Alicia.

He shook his head, pushing away the memories and concentrating only on the moment. On Zor. And on the woman cowering in a cage.

The female was naked, and even from a distance, Rand could see the red welts on her back from where the daemon had removed long strips of skin. Zor would pull off every inch, feeding on her pain until the flesh was gone and it was time to kill the woman and find a new one.

Five females. Six counting this one.

A muscle in his jaw twitched. There would be no more.

He checked his perimeter, finding no sign of Zor, then approached the cage.

"Non." The woman scrambled backward, eyes as wide as quarters.

"I'm not going to hurt you," Rand said in the woman's language. He studied her face, but didn't recognize her. "Je suis un ami."

She remained in the corner, as far away as possible.

He crouched down and inspected the cage. Straw littered the floor, along with a tattered blanket and a dish filled with kibble next to a bowl of stale water. One lone water bug moved across the surface, disturbing a thin layer of grime.

After a moment of searching, he found the hidden hinges as well as the lock that kept the cage sealed. He tugged at the door, but it didn't give.

Apparently he should have brought C-4 and a det cord, and left the Ka-Bar behind. He peered at the woman. "La clef?"

A hint of hope fluttered across her shell-shocked features. "Je ne sais pas."

Fuck. Most likely Zor kept the key on his person. Still, he scanned the small room, just in case.

Nothing.

Two ancient swords hung on the wall, forming a cross above a stone coffin. As Rand considered the blades' usefulness for freeing the woman, a new sound caught his attention. The rough scrape of stone against stone.

The woman's cry of "Monsieur!" filled the chamber

as Rand spun toward his attacker, the switchblade extended and tight in his hand, as comfortable as an extension of his own body.

He sliced through the para-daemon's shirt and knocked the bastard backward, but not before the para-daemon grabbed the hilt of the Ka-Bar sheathed at Rand's thigh, taking the knife with him as he tumbled away. Zor's reflexes were sharp, honed from his recent feeding, and the monster sprang back to action almost immediately. Greasy strands of pure white hair hid his face as he crouched near the opening to the tunnel he'd come through.

"Running, Zor? Go ahead. You won't last long."

"Against you? I'll barely have to strain myself."

"I wouldn't bet the bank." He was being arrogant, and he knew it. Unlike most weren, Rand couldn't intentionally summon the change that merged wolf and man, elongating his features, stretching his muscles, and turning him into a wolf-man that resembled the creatures from childhood horror flicks.

He changed only with the full moon, and when he did, he lost himself entirely, his body shifting into the form of a preternaturally strong gray wolf, his human mind lost inside the mind of the animal.

But even though he couldn't change at will, the wolf lived within him always, drawing power from the pull of the moon, and tonight 72 percent would do just fine.

Arrogant or not, Rand knew he wouldn't lose. The beast within wouldn't allow it.

Zor would die tonight, and Rand would savor the killing blow.

The para-daemon seemed to hesitate, and for a second,

Rand thought that Zor would bolt. He didn't. Instead, he attacked, leading with Rand's own knife.

Rand cut to the side as the beast lunged, the blade slicing through the back of Rand's shirt and the flesh of his shoulder blade. The wound was hot and deep and stung like a mother, but Rand ignored it. *Not the time; not the problem.* Instead, he rolled over, taking his weight on the wound as he kicked up and out, his heel intersecting Zor's wrist, forcing the son of a bitch to drop the knife, which skidded across the stone floor until it was lost in the shadows.

His own blood stained the blade now, and Rand could smell it—covering the steel, seeping into the floor, soaking his shirt.

He breathed in deeply, the scent and the pain rousing him, thrusting him into the warm, familiar black where nothing mattered but the kill.

He sprang up, determined to kill the para-daemon right then. The daemon might be older and stronger, but Rand was certain Zor underestimated him. In the ancient daemon's mind, a werewolf barely twelve years into the change hardly posed a threat.

Sure enough, the creature leaped forward, wiry muscles propelling him high into the air. He lashed out on descent, his kick soundly intersecting Rand's chin. The blow sent Rand's neck snapping back, but he didn't falter, managing to snag the beast around the ankle and sending him to the ground.

Rand pressed the advantage. He lunged forward and slammed his knife through the para-daemon's gut, releasing a gush of snot-yellow liquid through which ran thin strands of crimson blood, together but separated, like oil and water.

The scent of blood rose, and the wolf within Rand snapped and growled. But it wasn't the wolf who would take Zor. It was the man—and the animal inside him.

He leaned in close, hot breath on Zor's ear. "If I could destroy you six times over, I would, you twisted motherfucker." He gripped Zor tightly around the neck as he straddled him, his knees crushing into the beast's sides as he kept him pinned to the ground. "Six long, slow deaths for each of the females you tortured. Six trips to hell and back. Six times you would look into my eyes and know that I'm the one who brought you down."

"Destroying the mortal shell will not destroy me, you foolish animal." Zor's eyes filled with loathing. "You, however, will stay dead."

His body seemed to explode from within, the force of the assault tossing Rand backward and knocking the blade from his hand. Zor leaped to his feet, larger now, all sinew and muscles and taut, tight skin, his body as good as new. His eyes glowed a savage orange, and when he spat at Rand, the spittle ate a hole in his shirt. *Acid.*

Well, shit.

"Playtime is over, wolf cub. Time to die."

He charged, and Rand didn't even have time to wonder how he'd so quickly lost the advantage. He could only react. Could only trust his training and his strength and the cunning of the wolf inside. He spun out of the way, slamming his chest against the side of the tomb under the crossed swords. He reached up and grabbed them.

Rand couldn't see the daemon behind him, but he could smell him, could feel the shift in the air, and without thinking, he extended the sabers at his sides, then whipped around, scissoring his arms as he did so. It worked. The steel sank into Zor's gut, too dull to cut all the way through, but it didn't matter. Rand had him now, and he used the force of the blow to knock the bastard backward.

Zor fell, his eyes wide with surprise, and he had time only to haul back and spit before Rand pressed his foot on the creature's forehead, held him still, and used the sword as an ax to chop off the creature's head.

"Told you not to bet against me, you worthless piece of shit."

Only after the head rolled to the side, eyes staring blankly, did he realize that a bit of the spittle's spray had landed on his face. Rand reached up and wiped it away, ignoring the acrid scent of burning flesh as he bent to pick up his switchblade. Then he turned to the woman, whose wide eyes contemplated Rand with an expression usually reserved for quarterbacks and MVPs.

"I'll get you out," Rand said. When a search of the daemon failed to turn up a key, he lifted the head, jammed the blade of his knife into the back of the beast's throat, and then used the acid that spilled from the ripped salivary gland to eat through the lock.

The door swung open, and he took off his shirt and tossed it gently at her feet. She bent slowly, then put it on, the hem hanging down almost to her knees. She stood in the doorway of the cage, looking at him as if waiting for a signal.

Rand rolled the head across the tomb, out of sight.

Then he retracted the blade. "Il est fini." He turned toward the door, then back to her when he realized she hadn't moved. "Allons-y. Vous êtes sûre."

Slowly, very slowly, she walked toward him, pausing a few feet away. "Mon mari?"

"We'll find your husband," Rand promised. "We'll go right now."

Her eyes flickered, as if trying to smile, and she reached for him, wanting comfort, but he wasn't the one to give it. He'd given her life; that would have to be enough.

Slowly, she lowered the hand.

"Let's go," he said, then saw her eyes widen with fear. In one motion he turned, shielding her petite frame as he flipped open his blade. He let it fly toward the tomb's doorway, only to have it knocked aside by the strong arm of the man standing there.

"Have I been so poor a leader that you would seek to take me out with a blade to the heart?" Gunnolf asked. He reached down to pick up the knife, then slid his fingers along the blade's edge, drawing a thin line of blood. "A steel blade will render no permanent harm to a werewolf, lad. You know that, aye?"

"That was a warning," Rand said, inclining his head both in respect to his leader and to hide his amused grin. "But next time maybe you shouldn't sneak up after a fight."

"Och, aye. You have me there." He crossed the room in three long strides, his wild mane of fiery red hair more suited to a Viking than to a political leader. Not that the Shadow Alliance was a typical political entity. Nothing within the shadow world was typical.

It had been Gunnolf who'd found him, confused and angry and changed. Gunnolf who'd fed him and sheltered him. Gunnolf who'd taught him what he now was—as much animal on the inside as he'd always been on the outside.

And it had been Gunnolf who'd given Rand a killing role in this new world, a role he understood and a part he could play with ease.

Gunnolf glanced down at the woman, who now stood behind Rand, clinging to his shoulders. "Do you know who I am, lass?" Gunnolf asked, compassion softening his sharp features.

The woman nodded, stepping close, finding the comfort with Gunnolf she hadn't found with Rand. "Oui."

"She needs to find her mate," Rand said briskly. "And she needs a medic."

"It will be done." Gunnolf pressed a hand to the woman's shoulder, then glanced down at Zor's body. He shot Rand an ironic smile. "You found the bastard, then?"

"I did."

The alpha turned slowly, taking in the tomb, the cage, the rank smell of death and decay with casual acceptance. "You took a hand to the matter yourself, I see," Gunnolf said, his meaning clear. Rand had gone after Zor without official sanction. Without involving the Preternatural Enforcement Coalition, the organization with jurisdiction over all the shadow creatures.

"Yes, sir. You wanted the problem solved, and I solved it."

"Aye," Gunnolf said slowly. "You did right." He

paused, stroking his chin. "There is another matter. A delicate one."

Rand stood at parade rest, his hands at the small of his back in a long-practiced show of respect.

"There are not many I can put on this task," he said, shooting the woman a quick glance. Rand understood his alpha's shorthand. He was referring to the *kyne,* a secret group of warriors assigned to each of the Alliance representatives. "Of those I can ask, you are the one I want."

"Sure. Whatever you need." Gunnolf said nothing, and the heavy weight of dread settled on Rand's shoulders. He shook his head. "Oh, shit, no. Not that."

"I haven't asked."

But he had. Even in silence, Gunnolf was asking him to do the impossible. "The answer is no."

Gunnolf looked pointedly at the female. "Let us return the woman to her pack, and then we can discuss this."

Rand squared his shoulders. "Now."

Gunnolf's shoulders dropped, and for a moment Rand thought he'd pushed too far. Then Gunnolf lifted his chin, and though Rand saw compassion in his alpha's eyes, what he saw most was determination. This wasn't a request; it was an order.

"I have another job for you, Rand. I need you to return home to Los Angeles."

CHAPTER 2

Give me something, dammit. A flicker. A flash. Any goddamned thing.

Agent Ryan Doyle kept his eyes closed, one hand pressed against the body's forehead, the other pressed against its heart. Usually he despised his gift. Today he hadn't even hesitated before kneeling by the body. Seven humans, brutally slaughtered. Necks punctured. Blood drained. And not one goddamned suspect.

"Anything?"

He rocked back on his heels and looked up at his partner. He didn't have to say it, Tucker could see the answer in his face.

"Fuck."

Doyle nodded in agreement, then rose, nodding to the ME and his team hovering nearby. Time to let forensics take over. "Seven corpses, and we don't even have shit from one of their heads." As a percipient daemon, Doyle had the ability to snatch the last experiences from a body's lingering aura. A handy tool for an investigator, especially in situations where the victim actually saw his killer. But the skill wasn't without flaws—the weakness that overcame him after he plucked those last few moments from a victim's head, the nourishment necessary to get his strength back.

Souls.

He scowled. Every time he did his goddamned job, he was reminded of what he was. What he always would be. A daemon. A soul-eater.

Fuck.

Tonight, though, he would have gladly paid that price.

Except there was nothing there. They were too late. Because once the aura faded, he was shit out of luck.

The first five victims had been a wash, the human cops getting to the bodies and putting them through their investigative paces, and finding less than nothing. It wasn't until victim number six was discovered ten days prior that one of the human liaisons to the PEC had gotten a clue and notified Division 6. In Doyle's opinion, the delay qualified as a major interagency fuckup, but at least things were on track now. Jurisdiction had been officially shifted, and now the case fell under the auspices of Homeland Security—the agency inside which the American arm of the Preternatural Enforcement Coalition existed as an off-the-books division known only to humans in select key positions.

Doyle looked down at the corpse, now glowing in the harsh lights put up by the crime-scene techs. The medical examiner, Richard Erasmus Orion IV, had moved in beside the body and was scraping samples of ash into small glass vials, which he then handed to his assistant, Barnaby. The ash had been at the last four crime scenes, its source still unidentified. Possibly it had been at the earlier scenes, too, but the bodies had remained undiscovered for days, and the scenes had been well contaminated by animals and weather by the time the techs had arrived.

"This is so fucked up," Tucker said.

Doyle shoved his hands into his pockets. "Ain't that the truth."

"Sure as hell looks like a vampire kill," Tucker said, squinting down at the body. "Not a clean one, though. Throat's ripped out. Blood gone."

"Occam's razor," Barnaby said, his elven eyes narrowing as he wrote on one of the vials with a Sharpie.

"Come again?" Tucker said.

"The simplest answer is often correct," Orion said, not bothering to look up from the body. The ME always took exceptional care of the bodies in his custody, but tonight his examination went beyond meticulous. Understandable. The victims were human—and so was Orion.

He carefully scraped the dirt from under the victim's fingernails into a vial, then handed it to Barnaby. "As Tucker said, the simpleminded, knee-jerk reaction is to cry vampire. Even though in this case, the simple answer may not be the correct one."

"Simpleminded?" Tucker looked between Doyle and Orion. "Did he just insult me?"

Doyle ignored his partner. "So why not vamps?" So far Orion had withheld his formal report, claiming that his tests were inconclusive. If the ME finally had something solid, Doyle wanted the details, especially if the ME was giving a pass to the bloodsuckers. Despite the party line about how most vamps had reined in their daemon, Doyle knew damn well that in some it only took one little push to force the daemon to the surface. And a vampire with its daemon unbound was more than capable of killing seven humans. Or worse.

The medical examiner hadn't answered the question, so Doyle pressed. "Why not vamps?" he repeated.

"I haven't ruled out vampires," Orion said. He stood up, pressed his hands to his lower back, and stretched, his spine popping as he let out a low, grateful sigh of relief. "Unfortunately, I can't rule out anything." His voice was level, but strained, frustration bubbling just below the surface.

"Why the hell not?"

"Because with the evidence sitting in my lab, I can draw no firm conclusions. A whole slew of samples, and the DNA doesn't tell me a damned thing."

Doyle glanced at Tucker, who shrugged. "Contaminated?" Doyle asked.

"No," Orion said. Then, "Maybe. It's like nothing I've seen before, and after fifteen years working for the PEC, I've seen a lot."

"Well, what the hell are you seeing?" Doyle asked.

"We're hitting a few markers that suggest vampire," Barnaby said, looking up from the vials he was labeling. "But the rest is a mess. Like it's something else entirely."

Doyle noted the kid's smug expression and narrowed his eyes. "You've got a theory."

"Therians," Barnaby said, referring to the broad species of shape-shifters that included werewolves, were-cats, and the like.

Orion shook his head slowly, as if both amused by and exasperated with his protégé. "Therians aren't any more likely than vamps," the ME said.

"What about the rumors?" the elf demanded. "It's all over the street that Gunnolf's behind all of this."

Orion held up a vial of ash. "This is evidence," he said. "Rumors aren't."

Barnaby turned to Doyle as if looking for an ally. "But that's got to be it, right? Gunnolf's back to his old tricks?"

Doyle stayed silent. He'd heard the rumors, too, and he wasn't discounting them. But as the ME said, rumors weren't evidence.

The elf frowned. "I don't get you. I mean, it makes sense, especially after what Gunnolf pulled six months ago. All that shit about killing off a bunch of humans and making it look like vamps did the deed. The whole idea was to make folks think Tiberius didn't have a handle on his territory, right?" he asked, referring to the vampiric liaison to the Alliance and governor of the L.A. territory. "So all this is just him trying again."

Doyle bit back a curse. Trying to contain information in the PEC was like trying to herd tree nymphs. "Gunnolf backed off."

"You trust a werewolf to keep his word?" Barnaby asked.

Doyle was saved from conceding the point by the arrival of the transport team, and Doyle and Tucker stepped back as Orion and Barnaby finished with the body and prepared it for the ride to Division. The rest of the forensics team swarmed in next—agents trained in the human approach to trace evidence and those skilled in looking for the various markers that indicated death by preternatural means. Doyle gave them his standard lecture, reminding them that unless they wanted to finish out their lives with certain limbs removed from their bodies, they'd do well to apply themselves 110 percent.

With the team sufficiently terrorized, he stepped away, then glanced around the area, as if a quick resolution to this mess could be found in the grass or the trees or the soil that made up the area inside the crime-scene tape. Beyond that boundary, reporters hovered near the uniformed PEC officers who stood tall and straight and tried to look like humans.

He recognized one of the reporters—a wisp of a girl with short cropped hair and an expression of firm determination. She stood now pressed up against the tape and waved her recorder, and even over the cacophony of the crime scene, he could hear her swearing to the officer that Ryan Doyle knew her and wouldn't mind a few questions and couldn't they please just let her through?

Despite himself, Doyle smiled. He didn't have one goddamned clue who the girl was, but she must have picked his name up from somewhere, and she actually had the balls to try to turn that tidbit of information to her advantage. Clever, but too bad she was shit out of luck.

"Want me to get rid of them?" Tucker asked, following Doyle's gaze to the onlookers. He cracked his knuckles, then rolled his neck, perfectly mimicking a boxer getting ready for a fight. "I can send them all down the road to Disneyland. Or skinny-dipping off the Santa Monica Pier. They'll snap out of it in a few hours and wonder what the hell they're doing. And what do you bet someone posts a few pictures of them in the meantime?"

"Tempting," Doyle said, because using Tucker's mind-control hoodoo sounded pretty damn appealing right then. "But—*oh fuck me.*"

"What?" Tucker asked, then turned in the direction Doyle was looking and saw the couple striding purposefully toward them. "Oh."

"*Him* you can get rid of."

"I thought you and Dragos had found your happy place."

"I've acknowledged that he's not a walking plague upon the earth," Doyle conceded about the vampire he'd once called friend. "But that doesn't mean I want to prance through the daisies with him, and I sure as hell don't want him at my goddamned crime scene."

"Gentlemen." The woman with Dragos didn't even slow, just signaled for them to keep up as she retraced their path toward the body. Doyle didn't begrudge her a look at the victim. He'd had his doubts about Sara Constantine when they'd first met, but he'd learned soon enough that she was a top-notch prosecutor, even if her initial training had been in the District Attorney's Office instead of within Division. And even if she had dubious taste in men.

Respect, however, didn't ease over into taking her shit, and he reached for her elbow and tugged her to a stop. She complied, one eyebrow lifting in question. Her skin was pale, almost translucent, with the ethereal glow of the recently turned. Her coal-black hair was pulled back into a practical ponytail, but a few strands had escaped and now curled around her face, softening her no-nonsense expression.

Doyle focused on Dragos, who stood tall beside his mate. His words, however, were for Sara. "You want to tell me when you started dragging loverboy to crime scenes with you? Last time I checked, he wasn't clocking in at Division."

"You're right about that," Dragos answered, the words flat and even, but masking an underlying hint of amusement.

Doyle wanted to punch him, and not because Doyle's famous temper was peeking out, wanting to kick ass and take names. No, where Lucius Dragos was concerned, punching just seemed like the best option on the table.

He reined it in. "Not in the mood for twenty questions." He faced Sara. "What's going on?"

"What do you think?" she snapped. "Division isn't calling the shots anymore."

He started to ask what she was talking about, but he didn't need to. The answer was coming straight toward them—a white mist drifting over the low-cut grass, eerily illuminated by the not-yet-full moon. As Doyle watched, the mist seemed to rise, then take form, the soft, shadowy edges hardening into the powerful form of an ancient master vampire.

Tiberius stood tall and proud, his hair as black as his eyes, and his eyes as black as the night. He turned to face Doyle, then Tucker, then Sara, then Luke. Only when he reached the last did he nod briefly in acknowledgment.

"My lord," Luke said, and beside him, Sara inclined her head.

Doyle didn't. Governor or not, Tiberius had materialized at *his* crime scene in full view of humans, and that shit was dangerous. He glanced again toward the clutch of reporters, but saw that they were each looking elsewhere, their attention clearly diverted.

Doyle felt a reluctant tug of respect. As usual, Tiberius had the situation firmly under control.

The governor said nothing, but instead moved past Doyle to where the techs were still scouring the scene. As the vampire approached, the team scurried away. The governor paused a proper distance from the scene, and Doyle had to give him props for not stepping in like an ass and contaminating the area.

Then Tiberius turned, and his cold, coal eyes found Doyle in the darkness. "You are the investigator assigned to this matter?"

Doyle shoved his hands into his pockets. "Yeah."

Tiberius didn't move, but his attention shifted to Sara. "And you are the prosecutor."

She came to stand beside Doyle. "I am."

"Ten days," Tiberius said, his voice as hard as his expression. "I expect answers in ten days or heads will roll."

CHAPTER 3

Rand killed the Ducati's engine and leaned back, his feet planted on the asphalt as he balanced the bike and looked across the street at the puke-green apartment complex. Jacob Yannew was in there. Apartment 212, shared with five other therians. A pack-dweller, unlike Rand, who chose to live alone, roam alone, hunt alone.

Right then, Rand needed Jacob alone.

The little shit was the reason Rand had come back to Los Angeles. "The wee devil's kept a low profile," Gunnolf had said, "but it's him who's telling lies behind me back."

Rand intended to find out why.

He pulled out his smartphone and opened the file on Jacob that Gunnolf's assistant had transmitted en route. He'd already memorized his target's stats, but he reviewed the information anyway, the rote action part of a familiar routine. Five foot two. Mouse-brown hair. One eye scarred shut, the result of a knife fight two years before he'd been changed.

Jacob Yannew had lived in the gutter before the change, and he lived there still, his days spent panhandling on the city's busy corners, and his nights spent roving the town, sucking down hard liquor at the various therian hangouts. He was a known snitch, not above sharing information he'd learned about his fellow therians with the PEC—at least not as long as the price was right.

Unfortunately, his snitch status went hand in hand with a reputation for being in the know. He'd started spreading rumors about Gunnolf and the dead humans, and because it was Jacob talking, the other therians had believed and the rumors had spread.

Rand knew better. And what Rand wanted to know was why Jacob had started spewing lies in the first place. Jacob had no reason to hold a grudge against Gunnolf— not one that the alpha was aware of, anyway. To Rand's mind, that meant someone was pulling Jacob's chain. Tonight, Rand would find out who.

Find out, deal with the problem, and get the fuck out of L.A.

He checked his watch, then swung his leg off the bike as the minute hand clicked into a perfectly vertical position, marking ten o'clock on the nose. He waited sixty seconds, then crossed the street at the same time Jacob emerged from the apartment's main door for his late-night round of drinking. He turned north toward the cross street and the corner bar that catered to humans, but was still Jacob's habitual first stop.

Rand fell in step behind him, his contempt for his prey rising when Jacob didn't note his presence. A fucking werewolf and he didn't catch the scent of a tail. *Useless bastard.*

Rand lengthened his stride and caught up to Jacob just outside the bar. As Jacob pulled open the door, Rand stepped close behind and caught Jacob's free arm with an iron grip. With his right, he pressed the point of his Ka-Bar into the small of the wolf's back.

"Jacob Yannew," he said easily. "Step into my office."

The little weren stiffened, but Rand pushed them both through the door. Jacob might force the change—most weren could summon the wolf at any time, the full moon not withstanding. But this wasn't a therian bar, and changing in front of humans was not only reckless and stupid, it was illegal. And Rand didn't think a weasel like Jacob had the balls to flaunt the system.

"Sit," he growled, shoving the weren into a dark booth. "Talk."

"I want a whiskey," Jacob said, and Rand had to smile. It wasn't exactly backbone, but it was something.

"I want to be out of this hellhole," Rand said, sliding easily into the seat opposite. "But I'm learning to live with disappointment."

The bastard hawked up a wad of phlegm and spat at Rand. It missed his face—which was good for Jacob's overall life span—and landed with a wet splat on his collar. Rand wiped it away, his eyes never leaving his prey's.

"You know who I am?"

"I know you're in my face."

"I'm Gunnolf's," he said, and watched as the face crumpled. And then, almost as quickly, shifted back into snarling indifference.

"Good for you," Jacob said. "Now get the fuck out of my face."

"Not just yet." He leaned back in the booth, his quarry across from him. "Word on the street is you've got a big mouth."

Jacob said nothing.

Rand frowned at the irony. "Maybe word on the street was wrong."

"Fuck you."

Rand leaned forward, his eyes never leaving Jacob's. "You've been spreading rumors about Gunnolf and dead humans. I want to know why."

"I don't know what you're talking about."

Fast as lightning, Rand lifted his foot under the table, then jammed it forward, closing the distance between them. His heel intersected Jacob's crotch, but he didn't slow, not until there was nowhere to go, and Jacob's puny balls were crushed beneath his heel.

He maintained the pressure and smiled congenially, the other bar patrons oblivious. "Talk," he said.

"You'll pay for this," Jacob sneered.

Rand ground his heel, saw pain rise in Jacob's eyes. "Maybe," he admitted. "But not today. *Talk*. Or never get it up again. Your choice."

Jacob spat on the table, but that was just posturing. Sure enough, he scowled at the tabletop, then lifted hooded eyes filled with malice to meet Rand's. "You're howling at shadows, boy."

"Am I?"

"I'm not the one you want."

"Then who is?"

"Don't know."

Rand bore down with his heel, and Jacob's fingernails dug into the hard wood of the booth.

"Goddamn you, I don't. Older. Weren. Smelled like damp and moss. Only saw him the one time. Figured him for an Outcast," he said, referring to shunned therians forced to live outside the formal shape-shifter community, their privileges stripped along with their money and even their identities. Known only as Outcast, the creatures were forbidden to interact in either human or shadow society, and any therian caught interacting with an Outcast could be shunned himself.

Apparently that possibility didn't bother Jacob, who merely shrugged. "Old bastard paid damn good."

"When did you see him?"

"Weeks ago. He tossed a C-note into my can when I was working down on Hollywood. I noticed 'cause that kind of scratch makes an impression, and he was the only therian I'd seen that day. I caught his scent, you know."

"He hung around? Talked to you?"

"Shit no. Was a message scrawled across Ben's face. Big black numbers all graffiti-like on that hundred-dollar bill."

"What numbers?"

"Phone number." Jacob rattled it off. "Said it was a pay phone. He picked up when I called. Told me what he wanted. I never saw him after that."

"Name?"

"Hell no."

Rand considered him, nostrils flaring as he took in the scent. There was fear and sweat, but nothing to suggest Jacob was lying. Considering the little weren valued his testicles, Rand figured he wouldn't risk a lie.

"Why?"

Jacob rolled one bony shoulder. "Figured he wanted to fuck with Gunnolf."

That about summed it up. Rand leaned back, but didn't move his foot. "And did he have the scent of blood on him? When he dropped Ben Franklin into your can?"

"You mean is he killing the humans? Don't know; don't think so."

Rand cocked his head. "Why not?"

Jacob looked him hard in the eyes. "Wasn't the scent of blood I caught on him. Was the scent of vampire."

It was the most interesting revelation that Rand was able to extract, despite ten more minutes of ball-crushing interrogation. Interesting because vampires and weren tended not to mingle—at least not unless the mingling was laced with fighting.

"Go," Rand finally said, moving his boot down to the ground. "And don't let me see your face again."

Jacob's face twisted, and Rand was certain the little weren was biting back a burning desire to fire off a stream of insults. Wisely, Jacob kept his mouth shut, then left through the front door.

Rand waited a moment, then slipped out through the back, ignoring the sullen, questioning stares of the humans working in the kitchen.

He exited into an alley, then walked slowly to where it intersected the street. He stayed in the shadows, listening, and caught the distinct sound of Jacob's steady footfall moving toward him.

He drew in a breath, readying himself, and when the weren passed, Rand stepped silently out, clasped his left hand over his prey's mouth, and yanked the disloyal, backstabbing asshole back into the shadows.

Jacob tensed in his arms, a werewolf summoning the change.

But there wasn't time. Rand's knife was already at his temple, and with one quick thrust, he drove it home.

Jacob crumpled to the ground, one loose end expediently taken care of. Then Rand walked away, the darkness swallowing him.

He didn't look back.

CHAPTER 4

There was nothing remarkable about Orlando's. A low building painted a dull shade of gray, it covered two commercial lots in an area just north of Pico that had managed to retain its seedy character despite the economic boom all around it. The paint had peeled off in a number of places, revealing the white stucco underneath, and the letters in the neon sign tended to flicker, as if in silent disapprobation.

That shabby facade was exactly the way Lissa wanted it, the uninviting exterior meant to discourage anyone who wasn't already aware of the nature of the business inside.

For the most part it worked. A few humans wandered in—junkies looking for a fix, college kids playing at being streetwise and cool—but the bulk of the patrons walked in the shadows, and understood what was being traded inside.

The once-cavernous building had been divided into distinct sections, with the main room split down the middle by an arrangement of Art Deco–style tables that arced around the U-shaped stage, separating the dancers' area from the polished oak bar accented by a neat line of retro bar stools. The north corner of the building had been partitioned, then divided into twelve small but plush taking rooms, each carefully designed to put the clients at ease.

The basement rooms were more austere, designed for practicality rather than for pleasure. Even so, Lissa had taken great steps to ensure that her girls were comfortable during the extraction.

After all, she wanted her employees to be happy, and she wanted her clients even happier. Happy enough to return again and again. In the end, she thought, that was what business was all about—a mutually beneficial transaction. Some people traded goods. Some traded services.

Lissa traded souls.

Considering she was a succubus, the fact that she was in the soul-trading business was hardly breaking news. But as far as she knew, no other succubus had managed to buy her way out of the cortegery, the court of succubi owned by a particular trader. And certainly no other succubus had managed to scrape and claw her way to owning a licensed, bonded, and sweetly profitable soul-trading enterprise.

Then again, as far as she knew, no other succubus had Lissa's particular skill set—a dangerous gift, and one she guarded closely, but used when she had to. When it was important. When it tilted the balance in favor of her girls.

Lissa stood now in front of the glass that made up an entire wall of her private office and looked down on Anya, the newest addition to the club. Lissa had risked more than usual to get the girl, and knew she'd do it all over again if she had to. The girl was strutting her stuff with confidence, her allure cranked up high and working its magic on the slack-jawed men at the table, who wanted nothing more than to hand Anya both their money and their souls.

Lissa surveyed the five males closest to the stage—two para-daemons, a jinn, a shape-shifter, and a vampire. She ruled out the vampire and the para-daemons immediately. Their souls were buried too deep, clinging to the dark underbelly of the daemon. Anya's week had been stressful enough. Tonight she needed an easy hit. The shape-shifter, she decided.

"Marco," she said, speaking into the microphone that led into her security chief's ear. "When the set is over, tell Anya that table three is hers. The taking room's available whenever he's ready." She cast another glance toward the girl. Despite Anya's smile, Lissa couldn't help but notice the worried way her eyes kept darting to the front door.

Fear. Anya was afraid he'd come after her.

Lissa shivered, understanding the girl's fear. Hell, the thought made her tremble, too, and once again she cursed herself for not being more careful. She told herself she didn't regret what she did to free the girl from Priam's vile clutches, but the truth was that she'd let her temper and her concern for Anya fuel her actions. There were better ways. More subtle ways.

Ways that wouldn't potentially return to bite her in the ass.

She knew that, but with Priam she'd ignored her own judgment. She'd told him what she knew about him—and she'd demanded the girl in exchange for his silence.

Blackmail, pure and simple.

The game wasn't new to her—unlike her peers, when Lissa took a piece of the soul, she also took information.

The skill came as naturally to her as breathing, and when she was younger, she'd assumed her gift was no different than anyone else's.

When she'd realized how wrong she was, she'd also realized how easy it would be to use her particular skill as a lever to move her world—to free herself first from the cortegery, and then to free other girls. Girls who were being beaten by their traders or forced to take so many souls that they lost the joy that came with the soul-catch and felt shame as keenly as the soreness between their legs.

Shame should not be within the province of a succubus. They were an elevated species, commanding desire and respect. Succubi had held kings and countries in thrall, and Lissa had dedicated herself to freeing herself and other girls from the service of traders who didn't understand that very basic fact.

Her demands were always made anonymously—and always for cash. She never bargained for a girl by holding explosive information over a trader's head. But she'd take money from her various marks, then turn around and use it to buy freedom for as many girls as she could.

With Priam, though, she'd used what she knew about the trader against him directly, demanding Anya in exchange for her silence. She'd been stupid—letting temper overshadow reason—but she couldn't help it. Not after she saw the way he'd forced Anya to take from a client right there on a dais in the middle of his club, while other patrons paid for the so-called privilege of watching.

A stupid, knee-jerk reaction that she deeply regretted. But it had worked. Priam had deeded Anya to Lissa, but he hadn't done it happily, and now the girl was afraid of reprisals. That wouldn't do. Lissa was willing to shoulder the fear for both of them. Anya deserved to finally have peace.

She spoke again into the microphone. "Tell the E Team to fully credit table three's account, but not to perform the extraction."

On the floor, she saw Marco tap his earpiece, then tilt his head up to look at her. "Say again, Sparrow."

"I want Anya to keep as much soul as she takes," she clarified, knowing firsthand the sense of peace that came from absorbing and retaining a decent-sized piece of soul.

Confusion flickered over Marco's face, and Lissa understood why. Normally a girl would entertain the client in the taking room, pulling bits of his soul into her while the male enjoyed the pleasure of her company.

Later she would slip away to the basement, where the E Team would carefully withdraw the fragments of soul, leaving the girl only the nourishment that kept her strong and very nearly immortal. The client paid for the privilege of lying with one of the girls, but also got house credit for the amount of soul tendered.

Then Orlando's would sell the souls on the open market, usually at a nice profit.

So for Lissa to tell Marco not to have the E Team perform the extraction went entirely against her business model. But to his credit, he didn't ask for an explanation. Orlando's was hers, and Marco's job was to do as she asked, without question. It was a job he did well.

Today Lissa didn't mind giving up some profit. Anya needed that boost, that push toward euphoria, and if

Lissa lost a few credits on her profit-and-loss statement, then so be it.

As she watched Anya work, Rhiana—Lissa's closest friend and the senior girl working the floor—cocked her head toward the shadowy area in the front of the club where people tended to pause or mingle before making up their minds to head to the bar or to the tables by the stage.

Lissa peered into the dark and saw immediately what had troubled Rhiana—two clusters of bristling males, standing too close together to be friends, the tension between them so thick she could feel it even from her office. Even behind the glass.

Three vampires about to face off against three werewolves.

Not in her club they weren't.

She grabbed her jacket from the brass-and-ivory rack and slid it on as she crossed to the door, her heels clicking on the polished wood floor. Given the gang wars that frequently sprouted up between the fangs and the furs, vampires getting in the face of werewolves was not a good thing.

By the time she reached the club level, Marco had shifted his post to a few feet in front of the males. He wouldn't interfere—he knew better than to ever interfere without her specific signal—but his presence was sufficient to cause the two clusters to break apart. *Good.*

She glanced around the club, ensuring that the tension that had sparked in that corner hadn't tainted the overall mood of the place. As far as she could tell, though, none of the patrons had noticed the brewing trouble.

None, that is, except one.

He stood a few feet from the end of the bar, his face partially lit by the dim light reflecting off the liquor bottles that lined the glass shelves behind the bar. Hard angles dominated his face, the only softness around his mouth. His smile was probably dazzling, but the harshness in his eyes suggested that he didn't smile often.

His scalp was shaved, his skin the color of milk chocolate. And except where the light touched him, he seemed to melt into the shadows. He radiated mystery and power, and considering the types of creatures who frequented her club, Lissa had to admit that was saying something.

She had no need to ask; she knew that he was therian. There was no mistaking the wolf inside him. It was there in the deliberate way he watched the room and the muscular grace with which he moved.

As if he felt her watching him, he turned. His eyes met hers, and she saw the restrained beast staring back at her with animalistic hunger. She gasped, fighting a tug of sensual pleasure so intense and unexpected that she had to look away, then wipe her damp palms on her linen slacks.

Anger that he could create a weakness inside her warred with a secret excitement. It was the nature of a succubus to entice, and with each rebirth, succubi were trained not to feel lust. A succubus desired the soul—it was her life, her nourishment, and her most intense pleasure. She was a gift to a man, but it was his soul, not the man, that stirred a succubus's pleasures.

That, at least, was usually true. Right then, though, it was the man himself who was pushing Lissa's buttons.

And that made the weren male both intriguing and dangerous.

Lissa had never shied from danger, and now she lifted her chin, intending to meet his look with one of her own. The kind backed with all the power of her nature and targeted to bring a man to his knees.

He was gone.

She frowned, his unexpected absence troubling her as much as his presence had. Intellectually, she knew that some males were immune to the sheen of the succubi, but she had never met such a man, at least not that she remembered. For that matter, there was no reason to think that *this* man was impervious. She wasn't close enough to him to have any sort of real effect, and she hadn't even tried to ramp up her charms.

But he'd looked at her as though she'd turned it on full throttle—and then he'd walked away.

She didn't want to know a man who could walk away from her despite that heat. A man like that was danger. A man like that could wrest control right out of her hands.

She tapped a finger on the back of a chair, undone by a sudden desire for a cigarette, not to mention the urge to turn around and look for him.

No.

She had a million things to do in her office, and now was as good a time as any to start them.

Determined, she turned, intending to head up the stairs. Instead she found herself only inches from him. She gasped, breathing in the smell of him, dark and woody and utterly male. "Nice place," he said, looking only at her.

"We strive to keep the customers satisfied."

He took a step closer. "Do we?"

Her breath hitched as he tilted his head to the side, the angle enhancing the feral quality that clung to him. He was watching her like prey. Like a conquest. But she wasn't a prize to be won. Not anymore. Not ever again.

"Your guard handled that situation well."

For a moment, she didn't understand, then realized he was talking about Marco deflecting the vamp/weren scuffle. "Friends of yours?"

"No."

She lifted a brow. "So you didn't come to babysit the young pups. Maybe you're here for happy hour?"

"That depends on how happy you're going to make me."

She ignored the way his words worked on her, easing over her like warm honey, overflowing with sweet promises. Instead, she forced herself to take them at face value. He was a client and he was in her club and what he wanted was perfectly clear. They were negotiating now, and that she could handle.

With a broad gesture, she laid the club out at her fingertips. "Let me take you around. I'm sure we can find a girl that pleases you."

She took a step, but he stopped her, his hand closing over her forearm. The shock of his touch ricocheted through her, and she took a second to adjust her expression before she turned back to him.

"I'm already pleased." Once again, his eyes took her in. This time, though, they traveled slowly, his inspection as intimate as a caress. The hot gaze moved over her breasts, then slowly, so slowly, down to her thighs.

Lissa forced her voice to stay steady, determined to keep a businesslike demeanor. "I'm flattered, but I'm the owner."

"Yeah."

"I have a very limited clientele."

"Really?"

He wasn't making it easy. For that matter, *she* wasn't making it easy. Her thighs tingled in anticipation of something that was *not* going to happen, and she felt a bead of sweat drip down the back of her neck. She reached up to wipe it away, her fingers brushing over the quarter-sized scar just beneath her hairline, a reminder that in Orlando's, she was the one in charge.

She straightened her shoulders. "We have policies, Mr. . . . ?"

"Rand. Vincent Rand. And policies can change. It's your club. That's a perk of being the boss. You can do what you want."

He had a point. But no. Absolutely no. And not because it was bad precedent, and not because she had another client engagement lined up; she didn't.

No, she was turning him down because of the way he made her feel. Just being near him was like approaching a charged fence, as if her body could sense the hum of power even before she touched it. He was as dangerous as that fence, too. Touch him, and she wouldn't be able to let go. Grab on to him, and his heat would burn her straight through.

This was lust, plain and simple, and that wasn't acceptable. So what if he looked at her with heat in his eyes? What man didn't? Of course he wanted her—her nature, her raison d'être, was to be an object of desire for males. But that didn't mean she had to fulfill those desires, not when another one of her girls would serve that purpose just fine.

"I *am* doing what I want, Mr. Rand," she said firmly. "Let's go find you another woman."

Surprise crossed his features, and she felt the thrill of a minor victory. Apparently he was a man used to getting what he asked for.

"I want you," he said, and she fought an unexpected rush of pleasure.

"And if I don't want you?"

He pressed a hand to his chest. "I think that would break my heart."

With her most seductive smile playing on her lips, she leaned forward and caressed his cheek. "I guess you'll have to learn to live with disappointment."

CHAPTER 5

Lissa pushed the werewolf out of her mind as she eased through the room, circumnavigating the sea of tables, shaking hands and doing kiss-kiss greetings, giving her girls an encouraging smile when they passed by, and peering into the dark corners. She told herself she wasn't looking for him; she was simply confirming that all was well. That any growing tension among her clientele had been soundly quashed.

It was, she thought, the first time she'd told herself a flat-out lie.

Frustrated with herself, she cut across the center of the room toward the stairs leading to her office. She was passing the stage when she heard a sharp gasp, and turned to see Anya sitting stiffly in a customer's lap, her face pale and her eyes as wide as an animal caught in the hunt. Not because of the shape-shifter who held her, but because of what the girl was looking at across the room.

Priam.

The para-daemon stalked toward them, his huge body cutting a path through the crowd. His silver-gray hair stood out in lacquered spikes that looked as tough and unbendable as the patchwork of scales that covered his face. He had a flat nose, like a snake, and his nostrils twitched as he pointed a long, bony finger at Lissa, then smiled, showing sharp, gray teeth. "You and me, girl. We need to talk."

"I have nothing to say to you," she said, stepping closer and forcing herself to look up and meet his eyes.

"Oh, you'll talk to me," he said. "We're going to have ourselves a nice little chat."

◆

From the shadows, Rand watched as Lissa lifted her chin and got right in the lizard daemon's face.

Lissa. He'd learned her name from a business card near the entrance, and there was no mistaking her as the club's owner.

He'd come into Orlando's just to get a drink and clear his head. He'd tracked the pay phone that Jacob's mysterious Outcast had used to this neighborhood, but the lead had been a dead end. The phone provided no new information—no scent to follow, and none of the nearby vagrants had anything useful to say.

He'd seen the club's sign, caught the scent of those in the shadows, and stepped inside with the goal of finding whiskey and a moment of peace in which to gather his thoughts. One look at Lissa, though, and he'd known that peace would be a long time coming.

He could still feel the shock waves from the sensual punch to the gut that had hit him the first moment he'd seen her. A punch that had settled low and hard as he'd talked to her. Her voice had teased him, and although she had been careful to reveal nothing, he'd caught the scent of desire, and it had gone straight to his cock.

She was exquisite, with golden hair and pale blue eyes the color of his Aunt Estelle's favorite curtains. His life had been asphalt and camouflage, not blues and golds, and he wanted to stand there and simply watch her.

She carried herself with an attitude of command, in charge of the very air that filled the place. He knew that, because she took his breath away.

He'd had his share of exquisite women. Exotic women from all over the globe, some human, some not. Women he'd met in bars, who'd looked at him with lust in their eyes, and he'd pulled them to him, giving in to an animal's need to rut.

Those women, for all their beauty, hadn't done anything for him. Lissa had.

The other women he'd taken because he wanted to get laid, and any girl would do.

With Lissa, he wanted *her*. And he counted the fact that he didn't have her right then among the bigger frustrations in his life.

His fingers itched to touch her. To strip off her clothes and see her naked. To drive himself deep inside of her.

A trick. Only a trick.

No part of the way he felt was real—nothing except for the way he'd gotten hard. But the simple reality was that he'd been slammed by a succubus. She'd suckered him into the net of her spell and reeled him in. He knew that; was positively sure of it. But right then, he didn't give a shit. He'd taken women to bed for a lot less than that, and whatever the cause, he wanted her. Craved her. Wanted her scent all over him, and his all over her.

Wanted to tease her flesh and raise her desire, taking her to the edge and then watching her explode.

Not now, though. Not here.

Her refusal may have disappointed him, but in the end he had to be thankful. He'd come to Los Angeles for only one reason: to find out who was blaming Gunnolf for dead humans. And why.

He still had work to do.

"You look like a man with something on his mind."

A girl stood in front of him holding a tray with two empty glasses. Like the girl at the front door, this one wasn't a succubus. He looked at her, his mind still on his purpose tonight.

"Do you want a taking?" She slid the tray onto a table, then pulled out a small PDA. "Jayla has the next hour free, and she's exceptional at making men forget their troubles. At least for a little while."

"No." He shook his head, then stepped forward, forcing her to move back to get out of his way. "I'm not interested."

Except he was . . .

Not in Jayla, but in Lissa. In her, he was damn interested.

The waitress smiled, as if she knew a secret that he didn't. "When you change your mind, come and find me. I'll get you set up." She didn't wait for him to reply, just stepped away and melted into the crowd.

He shifted, the thought of Lissa pulling him tight, making him restless. Within, the wolf snapped and shivered, wanting her.

She stood in front of the lizard man, her body erect and her expression protective and resolute. Tension arced between them, and her face was tight, masking fury.

Not his problem.

Rand had enough on his plate without worrying about the business concerns of a succubus. He needed to leave. Needed to learn which Outcasts were lurking around Los Angeles. Needed to contact his local assets and pull together a street team.

He stepped from the shadows and moved toward the door, passing close enough to pick up the thread of their conversation.

"I should drag your little Anya right out of here," the lizard was saying. "You can't keep what you took by trickery."

Lissa's eyes flashed dangerously. "Be careful what you insinuate."

"I insinuate nothing," the lizard said.

"Apparently not, since I don't have a clue what you're talking about," Lissa said boldly, but Rand knew she was lying. So, obviously, did the lizard man.

Rand tensed, his muscles on high alert. He glanced around, wondering where the hell her security force was. He'd seen several of them wandering the room, taking care of small problems, their black T-shirts with SECURITY stamped in white making them hard to miss, but not one was nearby now.

What the fuck?

He told himself it wasn't his problem. That he needed to keep walking. He wasn't security, and the woman wasn't his responsibility. But he stayed rooted to the spot, his body refusing to accept his own rational commands.

"You know damn well of what I speak, you insufferable bitch." The lizard lurched forward, his face contorted, his hand going to her shoulder.

Dammit.

In a flash, Rand was at her side, his actions propelled by human fury as much as by the wolf within. He wrapped one arm around the lizard's throat, cutting off his air. At the same time, he used his other hand to grab hold of the creature's arm, jerking it off Lissa's shoulder and twisting it behind the slimy reptile's back.

Then he leaned in close and whispered in the bastard's ear. "I suggest you keep your hands to yourself."

And that was when he heard it—the soft click of a hammer being pulled back. And after that, he felt the cold press of a steel muzzle pressed firm against his temple.

CHAPTER 6

"Let him go," Lissa said. She held the weapon firm, relieved it wasn't shaking. Priam scared the shit out of her, but as long as she didn't let it show, she could still come out of this on top.

Rand didn't comply. Instead he turned his head, ignoring the barrel she had pressed against his scalp, and looked at her with heated, steady eyes.

"*My* place," she said. "And nobody pulls that shit in my place unless I say so. Nobody except me."

For a moment, he did nothing. Then he released Priam, shoving the para-daemon forward as he let his arms drop, suggesting that the reptilian trader was little more than garbage.

It was, thought Lissa, an astute assessment.

Priam turned to launch himself toward the werewolf, but she shifted the gun faster than he moved. "Don't even think about it."

The para-daemon froze, his already ugly face hideous now that rage and embarrassment flooded it. All around them, the club's clients were looking on, whispering among themselves. Some afraid, some wary, some merely enjoying the show.

"Sorry if I interrupted your little party," Rand said, his words even. He hadn't moved when Priam had leaped at him, and now he looked solely at her with the same heat she'd seen earlier. "I thought you needed help."

"I don't," she snapped, then signaled to Marco, who was at her side within seconds. Unlike Rand, he knew not to butt in until she signaled for help. She lowered the gun, silently passing responsibility for the para-daemon to her chief security officer.

"Escort Priam to my office. We can finish our chat there."

"Of course." The beefy troll nodded at Priam. "Move."

As soon as the para-daemon was gone, she relaxed. For a few moments, at least, she could think. Or she could try. Rand was messing with her head, too, albeit in an entirely different way.

He glanced down at the gun. "Bullets can't harm me."

She raised an eyebrow. "These are magic bullets."

His eyes widened, and she laughed, surprised by how delighted she was to have won a reaction. "Okay, not magic," she conceded. "But specially made. Wooden bullets coated with pure silver. Kill most therians and all vampires, and do significant damage to pretty much everyone else."

"Clever. You thought of that?"

"Believe it or not, there's a brain under the blond."

"I believe it." His gaze remained steady, his attention making her feel hot and needy, the way she felt when a soul first slipped free and started to twine around her.

"You need to leave."

He made no move toward the door.

She sighed. "Fine. Stay. Order a drink. Try an appetizer.

But pull that kind of shit again and you'll find that you're no longer welcome through the front doors." She flashed a cool smile. "I'll regret the potential lost profit, but eventually I'll get over it."

"But would I?"

She bit back a smile. "Right. Well. Thank you for coming to Orlando's." The words sounded idiotic, and she fought not to wince. "Enjoy the rest of your evening."

She had more pressing things to occupy her attention than a man who could twist what she was around on herself, making her feel the same rush of desire that men felt around her. Making her lose sense and reason the way they did when they were in her arms.

She started moving toward the stairs, then paused at the base, fighting the urge to turn around and look at him one last time. She gathered her strength, kept her focus, and marched purposefully up the stairs toward her office door.

At the threshold, she hesitated, trying to decide how she was going to play this. She'd made a huge mistake when she'd showed her hand with Priam, but he couldn't possibly know that she'd gotten her intel about him out of another client's head. That secret she'd kept buried deep.

He was just pissed off that she'd played the blackmail card, but she could handle pissed off. Priam had a lot to lose, too, and a lot of secrets he wanted to keep buried. That, at least, would make this more of a negotiation and less of a bloodbath.

She hoped.

Emboldened, she pulled open the door, and immediately Priam rushed toward her, pushing past Marco. Her security chief didn't stop him; Marco understood the rules.

"Sit," she said to Priam, pointing to a chair.

He didn't sit, but he moved to the chair and stood beside it.

She pretended not to care. "Thank you, Marco. That will be all."

He nodded, then closed the office door firmly behind him.

Lissa crossed to the window so that the entire club was behind her. *Her* club.

"We have much to talk about," he said.

"We have nothing to talk about. Fuck with me, and I'll tell the PEC exactly what I know. Do you think your license will hold up when the PEC learns what you've been doing? That you've been tucking entire souls away for black-market trading? That you've enticed unknowing *humans* into your club and taken their souls as well?"

"You will keep your nose out of my affairs, girl."

She fought the urge to lick her suddenly dry lips. "As long as you're hurting your girls, you're going to have to deal with me riding your ass."

"No," he said, his voice so low and calm and assured that it sent shivers racing through Lissa. "Things have changed since yesterday."

With extreme effort, she kept her face passive, but her pulse was pounding, throbbing against the scar on her neck as if a reminder. A scar that had once been a brand, marking her as one of the cortegery. "What things?"

"Perhaps I'll be the one going to the PEC. I think they'd be very intrigued by your operation."

"Go ahead," she said. "Tit for tat. You tell on me, I tell on you. I'm saving abused girls. You're stealing entire human souls. Who do you think will end up in their crosshairs?"

His lips pulled back in a parody of a smile. "You misunderstand. It's not the fact that you have a tidy little blackmail scheme that will make the PEC drool. It's how you get your information in the first place."

The air in the room grew thicker. *Don't react. Don't do anything. Just play the game.*

She looked at him, her gaze as steady as her breathing. "I already told you. I learned about you from a source."

His lip curled into a sneer. "You stole your information," he said. "Right out of your source's head."

"Don't be absurd." He couldn't know that. How could he know that?

But he did. Somehow, he'd found out her secret.

Her mouth had gone completely dry, and her fingers twitched, itching to reach for the gun she'd holstered under her jacket. To make this problem go away. But that would be trading one problem for twenty, and as much as she wanted the son of a bitch dead, she wasn't that desperate.

He moved closer, his expression full of menace. "Don't even think about lying to me," he said. "I know you, Lissa." He met her eyes, his dark with purpose. "I *know* you. *Elizabeth.*"

Breathe, dammit, breathe. But she couldn't. Her lungs simply weren't cooperating.

"I think you look even better as a blonde," he said casually. "Although your coal black hair against your fair skin used to drive the men of the court to their knees. They used to beg me for a moment with you. Not even sex. Just a moment. Did you know that? Do you remember?"

She stayed silent, sickened by the reality he was setting out in front of her. *She'd once been in Priam's cortegery. She'd once been among the girls that he'd used and abused.*

Though the effort cost her, she lifted her chin. "Even if what you're saying is true, that was a lifetime ago, maybe more than one. It has nothing to do with today."

He ignored her. "They have ways, you know. Ways of testing. Ways of finding out what kind of gifts you have. Is that what you want, Elizabeth?"

"I don't know what you're talking about."

"Of course you do." He moved to the window and stood looking down at the club she so cherished. "You've put together a fine establishment here, my dear. I like to think perhaps a bit of my business acumen rubbed off on you, even if only subliminally."

"If you've rubbed off on me at all, I'll have to take a bath in acid simply to remove the slime."

"Ouch." He turned toward her. "Not your best comeback. Perhaps I've rattled you more than you care to admit?"

She said nothing.

"I didn't realize it was you," he said. "Now that it's so obvious, I feel like such a fool. For years we've been working in the same city, and for years you've been poaching girls from other traders across the globe. I never even gave it a thought until you came poking around for Anya." He tilted his head to the side, as if examining a painting. "When you walked into my office yesterday, something struck me as familiar. Nothing concrete, though. Not then. But you knew my secrets, and I couldn't figure out how. You see, I share very little with my business associates, and they are loyal to a fault. They know that the punishment for loose lips is their own sinking ship."

"You must be so much fun to work for."

"So how could you have learned about my operation?" he continued. "Honestly, I didn't have a clue. But I could picture you standing in front of me, your blue eyes blazing like Arctic ice. That was what did it, you know. I couldn't shake the image. Those eyes, Elizabeth. Those eyes."

She swallowed, understanding. With each life, a succubus was born into a new body. Her look would change—the shape of her face, the color of her hair. But her eyes would always remain the same. Even her name followed her through lifetimes, the guardians of the birthing mist ensuring that the name followed the essence. There was, after all, power in a name.

She'd abandoned her name. Somewhere along the way, she'd abandoned Elizabeth for Lissa. When? Why?

She pushed it aside. Right then, her name was irrelevant. "So you knew me," she said. "So what?"

She knew what he was going to say. He knew her secret; he'd known it for lifetimes. But she had to hear the words. When he said them, though, she didn't feel any sense of relief or lessening of the pressure pushing against her. She'd thought she'd be able to step back and evaluate once all the cards were firmly on the table. She'd been wrong.

I know how you take secrets, Elizabeth, he'd said. *I know, because you used to take them for me. For us.*

What he said disgusted her, but there was no point in denying. He would want that. Want her cowering in fear. She wouldn't give him the satisfaction. "If you get the PEC poking around in my business, I can assure you I'll return the favor." He'd been nervous enough about the prospect to give her Anya. Maybe he was still twitchy enough to negotiate.

"You won't do that," he said, his thin smile suggesting victory.

She remained still, not willing to show defeat even though she knew damn well that she'd lost.

"You have too much to lose," he continued, as if her decision hadn't already been made for her. He pressed his palms flat on her desk and leaned in close. "All of those little girls you've tried so hard to protect, for instance." His breath smelled of dead fish and sour milk, and she turned her head away, trying not to gag.

"Do you think the PEC will simply release you?" he pressed. "Do you think they'll let you keep this club? If you're lucky, you'll be executed—that's hardly a punishment for your kind. And if you're unlucky . . . ?" He trailed off with a shrug. "I'm sure the PEC could put someone with your talents to use. And I'm sure that in exchange for your services you'll even get a blanket in your cell."

He was right, and she moved her hand away from her waist, away from the gun, and pressed it flat on her desktop. Then she looked up at him, not bothering to hide the disgust she felt. "What do you want?"

"I need you to do something for me." He smiled coldly, revealing rows of sharp teeth. "For old time's sake."

CHAPTER 7

"You want to tell me why I'm here?" Sara asked, her arms crossed as she looked from Doyle to Tucker. The alley behind the human bar smelled like piss and rotting food, and so far the para-daemon hadn't been forthcoming with explanations. As a prosecutor, Sara didn't usually visit crime scenes, and her presence at the scenes of the last two dead humans reflected just how seriously Division was taking that investigation. Tiberius had even authorized use of an Alliance Seer, but the creature hadn't been able to find any more evidence than Division had turned up.

Right now, though, she wasn't looking at a dead human. Instead, she was looking at a dead weren. More specifically, she was looking at an empty section of concrete where a dead weren had been until the techs had carted his body off to Division's morgue.

Doyle might be a pain at times, but he wasn't stupid. If he'd dragged Sara—and Luke—from Beverly Hills to Sun Valley, there was a reason.

"What I want," Doyle said, "is to know why *he's* here." The investigator cocked a head toward Luke, as if Sara needed the interpretation. She knew why Doyle was pissed. Honestly, she was a little pissed, too.

"Why do you think? You heard Tiberius. He wants

answers, and he's appointed Luke as the Alliance liaison for this investigation."

Doyle looked at Luke. "Won't this be fun."

"Humans are dying, Doyle," Luke said. "Tiberius is concerned."

"Tiberius is concerned that if humans keep on dying, it's going to look like he doesn't have control of his territory."

Sara took a step toward Doyle. "Forget the damn politics. What Luke said is right. Humans *are* dying, and whatever his reasons, Tiberius doesn't want any more human deaths on the PEC roster. Neither do I," she added, silently daring Doyle to contradict her.

He didn't. Doyle knew damn well that she wasn't even a year away from being human.

For a pregnant moment, no one spoke. Then Tucker stepped forward. "We may have caught a break," he said. His voice was low, without its usual tinge of sarcasm, and Sara reminded herself that Tucker was human. Now he was even more human than she was.

"Tell me."

"Getting the call was plain, old-fashioned luck. The body had ID, the human cop radioed it in, and our computer caught the name. Body was still warm when we got here."

"I'm listening," she said, but she transferred her attention to Doyle, and this time she noticed the fatigue in his eyes and the sallowness of his skin. Noticed, too, the way he leaned against the stucco facade, not quite as casually as she'd thought at first glance. "He saw something."

"Not much," Doyle said. "But enough." He held out a hand, and Tucker passed him a bottle of water.

"You need a fix, man," Tucker said, but Doyle shook his head.

"I'm okay. Didn't have to go deep."

"Doyle . . ."

"No." He took a long sip, then continued. "Vic's name is Jacob Yannew. He's a snitch, on our payroll, though he wasn't above passing bad intel if the price was right."

"You got a lead from Yannew, you double- and triple-checked it," Tucker added.

"So maybe he double-crossed the wrong person," Sara said. "Did you see a vision of his killer?"

Doyle shook his head. "No. Just images and emotions of what he was doing before. And a name."

"What name?"

Victory lit in Doyle's eyes. "Gunnolf. He was scared shitless of Gunnolf's man in Los Angeles."

"Really?" Sara said, glancing quickly at Luke. "Gunnolf hasn't had a man in L.A. for a while."

"We talked with the bartender," Tucker said. "Turns out this ain't such a great neighborhood. The owner keeps a security camera running. Does a sweep of the tables, and it happened to catch our vic having a not-so-friendly chat with another weren."

"Have you identified him?"

"Vincent Rand," Doyle said.

"I've heard the name," Luke said. "He's been Gunnolf's right hand for over a decade. Rumor is he's got a special talent for wet work."

"Maybe you two should have coffee," Doyle said.

Luke ignored the dig. "He works out of Paris."

"Well, he's here now," Doyle said.

"I made a few calls," Tucker said. "And it's looking more and more like our vic was telling anyone who'd listen about how Gunnolf killed those humans."

"And now he's dead," Sara said. "Interesting. Did Rand shut him up because he was telling the truth, or because he was spreading lies?"

"Or some other reason," Tucker said.

"So let's bring Rand in for questioning," Sara said. "We've got enough to charge him with Yannew's death. Let's see what else we can sweat out of him."

"You won't get much," Luke said. "He doesn't sound like the type who'll simply roll over and talk."

"Hate to admit it," Doyle said to Sara, "but I agree with your boy."

So did Sara. She cocked her head and peered at Tucker. "Why can't you step in, twist a few knobs in his head, and convince him he wants to reveal all?"

"Big job," Tucker said. "And there's no way to be sure he shares everything. If he's a strong-willed son of a bitch, he may hold something back and we'd never know."

"Forget Tucker," Doyle said. "For that matter, forget charging Rand. At least for right now. Instead, we play him."

"How?"

"We send in someone who can take the thoughts right out of his head."

"Good luck with that," Tucker said. "It's not a common gift, even less so if you're looking to be sneaky in there. This guy realizes someone's poking around in his head, and it's all over before it began."

"No worries there," Doyle said. "I've been thinking. Got someone in mind."

"Who is he?" Sara asked.

"Not he. *She*. Her name is Lissa. And I can guarantee that she'll cooperate."

CHAPTER 8

Lissa leaned against the rough stucco and lifted her chin, her eyes closed, wanting to feel nothing except a cool summer breeze across her skin. Longing for it to whisk away the lingering stench of Priam and the deal she'd made with him.

The air did not cooperate.

Instead of comfort, the breeze carried the fetor of garbage and debris, the unpleasant miasma of things that rot in alleys, hidden from the delicate sensibilities of those who might pass in front of the buildings.

Like we hide from the humans.

Frustrated, she brushed the thought away. She didn't usually concern herself with the human world; there was enough within the shadows to occupy her, and what would be the point? A complete human soul might bring a fortune on the black market, but that wasn't a game she played, not even if that soul could buy the freedom of ten girls. There were lines she wouldn't cross, and the idea of taking an entire human soul was simply wrong, the act of doing it transforming her into the kind of monster about which humans whispered.

And whisper they did.

She knew it, as did everyone in the shadow world.

Some humans knew the truth about the shadows, of course, but most did not. Most had only a hint, a feeling.

Something glimpsed out of the corner of their eye. Something remembered from a nightmare.

Most humans were afraid of the dark and made up stories about what lurked in the shadows. Ghoulies and beasties that would come to them in their beds. Come and steal their souls away.

She shivered, knowing she was what they feared. Knowing the stories were true.

To a human, she was the monster. But in her own world, she was . . . what?

The answer came quick—*an entrepreneur*.

She smiled at the thought, because it was true. She had no desire to sacrifice the life she'd built, and she hated that Priam had put her in the position of having to protect it. That he'd turned the tables and was now blackmailing her, threatening to turn her in to the PEC if she didn't get into a certain human's head and take that human's soul.

Damn Priam all to hell.

For one brief instant, she wished there was someone to whom she could go for help, but she quashed the thought almost immediately. There was no one, and wishing wouldn't change the fact that although she was consistently surrounded by people, when it counted, she was alone, and always had been.

She'd do what she must, and she'd deal with the consequences when they came.

Her fingers twitched, longing for a cigarette. She didn't smoke, but some deep buried memory surfaced, calling to her mind the sharp taste of tobacco on her tongue, her lips tight around the shaft of a cigarette as she inhaled, feeling the sweet smoke fill and warm her.

She wanted that now—that internal warmth. In memory, it seemed almost safe, comforting.

But she'd never smoked in this life. Not because of the surgeon general's warnings—that hardly seemed relevant to someone like her who would continue living in some form or other until the end of time—but because she refused to let her girls smoke, wanting their breath and clothes to smell fresh and clean for the clients.

Her girls.

Everything circled back to her girls.

With a small sigh, she turned to go back into Orlando's through the service door beside her. She hesitated, though, when she heard male laughter echoing up the alley toward her. Young males. A group of them, out for a night prowl.

From the sound, she couldn't tell if they were human or shadowers, and though it really didn't matter, something compelled her to stay and watch. She glanced toward the end of the alley, certain the group would come into view. She didn't see the young men, but as she looked past the end of the alley to the street and then to the building on the other side, she saw something shift against the brick wall, edging slightly into the dim light cast by a nearby traffic signal.

Her breath caught in her throat, and her body tightened with disturbing awareness. *Rand.* Her nipples peaked beneath her thin blouse, and she cursed the unwelcome desire that shot through her, hot and fast and so unexpected it made her knees weak.

She didn't know why he affected her as he did, but she did know that she didn't like it.

No. That wasn't true. She did like it. *That* was what she didn't like.

Deliberately, she stepped away from the wall, intending to cross the alley and confront him. She wasn't entirely sure what she would say—once he was outside, he was entitled to stand wherever he damn well pleased—and yet she wanted to know why he chose to stand in front of her club. She doubted that he would tell her, but she took another step anyway. And then another, and another, until she came to a stop in the shadows at the end of the alley, only a few yards from where it intersected the sidewalk.

She was certain he'd been watching her approach. The shadows in the alley hid her, but he was therian and could see well into the dark. He didn't move, though. Did nothing, in fact, except readjust his position against the wall.

Inexplicably frustrated, she drew her fingers through her hair and stepped forward, stopping just shy of the sidewalk and the light that bathed it. This time, her hesitation had nothing to do with Rand. The young men she'd heard earlier were clustered on her left, their words now clear. Their faces, too, and she recognized them as the group that had been in the club earlier, butting heads with the vamps.

"—should go back in," one of the males said, as Lissa slipped back into the shadows, prepared to get a customer's view of her club. "The females in there . . . I mean, damn, they were so hot." He turned his head, his nose making an arc through the air as if trying to catch the scent of the night.

"Shit yeah, they're hot," another one said. "They're

almost all succubi. They're *supposed* to be hot. Even if they were ugly as a monkey's butt, you'd think they were hot if you've got balls. That's the *point*."

"So they're not really hot?" the third one asked, this one smaller and skinnier than the others. "Like they're hags or something, and it's just an illusion that their faces look better than dung, and their boobs don't sag to their waists?"

In the shadows, Lissa pressed her hand over her mouth to hide a snort of laughter.

"Great *magnus lupus*, Tremaine, are you that much an idiot? They're still girls, not harpies or wraiths. And I bet even without the sheen they look a hell of a lot better than Sylvia."

The one called Tremaine bristled. "You keep her out of this, Gregor."

The first one snorted. "Go in, Tremaine. Find out for yourself. Then we'll see if you still sing Sylvia's praises."

The other two boys laughed raucously, though Lissa thought they sounded a bit nervous, too. They were therian, of course, but they were also young. And considering how comfortable they were discussing the ins and outs of the shadow world, she assumed they were all born werewolves, not made. In her experience, made weren tended to be edgier, uncomfortable in their own skin, and often had something to prove.

She glanced across the street and saw that Rand still stood there. *Him, for example.* She'd bet a week's profit he'd been made, the weren virus ripping through him. Changing him. Bringing a bit of the dark into his soul.

Though she walked through the human world daily, she'd never lived as a human, and for a moment she wondered what it had been like for him, being pulled away from everything he knew and thrust into the world of fairy tales and nightmares. Probably not one of his better days.

On the sidewalk, the first boy gave Tremaine a shove. "Get on with you, then."

"Stop it, Ash," Tremaine said. "You're fucked in the head if you think I'm going to sell my soul."

Ash laughed. "Little wimp, it's only a piece. You keep the bulk of it, and don't even miss what's gone. And, man, is it worth it," he said, cupping his hand in front of his groin and pantomiming sex.

"It's almost like a community service," Gregor added. "You don't want soul-suckers wandering the streets, do you? Maybe cuddling up close to your Sylvia? They gotta have someplace to come for a snack."

"Fuck that," Tremaine countered. "They destroy you, you know. Suck you dry. You can lose your mind to a succubus. She takes all of your soul, and there's no going back."

Even in the dim light, Lissa could see Ash roll his eyes. "That's bullshit."

"It's true," Tremaine said, and Lissa fought the urge to back up the small werewolf. He was right, after all.

"What a load of crap," Ash said. "And even if it was true, they're not allowed to take a whole soul. It's against the Covenant."

"You trust them to follow the rules?"

Gregor shook his head. "Holy shit, Tremaine, you're a pansy ass. And one hell of a lot more stupid than you look."

"That so?" Tremaine said, taking a menacing step toward his friend. "Then *you* go in."

"Better believe I will," Gregor said. "I could use a solid poke. Been awhile." He took a swaggering step toward the door, then stopped as it flew open in his face and a black-clad figure stepped out, his shoulders broad, his eyes sunken, and his face as hard as if it had been etched from stone.

A vampire. More specifically, one of the same vampires the weren boys had been butting heads with earlier. Another followed, this one shorter but equally foreboding. Great. Apparently Lissa hadn't prevented the problem, only delayed it. Which, frankly, was a pretty apt metaphor. Because despite the treaties and agreements and covenants established after the Great Schism, fighting between the shape-shifters and the vampires bubbled to the surface with predictable regularity.

"Get the fuck out of here," the second one said to them.

The three male werewolves seemed to age as Lissa watched, the soft edge of boys being boys disappearing, replaced by the harsh wariness of hunters.

"Fuck you," Ash said, taking a step toward the vamps. Gregor and Tremaine took positions at his flank, even Tremaine now giving off a soldier's vibe. Whatever hesitation he'd had about sleeping with one of her girls didn't wash over into his street life. He was ready to defend himself. To the death, if necessary.

The lead vamp stepped forward, his mouth cut into a harsh smirk. "Look what we've got here," he said in a voice like acid on sandpaper. "Some pups loose on the street." He cast a careless glance toward his companion. "Got any doggy bones?"

When he turned back, Ash's fist intersected his nose. Lissa sucked in a noisy breath, but neither the vamps nor the weren appeared to have heard her. Across the street, she saw Rand straighten, and even from that distance she could tell that his muscles were tense and ready, expecting a fight to erupt.

She expected it, too. Considering her mood, she wouldn't mind getting in a few blows herself.

She stepped away from the wall and into the light right as the first vampire shoved Ash. The weren snarled, then lunged for the vamp, who met him midway.

"Keep your hands off of me, you damn walking corpse."

The vamp moved faster than Lissa could follow, flipping Ash around and curling his arm under his neck. She could see the vamp's eyes, dark and dangerous, the thin control reflected in his face clearly about to snap. "This is our territory," the vamp whispered.

"Tiberius might be the governor, but we can go wherever we damn well please."

"That a fact?" the shorter vamp retorted. "You want to survive puppyhood, haul your ass over to Paris and stay the fuck out of our city."

The other two weren stepped in, pulling stakes from pockets inside their coats. The vamp holding Ash looked at them and grinned. His partner moved closer, his motions quick and choppy, as if he was holding in the devil, and once he set it free, he'd be destruction personified.

Shit.

She wasn't the only one who thought so, and with dual ferocious howls, Tremaine and Gregor leaped upon the vamp, even as his partner fell upon them.

"Hey!" she called, to absolutely no effect. She itched to take a punch at one of them, but while her temper might be flaring, her brain was still functioning.

Across the street, Rand stood still, watching.

She clenched her teeth, ignored him, and focused on the battle going on in front of her. A loud cry of pain burst out, and then a hand followed, fist closed, hair clutched tight in the fingers. Holy crap, they were going to rip one another to pieces.

Once again, she felt the gun at her hip. This time, it made sense.

She lifted it, aimed toward the sky, and fired.

The brawlers burst apart, faces red, teeth bared. They stared at her, breathing hard.

"Get the hell out of here," she said, lowering the gun and leveling it at each one in turn. "This fires silver," she said to the werewolves, then turned to the vamps. "And wood."

The large vamp met her eyes and grinned icily, then took a single, menacing step toward her. A chill ran up her spine, but she didn't waver.

"I'll do it," she said. "I'll end each and every one of you if you don't get the fuck away from my club." She didn't have to fake the passionate certainty that buoyed her voice. Right then, she meant every word she said.

The vamp's lip lifted in a sneer that twisted with pain as Ash smashed his foot down, then took off running down the sidewalk with his buddies.

"Go," she said to the vamp. "Follow them, or don't. I really don't care. But you're not pulling that shit here."

The second vamp narrowed his eyes, but the tall one who'd been holding Ash regarded her silently, then nodded. She held her breath until he and his companion headed down the street in the direction the weren had run.

She turned—and found Rand standing right behind her.

"Merde!" The curse slipped out without thought.

"French," he said. "Comment ça va?"

"I haven't got a clue what you just said." She frowned, troubled that she'd cursed in a language she didn't speak, then turned to head in the opposite direction. "If you'll excuse me."

"Wait." His voice was low. Commanding.

She stopped, her back to him, and closed her eyes briefly in an effort to control her temper. Then she turned calmly and faced him, forcing herself not to reveal the shock of awareness that ran through, lighting her senses from nothing more than his proximity. "Who the hell do you think you are?"

"Vincent Rand," he said, his face placid, but amusement sparking behind fathomless eyes. "We met earlier."

"So we did." She glanced over her shoulder in the direction the vamps and weren had disappeared. "Thanks so much for the help."

His sudden laughter caught her off guard, and she crossed her arms as she adjusted her stance and met his eyes with her most imperious gaze. "Did I say something funny?"

From the way the corner of his mouth twitched, she was certain the answer was yes. "The last time I stepped in, you put a gun to my head."

"I see your point." She glanced down at the sidewalk, unwilling to let him see her smile.

"Lissa." His voice was low. Rough. And as she looked down, she saw the black leather of his boots glint in the streetlight as he took a step toward her.

She swallowed, hating that her control had faded. She lifted her head, forcing her expression to remain cool.

"You weren't in any danger," he said.

"And if I was?"

He didn't falter, but met her eyes, and when he spoke, she heard the truth in his words. "They'd all be dead."

Her breath hitched and every instinct within her told her not to believe him. Men didn't protect. The strong ones captured. Controlled. And the weak ones lost themselves in her sheen.

This one did neither. Instead he stood and looked at her, as if she were something he wanted but didn't dare take.

"Why are you here?" she asked.

He didn't answer. Instead, he reached out, his fingers gently brushing her cheek. And then, after a moment that seemed to last forever, he turned, walked down the sidewalk, and didn't look back.

CHAPTER 9

Rand slid the Ducati into the lot and killed the engine. He'd left Orlando's planning to grab a few hours of sleep, but had ended up here at the cemetery instead, his mind full of Lissa. He told himself he didn't want her in his head, and yet there she was, filling his thoughts and tightening his balls. Making him want to sink inside and feel her tighten around him.

She's a succubus. There's nothing there. Nothing real.

He should know, right? He knew all about illusions.

He got off the bike, then moved in long strides, the gravel of the parking lot crunching under his feet before he stepped onto the well-tended lawn. He passed quietly down the maze of paths until he found her grave. *Alicia Rand. Beloved Wife.*

Beloved. He traced his fingertip over the word etched deep into the marble. This was the first time he'd seen the grave marker. His Aunt Estelle had taken care of those details while he returned to his unit in Bosnia. Now he had to wonder if his aunt really thought that Alicia had been Rand's beloved wife, or if Aunt Estelle somehow knew—in the same way that she had always known when he'd snuck back to Inglewood to hang with Rollins and his gang, the Crew—that he'd never really loved Alicia.

In his world, men didn't have time for love. They killed, or they got killed.

Hell, from diapers he'd been told that to be a man was to protect his turf—with his fists, with a gun, with whatever it took.

He'd gotten his first tat when he was eight—a black X on his wrist. A kill tat.

It had been Paulie who hadn't understood the game. Paulie who'd stolen the shit from Rand's cousin, Rollins, who then expected Rand to take care of the problem and pop his cherry all with one shot.

They said you never forgot your first kill, and it was true.

There'd been a flicker in Paulie's eyes, the .22-caliber hole in his forehead, and an eerie stillness in the air. Rand didn't eat for three days, because there was a stone in his gut that wouldn't go away. But eventually he ate, eventually the air moved again. And eventually he killed again.

Over time, it had gotten easier. Lots easier. And by the time a rival gang's bullet killed his mother and he went to live with Aunt Estelle in Pasadena, he had three X's, a complete set, marking him as one bad motherfucker.

Nobody argued with Rand.

He was a fighter. A stone-cold killer with no heart to give. Not to his aunt, not to Alicia, not to anyone.

He was the job. He was a killer.

He was the wolf.

On the ground at his feet, flowers spilled out of an overturned vase. He bent to pick up a rose, the petals still soft. Even after all these years, someone still brought flowers to her grave. He clenched his fist, a thorn biting into his palm. She'd loved him, but he'd never understood why. He'd married her because that was what you did when you knocked up a girl, and because she was pretty and banging her felt pretty damn good. He'd wanted to love her, but that wasn't in his blood.

He'd left because the military was where he belonged, and he'd slid easily into Special Ops.

And then he'd gotten the call from Rollins and all hell had broken loose.

Rand had gone home within days of getting the news of Alicia's death, his buddies walking on eggshells around the badass Rand who had to be broken inside. But he wasn't grieving—he didn't feel a goddamned thing except guilt for his lack of grief.

He wasn't a man. He wasn't a husband. He was soulless. Unfeeling.

A cold-blooded animal.

And within weeks of Alicia's death, a werewolf's bite would change his body into the beast he truly was.

Inside, he could feel the heart of the wolf, snapping and biting, impulsive and wild. Things that got a man dead if he wasn't careful, and Rand was always careful.

He took a deep breath, pulling control back in from the depths. Fighting the goddamned tug of the wolf.

Slowly, deliberately, he knelt down and returned the rose to the grave.

The wind shifted, blew across his skin, his nerves responding with life, with change. In an acre of death, he was the only thing alive.

The persistent image returned to his mind—a mane

of blond curls, a patrician nose, and an attitude that rivaled a Wild West sheriff. Heat swept through him, filling his limbs and coloring his thoughts.

He pushed the image aside and pressed his fingers to the cool, smooth surface of the gravestone as if in tribute. "No," he said simply. "No."

◆

"No way in hell I'm working with that bitch," Xeres said, lurching to his feet as Gunnolf's woman, Caris, slipped through the doorway of Rand's de facto office in the back of the Slaughtered Goat. The pub's owner, a burly daemon named Viggo, had married one of Gunnolf's cousins three decades prior, and since that time the pub had become the informal gathering place of Los Angeles therians. The building itself was old, ramshackle, and tucked away in a run-down area of Van Nuys. It smelled of sweat, beer, and trouble.

All in all, Rand felt right at home.

From his seat behind the desk, Rand shot Xeres a hard look. "She's part of this team," he said as Caris sat down, apparently unperturbed by Xeres's outburst.

"She's a vampire," Xeres retorted. A born werewolf who'd been found orphaned at the age of four, Xeres had grown up within Gunnolf's inner circle. But he'd lived in Los Angeles long enough now that Rand knew he'd be an asset. "Just one more fucking bloodsucker."

"She's a vampire," Rand agreed. "And she's working with us." He kept his voice level and his face masked. Caris was Tiberius's former lover, and now she was Gunnolf's woman—a switch that had raised plenty of eyebrows and hadn't done a damn thing to smooth the friction between the groups. And although Rand didn't entirely trust her, she had her uses, especially in light of Jacob's claim that the Outcast planting the rumors had the stink of vampire.

Besides, if he was working with her, he could keep an eye on her.

Xeres's eyes narrowed, but he sat back down, the action punctuated by a snort of displeasure. "Can't fucking believe this," he muttered.

Beside him, Bixby lifted one thin shoulder. Scrawny, with bulging eyes and pasty skin, the were-cat also had mad tech skills. "Looks like vamp kills. Could be vamp kills. Girl can get in. Find out. Got the contacts, don't ya know? So we use her. Smart that way." He beamed at Rand like a dog waiting for a pat from his master's head.

"And this one's just a pain in the ass," Xeres said, hooking his thumb toward Bixby. "Shit, Rand. Are you running an investigation or putting together a comedy troupe?"

"I suppose you'd be the headliner?" Caris asked, crossing her legs to reveal a mile of thigh under the short leather skirt.

"Fuck you."

"Your eloquence never ceases to amaze me."

"Enough," Rand said. "Everyone in this room is here for a reason. You want to second-guess me? Fine. There's the door. But in this room, on this crew, I'm the motherfucker in charge."

He caught Xeres's eye and waited for the huge werewolf to argue. Xeres stayed silent, and Rand nodded in satisfaction.

"Good. We all know the deal. Seven deaths, with number eight coming, and all hell about to break loose at the Alliance. We have one advantage over the PEC investigators," he added. "We can rule out Gunnolf. But if we want to make sure he doesn't get kicked out of the Alliance, then we need to find the real perp." He relayed what he'd learned from Jacob. "Either this Outcast feeding him intel is our perp or he's taking advantage of the situation to spread rumors. We need to know which, and that means finding him." He looked at Xeres. "You start with that angle. Track down all the Outcasts in L.A. and the surrounding counties. We'll go through and eliminate them one by one."

Xeres barked out a laugh. "Shit, man. It's not like they're in the fucking Yellow Pages."

"We find them, we interview them," Rand reiterated. "No one goes completely under. As for you," he continued, shifting his attention to Caris, "I want you to—"

"Focus on the vampire angle," she said, interrupting.

"Got it in one."

"You really think the local vamps are going to tell me anything?"

"I think you still have friends," Rand said. "And if not friends, then connections. Pressure points. You take what you know about the local vamps, and you sort through it, you ask questions, you come up with a solid list of bloodsuckers that we need to talk to. And you do it fast."

"The most likely vamp would be rogue. But a rogue doesn't prance around the city leaving an engraved calling card."

It was an angle Rand had already considered. A

rogue vampire was one whose daemon was out—a vampire who would kill indiscriminately, without either conscience or concern about the law. A rogue was already marked for execution, after all. And the daemon cared about nothing but the kill.

Rand ran a hand over his scalp. He understood the rogues.

"Are there any known rogues in the area?"

Caris looked at him evenly. "That's not something Division advertises. The general public tends to get worked up at the thought of a rogue running around town."

"That's not an answer, Caris."

Her eyes flashed irritably. "I don't know. Sergius went rogue when he was in L.A., but there's no reason to believe he stayed."

"Fair enough. But is there any reason to believe he's gone?"

Caris didn't answer, and Rand turned to Bixby, letting Caris stew, then ordered the were-cat to target all the other therian hangouts in the Los Angeles area. Buy drinks. Mingle. Melt into the shadows. Whatever it took for Bixby to hear what the locals were saying. If an Outcast had planted rumors with Jacob, maybe he'd hit up other therians to spread the dirt as well. "And you're on point for tech work, too," he added. "Xeres or Caris need something hacked, you drop what you're doing and help them out."

"I will, I will. Yes, I will," he said. "But what if the killer ain't from the shadows? What if it's just a human killing humans?"

"It's a possibility," Rand said. "But the PEC stayed

out of it until body number six. Someone at Division took their time deciding that our killer walks in the shadows, and the odds that they're wrong are slim." He shot a hard grin at Bixby. "But actually, you've just laid your finger on another angle. I'm working on a way into the PEC. I want to find out what sort of evidence is stacking up."

"Good luck with that," Xeres said, his expression clearly suggesting Rand was dreaming. Division employees were notably tight-lipped. But it only took one chink to start a leak, and Rand was willing to start tapping.

As soon as the meeting wrapped, Bixby followed Xeres out, muttering vaguely incoherent requests for a ride, which Xeres appeared to ignore.

Rand turned back to the desk, preparing to grab the keys to his Ducati, then realized that Caris was still in her chair, legs still crossed, eyes fixed right on him. "Hanging around?" he asked.

"If you've got a problem with me, I think we should get it out in the open right now."

He grabbed the keys and took a step toward the door. "No problem."

"Dammit, Rand, don't walk away from me."

He stopped and turned back to her.

"Let's get it out," she said.

"Nothing to tell you."

Her face hardened. "When have I ever once given you reason to distrust me?"

"Where do you go?"

Her brow furrowed and he noted that she leaned slightly backward. "What?"

"You leave. Sometimes for days. You did it in Paris, on and off for the last year. Maybe longer. And I've asked around—you do it here, too. It's a simple question. Where do you go?"

"You've been keeping tabs on me?"

He stared at her.

She shook her head, then pointed a finger at him. "Fuck you," she said. "It's the weren curse. Makes you all a bunch of low-life idiots. Next time you're so damned interested in what I've been doing, try gathering your balls and just asking me."

"I am asking."

A muscle in her cheek tightened, and she broke his gaze for the briefest instant, but whether because she was trapped or frustrated, Rand couldn't tell, and he didn't have time to think about it, because she was moving forward, getting right in his face. She smelled fresh and woodsy, like a forest after a rain, the enticing scent counterbalancing the ice in her voice. "It's none of your goddamned business. But it doesn't have a thing to do with this."

"And I'm just supposed to believe that? Why? Because you're fucking Gunnolf?"

She reached out and slapped him hard across the cheek. "The point of this team is to save Gunnolf's ass, so I'll stay on it. But you should learn to watch your language."

"I'll make a note of it."

She turned on her heel and stormed out of his office. He watched her go through flat, emotionless eyes. He didn't have any proof—just a gut-level feeling that she was holding back. As far as he knew, Caris had no motive to backstab her mate, but something was going on with her. Something she was determined to keep secret. Too bad he didn't give a shit what she wanted. He'd come to Los Angeles to do a job. And if that meant poking his nose into Caris's business, then that's what he'd do. His loyalty was to Gunnolf, not Gunnolf's mate.

And if his investigation revealed the worst? If it turned out that she'd betrayed Gunnolf and was somehow behind the murders? In that case, she'd be dead.

He didn't particularly want to kill a female—even a female vamp—but if that's what it took to protect Gunnolf and the weren community, he would do it without hesitation.

♦

There were daisies on the reception desk of the small home office in Pasadena. Daisies on the desk, floral paintings on the walls, and a tiny shop bell hanging over the door that had jingled when Rand entered. The place was sterile and familiar and so goddamned human it made his head ache. Even the smell reminded him of his Aunt Estelle's living room, which reminded him of Aunt Estelle, which reminded him of the life he'd left behind.

A life that had chugged along under his aunt's hawkeyed inspection less than two miles from this very spot.

A side door opened and a girl walked in, wearing jeans, boots, and a long-sleeved T-shirt. Her forehead was furrowed in concentration as she tapped the keys on her phone with fingers covered by thin, gray gloves.

"Just a sec, just a sec," she muttered, apparently talking

to him, but keeping her eyes on the phone. After a few curses, she hit a key triumphantly with a shout of "Ha!" and looked up at him, her grin broad. "Sorry about that. Had to finish."

"Text message?"

"Online chess. Badboy2682 nailed me last week, but he just learned that payback is a bitch." Her mass of short curls bobbed as she tilted her head to the side. "So you must be Rand."

"And you must be Petra."

"In the flesh."

He waited for her to offer her hand, the way his Aunt Estelle would have done in her picture-perfect living room. Instead, the girl gestured to one of the small chairs in front of the desk. As he took a seat, she hauled herself up onto the desktop and let her legs hang, her heels brushing the polished cherry wood. All in all, the girl was nothing like what he'd expected, and he had a hard time imagining that the petite female with the wide eyes and wild curls was really a witch or a PI. Or that she could get her hands on information the PEC wanted to keep hidden.

"You didn't tell me much on the phone," she said. "Now's the time."

He hesitated.

She shook her head, looking exasperated, then spread her arms wide to encompass the room. "I work in both worlds. Humans need something to relate to. Although I might have gone a little overboard with the flower theme." She pursed her lips as she pondered the brightly framed watercolors, then shrugged nonchalantly. "Oh well. It's not like it's hurting business." She hopped off the desk and stood. "Come on."

Curious, he followed her back the way she'd entered, and found himself in a much more dimly lit hallway. A man stood there, tall and lean, his expression hard and his eyes never leaving Petra.

"My bodyguard," she said, her voice dripping with irony. "Otherwise known as my brother. Kiril, meet Rand."

Kiril nodded in greeting, then followed them into a small room, this one lit with candles. Strange objects lined glass shelves, and ancient books—everything from grimoires to mythology textbooks—teetered on table-tops. The room smelled of herbs and smoke, the air tingled with lingering magic, and Rand fought the urge to leave. He may have been thrust into the shadow world, but his role was one he understood, one that dealt in concrete things like life and death.

Magic twisted reality, making him think of Ouija boards and *The Exorcist* and the kind of creepy shit his aunt had said over and over was a slap in the face to God.

He grimaced. Aunt Estelle would surely think he was a slap in the face, too.

"What exactly are you wanting my sister to do?" Kiril asked.

He looked at Petra's brother, his mind back in the game. "I want her to get information."

"That's what I do," Petra said, sitting down on a velvet-covered chaise. She leaned back, as if relaxing, but her sharp eyes never once left him.

"What kind of information?" Kiril asked.

"The kind the PEC wants to keep confidential," Petra said. "He explained a little when he called. Now he's going to tell us the rest. Aren't you?"

He took another look around the room, with its trappings of magic and atmosphere. That shit might give him the creeps, but this was why he'd come to her. Because she walked in that world, and right now he had to use everything the shadow world had to offer. "I guess I am," he said, then told her what she needed to know. "Can you do it?" he asked, when he'd summed up the basics.

"Not easy getting information Division wants to keep quiet," she said. "And nobody in the shadow government wants rumors about who's killing all these humans floating around. Especially not in this climate," she added. "I mean, what with the therians and the vamps being so snappish."

"Snappish?" he repeated, unable to hide his amusement.

She shrugged. "That's what it looks like from my perspective."

"What perspective is that? An investigator? A witch?"

"A little of both. Mostly just as a human. It's like watching something brew in South Central."

"Yeah," Rand agreed, knowing firsthand what she meant. "It is."

"You'd know," she said. "But you're a long way from Inglewood these days."

He flinched, her words taking him by surprise.

"I like to know who's hiring me," she said simply.

He frowned. His story was his, not out there for nosy investigators to poke into.

But it was a nosy investigator that he needed, and his past was hardly secret. Only his Black Ops missions as a human and the *kyne* assignments he did for Gunnolf.

"Can you get me what I need?"

"Of course."

"I'll throw in a bonus for speed."

"I'll work fast. And I'll let you know what I've got tomorrow." She stood up. There was nothing left to be said.

Kiril leaned against the door. As far as Rand could tell, he hadn't moved a muscle—at least not until Aunt Estelle's training kicked in and he held out his hand to shake Petra's. Then Kiril bristled, his eyes narrowing as he took one step forward.

Petra took a step back, eyeing his hand as if it would bite. Rand dropped his hand, and Petra smiled. "I think we'll work together just fine," she said.

He didn't press. He'd lived in this world long enough to know that some secrets didn't need to be shared. By the time he was back on his Ducati, Petra's secrets weren't even on his mind. Instead he was preoccupied with the PEC's secrets, and his hope that by tomorrow Petra would have a few answers.

Just in case she wasn't as good as she thought, Rand had a contingency plan. He pulled the bike over long enough to make a call to an old buddy who'd left Gunnolf's inner circle to go be all respectable within the walls of Division 6 itself. The odds that his friend would risk his ass to feed Rand information were slim, but Rand could be persuasive when he needed to.

He was about to fire up the bike again when he saw the Wash 'n' Go and realized he was only two blocks over from Morningstar Drive. Aunt Estelle's street. *His* old street.

He should go see her. She'd loved him, after all. Despite everything he was, his aunt had truly loved him.

He popped the clutch and started the bike, then drove the short distance to the house. It looked the same as always, its porch railing painted yellow to match the chrysanthemums that bloomed in the brightly painted pots. *Home.*

He should go up. Knock on the door. Hug his aunt and tell her—

Tell her what?

This was the woman who'd literally hauled his ass out of the gang territory. Who'd verbally ripped him a new asshole when she'd learned that he'd snuck back to see Rollins. The woman who'd made him gargle dish soap if he used gang slang around her, which cleaned up his language but not his habit of sneaking back whenever he could. The woman who'd grounded him, threatened him, and finally praised him when he'd joined the army, so happy that he wouldn't end up like those animals in the gangs.

Those animals . . .

So what was he supposed to tell her? That he'd become exactly the thing that destiny had picked out for him? An animal?

Or maybe that he lived in a supernatural world now? With daemons and witches and goddamned werewolves.

Oh, yeah. That would make her so fucking proud.

He'd become everything she never wanted him to be . . . and then some.

A shadow moved behind the curtains. His aunt, doing her daily dusting. He watched a moment longer, wanting to see her, but knowing she wouldn't want to see the man he'd become. As far as she knew, he was still overseas, going where Uncle Sam sent him. Best to let her keep thinking that.

A pang of regret shot through him, but he buried it under the roar of the engine and the slap of wind on his face as he tore off down the street. He opened the engine up on the highway, then maneuvered over to the Pacific Coast Highway and roared up past Malibu. After a while, he did a hard U-turn, putting the ocean on his right, and followed it down to the 10. He cruised inland, searching for something that the power and speed of the bike wasn't satisfying. Seeing his aunt's house had left a hole in his gut, and he needed it filled. Needed a release. Needed to forget.

He hadn't realized he was thinking of Lissa until he found himself pulling up in front of Orlando's. Then he realized she'd been in his head all along, hiding in his mind, tempting him with delicious promises. And, yeah, he was tempted. He wanted her, plain and simple. And the fact that she'd flatly and resolutely turned him down wasn't going to fly tonight. She was the one he wanted, and she was the one he'd have. And if persuasion wouldn't work, then he was damn certain money would. After all, Lissa was clearly a businesswoman.

He left his bike on the sidewalk, ignoring the protests from the woman working the door. "I need to see Lissa."

She switched her scowl from the bike to him. "Lissa's not on the premises tonight."

"What?" He'd come for her. She had to be there.

"She's not here. Can someone else help you? The floor manager, perhaps?"

"No," he said. "No one else."

Numb, frustrated, and horny as hell, he thanked the girl, his voice calm and steady.

Inside, though, he wasn't calm.

Inside, the beast roared.

CHAPTER 10

"Could you repeat that?" Nicholas Montegue stood on the stone patio of Luke's Malibu house, looking out at the raging sea. His mind tried to process his friend's words, but they fell like marbles to the ground, rolling away before he could grasp any meaning.

"Elizabeth," Luke repeated. "She's alive again."

"I see." Nick turned and pressed his hands against the railing, his emotions roiling. *Lissa.* Could it really be true?

A low anger rose within him, threatening to call out the daemon he had for so long mastered. In the distance, waves battered the shore beneath a star-filled sky.

"I thought I should tell you."

Nick didn't answer, the anger swallowed by the hunger of a desire still ripe after all these years, still sharp despite the hurt that should have dulled the need to nothing more than a memory.

His mind had drifted back. To Paris. To the years before the revolution. He could remember the first time he'd seen her among Baron de Villefort's cortegery. The silk cerulean gown hugged her curves, accentuating her breasts and her tiny waist. She stood in a cluster of males, her dark curls brushing pale shoulders, her cheeks blooming as she blushed prettily at what was surely a series of off-color jokes, not fit for a lady of the time, even a lady of the cortegery.

He'd asked her to dance. She'd accepted. And he had fallen under her spell.

As he stood now, staring out at the sea, he had to admit that the spell had never lifted.

He closed his eyes and imagined her face, her Caribbean blue eyes. Even now, he could feel the touch of her fingers upon his skin. He recalled the way she made him laugh, and the way she would sit with him, listening to him speak of his passion for the stars, for philosophy, for the science of their time. They would talk for hours, her quick wit challenging him, setting fire to his mind even as her curves caused his body to burn.

Most of all, he remembered the way she had smiled when he had told her that he loved her. And he remembered the way his heart had shattered and his daemon had roared when he learned that she'd taken plans from his head, then sold them to the very creature he'd been hunting. A creature who'd used the knowledge to turn the tables on Nick and his team.

It had been a bloodbath, a fucking bloodbath, and one that Nick had barely survived. His team hadn't been so lucky.

He had not killed her, though his anger nearly pushed him to it. He couldn't, and instead, he lost himself, the daemon rising. Destroying.

He'd killed—oh, yes, he had killed. But he had not harmed Lissa. Even the daemon could not bear to destroy the one creature in all the world who had brought Nicholas such happiness. And such pain.

And so she had lived on, while Nicholas had sunk

deep into the daemon's madness, farther than he had ever fallen before, so far he almost lost himself forever.

"Nick?"

"I had heard that she died," he said, his voice strange. "Years later I heard that she died only weeks after I— after I lost myself." He turned to face Luke. "I hadn't heard that she had been reborn."

"Would you have expected to?" His friend's voice was gentle. Of all of those close to Nick, only Luke and Serge knew the way that she had betrayed him. And only Serge understood fully what that betrayal had cost him.

"No. But it—it is a shock." He turned, facing Luke, determined to push away the memories, to gather his wits. "Does she remember?"

"I don't know. I doubt it. Most only remember bits and pieces, don't they?"

Nick shrugged. He had known the women of the baron's cortegery, but that hardly made him an expert regarding the multiple lives of succubi. "Have you seen her?"

"No. Apparently she owns a soul-trading club. Orlando's."

"I've heard of it," Nick admitted. "I had no idea it was hers." No idea she was in Los Angeles, so close he could have reached out and touched her. Seen her.

An invisible band tightened around his chest, and he turned once more toward the violent waves. "How did you learn this?"

"Doyle," Luke said, the harshness in his tone reflecting his feelings for the para-daemon.

"What about Doyle?" Luke and the para-daemon

had been friends once, and after what had happened to Sara, Nick had thought they would be again.

Not quite.

"Apparently he frequents Orlando's. He's crafting an operation around her. A sting for later tonight. We need her skill, Nick. Her particular skill."

"Then she still has the ability, even in this life?"

Luke nodded. "Doyle believes so."

"And she's using it?" His daemon writhed and shifted as he wondered whom she was fucking, who her new mark was.

"Yes."

"And yet the PEC hasn't arrested her?" His words came out clipped, and he realized he'd closed his hands into fists, fighting the image of her that had risen in his mind.

An image that had, for more than two centuries, been alive in his dreams.

"According to Doyle, they've been watching her for years."

Nick heard the compassion in Luke's voice and hated it. "So the PEC simply chose to ignore her crimes? It is still a crime to steal information from a man's head, is it not?"

"It is. But if Division's knowledge of that crime can provide leverage . . ."

"They were waiting," Nick said. "Waiting until they needed to use her as an informant. Then they play the prosecutors' game and arrest her and threaten her with prison, with bondage, even with death. And once she's quaking with fear, they offer her an out. Do this one thing for us, and we will forgive your crimes. Work for us, and have your slate wiped clean."

Luke's smile was thin. "You almost sound like an advocate for the defense."

"Fuck you."

Luke laughed, and Nick actually smiled.

He wouldn't admit it out loud—could barely even admit it to himself—but he had never stopped loving her. Despite the sting of her betrayal—despite the cold hate he'd let brew within him—he loved her as he'd loved no other woman before or since.

And now he knew how to see her again.

"I'll represent her," he said.

Luke's expression darkened. "I don't think that's a good idea."

"I don't recall soliciting opinions on the matter."

"Nicholas—"

"No. She is about to be arrested, charged, and threatened with prison. She is about to be asked to do something for the PEC, and though you have not told me what, I expect that not only is it dangerous, it is necessary. This woman is about to do something for Division that it cannot do with its own resources. There's value in that, and I will not have her unrepresented, or incompetently represented. I will be there, Luke. I will protect her interests."

"Tiberius won't allow it."

"Fuck Tiberius."

Luke cocked his head.

Nick sighed. "Tiberius will agree, I'm confident."

"He assigned you to search for Sergius."

There was no reproach in Luke's words or his tone,

but Nick cringed nonetheless. "For six months I've been all over this goddamned earth. I've chased rumors and shadows and trails of dead bodies. I've found nothing." The failure ate at him. After Lissa's betrayal, it had been Serge who'd combed the countryside, following Nick's trail of destruction. It had been Serge who'd risked the rising of his own volatile daemon by capturing Nick and forcing him into the Holding. It had been Serge who'd remained at Nick's side for four months in the bitter cold of an alpine cabin, not leaving until Nick was himself again, still tender from Lissa's betrayal, but no longer staring into the dark maw of madness.

"I hope he is out there, Luke, so help me, I do. But at this point, I fear that our friend is dead. Or worse."

Luke eyed him sideways. "Then you're afraid of it, too?"

Nick nodded, then sighed. "I have no proof. Not even one shred of evidence. Hell, I don't even have any proof he's here in Los Angeles, but you know as well as I do that if anyone in this world can hide himself away, it's Serge."

"You think he could be killing the humans."

"I think we can't ignore the possibility. His daemon's surfaced, Luke. There's no way that's working out to a pretty picture." Nick thought of the dead humans, each one lying cold in a grave because Nick had failed to find his friend.

"If you're right," Luke said, "then Serge really will fall to the PEC's stake."

"I know." Though Tiberius had assigned Nick to bring Sergius in, Nick had accepted the job so that he could help his friend to control the daemon, to fight his way back through the dark, and then, he hoped, to persuade Tiberius to withdraw the order to execute. But now, with Tiberius's governorship hanging in the balance, Nick knew damn well there would be no reprieve.

Luke said nothing, simply stared out at the white-capped waves of the Pacific.

"Tiberius will agree," Nick said, more firmly this time. As if firmness could make it so.

"She betrayed you, Nick. She betrayed you in the most horrible of ways. Why the hell are you doing this?"

Nick looked out over the foaming ocean. "Even the guilty require representation."

"Why are you doing this?" Luke repeated, not buying Nick's bullshit.

Waves pounded against the beach, and Nick felt something hot unfurl within him. Embers of desire. A hint of excitement. "Because I can."

CHAPTER 11

For her girls, Lissa reminded herself as the man—*Claude*—cupped his palms over her bare breasts. *This was to protect herself, and her club, and her girls.* She straddled the human and forced herself to feign enjoyment as his hands stroked her rear.

Usually, she didn't have to pretend. There was pleasure in sex, although nothing as amazing as taking a sliver of soul, the sublime twining of the soft ribbons around and through her. Nothing matched the exquisite joy that filled her when bits of soul danced along her skin and slipped in through her pores.

How could anything match that? Certainly not the mere joining of bodies.

But as crude as such joining might be, she couldn't deny the sweetness that accompanied the act. The sensual meshing of bodies, the touches and caresses that brought such delicious satisfaction.

But it was a physical pleasure, never more. She wasn't entirely certain what that "more" would feel like, but in the classic movies she adored she could see that spark in the characters' eyes. An adoration and connection that was based on more than a physical coupling. She wanted to experience that. To hold that bit of "more" in her hands and cherish it. She couldn't, though. She knew that. That was love, and succubi weren't wired that way.

She leaned forward, her back arched as his hands traced up her spine and his body shook with pleasure.

She stifled a sigh.

Today she could only go through the motions, counting down until the moment when his soul broke free and the genuine ecstasy of the taking would spread through her.

Priam expected her to take all of it. That was his demand. Lissa was supposed to take Claude's entire soul, along with the information in his head. Do that, and Priam would leave her alone.

Lissa didn't believe the daemon for one minute.

If she took Claude's entire soul, then Priam would have one more mark against her—and a damn potent one, too.

So Lissa had told Priam she agreed to his terms, but she didn't really mean it.

She'd take a piece of Claude's soul—why not? She took pieces of soul all the time. Usually she took with consent, but it wasn't as if she would be hurting the human. Humans lived with mangled souls all the time and never even noticed.

And as long as she took a piece of soul, she could get the information from his head, and Claude would never even know it had been stolen.

But the entire thing? No way. No fucking way.

And when she saw Priam again, she'd be the one in charge. Claude would still have his soul, Priam would have nothing new to hold over her head, and she'd dangle the information he wanted against her freedom from any future bullshit demands.

Her plan would work.

It had to work.

Beneath her, Claude moaned, so very close to finishing.

Thank heavens for that.

Sometimes, if it took longer than expected to withdraw a client's soul, she would try to find the sweetness of intimacy in her own imagination, replacing the man beneath her with a faceless male who had recently entered her fantasies. An unknown man who could bring her to her knees with nothing more than a glance, and whose touch brought the same pleasure as the twining of a soul.

Beneath her, the man writhed, small moans of pleasure rising up to meet her. She arched her back again and drew in a breath, hoping she appeared to be enjoying herself, when really she was escaping into the waiting arms of fantasy.

She could see him in her mind, a figure, dark and faceless. Yet somehow she knew that he was watching her with that sensual intensity. He moved forward, and for the first time, she caught a flash of his eyes, so brown they were almost black, and full, clever lips that were designed to pleasure a woman.

His shoulders were broad, his skin like coffee touched with a dab of cream, his arms tight and strong. And though he moved toward her in her mind, she knew he wouldn't come so far as to step out of the shadows. The man in her fantasy never did, always staying in the dark, his face hidden even when he touched her, even when he bent down to kiss her.

He did that now, his face easing forward in her

imagination, but this time, the shadows slipped away as his features slid into the light.

Rand.

She gasped.

"Oh, yes!" the man beneath her said.

She ignored him as Rand smiled in her mind, slow and sensual and full of decadent promise.

She wanted to turn away. Wanted to escape the inescapable realization that he'd so cleanly and deeply gotten under her skin. Men craved *her,* not the other way around.

Panic quickened her pulse. The iron-tight grip she'd kept for so long on her control had loosened, and if she let it slip any more the world she'd worked so hard to piece together would unravel.

And yet there she was, losing herself in ecstasy. She could feel Rand's hands on her breasts, his thumbs caressing her nipples. She gave in to pleasure, arching her back, wanting more. Wanting his hands everywhere. Wanting his lips on her skin. Craving the tingle of electricity that could shoot through her body from little more than the brush of a finger.

He could give her that.

She trembled at the thought, somehow knowing that Rand's touch would fill her in ways she'd never experienced, in ways not even matched by the gentle thrill of a soul twining around her, those vibrant strands of orange caressing her, filling her. Making her warm. Taking her higher and higher to the kind of ecstasy that lived only in dreams.

In her mind, his lips met hers, his mouth hot and demanding.

"Oh, yes, baby!" the man cried, but in her mind, it was Rand's hands touching her. Rand's fingers stroking her. Her body thrummed, not from the sex, but from what was coming—what she was made for. *The extraction of the soul . . .*

A low groan filled the room, and Rand's image faded, pushed aside by the power building within her, rising, filling, *taking*. And then there it was—the whisper of the man's soul rising in thin strands to twine around them. Thinner than she'd anticipated, like cotton candy stretched to the limit, but still vibrant, still *soul*, and she tilted her head back and thrust her arms out, taking it into her, her eyes closed as she used her mind's eye to watch the way the strands twisted and twined around her, caressing naked flesh, joining and melding until she was more than she'd been before. *Exquisite.*

It was times like this, in the taking, that she truly loved what she was. There was life here. Joy. And through the veil of the soul she could see all the beauty of the world.

Beneath her, the man's body trembled, the ultimate pleasure rising up to meet him. "Almost there," she whispered, as she pressed the heels of her hands to her forehead—summoning the dark trick that made her so different from all her peers. As she did, the man shifted beneath her and she realized that the delicious orange strands were fading, losing form. If she took his thoughts, she'd have to take the rest of his soul, and she couldn't do that. Even taking a smidgeon without consent was illegal, but if she drew out the entire soul, the penalty under the Covenant was death.

Fear prickled over her. A creature without a soul was mangled. Wrong.

Some simply hollowed out. Empty and lonely and full of despair. But some were nothing short of evil.

Screw Priam and his secrets, she thought, trying to get off. But the man tightened his grip on her hips and pumped. She bit back a curse, panic threatening, and tried again. Claude wasn't about to give up the prize—he was close, and he was strong, and he was determined.

Sweat broke out in beads on his red face, the orange strands of his soul waving around him, seeking Lissa. She twisted, trying not to be the creature she was, but there was no stopping it—if he was coming, then his soul was sliding into her.

"Stop! Dammit, you have to stop!" But he was deaf now. Deaf and pumped up on the ecstasy of sex and not about to let her go. He grabbed her hard at the hips and tumbled sideways, trapping her beneath him and pumping, pumping, not stopping the pumping. His soul was little more than wisps now. If he actually came, he'd lose it all, and no one would believe that she'd tried to stop. She beat at him, but his grip was like iron. He was fucking himself out of humanity and not even knowing it, and cold terror iced her skin. All she wanted now was to get out of there. Get away, and forget she'd ever—

"Oh, yeah, baby, fuck yes, yes, yes!"

"No!" She clawed her way out from under him, as the last remnants of his soul engulfed her. *It was over.*

She scrambled free, breathing hard, terror completely overshadowing the sweetness of the soul that even now seeped into her pores.

"Where the *fuck* do you think you're going?" Claude

was right there, standing over her, and then his hand smashed down, catching her hard across the cheek and knocking her sideways. She gasped, looking up into flat, dead eyes as he kicked her hard in the stomach. She curled up, hugging her knees, protecting her middle as she summoned the preternatural strength that usually flowed through her after a soul-taking. But there was no strength. His soul had been too thin to give her power, and she was going to have to fight on her own.

"Should kill you right now, I should," he howled, and she searched with her eyes, trying to find something within reach that she could use as a weapon. Something that would stop the psychopath she'd just made.

Nothing.

She heard him behind her and tensed for the next blow. She'd grab his foot and yank him down. She'd run. She'd get the hell out of there. It would work. It had to.

Except she never had the chance to try. The blow didn't come.

Instead, she heard the door open, then slam closed. Slowly, she shifted, then sat up.

The room was empty. His clothes were gone.

She drew in a breath, forcing herself to focus. She'd clawed her way out of the cortegery. She'd done the same for dozens of girls. She ran a successful business, and no one messed with her because they knew she could hold her own.

Well, that wasn't going to stop today. She was damn well going to get a grip.

She pulled on her dress, talking herself through the steps. Arm, arm, zip. Now shoes. Now purse.

She smoothed her hair, then moved to the mirror to check her makeup.

Tears, she saw, streamed down her face, and for the first time, she realized she'd been crying.

Stop it.

With the back of her hand, she brushed the tears away, then used the edge of her thumb to wipe away the mascara that streaked the tender skin beneath her eyes.

After a few more ministrations, she decided that she looked passable. She'd go down to the lobby and meet Priam. Not her original plan, but she'd make it work. She really did have Claude's entire soul—and she'd damn well use it to negotiate the daemonic bastard right out of her life.

Finally ready, she pulled open the hotel room door and found herself staring at the familiar face of a lanky para-daemon.

A finger of fear snaked up her spine as she tried to remember how she knew him. She tamped it down, managing to conjure a bright smile. She tried to step past him, but he moved in front of her, blocking her way. "If you'll excuse me, I'm running a little late."

"No can do," he said, pulling a thin leather wallet out of his pocket. He flipped it open, revealing the shiny silver badge of a PEC investigator. "Agent Ryan Doyle. And right now, Lissa, we need to talk."

CHAPTER 12

Sara watched the woman through the one-way glass. She'd expected Lissa to be scared. To draw into herself or beg for counsel or scream that she didn't belong there.

The succubus did none of that. For the last two hours, she'd done nothing except sit tall and straight, her hands clasped in front of her on the battered metal table. Once or twice, she looked toward the glass, as if she could see Sara standing there. Nothing shifted in her expression, but Sara saw a strength that she admired.

She didn't want to admire it. The woman took souls, after all. And, yeah, Sara might drink blood now, but souls were . . . well, *souls*.

Now I lay me down to sleep territory. The very essence of life, the eternal kind of life.

So how the hell could this woman just take them?

"You're still clinging to your old-world beliefs," Luke said beside her.

They were alone in the antechamber, and she leaned against him, her eyes still on Lissa. He drew his arm around her and pulled her close.

"My thoughts aren't my own anymore," she said.

He kissed the top of her head. "Does that bother you?"

She tilted her head back, then smiled at him. "No."

"The soul trade has been around since the beginning of time. Without it, creatures like Doyle would be much more of a danger to humans than they are. And the succubi need souls, too. Not for nourishment, but—"

"For what?"

"They live, they die, they are reborn. Souls lengthen their lives. Enough souls, and a succubus could become essentially immortal, just like us."

Immortal. She'd wanted it—wanted Luke and everything that having him meant—but it was still new, and a lot to get used to.

"But to take it, even to give it away . . ." She trailed off, shuddering. "We're talking about souls, Luke. *Souls.*"

"Any person—even those of us in the shadows—can willingly give up our soul. Tragedy can rip it. Love can expand it. It is not a constant thing. It can be shared. Worn. Treasured. And as long as some is left, it can grow." He brushed her cheek. "I feel your soul within me all the time."

Her throat felt thick. "Luke."

"But like everything else, there are rules, and taking without permission is a crime. And taking the entire soul is unforgivable."

"I know the law, Luke. I'm not talking about that. I'm—"

"Talking like a human. I know. But you're not human anymore."

"No," she admitted, then squeezed his hand. "But I still feel like I am."

His arms tightened around her, drawing her close and offering love and support and understanding. She closed her eyes, accepting what he was willing to give, then opened them again when she heard the click of the door. Doyle stepped in, followed by Nick, and Sara slid out of her husband's arms and back into the role of prosecutor.

"Wonder boy here says he's going to represent the defendant."

"Is he?" Sara crossed her arms over her chest and smiled. "This will be just like old times."

"Except that my client isn't going to face a courtroom. She's going to be the picture of cooperation."

"Does she know that? For that matter, does she know you?"

"She will soon."

"Can we get moving?" Doyle asked.

"Would you rather I interview her?" Sara asked.

"Why?" Doyle asked. "She's going to be my CI."

"Things have changed," Sara said. "When we first talked about using her as a confidential informant, you said she was running a blackmail scheme." She thought of the report she'd received less than an hour earlier from the two officers who'd tailed Lissa's mark from the hotel. She stifled a shiver, unable to get the images the officers had sent to her phone out of her mind. "What we just learned changes everything."

"And what did you just learn?" Nick asked, glancing between her and Doyle.

Sara shot him a cool look. "Need to know, Nicholas. And until she formally retains your services, you don't need to know."

"All it changes is our lever," Doyle insisted, handily ignoring Nick. "She'll cooperate now. She won't even think of hesitating."

The point was valid, but that didn't mean Sara had to like it. "Still . . . she's a succubus. And you're male." She glanced at Luke, hoping he'd back her up. "I really think I should be the one going in."

Doyle snorted. "I'll grant you she's a hell of a looker, but I'm blind to a pretty face."

"She's more than a pretty face," Sara said. "Dammit, Doyle, this isn't a—"

Luke's hand rested on her shoulder, silencing her as much as his soft words. "Doyle's a soul-taker, too. That gives him an edge dealing with succubi."

"I see," she said, though she really didn't. "And you?" she asked, turning her attention to Nick. "You can't cut any deals, so you're really not my problem, but do you want to just waltz in there with a woman who can wrap you around her little finger?"

"That really won't be a problem," Nick said, his expression tight.

Frowning, she looked at Luke, who shook his head a fraction of an inch.

Sara nodded at the door. "It's your party. Don't cross any lines, Doyle," she added with a quick glance toward Nick. "Her attorney plays hardball."

♦

Lissa's nerves were shot. Agent Doyle had handed her off to some administrator who'd passed her off to someone in a uniform who'd dumped her unceremoniously into this interview room. She wasn't cuffed to the table, but she also wasn't free to leave. She knew. She'd tried the door.

No one, however, had told her why she was there.

At first, she'd been sick with fear. But once she was settled in the backseat of Doyle's eyesore of a car, she realized that this couldn't be about Claude's soul. There was no way—no way in hell—that Division could know she'd taken all of it. After all, it wasn't as if souls were equipped with little tracking devices and folks at the PEC spent their days monitoring them on a big green board.

Maybe they knew about her blackmail scheme? Maybe Priam had ratted her out after all?

She didn't know, and she was almost to the point of going mad from speculation when the light above the door shifted from red to green and Agent Doyle sauntered in, a folder tucked under his arm, followed by another male. She paid little attention to the second male, though; finally, she remembered how she knew Doyle. "You come to Orlando's," she said. "I recognize you now."

"I've got a long-standing open account," he confirmed.

She leaned back in her chair. "Apparently I need to pay more attention to who my staff is authorizing with account privileges." She turned to the other male, a vampire, and very easy on the eyes. Like Doyle, there was something familiar about him, but she was certain he'd never set foot in her club.

"Who are you?"

"Nicholas Montegue. Your advocate."

The hair on the back of her neck prickled, but she forced a casual retort. "Funny. I think I'd remember hiring an advocate."

"Trust me, you want to retain me."

"Trust *me*," she countered. "I make my own decisions when it's my ass that's on the line."

Doyle pulled out a chair, then flipped it around and straddled it. "Hire him, fire him, I don't care. But right now we need to talk. You want counsel, then go with this guy. You can toss him out on his ass later. You want to waive your right to an advocate, that's fine, too. Just say the word and we'll bruise his ass up now."

She ran her tongue over her teeth. "And if I want counsel, but just not *this* counsel?" She had no reason to shun Montegue, but she felt a lingering discomfort around him. A hint of a memory, a feeling. Something just out of reach.

"No problem," Doyle said, standing back up, his rangy features schooled into an expression of complete cooperation. "I'll have a phone brought in. I'm sure you'll be comfortable waiting here a little while longer until your advocate shows." He cocked his head toward the door, his eyes on Montegue. "Looks like you've been spurned, buddy boy."

"Lissa . . ."

She said nothing, watching as the men exchanged glances. She eyed the glass, wondering who was outside, watching the show within. The *Lissa Show* in this small cement room, with its drab gray walls and hidden cameras.

Every minute she was in here was a minute she wasn't at her club supporting free enterprise and a capitalist economy. The world needed her. Her girls needed her.

Doyle pulled open the door, gesturing for Montegue to leave. She held out a hand, stopping him.

"Why?" she said. "Why do I want to retain you?"

Montegue looked at her, just looked, and the gaze lasted almost longer than was comfortable. "Because I'm the best."

She was certain it wasn't what he'd planned to say, but she didn't call him on it, because during his hesitancy she'd realized the truth: She did know him. Not from this life, but from the past. She didn't remember him—had absolutely no clue who he was or how she knew him—but she was certain she was right.

She licked her lips, then nodded. "All right. For the time being at least, I'm represented by Mr. Nicholas Montegue."

Doyle let the door fall shut, then returned to his chair. "Glad we got that worked out. Big load off my shoulders, that's for sure."

She glanced at Montegue, who remained standing. "I'd like to know why I'm here."

"The charges, Doyle. My client has a right to know exactly why you brought her in. And," he added with a sudden harshness, "why you're keeping her here."

"Exactly?" Doyle repeated. "Well, *exactly*, we brought her in on twenty-seven counts of extortion, all in violation of the Fifth International Covenant."

She swallowed, not quite able to believe what she was hearing. "Twenty-seven?"

"We've been watching you for a long, long time, Lissa," Doyle said, his tone calm while his words brutally exploded all of her fantasies that she'd been operating so well under the radar.

He cracked his knuckles. "Tidy little side business

you've got there. Gather the info, blackmail a few lowlifes, help those poor girls."

She opened her mouth to defend her actions, but his talk of lowlifes and poor girls stayed her tongue. Better to keep quiet and see where this was going.

"Interesting," Montegue said.

"What's that?"

"That you've been watching for so long, but now you choose to arrest." He stood behind Lissa, his hands on the back of her chair. "This isn't about what she's done, it's about what you want. So lay your offer on the table, Agent, and my client will decide if she's willing to play."

Lissa fought not to smile. Apparently, she really had chosen the best.

Doyle shrugged. "Maybe we just didn't feel like bothering before. Division doesn't arrest for every crime, and we plead out a lot of cases." He stood up. "You're right, though. A plea sounds like the way to go on these charges. On the other, though—"

"What other?" Montegue asked, as Lissa stiffened, the fear that had started to fade rushing back.

Doyle had been holding the folder. Now he tossed it onto the table. It stayed closed, but the papers inside shifted, the edges of a few peeking out. A white border around something gray, like photographs. Lissa swallowed, suddenly terribly afraid of whatever was inside that folder.

Doyle nodded toward the tabletop. "Gotta admit we weren't expecting this." He lifted his head to look at Lissa. "We went to the hotel for you, had a warrant for those twenty-seven counts all nice and neat in my pocket. Brought you in, sat you down, figured we'd have ourselves a nice little chat. And then, while you were in here, and I was out there getting all my ducks in order, we learned this." One solid tap to the folder.

"I have to tell you, I didn't doubt for a second you'd be willing to cooperate with us, but they weren't so sure." He glanced toward the mirror and whoever was out there with Lissa locked in their sights. "Now we all know damn well that you're going to be cooperative. Very cooperative."

They knew. There was no other explanation. They knew what she'd done to Claude.

Montegue, however, didn't. "You want cooperation, I suggest you drop the mystery and tell us the facts," he said. "My client's not inclined to do anything for you simply because you like to hear yourself talk."

Doyle's thin smile reeked of victory. "Our final charge," he told Montegue. He flipped open the folder, then ran his hand over the stack of papers, effectively spreading them out. Lissa's stomach tightened as she looked at the array of gruesome images of bloody bodies, saliva forming in her mouth. Dear God, she was going to lose it.

She turned away and found that Montegue had moved even closer. He cupped her head, and she took the comfort willingly, resting her forehead against his thigh. His fingers twined in her hair, the gesture soothing, and she stayed there, breathing deep through her mouth, willing the nausea to pass.

"Olivia Perkins," Doyle said, his voice monotone as he rested his index finger on a photograph showing a toddler. "Strangled with a curtain sash. She had it the easiest." His hand moved to the next picture. "Timothy

Perkins. Throat cut. Made a mess of it, though. Boy was twelve and big for his age. He put up a fight. Didn't do any good." The finger moved to the next. "Amanda Perkins. Pregnant. Stabbed in the chest. Can't see it from the picture—what with all the blood—but her heart was ripped out." One photo remained. "Claude Perkins— I think you know him? Put a bullet through his head. I like to think it was remorse that he'd just killed his family, but I don't know that a creature without a soul feels remorse. I think the son of a bitch was just fucked up."

Lissa opened her mouth, wanting to say something, wanting to cry that this wasn't real, and that she'd only seen him a few hours ago, and he couldn't possibly have done this. But she knew that wasn't true. She'd taken his soul, and Claude Perkins wasn't the kind to sleepwalk through the rest of his life. He was violent, and hard, and without a soul there was nothing to hold that violence in.

She closed her eyes.

"Hard to look at, isn't it? Hard to know you played a part. That he rushed home from his oh-so-cozy encounter with you, and without even a second thought murdered his entire family. Do you know he killed the dog, too? Didn't bring in that picture. Maybe I should have."

"Careful," Montegue said.

Doyle narrowed his eyes as he spoke to Montegue. "This is our final charge. The complete extraction of a soul from a human. That's a Class 5 violation, and she's looking at life in prison." Doyle turned to look her straight in the eyes. "No execution for a succubus. That's too much like a do-over."

The walls seemed to move in closer, the temperature rising. She still wore the sleeveless black dress, and she felt a single drop of perspiration trickle from under her arm down to her waist. She opened her mouth, found it too dry to speak, and tried again. "I'd like a moment to talk to my advocate." She met Doyle's eyes—dark, weary eyes that saw way too much. "I'd like the recorders off."

Doyle stood up. "Hey, you want it, you got it." He paused at the door and looked back at her. "You made a big mistake, kid, but I like you. Like your establishment. Orlando's is the only soul-trading club I can walk out of without feeling like I've got a layer of grime on me. I want to help you out here. I really do."

She swallowed, wondering if he was playing good cop, who'd be coming in to take the other role.

The door clicked shut, leaving her alone with Montegue.

He took the chair and sat opposite her, then he leaned back casually, as if they'd just finished dinner and were waiting for the waiter to arrive with brandy. "I'm your advocate no matter what happened," he said. "But to best represent you, I need to know the truth. All of it. There's a deal on the table somewhere. A sweet one, I think, that will make all that go away."

She turned to the photos. "Nothing will make that go away."

"You're right," he said, his voice softer. "And nothing will bring that family back. But we can spare you the life sentence. To do that, though, I need all the ammunition. And that means all the facts. You get that?"

She nodded. She didn't want to tell him—wanted to

keep the whole thing locked up in a box—but she wasn't naive. She knew how this worked. And, yeah, she wanted to cut a deal. The best one Montegue could make.

"There's another trader. Priam. He's the one who set me up with Claude." She drew in a breath. "He threatened me. My club. My girls."

"How?"

She told him. "I didn't know his soul was so thin, I swear. And when I realized and tried to stop—" She broke off, remembering the way Claude had held on to her, not letting her move, not letting her get free. "He wouldn't let me," she said simply.

"Why did Priam want you with Claude?" he asked, though something in his tone made her think that he already knew the answer.

She hesitated only a moment, then told the truth. "Priam wanted me to get inside his head. Claude wasn't the nicest of men," she added, her eyes drawn once again to the photos. "Priam wanted all the dirt."

"Why?"

"Blackmail, I assume."

"And you can do that? Get inside someone's head?" He didn't sound surprised.

"Yeah."

"They know that, Lissa," he said, his words chilling her. "That's why you're here talking instead of in a cell waiting for trial."

"I'm scared," she admitted.

"I know." Montegue stood. "I'm going to go out and talk to them for a moment."

She pulled a frown. "Tell them to arrest Priam. I've taken one entire soul. He's taken dozens."

"Actually, I was told they're already on that. I don't think he's been apprehended yet. What about you? Is there anything you need right now? Anyone I should contact?"

Inexplicably, she thought of Rand.

She looked down at the table. "No," she said. "There's no one."

He left, then returned a few moments later, trailed by Doyle.

Doyle straddled the chair again. "There's an easy way out of this, Lissa. Clear your name. Drop the charges."

She glanced at Montegue, hardly able to believe what Doyle was saying.

"Hear him out."

She drew in a breath. "I'm listening."

"You're aware of the murders? The humans that keep turning up dead, throats punctured and bodies drained?"

She looked between the two men. "What does that have to do with me?"

"What have you heard?"

"Nothing really." She shrugged. "I try to avoid gossip. There's not much of a market for rumors."

"It's my job to think about it," Doyle said. "To pursue all leads, all avenues. But to get to the truth, you have to go to the source. You should know that better than anyone."

Her cheeks warmed, but she held his gaze. They already knew what she could do. For that matter, what she could do was the reason they were offering a deal. "So?"

"So if I want to know what the weren are up to, my best bet is to get close to their leader."

"I'm sure you two will hit it off great."

"Hell yeah. I'm a personable kinda guy. But time is of the essence, and I'm thinking you might make inroads faster than I could."

"Inroads," she repeated.

"Like I said, we've been watching you for a while." He tapped his skull. "Nice talent you have there. Put it to good use, and I can see these charges disappearing."

Her excitement at walking out of Division a free woman warred with her fear of what they wanted her to do. "Their leader, you said? You want me to get into Gunnolf's head? Are you nuts?"

"Not Gunnolf," Doyle said. "He's in Paris. We're interested in one of Gunnolf's men. Just rolled into town. We have reason to believe he took out one of his own for spreading rumors that Gunnolf's behind the killings. We want to know why."

She licked her lips. "You're wondering if he killed because the weren was telling the truth, or because he was spreading lies."

Doyle tapped his nose. "Smart girl. We figure our boy's here to poke around, and we want to know what he knows."

She leaned back in her chair. "Unbelievable. You just threatened to charge me for getting into people's heads. Now you want me to do it for the PEC?"

"You want to debate moral quandaries," Doyle said, "I'll step out of the room and you and Montegue here can have at it. He's erudite as shit. Me, I just want to stop a killer."

She ran her hands through her hair, then looked at Montegue.

"It's a good deal," he said, then met Doyle's eyes. "But we want better. If she does this, immunity for all past offenses as well. Clean slate starting from the moment she's done."

"I can live with that," Doyle said.

"Lissa?" Montegue asked. "We're not going to get better."

"It's not like there are little filing cabinets in people's heads—I can't just tug open the drawer marked Human Murders. I might not find anything at all. I might have to try more than once. And each time I try, I have to take a little bit of soul."

"I guess you'll have to work fast. You in?"

There wasn't any argument she could broach, any war she could wage. They held all the cards, and if she wanted to keep her girls safe and herself out in the world instead of behind bars, then the only thing she could do was agree.

"Looks like you people have me by the balls," she said. "Who is he?"

"Name's Rand," Doyle said as Lissa stifled a gasp. "Vincent Rand."

CHAPTER 13

"She doesn't remember me," Nick said as he and Luke slid through the dark of the Red Line tunnel, searching for any sign of Serge within the long, subterranean miles.

"Did you really expect that she would?"

Nick considered the question. "No," he said. "I envy her that."

Luke stopped, his eyes narrowing as he looked at Nick. Nick turned away, not wanting his friend to see his expression and knowing that despite the dark, Luke could see everything perfectly clearly. Everything in the tunnel, and every thought on Nick's face.

They knew each other too damn well.

Nick continued walking, his eyes scanning the dark, searching for Serge. "Do you remember our years in Europe?"

Luke's laugh was low, and held little amusement. "Some years I remember better than others," he said. Nick nodded, understanding. Luke's daemon had come out hard and powerful, and for Lucius Dragos, much of the past was lost to a red, bloody haze.

"I spent so many years searching for immortality," Nick said. "Before the dark lady's kiss it was all that I wanted, and after, I kept searching, wanting to perfect what I already had. I had brilliant mentors, men who are revered even today, and whose minds I still cannot completely fathom."

"Right now, it's your mind I'm not fathoming."

Nick fought a smile. The subtleties of alchemy held no interest for Luke. "I find it ironic that in many ways Lissa now has what I want."

"Lissa dies, Nick. Over and over again."

"But she's reborn," he said. "And without painful memories."

"You'd willingly forget her?"

Nick hesitated, remembering the depths of her cuts to his heart. Wounds that still ached. If he could, would he erase those memories and heal those wounds, knowing that he would erase the good times, too?

"Perhaps not," he admitted.

"Keep the good memories," Luke said. "But let the woman go."

Nick nodded, but said nothing. That was the real trick, wasn't it?

"We're almost to the Vermont station," Luke said after they'd walked in silence for a while. "Shall we go on, or stop?"

"Stop for now," Nick said. "Did you notice anything odd about this section of track?"

"No rats," Luke said immediately.

"And no homeless." They both knew what that meant.

Serge had been here. And not that long ago.

Soon Nick would find him.

What he would do if it turned out that his friend really was killing the humans, though . . .

About that, he really wasn't sure.

♦

"Yo, soldier boy, get your ass over here."

The low, harsh voice came from behind him, and Rand turned, his growl dying in his throat when he saw J. Frank Murray sitting at the Slaughtered Goat's only circular booth, a wood nymph curled up on his lap.

The werewolf watched him coming, then shifted the girl and stood up, one step forward putting him right in Rand's face.

"I thought I told you never to call me that," Rand said.

"And I thought I told you I don't give a shit."

They stood for a moment, each staring the other down. Behind Murray, the nymph shifted nervously in the booth, her eyes darting repeatedly toward the door.

A werewolf at a nearby table shifted his chair away, and a were-cat at another table took her drink and headed across the room.

A beat. Then another. Until finally, Rand couldn't stand it any longer.

"Murray, you son of a bitch," he said with a laugh. "How the hell are you?"

"Good," Murray said, clapping him on the shoulder. "Damn but it was good to get your call. Shove over, baby," he said to the nymph as he cocked his head toward the bench. "My buddy's going to join us. This man and I go way back. Way back."

"It's been, what? Six years?"

" 'Bout that," Murray said. "Remember Istanbul? The twins?"

Rand chuckled. He'd started out the evening with the

red-haired twin, woke up in the morning with the dark-haired one, and sometime in between he'd had both of them, and at the same time. Now he couldn't even remember their names, but at the time, they'd sure as hell smoothed out his night.

He lifted his hand, signaling to Joe, the bartender, to have one of the girls bring a round over.

"So how goes life in the big city?" he asked. He'd met Murray in Europe, only a few weeks after he'd begun pulling special missions for Gunnolf, when Alicia's death was still raw and the anger at having the curse thrust upon him was still fresh. Murray wasn't *kyne*—wasn't part of the elite team that each of the Alliance leaders controlled—but he was a damn solid werewolf, and good in a fight.

He was also, Rand hoped, a potential resource, but Rand knew better than to show his hand too early. That, they'd ease into.

Unlike Rand, Murray was a born werewolf, with a weren father and a human mother, and the human side meant that he had a sense of what Rand had lost.

"Would you believe I'm working for Division?" Murray asked. He barked out a laugh. "After all my years of freelance, they got me on the inside."

"I heard you'd gone respectable," Rand said as one of the girls, Mia, slipped the beers onto the table.

"Never happen," Murray said, a statement that Rand believed. Murray hadn't ever been straitlaced. And while he'd never been caught breaking the law, he knew how to bend it. "But the job gives the illusion of respectability." He gave the nymph a squeeze. "And I'm in the RAC Division—Recon and Capture—and the uniform makes the females as slippery as seaweed." The nymph giggled. "It's the big boys that get the best prizes."

"We should talk," Rand said. "About your job. What you do. I'm interested."

Murray's head tilted slightly. "Thinking about becoming respectable yourself?"

"Never happen," Rand said, echoing his friend. "Got something else on my mind."

"Do you, now?" He patted the nymph's rump. "Go make a friend, sweetheart. Someone willing to cuddle up despite this boy's ugly face." He shot Rand a wicked grin. "We'll double-date."

Rand said nothing as the girl slid out of the booth. She didn't look happy, but she clearly knew the score—the conversation had turned, and she wasn't welcome anymore.

The benefit of the back corner booth was its isolation, but Murray lowered his voice anyway. "You called me, bro. Lay it out."

"I need intelligence," Rand said. "From someone with your unique placement."

"That a fact?" He downed what was left of his beer. "What kind of information you looking for?"

"Interesting shit going down in L.A. these days."

"The dead humans," Murray said. "Bad all the way around."

"That it is. Would be good to know the PEC's got a handle on it. That they're making progress in the investigation."

"Wouldn't it, though?" Murray said, his voice edged with exasperation.

"You're not in that loop?"

"That loop is sealed tight as a virgin's ass. Tiberius is on it personally, and the investigative team is playing it close to the vest." He met Rand's eyes. "And not one werewolf on the whole damn team."

"So the rumors are true? They really think it's a therian plot?"

"Hell, who knows? They're sure as shit not dragging me into the loop."

"I hear you," Rand said, pushing down his disappointment. "If the circle widens, though . . ."

"Can't risk my newfound respectability," Murray said. "But if I hear anything, I might be able to meet you for a beer."

"Anything you got," Rand said. "And I'll owe you."

"Vincent Rand under obligation. Almost worth risking my ass." He reached for the nymph's beer and finished that off, too. Then he held up his hand and signaled for the waitress and the nymph to return. She slid back onto his lap, and he sighed, long and deep. "I gotta tell you," Murray said. "Those vamps? They don't know shit."

"About the dead humans?"

"About life," Murray said. "They spend their whole existence holding the daemon in. But we," he said, gesturing between the two of them, "we come alive when our beast comes out." He closed his eyes. "Ninety-nine percent tonight. Just one more turn of the earth to absolute perfection."

He tilted his head back and breathed in deep through his nose. "Damn, but I love a full moon." He looked straight at Rand, and from the gleam in his eyes there was no question that he meant it. "That tug. That pull.

The way it feels when your nature rips free and you become the wolf—it's like being born all over again." He sighed. "Fucking perfection, man."

He hooked his right arm around the nymph's shoulder and pulled her close, his hand slipping down inside the thin material that made up her blouse. A soft smile brushed her lips, but otherwise she didn't react to the way his fingers grazed over her nipples.

Rand stayed silent. There was nothing about a full moon that he loved.

Across the table, Murray drew his head up as he sniffed the girl's hair, his body shaking with what had to be a shiver of damn doggy ecstasy. "Oh, yeah, baby. Me, too." He closed his eyes and let his head fall back against the upholstered bench.

"Yes, indeed," Murray continued, then brushed his lips across the girl's ears. She began moving back and forth in a rhythm that matched Murray's fingers on her breast. She'd edged in closer to him, and though Rand couldn't see below the tabletop, he was certain she was straddling Murray's thigh, gyrating against him.

"What was I saying?" Murray asked. "Oh, yeah. How about it, buddy? For old times' sake? The moon's going to rise in a few hours, and at ninety-nine percent we can give a female one hell of a ride. Fiona can find a friend, and even if she doesn't, I think she's feisty enough to share. You game?" As if to prove Murray's point, Fiona tilted her head and winked.

Hell yes, he was game. He needed to get loose, to forget. To set free the pressure building up, rising in him, and from more than the damn moon's orbit. It was coming, no denying that, and the animal in him wanted to be free. Wanted to mate.

Wanted to fuck.

Not love, not a connection. Just pure, animalistic sex. A few moments when he could lose himself. When he could find the oblivion of ecstasy, the cleansing of pleasure, and even the subtle allure of pain.

Oh, yeah. He was most definitely game.

He slid out of the booth, right behind Murray and the nymph, who didn't bother straightening her clothes. Mia fell into step beside them. "Hello, stranger."

He grinned, taking in the short skirt and low-cut top.

"You should slow down, you know?" she said, a tease in her voice. "You'll never find the right girl if you're too busy tossing her aside to get to the next girl."

"I'm not looking for the right girl."

Her smile widened and she trailed a finger down toward his crotch. "Lucky you ran into me, then, isn't it?"

"I guess it is. Come on."

They were halfway across the room when the door opened, and Lissa stepped inside. He froze, looking at her, as a current of heat ran through him. She stood in the doorway a moment, and only her eyes moved as she studied the place. When her gaze fell on him, she smiled. The slightest curve of her lips, but a smile nonetheless.

But her eyes didn't linger, and without looking at him again, she crossed the floor toward the bar. She wore jeans and a simple white T-shirt, under which he could see the outline of a lacy bra. Her mass of curls was tied back with a white ribbon. She looked completely casual and totally elegant, and damn if his fingers didn't itch to touch her.

He clenched his hand on the back of a nearby chair, watching the curve of her ass as she moved across the room, and cursed the longing that was building inside him. It was different, dammit. Different from the way his body tensed at the thought of taking Fiona into the back and letting the beast go wild. Different from a quick in-and-out with Mia in his office.

He didn't just want a girl, he wanted *her*, and no substitute would suffice.

It's because she's a succubus. That's what they do. They mess with your mind.

Maybe so, but right then, he could deal with that if it meant he got to touch her.

He felt himself start to turn, trying to catch just a glimpse from the corner of his eye. *Damn him.* Was he really thinking about risking his concentration on this mission because the lure of a succubus tugged at his cock? What kind of weak-ass fool was that?

He closed his eyes, and when he opened them again, he saw Murray looking at him curiously. He shook his head, not looking at Fiona or Mia at all.

He was done here.

He caught Murray's eyes. "Later, bro."

"Rand?" Mia pressed her hand on his arm.

"Go back to work."

He turned, ignoring her confused whisper to Fiona, then headed toward the door in the back. He never looked at Lissa; somehow he knew that if he turned around right then, he'd see her watching him. He pulled open the door and stepped into the hallway that led past his office to the alley and to his Ducati. He needed to get the hell out of there.

He hesitated in the doorway. One moment, then another.

He didn't turn around.

CHAPTER 14

"Vodka," Lissa said, then closed her hands around the cool glass as soon as the wiry bartender slid the drink in front of her.

She'd felt it again as her eyes had passed over Rand. A ripple of electricity. A sizzle that snaked through her, making her aware of her own skin, suddenly sensitive to even the air around her.

Focus.

She lifted the glass and took a long, slow sip, knowing he was back there. Knowing he was watching her.

Good. Let him stew. The longer he waited, the more he wanted. And she needed him wanting her bad. Because she'd come to the pub for only one reason: Division held the trump card—for the moment. And while she might not like it, she was not only going to play, she was going to win.

Get the guy, get the information, and get the hell out of there.

How hard could that be?

Not hard at all, considering what she had riding on it.

Hell yes, she'd cooperate.

She hated the thought of being used—by Priam, by Division—but she wasn't foolish enough to believe she had any choice in the matter. And that it was Rand she was targeting added a whole new level of insult. A man she really didn't want to see again. No, that wasn't true. She *did* want to see him again. It was that very desire she didn't want.

Now, though, it didn't matter. Not only was she going to see him, she was going to sleep with him.

Just like back when she was in the cortegery, someone else was calling the shots. She hated it, but once again, she was trapped.

Were it just her life and livelihood on the line, maybe she could negotiate. For that matter, she could run. Not all of the PEC's divisions were as stringent as Division 6, and she'd always had a fondness for the Yucatán Peninsula.

But that really wasn't the point. She'd built a life in Los Angeles. More, she'd helped her girls build their lives. And she'd be damned if Division was going to strip her of that.

She sighed, then took another sip of vodka. She didn't turn to look at him. Not yet. Instead, she kept her gaze perfectly straight.

But he was back there. Watching her. Wanting her.

She was certain of it.

He might have turned away from her at Orlando's, but she'd seen the desire flare in his eyes. Seen it again in the street in front of the club. He wanted her, and he wasn't going to be able to fight that desire for long. Men never could.

Get in. Get out. Get home.

She'd get Division what they wanted and be done with it, and with any luck, she'd be back at Orlando's before the change in shift.

She took another drink and decided he'd suffered enough. Time to give the male some satisfaction.

She shifted on the stool, then looked over her shoulder, her sultriest smile dancing on her lips.

He wasn't there.

He wasn't there.

Something cold and unfamiliar settled in her gut, and she clutched the edge of the bar for balance as the world rocked beneath her.

Well, damn.

♦

Lissa wasn't sure if she was insulted, pissed, or just plain baffled.

Not that it mattered. The fact was that she needed his thoughts—and that meant she needed him in bed.

He wanted to ignore his attraction to her? Fine. He could do that tomorrow and the next day and the next. But right then, she intended to make him stupid in lust with her.

Time to call upon her particular talents and ratchet up the charm that could beguile even the most stalwart of men. A seductive fascination that throughout history had inveigled kings to abandon their thrones and seduced warriors to fight their allies.

Time to turn it on high and watch as Rand fell gaga at her feet.

Ready, she slammed back the remnants of her drink, then slid off the stool. She peered around the smoke-filled room, searching the faces in the shadows to make sure he hadn't simply faded into the background. She didn't see him, and for a moment she feared that he'd gone out the front door and that this mission of hers had reached a dead end, at least for tonight.

No. This ended now. He had to be there—he had to be in the building even if she had to conjure him by the sheer force of her will.

She saw a simple metal door against the far wall, a stack of beer crates teetering beside it. Something had been stenciled there in faded black letters, and as she got closer, she could read the two simple words: No Admittance.

How fitting.

He'd gone through there, and now, so would she.

A petite girl with curly purple hair and a bar tray tucked under her arm eased in front of her, one firm finger pointing at the faded sign. "Hold up there, sister," she said. "Can't you read?"

Lissa smiled and straightened her shoulders. And then, just because she could, she turned it on, just a little. "Rand's waiting for me," she said.

"That a fact?" The girl dragged her teeth over her lower lip, then looked Lissa up and down, approval in her starstruck eyes.

"You don't believe me?"

"Oh, I do. I guess we've got something in common, huh?"

Something cold swirled inside Lissa, and she frowned when she recognized it—jealousy.

The girl's eyes turned soft, her mouth pursing. She took a step toward Lissa. "I'm Mia. I've got a break coming up. Why don't I buy you a drink and we can exchange notes?"

Lissa forced a smile, fighting the urge to slap the girl's face. A ridiculous urge, considering she'd intentionally turned it up and, in the doing, turned Mia on. But that jealousy—foolish, stupid jealousy—was still there under the surface, and all of that dark emotion converged on Mia, who had no preternatural allure whatsoever, yet Rand had chosen this girl and had ignored Lissa.

It didn't matter. He didn't have to like her, he just had to sleep with her. And that meant she needed to get through that door.

She relaxed, letting her muscles grow soft and her smile grow bright. "A tempting offer," she said. "I'll take a rain check." She bent over and pressed a soft kiss to the girl's cheek, and when she pulled away, she could still hear Mia's sigh echoing in her ear. Then she opened the door and stepped over the threshold. As soon as it clicked in place behind her, she relaxed, dialing down the sheen. A small knot of satisfaction displaced the lingering jealousy, and she allowed herself a victorious smile.

A corridor stretched out in front of her, ending at a metal fire door that opened, presumably, on an alley. The hallway was lined with four doors, two on each side, each standing half open and all except one revealing a darkened room.

The room with the light on was the last door on the left, and she moved toward it, then paused to smooth her hands down her waist and hips. She closed her eyes as she drew them up, cupping her breasts only briefly as her hands passed up and up, easing over shoulders and neck, her fingers twining in the soft strands of her hair, until finally she raised her hands high. She stretched her body tall, letting the power surge through her, feeling the raw sensuality, and knowing damn good and well that no one—not Rand, not anybody—would be able to resist her.

Oh, yes. She was ready.

She stepped inside the office with the charm turned up full blast.

He wasn't there.

She bit back a curse and eased into the hall again. He had to be here. If he'd gone out the front, the girl would have said something.

She was about to backtrack to check the darkened offices when she noticed that the fire door wasn't completely shut. No light was coming in through the crack, and because the end of the hallway was in shadows, she hadn't noticed the thin strip of night.

Slowly, she pushed open the door, relieved when it didn't squeak. She stepped out, the cool night air a shock after the heavy, smoky interior. She'd imagined that he'd be leaning against the door, looking smolderingly sexy and waiting for her to step out into his arms.

He wasn't, and she sighed, letting her eyes adjust to the dark as she glanced around the shadowed alley. The only light came from around the corner, a sputtering bulb that was trying to penetrate the darkness and mostly failing. The anorexic yellow light did manage to illuminate a flash of chrome, and when Lissa peered harder, she saw that the chrome was a bumper and that the bumper belonged to a motorcycle.

She headed in that direction, simply because there was nowhere else to go. If the folks at the Goat parked back here, Rand was most likely long gone. She wasn't yet willing to accept that conclusion, though, so she stepped away from the door and began crossing through the shadows toward the lone bike, hoping she'd find him. Hoping she could manage to end this nightmare tonight.

Damn Priam. Damn Division.

And for that matter, damn herself for not realizing that the PEC had figured out her secret a long time ago.

The brick facade of the pub rose up on her right, and as she walked in that direction, it seemed as if the brick melted away into shadows. She realized that she was passing the delivery entrance, a short, dark driveway that butted up against another door that led to the kitchen. The ragged circle of light cast by the sputtering bulb stretched out across the alley, and she eased toward it, prepared to step into the light.

She didn't make it. An arm wrapped hard and firm around her waist, and she felt herself being jerked backward—hard.

She tried to scream, but she couldn't because of the hand clasped over her mouth. He pulled her close, pressing her body against his. A large man, with a hard body and a musky scent half hidden beneath the smell of alcohol and tobacco that lingered on his clothes.

Her heart pounded wildly in her chest as she struggled. With a violent jerk, she tilted her head up and found herself looking deep into the eyes of her attacker—*Rand*.

"Lissa," he whispered. And then his mouth closed hard over hers.

CHAPTER 15

Hunger. Need.

They burned through him, making him hot. Making him hard.

With his mouth he claimed her, and with his arms he kept her, holding her tight as she struggled. Then her hands reached up, her fingers stroking his neck, cupping his head, and she lifted herself to her toes, her mouth as hungry as his.

Within, the wolf was rising, and he couldn't think. All he knew was want. All he felt was need. All he tasted was Lissa.

He drew back, savoring her moan as he broke the kiss. He pressed his hands against her face, his thumb brushing her trembling lip. She shifted, tried to taste and suckle, and the soft movement of her lips against his flesh made his cock twitch in fervent demand.

One breath, then another and another. It was all he could do. Just breathe, and try to force the animal back down as he called upon every ounce of strength he possessed to keep from descending into that primal place where nothing existed but the beast.

A thin sheen of sweat rose on his body as he fought, the effort to battle his own nature almost undoing him. *Breathe, damn you. Breathe.*

He breathed, and what he inhaled was Lissa. She smelled fresh and clean and cool, like grass after a rain.

But something else, too. Heat. *Desire*. Raw and needy, and mirroring his own.

"You won't walk away from me tonight."

She shook her head, the movement almost imperceptible. "I won't."

"I'll have you."

Her lips barely moved. "Yes."

He'd tried to walk away once already. He'd turned away from her sheen and left the pub. He'd gone out the back and he'd gotten as far as his bike. But the wolf had wanted, so he'd stayed, and his reward was finding her in the shadows. He knew he ought to go. But the wolf . . .

"Rand."

Her soft voice urged him in, her tone like a liquid promise.

He planted his feet. He wasn't going anywhere.

"Lissa," he growled, the beast rising and claiming, wanting to sink into her, desperate to shove those jeans down and lose himself, not in the hunt, but in the taking. The claiming.

Again, she lifted her face to his, her lips parted and soft. Had he bothered to think about it, he would have wondered about the triumphant gleam in her eyes.

He didn't bother. He only grasped the back of her head, then closed his mouth hard over hers. She responded immediately, moving in closer, pressing her breasts against him, the softness of her curves in stark contrast to the rigidity of his own body. Everything about him was hard, his muscles tense, his cock primed.

He knew only her. His mind was no longer his own, replaced by a singular demanding need.

Lissa.

Longing for her filled him, the heat of the need burning through him, setting the animal within on fire. She was right there, so clear in his mind, so perfect. He could see her, touch her, taste her. And he would. So help him, he would.

He slid his hands down, cupping her ass, pulling her in close so that the curve of her body rubbed tight against the bulge in his jeans. *Damn clothing.* The wolf wanted none of that. *He* wanted none of it. Only skin and desire and need and flesh. He drew his hands up, his palms warmed by the heat of her skin, his fingers stroking her back, then shifting toward her side until his thumbs felt the soft curve of her breasts and then the hard pebbles of her nipples beneath the lace of her bra.

Fuck that.

In one violent motion, he broke their kiss, then yanked the T-shirt over her head. Her blue eyes seemed to darken, as if the deepening desire was reflected in those irises. He saw her swallow, saw her lips part, and he couldn't stand it anymore.

He grasped her breasts, the firm buds filling his palms, the lace rough against his skin. His hand moved to her cleavage, and he grasped the simple silk bow. Grasped, and pulled—and as her bra ripped open, freeing her breasts to both him and the night, he cut off her gasp of delighted surprise with his own mouth, tasting the rising desire that was consuming them both.

It filled the air, a need that neither spoke of, but only acted upon. He could smell it, the need to claim and to mate. She was ready, and even before he slipped his hand down and stroked the soft flesh between her legs, he knew she was wet. The scent of sex was all around her, urging him on, begging him to take her, to claim her. To lose himself deep inside her.

Hell yeah, he would.

He took her by the waist, moving her lithe body until her back was against the wall, and her hands were on his face, pulling him in so that she could take his mouth in hers. No way was he going to deny her that. Right then, he wouldn't deny her anything, and from the scent of her desire, he knew she would deny him nothing as well. He would have her. Right then. Right there. Because damned if he could wait another minute.

His hands were on the button of her jeans when he heard her gasp and caught the scent of her fear. In the same instant, he heard his attacker and spun around to face him—to protect. And, yes, to kill.

He was too late.

The para-daemon lashed out, catching Rand across the face and sending him flying until his head smashed against a brick wall. The smell of his own blood wafted over him—and the last thing he saw before the world went black was the daemon grabbing the waistband of Lissa's jeans, and the terror that filled her eyes.

◆

She didn't realize she was screaming until the sound suddenly stopped, her breath knocked out when she landed roughly on the ground, gravel and debris digging into her bare back and shoulders. Priam loomed above her, the veins on his face bulging red and yellow with what looked like a thousand pinpoints about to burst from his skull outward through his skin.

"You goddamned *bitch*," he hissed, as the spikes broke through, sending daemon blood splattering down on her. "You think you can double-cross me?"

"I didn't," she said, though she knew the words were futile. "I swear."

He didn't believe her. Why would he? The PEC had shown up, and from his perspective, she was the one who'd called them to the scene. Hell, she'd thought the same thing about him.

"You think you can play me, *use* me? Do you truly believe the PEC will step in to save your pretty little ass?"

She tried to move, but it was no use, and he kicked out, knocking her feet out from under her as she scooted backward like a crab.

"You will die tonight, *Elizabeth*, and when you come back, I will own you once again."

She cringed, her terror like a thick red cloud, swirling around her, pulling her down into a hell she didn't understand and desperately wanted to avoid.

Memories. Goddammit, she'd bumped up hard against a memory.

Priam lunged for her, and she kicked out, landing a solid blow on his chin. It didn't matter. He just kept on coming, reaching down and grabbing her hair and pulling her to her feet as she gritted her teeth and forced herself not to cry out in pain. No way was she giving him the satisfaction.

A few feet away, Rand lay in a heap by the wall. No

sound, no motion, and for a moment, she feared that he was dead.

The thought left her head when Priam slammed his fist against her cheekbone. Her head snapped sideways, the place where he'd made contact feeling as if it was a pulsing, red bulge. That she was conscious amazed her almost as much as the fact that her facial bones weren't completely shattered.

She felt tears fill her eyes and hated herself for it.

"Nice, isn't it?" he asked, shoving her back down so that she landed hard on her ass. "The way you little bitches come back, time and again. All soft and malleable and full of potential as you emerge from the mist." His face contorted into a sneer. "I owned you once, you little cunt. Don't forget that. I owned you, and I used you. Oh, yeah. I *fucked* you."

He laughed, but whether he was laughing at the memory or at her disgust, she didn't know.

"You were mine, little girl. And not just in one life. I've had you over and over again, and when you're reborn, I'm going to make it my damn mission to find you again. You think you're so damned superior? We'll see how you like it when my cock's in your mouth and I own your ass. This life is nothing. *Nothing.* You've been mine before, and you'll be mine again, and so will all those girls you're so proud of freeing. You think they're free? They're not free, they're fucked."

The shivering started inside her and wouldn't stop, her breath coming in shudders as his words washed over her, scaring her and bringing back a past that she didn't want to remember. It wasn't her. *It wasn't.*

"Rip off those jeans and spread your legs, little girl,"

he said, his toe jamming at her calf, pushing her legs apart. "I want a taste before I send you back to hell."

"Fuck you," she said. Her voice was raw, ragged, and she knew that he could hear the fear. *Fine. Be afraid. But don't let it stop you.* "Get the hell away from me."

"Listen to the little girl grow a pair. Too late, Elizabeth. You're down there, you're weak as a goddamned kitten, and tonight I am not in a generous mood." He bent toward her, his eyes yellow, his mouth curved in a sneer.

She hawked up a wad of phlegm and let it fly, hitting him right beside the eye.

He froze, then wiped it away with the back of his hand. "That was a mistake."

He was on her in an instant, her body pressed against the asphalt, his knees hard against her waist, his hands closing over hers. She was trapped. Helpless. And though she struggled, there was nowhere to go.

She couldn't move.

He released one of her hands, and she lashed out, fingers stiff as she aimed for his eyes, wanting to gouge them out. Wanting to at least get in one serious blow if she was going to die.

By the gods, she didn't want to die.

Without realizing she was doing it, she turned her head toward Rand. His body twitched, but otherwise didn't move. She'd heard the crack of his skull against the brick wall, and now that she'd experienced the force of Priam's strength up close and personal, she knew damn well that even if Rand was alive—and that twitch gave her hope—he was in no condition to help her. By the time he regained his senses, she'd be dead.

As if to prove the point, Priam's free hand closed

around her throat, his thumb pressing against her windpipe. She tried to gasp, but even that was futile. The already dark night started to fade, and though she lashed out and pummeled him in the face, he didn't react. Didn't even blink.

He simply squeezed tighter until the world faded. Until life faded.

Until everything went black and she saw—she remembered—what life had once been like, and what it would surely be again.

"The human. Acquire his soul. Then end his life."

She blinked, looking down at bare feet that she knew belonged to her. She was clothed in rags. And into her extended hand, a smooth-skinned Priam placed an iron blade.

She dropped it, and the blade clattered to the ground.

"Pick it up."

"I can't—I can't do that . . ."

She flinched even before his palm crossed her cheek.

"Then bring him to me when you're done. I will finish the job for you, but you will pay the price." He traced his hand down over the thin rags she wore, twisting her nipple violently, then cupping her crotch in his hand. There was no question but that she belonged to him, and she made no move to protest. He was her master. She was his slave.

And that was simply the way it was.

CHAPTER 16

Fear.

The world came back into focus drenched with the scent of fear.

Her fear.

Her terror and his rage. Combined, they were one damned potent combination, and he was on his feet without even realizing he'd moved, letting instinct take over. The instinct of the animal combined now with the instincts of a soldier. A killer.

He would kill tonight as he always did. Without hesitation, without mercy, and just slow enough so that the para-daemon knew who brought death . . . and why.

The growl started low in his chest, a solid rumble that took on a life of its own. It built, louder and louder, until he saw the daemon turn and those yellow eyes widen ever so slightly with surprise.

"Too late," the para-daemon whispered, lifting Lissa by the neck. *Priam.* Rand had heard her call him Priam.

And right then, Priam's muscles were tensing, and Rand knew what the para-daemon intended to do—he was going to slam her head back and break her skull open as easily as a human could crack an egg.

He sprang, animal strength and rage driving him forward, sending him crashing against Priam's chest, knocking the para-daemon off her and freeing the hand from her neck.

He rolled to the side, then came up in a crouch, his movement punctuated by the thud as her skull hit the pavement and the small "aah" as she gasped.

She was alive, and for right then, that was enough.

Right then, he was only interested in the kill.

He let go, bursting forward as the wolf flowed through his veins, meeting Priam midway, their bodies colliding, then crashing to the rough asphalt in a flurry of skin and teeth and rock-solid punches. He felt his muscles changing, warming as lupine power flowed through his veins. He wished he could summon it, control it. He couldn't, but right then, the wolf was doing just fine on its own.

Beneath him, Priam's body tightened. The bastard wanted up, but no way was Rand giving up his advantage. He kept both hands tight on Priam's arms, but his head was free. As the bastard tried to rise, Rand smashed his own head hard against Priam's, snapping the para-daemon's head back and smashing his skull hard into the pavement.

The bastard howled, and Rand braced himself, wishing his knife wasn't inside the pub as he remembered the way Zor had changed in Paris. But except for the signs of fury, Priam didn't look about to burst out of his human shell.

Paris.

He couldn't reach his pocket, but he knew what was there—a coiled length of thin, strong wire. Always loaded, always armed. A soldier always had an out. If he could get to it now . . .

Not possible.

"You think you can best me, puppy?" Priam snarled, his silver hair now a crimson mass of blood and filth. "Do you think you have?"

"Yes," Rand said.

It was the wrong thing to say.

Priam's mouth stretched wide, and he lurched his hips up, the force of the action levering Rand forward. At the same time, the para-daemon jerked his head up, turning Rand's earlier move against him and colliding with Rand's skull with the force of a missile launcher. Stars exploded in front of Rand's eyes, and though he fought through the pain, it didn't matter. Priam had gained an advantage, and he pressed it, drawing back his now-free arm and landing a solid punch across Rand's jaw.

The daemon's angle meant that he didn't have much power behind the punch, but it was enough to knock Rand off of him, and as Rand rolled to the side, struggling to get his feet under him and get back into the game, he saw Lissa. She looked frantic, and her mouth was moving, but though he was certain she was screaming, he couldn't hear her. Right then, all he could hear was the cold rush of the fight in his head. The primal need to attack, and to kill.

And to survive, he thought, as Priam lunged, all fire and fury.

Knowing Priam would expect him to dodge, Rand met the assault full on, holding his ground until the bastard was right there, all claws and teeth and bluster. He got in a punch to the beast's snakelike nose. It would have smashed a human's, but on Priam it barely made a dent. The knee he thrust up into Priam's balls—assuming the creature had any—was much more effective, loosening the grip the para-daemon had on Rand's neck.

He snatched the advantage while he had the chance, bringing his hands up between the skin of his neck and Priam's palms. The daemon knew what he was about, though, and clutched tighter, cutting off Rand's air, making the world turn gray.

Fight. Push.

He strained, the muscles in his arms burning as he concentrated, willing his strength to focus, urging his body to cooperate. Break the choke hold—that was his single-minded purpose. Break it, and then break Priam.

He thought again of the wire in his pocket, pictured holding it tight against Priam's neck, cutting off the life of this beast who'd tried to hurt Lissa. Cutting off his air. Hell, cutting off his goddamned head.

It was an image worth fighting for, and the power of the wolf burst through him. He thrust his hands out, breaking Priam's hold, then flung his arms out and used Priam's own chest as leverage to push himself backward.

He reached toward his pocket for the wire, but he could already tell he wouldn't be fast enough. The para-daemon was practically on him, and all Rand could do was fight and hold him off and hope for another chance.

He got one.

Inexplicably, Priam stopped, his eyes going wide with surprise and pain.

Behind him, Lissa stood, her expression resolute, her breathing hard. And in her hand she held a rusty metal pipe, courtesy of the filthy alley.

It was all Rand needed, and he took the wire and readied it between his hands. When the beast had reconciled himself an instant later, Rand was ready . . . and Priam was blissfully unaware.

"Come on, you bastard," Rand taunted, and when the daemon complied, rushing at him full force, Rand lifted his arms and twisted around, looking for all the world like a man trying to avoid a blow.

That hadn't been his plan. Instead, he'd lifted the wire, then brought it down again. And now he was behind Priam—and the wire was stretched taut across the para-daemon's throat.

"Come on," Rand repeated as the wire dug into flesh, drawing the daemon's blood. His nostrils flared as the scent filled him, the wolf erupting as he tugged at the wire harder and harder.

Priam twisted, wild and senseless. He thrashed, trying to draw air, trying to get free, but Rand had the wolf now, and that wasn't happening. He had the advantage and he was holding on to it.

With a burst of strength, Priam jerked to the side, then thrust his body backward. Rand's grip didn't falter, but he let out a loud whoosh of air as his back slammed hard against the brick wall of the pub. It was a slight advantage for Priam, and he played it for all it was worth, stepping forward and slamming back, each slam costing Rand, his shirt ripping, blood spilling.

But each thrust cost Priam, too, because every forward movement drew the wire tighter and tighter, and when he made one more move to lunge—one more bid to slam Rand's head against the solid wall—Rand flexed his arms, drew the garrote toward him, and felt the sweet release of pressure when the wire finally cut through thick skin and then moved more easily through the soft insides of the para-daemon's neck.

Priam made one last gurgling noise, then fell forward. Rand held the garrote until the last minute, ensuring a clean cut to the bone, then let go, letting the body drop, propelled by its own weight. He stared, not wanting this to be over—not wanting a clean death. Wanting to not only kill but humiliate the male who'd stepped up and hurt Lissa.

Mine.

The word echoed in his mind—*his*, not the wolf's— and with one savage snarl, he grasped the daemon's head and ripped it the rest of the way off.

He sat back on his haunches, the scent of blood and victory fading to reveal another scent.

Her.

She stood a dozen feet away from him, her back pressed to the wall. Her face showed no fear, but he didn't believe the illusion. She was still afraid, all right. Only now, he knew, she was afraid of him.

He climbed off the daemon's carcass, moving slowly, his senses primed for any signal that she would bolt. He didn't want her to run.

He wanted her to stay. Hell, he wanted *her*.

And the wolf would take what he wanted.

"Run," he snarled, fighting it back. Before, he'd wanted to summon the wolf. Now he was desperate to call it off. He didn't want to be an animal with her.

She stayed.

"Run, damn you."

She took a step toward him. "Why?"

He cocked his head, nostrils flaring, his muscles still warm from the fight. *Primed.* Ready now for a different kind of workout.

"I scare you."

The slightest shake of her head. "You don't."

He sniffed again. "Bullshit."

She lifted her chin. "I'm not afraid of you." Her words were firm and clean, and beneath them, he caught a new scent. Faint, but growing stronger. *Arousal.*

The wolf preened. Wanting.

Hoping.

And still, the fear lingered.

"Then what are you afraid of?"

She moved toward him, two long steps bringing her a hairsbreadth away from him. So close he could feel her heat. So close he knew he couldn't resist anymore.

He hooked his arm around her waist and drew her to him. She gasped, and the scent of her desire flowed around him like a cloud.

"What are you afraid of?" he repeated.

"Me," she whispered. Then she rose up, pressed her mouth to his, and kissed him.

◆

She'd meant what she said, but right then, with his hands on her and his mouth hard beneath hers, she couldn't quite remember what had scared her so much. She didn't have time to think about it. *Couldn't* think about it, because her mind didn't work like that anymore. She'd been reduced to the purest form of passion, the most intense manifestation of desire.

She wanted him—and she knew with humbling certainty that if she looked at herself in the mirror, she would see in her own eyes the tumultuous desire she so often saw shining in the eyes of men.

A rampant, unchecked desire that promised pleasure as sharp as pain to satisfy a longing she hadn't even realized existed.

"You're afraid of the wrong thing," he said, his voice low and tense, as if he were a taut wire that could snap at any moment.

She saw the moment it did. Saw the heat flare in his wolven eyes. Saw the wolf move forward to take.

And felt the hard pull of his hands on her shoulder and her waist, yanking her to him, closing his mouth over hers. *Claiming,* whether she wanted him to or not.

She wanted.

By the gods, how she wanted. It wasn't supposed to happen this way. This was supposed to be business—get him in bed, get his soul, get into his head. But there was nothing businesslike about the way she felt, about the way she wanted him like she'd never wanted any other man, at least not in this lifetime. There was nothing planned or calculated about the way she melted against him, wishing she could be even closer, her fingers tugging at his shirt as shamelessly as one of her clients pawed at her clothes.

She didn't care. She simply wanted—and what she wanted, she would have.

Breathing deeply, she pushed away, her palms lingering on his chest as she did. A low growl of protest rose from his throat, and with that simple sound she learned everything that she wanted.

He was more than a man now—his eyes had turned pale green and ferocious in their intensity, a smattering of gray fur tufted at his wrists, and the skin of his palms had thickened like a canine's pads. Mostly, though, she saw the wolf in his movements and felt it in his touch. He was feral and needy, and she was the spoils of his victory.

She thought vaguely that her pride ought to be wounded. It wasn't. Instead, his base, animal need excited her. She had no power over beasts. He wanted *her*, and that simple fact was more erotic than any touch could or would ever be.

Slowly, she drew her hands up her torso, her eyes never leaving his face as she caressed her breasts, her nipples like pebbles rubbing against her palms.

A muscle in his cheek twitched and Rand felt the last strands of his control snap.

In one violent move, he pulled her against him, locking her in his embrace, reveling in the scent of her, her soft curves teasing the hardness that overcame him, turning him into nothing more than raw, desperate need. *Good*. He wanted to fight the truth hiding under the surface. Wanted this to be about nothing more than need; wanted this to be nothing more than physical. Nothing special. Nothing he couldn't take from a dozen other women.

He pressed her close, the movement hard and demanding and meant to remind him of who he was and what he was doing. Her body quivered against him as she gasped, the sound more pleasure than surprise, and the brush of her breath against his neck turned his body to steel. *Holy God, she was amazing.*

He slid one hand down soft curves until the swell of her ass filled his palm. With his other, he held her hair, pulling back until her neck was exposed. He nipped it, teeth trailing over her delicate collar bone, the hollow in her skin, and the lush fullness of her breast.

He closed his mouth over her breast, his tongue laving the hard nub, his mouth wanting to taste all of her, wanting to taste and bite and mark her as his, dammit, *his*.

She shuddered against him, arching up in silent demand, her hands snaking under his shirt, fingernails raking him so hard she drew blood. *There*. That was what he wanted. A violent, furious fucking that meant nothing more than what it was. Not special. Not right. Just sex. *Mating*. Raw and base and for no other reason than to scratch an itch.

He told himself all that, and while the wolf rutted and demanded, it was easy to believe it. He *had* to believe it, because he didn't want anything more. Couldn't go there. Couldn't play that game.

His breath came raw and ragged as a need burned through him, more intense than any he'd felt before. *She's a succubus. You don't fight the pleasures of a succubus. Go with it, have the best lay of your life, and then walk away.*

Her mouth closed over his, and whatever level of his brain had allowed rational thought short-circuited. There was no thought anymore. Just two bodies moving in unison, arms and legs tangled, tongues warring, bare skin pressed against useless hot cloth.

He fumbled for the button of her jeans, couldn't get the thing to cooperate, and ripped. She laughed, the sound like a caress, then took his hand and slid it into her jeans, easing his fingers down over sweat-slicked skin to her wet, slippery sex. He curved his hand, cupping her, realizing she wore no underwear, then thrust his finger deep inside her. One, then another, as she moaned with satisfaction and ground her hips, urging him on.

He couldn't take it any longer.

With her soft protests echoing around him, he pulled out his hand, then started to tug her jeans down over her hips. Her protests morphed into soft murmurs of "yes," and then a low "but we're in an alley."

"Do you care?" he asked, surprised to find he was capable of speech.

"No."

That was all he needed. All they both needed, and they fought with clothes until his shirt was open, his cock was free, and her jeans were tossed into a tumbled pile against the wall. He could see the flush on her skin, but it was her scent—musky and sweet—that tightened his balls and propelled him closer to her. She stood naked before him, clad only in her bra, and it was in such tatters it hardly counted.

Now. That was all he could think. Simply *now,* and he pulled her close, kissing her hard, all teeth and tongue until he tasted blood in his mouth. Her body burned against his, so hot, and so wet, and when he slipped his hands between her legs and spread her thighs, she grabbed his ass and urged him closer. "Now," she demanded, her word whispered like an echo.

He took her against the wall, his hands on her back,

her legs hooked around his waist, his knuckles taking the brunt of their rhythmic motion against the rough brick. Her hips pumped to match his own thrusts, and her body tightened around his, her nails biting into his back. He pulled her closer, his arm cupping her back as he slid one hand down between them, his fingers stroking her clit as they moved together. *Now.*

He could do this forever, he realized. Claim her and feel her quiver in his arms.

And even as that particular want formed in his mind, he heard her stuttered breath and felt the rhythmic tightening around his cock. He flicked his thumb over her clit, until she was like quicksilver in his arms, slick and wild and liquid, and even before the orgasm tackled her, he felt it: satisfaction, but something more, too. Something raw and intimate that scared the hell out of him.

CHAPTER 17

The orgasm ripped through her, a violent explosion that shook her body and filled her with light and color and a powerful pleasure that rivaled even the decadent sweetness of a soul-taking. No faceless fantasy man this time—he was right there, and she could see him, and she wanted him. Shamelessly, helplessly, fervently.

Maybe it was lack of oxygen to the brain from Priam's hands at her throat, but she'd wanted Rand with an intensity she'd never experienced before. Just the feel of his hands on her had been enough to send her over the edge, but having him inside her . . .

Oh, yes.

And now she wanted to wallow in the pleasure. To relish it and ride it out for as long as it would last. Rand's hands and body plying her, taking her to the precipice and urging her over again and again and again.

Focus. This was business. A job. And she needed to pull herself together, needed to fight through the languor in her mind and focus.

He'd been close, so close.

Close, but he hadn't come yet, pulling out so that he could focus on her pleasure. She didn't mind that, she realized as his fingers stroked her clit and his tongue danced over her ear, but so far only one tiny thread of soul had peeked out, caressing her skin and teasing her with the promise of more.

Weren men usually weren't much work, their souls close to the surface. But his seemed hidden away, as if blocked by some wall, the full strands not ready to burst free until he was close. She could take him there; she could take a bit of his soul, and slide deftly into his mind.

She could do exactly what she came for—only now she didn't want to.

Slowly, she traced her fingertips over his arms. She hadn't anticipated the way she would feel once she was in his arms. The way he got under her skin. The way he'd killed for her, stepping further out on a limb to protect her than any man ever had.

The PEC wanted her to betray him, and the fact that he probably wouldn't ever know didn't make it any easier. And the real irony? Priam was out of the picture. She was safe from him, and so were her girls.

But now *she* was the threat. Because the PEC knew what she'd done, and if she didn't cooperate, they'd shut her down.

Fuck.

"Lissa . . ."

It was only one word, but it was said with such powerful tenderness that she melted against him, fresh desire rippling within her.

His palm cupped her cheek. He'd slowed the rhythmic thrusting and was looking at her now with eyes that were soft with desire and sharpened with concern. Her heart twisted. He'd protected her, and now she was going to betray him. She hated herself, but in the end there was no option.

Slowly, she smiled—her lips curving, her eyes gleaming. How many men had she smiled at this way? How many men had she reached for, even as she was now reaching for Rand? And how many lips had she brushed across her own?

Only his.

She trembled against the thought, because although the answer was dozens—hundreds, thousands if you counted all her lifetimes—this felt as though it was the only time that mattered.

"I feel wonderful," she whispered, then pressed her palm against his bare chest. His shirt was open, but not off, and she slipped her fingers under the fabric, enjoying the sensation of cool cotton paired with hot flesh as she slid her hand down, lower and lower, over the waistband of his open jeans, until she finally curved her palm around velvet steel.

His cock twitched and tightened in her hand as Rand cupped the back of her head, tilting her face up to his. His mouth found hers, and she kissed him, long and hard, before pulling gently away.

"But I don't think we're quite even yet," she said with a tease, her hand stroking him. He was ready—so ready—and that simple touch was all it took to bring the animal out again. Not the wolf this time, or not completely. No, now she saw in him a familiar male wildness. A hunger and a need that she'd so often seen and yet had only experienced before in her fantasies, never with her clients.

Now she understood.

He grabbed her, pulling her to him, then kissing her hard. "Get dressed."

His voice was a growl of desire, yet his words sent both icy fear and cold relief through her veins. Fear that he didn't want her. Relief that she wouldn't have to betray him.

"Inside," he said, as if he understood her hesitation. "Office. Now."

They were both breathing hard as they struggled back into their clothes. Her bra was useless now, and she tossed it onto a trash bin. The sensation of sliding her T-shirt over her sensitive nipples made her bite her lip to hold in a moan, and the seam of her jeans against her sensitive sex was enough to make her come again right there. She wanted that—wanted him and the feeling and everything. And, yeah, inside sounded like a damn good idea.

They hurried to his office, the one right by the exit to the alley, and Rand slammed the door shut, flipped the lock, and had her on the couch and naked before she was entirely sure what had happened. He was on her, his own clothes abandoned, his body pressed over hers, his lips doing wonderful things to her neck and her shoulder. And his cock—it was right there. Hot and hard and demanding. And despite what she had to do, she wanted him with an unfamiliar, almost frenzied desperation.

She drew in a stuttering breath, trying to make sense of this new reality. He was on her—holding her so close and so firm that she couldn't move. It was all about him now, what he wanted and how he wanted it. And she was taking the ride right along with him.

Before Lissa even realized it was happening, she

tensed, small bubbles of trepidation popping inside her chest. "Let me up," she whispered, her voice as low and seductive as she knew how to make it despite the building panic.

His hands were on her breasts, and his mouth moved down to lave her nipple. She arched back, gasping with the pleasure despite the dark flood of fear, wanting to simply give herself over, but . . .

She pressed her palms against his chest, then took his lower lip in her teeth. A gentle nip, then a simple command. "Trust me."

His answering expression was all heat and promise and curiosity, and she pushed him up, the pressure in her chest lessening as she took the lead, straddling him as he sat back on the couch, her thighs against his, her knees pressed into the cushion. And the demanding, hard length of him pressed against her. With her hips undulating, she leaned forward, knowing her subtle movements were driving him wild—hell, they were driving *her* wild.

One hand pressed against his chest, her palm finding the skin warm and slick. She drew her fingers through the thin smattering of hair, enjoying the way it felt. Except for on their head, succubi had no body hair other than eyebrows and lashes, and there was something deliciously enticing about the maleness of his body. She was almost positive he'd been born human, and she wondered idly if his skin had been smooth before he'd transformed. How had it happened? Whom had he been before?

She'd probably never know, but she could learn about the man he was now. Slowly, she drew her hands up. His pecs were hard and firm, and she had no doubts about his strength. His shoulders were broad and she skimmed lightly over the muscles of his arms. He could snap her in two if he wanted, but from the look in his eye, that kind of punishment wasn't on his mind. More likely, he'd eat her alive.

The thought made her smile, and she looked away, turning her head to follow the path of her hand down his arm, because she didn't want him to see her amusement. The strength in his arms continued all the way down to his fingers. He wore no rings, no watch, but his wrists were not completely unadorned. The right one sported a tattoo—three X's in a row on the underside of his wrist.

She frowned, wondering about the import, but it wasn't a question that could stay long in her head, not with him naked beneath her. And when he pivoted his hips and the tip of his cock pressed hard against her, the last strands of curiosity evaporated from her mind, thrust aside by the need to have him inside her.

Control. Pay attention. Keep your head.

She would; she had to. But that didn't mean she wanted to—and it sure as hell didn't mean she wasn't going to enjoy what she could.

His hands were on her breasts, and as she arched back, he moved his mouth in, his hand snaking down to stroke her clit. She was wet—so wet—and she wanted him in a way she'd never wanted another man. "Now," she whispered. "Dammit, now."

He followed orders well, his cock sliding in past her tight muscles as she spread her legs, urging him farther and deeper. He pistoned his hips toward her, and she felt the shift of his hands to cup her rear, then the push of her own body as he thrust her hard against him. She let him maneuver her, working her body in tandem with his, their motions finding a hard-driving rhythm accentuated by the sounds of sex and breathing and rising pleasure.

"Lissa." His voice washed over her, low and desperate, and she clutched tightly around his neck as he slammed into her, moving her in the way that most pleased him, the way he wanted and needed.

The way she needed, too. Needed to see the passion in his eyes as his pleasure built and his cock filled her. She was so tight around him, her body urging him on, and she was *there*—right there—in the moment with him. With Rand. Not a fantasy. Not a faceless man. Not even with a soul to bring her pleasure.

She was with *him*, and the feeling was amazing, more fulfilling than the most vibrant of souls. Delicious. Decadent. *Spectacular.*

Harder and harder until she knew he was close. Knew from the way his body tightened and from the low noise he made in his throat, like a moan of pleasure combined with a warning against stopping. Most of all, she knew because of the wisps of soul dancing off of his skin.

They twined around her, a deep purple fading into a vibrant orange, like ribbons cut from a rainbow. She held her arms out and let the ephemeral, fragile strands twine around her. But it was slow and spotty, and with a start, she realized that the strands weren't only fragile, they were battered and weatherworn, ripped and patched, the bits and pieces barely clinging together. *Ripped. Somehow, Rand's soul had been ripped to shreds.*

A low, cold fear settled over her. Because he was close, dammit, so close, and if he was inside her when he came . . .

Flashes of Claude's murdered family filled her mind—*oh, sweet heaven, no.*

Not Rand. Dear God, he'd be nothing more than a killing machine. A mindless, violent animal. Without control or remorse.

That wasn't Rand. That wasn't the man who'd gone out of his way to protect her. Who stood strong and confident and—

No.

She couldn't do this. If he came while she had a grasp on even a thread of such a battered, minuscule soul, all that remained would burst from him and fill her. Surely the PEC couldn't ask that of her. They couldn't expect her to take a man's soul along with what was in his head.

Wait any longer and it won't be an issue . . .

His eyes were dark and savage. He was on the edge. Any more and—

She rolled off him, yelping when her shoulder slammed down hard on the concrete floor.

"Lissa! Jesus God, Lissa." With more agility than she would have expected from a man in his current condition, he was at her side. "Are you okay? What happened?"

"I—I fell."

He pulled her close, cradling her next to him. "Are you hurt? Let me see."

"It's nothing," she protested, but he wasn't listening. Instead, he was turning her, then gently caressing a tender spot on her hip. She'd have a bruise in the morning. A small price to pay for saving a man's soul. "It hardly hurts at all."

His hand gently cupped the injury, and he pulled her close, his mouth near her ear. "Do you want me to kiss it and make it feel better?"

A laugh bubbled out of her, erasing her fear that this would go all wrong. "It's an idea . . ."

"A good one, considering how close to heaven that bruise is." As he spoke, his fingers skimmed lightly from the bruise, over her hip, down the soft skin at her pubis, and then down lower and lower until she couldn't even think. "A kiss here?" he murmured, bending down to kiss the soft skin on her thigh. "Then a kiss there?"

Please, yes, please.

She didn't say it. Instead, she rolled away, gently pushing him off her, then curling her legs up beneath her.

"Lissa, I—"

"Don't." She didn't want to hear anything he had to say. Not right then. Not when she was the one ripping the moment to shreds.

Something close to anger sparked in his eyes, but it disappeared almost as fast as it came, and he inched closer, his eyes searching her face. For so long, she'd been an expert at hiding her emotions, yet right then she simply didn't have the strength. She didn't even try. Instead she ducked her head, put her arms around him, and pressed her forehead against his shoulder.

"We can't—*I can't.* Not tonight." She closed her eyes. *Not ever.*

"We can," he said, and the certainty in his voice was familiar. It was the same tone she used with nervous clients. But she wasn't nervous. She was trying to do him a favor. Him and his ragged soul.

His hand cupped her cheek, holding her steady when he kissed her, long and hard and so deeply and purposefully that she almost leaned into him, ignoring everything she knew about stopping and leaving and saving a soul he didn't even know was in danger.

She pulled away, her teeth tugging on his lower lip until the last possible moment because she didn't want to stop, but she knew she had to. "You do things to me," she said.

"Good things?"

"Unexpected things."

"Well, I do like to be different," he said, and she heard the smile in his voice.

She cocked her head and looked at him. She knew she should stand up and start moving—at the very least, they needed to decide what to do about the body in the alley—but all she wanted to do was stay with him.

"I think you do like to be different." She scooted back on the floor until her back was against the sofa and studied him.

"Why's that?"

"For one thing, you're not in a pack."

"I move alone."

"But you're a werewolf. I thought the weren moved in packs."

"Some do."

"What were you before?"

"A soldier," he said. "Special Forces." He almost smiled. "In a way, I still am."

She believed him. There was something hard about

him. Something raw and violent—and not just because he'd beaten Priam to a pulp. She'd called him dangerous in Orlando's, and now she could see just how astute that assessment had been.

"I was born the way I am," she said. "No mother, no father. We're just born into the mist." She shrugged. "But to you . . . the change . . . it must have been such a shock."

"That this world exists? That werewolves and vampires and daemons are real? Yeah. That was a shock."

He watched her, gauging her reaction to his words, and saw immediately that she had heard what he didn't say as much as what he'd said.

"But you, becoming a wolf, that part wasn't a shock?"

"No."

"Why not?"

He almost didn't answer. With any other woman, he knew he wouldn't have answered. But to Lissa he said simply, "Because it wasn't a change at all."

Her brow creased, as if she was trying to put his words in the proper order, and he felt a sudden pang of regret. She'd seen the wolf edge out. She'd understand now. And she'd know that he was as much an animal as the wolf.

He expected her to stand, then leave. Instead, she hooked her arms around her knees and looked at him, curiosity on her face, but no disgust and no fear. "What was your human life like?"

He didn't want to talk about it, but he didn't want her to leave. "Aren't they all the same?" he asked, trying for a joke.

"Are they?"

He sighed.

"Please. I'd like to know." She moved closer to him, then took his hand in hers. Her fingers traced the three X's at his wrist. "Is this from before?" she asked. "Or were you branded after the change?"

"Not a brand," he said. "A gang tat. One X for every kill." He glanced at her, but she didn't look like she was going to bolt.

"So you killed three times?"

"After three, they don't mark you anymore."

"Oh. Why?"

"No point giving the cops that much more ammo to land your ass in jail."

She nodded thoughtfully, as casual as if they were talking about the weather. "How old were you? When you got the first one, I mean."

"Nine. The third at ten."

"You got sucked in young," she said thoughtfully. "Something you couldn't get out of."

She was making excuses for him, and that pissed him off. "I didn't want out of it."

"No, why would you? That was the life you knew." She stood up, then grabbed his shirt off the floor and put it on. It hung to midthigh, and as she stood there hugging herself and shuddering slightly, she looked like a little girl, not like the hard-edged businesswoman he'd met at Orlando's, or even the sultry female who'd tempted and tormented and brought him to the height of pleasure. "I can't remember mine, not really, but I know it took me lifetimes before I finally figured it out."

"What?"

"The way out," she said simply, then continued before he could ask what she meant. "How did you finally get out?"

"My mother died," he said.

"I'm sorry."

"My aunt took me in, and moved me out of South Central."

"Where did you go?"

"A foreign land. Pasadena."

She laughed, and a knot of tension that had been building in his gut began to loosen.

"I don't think you were bitten in Pasadena."

"No. The Balkans."

"When you were a soldier?"

"Yeah, but I wasn't on duty. I was looking for someone in the mountain caves. But I found someone else."

"Long way from Pasadena. Long way from South Central for that matter."

"Closer than you might think," he said, thinking of the fighting, the death.

"How did you end up there?"

He shrugged, then went to the small refrigerator and grabbed two beers. "Let's just say Pasadena and I didn't get along."

"That's it? Why not just move to Santa Monica?"

He laughed. "It's a long story."

"I have no pressing engagements."

He looked at her, considering. "The truth is, I missed the old neighborhood. Even though my aunt busted my ass if I used gang slang or talked about my life back there, I kept going back."

"That's where your friends were."

"Friends, yeah. But it's like I knew who I was there. It was easy. Hanging with my cousin. Running jobs, banging my girlfriend, the usual shit."

"I bet your aunt was royally pissed."

"You could say that."

He could remember with vivid clarity the way Aunt Estelle had looked the first time she'd found out about his treks back to the neighborhood.

He'd cleaned up his language, was getting halfway decent grades in the dull-as-shit private school she'd shoved him in, and had pretty much transformed into a typical teenager. So it had been one hell of a shock when she realized it was all an illusion. His little white-haired aunt was more terrifying that day than his cousin Rollins had ever been. For a few days, she'd even managed to put a stop to his returns. But only for a few days.

"Everything really went to hell when I got Alicia pregnant."

"Alicia?"

"My wife."

"Oh." She took a long pull from the beer, her attention on the bottle rather than on him. "What happened?"

He hesitated, because he was running off at the mouth, her easy presence making him stupid. He tried to tell himself that was the succubus working, making magic and all that shit, but he didn't really believe it. It was just her, and he just kept on talking.

"Aunt Estelle dragged her up to Pasadena, too."

"Shotgun wedding?"

"Something like that. Set us both up in her garage apartment. Made us get married."

"How old were you?"

"Alicia sixteen, me barely seventeen."

"You were just a kid." There was sympathy on her face. "You must have missed your friends."

"Yeah. I did. Not Alicia, though."

"She was so glad to be out?"

"Oh yeah," he said. "Used to rip me a new one whenever I went back, hell even when I took a call from Rollins."

"Who?"

"My cousin. Alicia and Estelle, man, they couldn't stand that I was keeping my hand in that grime. They both released balloons the day I joined the army."

"I bet you were good at it."

"Hell, yeah." When he was inside—with the structure and the training and the weapons—he felt more at home than he had in his life. "By the time I turned nineteen, I was stationed in Serbia. By the time I was twenty-two, I was in Special Forces. I was damn good at what I did." Of course he was. In the streets, he'd killed for his gang. In the military, he'd killed for his country.

She met his eyes, her whole body hurting for this man and the tumultuous life he'd had. "And Alicia? The baby?" It was one thing to walk away from a human life, but to walk away from a child? Maybe because she'd never had parents, that seemed particularly horrible.

He ran a hand over his smooth scalp. "We lost it."

"Oh. I'm so sorry."

"It . . . it was . . . I don't know. Alicia's mom said it was probably for the best."

"God. Why? Because you got pregnant before you got married?"

He shook his head. "We were both sickle-cell carriers. She said the genetic risk was too high." He took another long pull of beer. "I really didn't like that woman."

"Rand . . ." She trailed off, not knowing what to say, so she said nothing. Instead, she took his right hand and lifted it, then pressed a kiss to his palm. Slowly, she put his hand down, then gently rotated it so that the tattoo faced upward. With the pad of her thumb, she traced the X's. "It's not a gang tat anymore."

"It is," he said. "It's a reminder that I'm dead to my old life."

Her heart hitched. "When you were infected, you mean? When you became a werewolf?"

For a moment he didn't answer, and she regretted asking the question. She had no right, especially considering what she'd come there for. Then he pulled his hand away. Her fingers slipped over warm, calloused skin, and then she was holding nothing but the air.

"No," he said. He turned away, and she studied his back, bare and etched with scars from injuries that she knew must have been made before he turned, before his weren biology could heal his injuries. He turned and faced her. "When I buried my wife."

Buried. She closed her eyes against the pain in his voice, understanding now why his soul was so fragile. He'd lost his love, and it had ripped his soul to shreds.

"I was out of it—the gangs, the neighborhood, everything my aunt had hoped. That wasn't me anymore, and I didn't want it to be."

"Something happened."

"Rollins had a friend in another unit stationed near me, and he'd told my cousin about a side gig he had going on smuggling heroin into the U.S. on military planes. Rollins wanted me involved. I told him to go to hell."

Her chest tightened with dread. She didn't want to hear the rest, but at the same time she couldn't stop listening.

"He told me I needed to watch myself. That I'd been his since I was five. That I'd killed for him, and that I belonged to him. And then he had Alicia killed to prove it." He drew in a harsh breath. "Told me Aunt Estelle would be next if I didn't get him the shit."

"You didn't."

"No. I came home. I went to Alicia's funeral. I hugged my aunt. And then I went to my old neighborhood and put a bullet in my cousin's head."

His words chilled her, but she would have done the same.

She met his eyes. "Justice."

"Two weeks later I was back in the Balkans, trolling the mountains looking for the cave where Rollins's friend hid his supply."

"That's when you were infected. You walked into a werewolf's hidey-hole."

"An Outcast," he said. "Nasty-tempered fellow. I don't remember much—the fever from the infection lasted over a day and the medics couldn't do anything but treat the weird-ass bite on my leg."

"Only a day?" From what she'd heard, most infected humans suffered for an entire month until the moon rose full again.

"About that. And for a month, I didn't realize what I was, but I was antsy, and I could feel the wolf inside. I didn't know what it was, but I knew it felt familiar. Then a full moon came."

"You changed."

"And Rollins's friend was found dead the next morning. Mauled. Completely ripped apart."

"You did it."

He lifted a shoulder. "I don't know," he said. "But I damn sure hope so."

She reached for him, held his hands tight, wishing she could provide comfort or peace. Wishing she hadn't walked through the door of the pub with a damn agenda.

She hadn't gotten any information out of his head, and with a soul as ragged as his, she would have to explain to Division that she doubted she ever could.

Would they make her try again? She closed her eyes, thinking of how futile the attempt would be. How dangerous.

But even so, she longed to see this man again. And so she couldn't deny the small, secret hope that Division would tell her to come back and try to figure out a way.

CHAPTER 18

It was fitting that he moved through the subway tunnels, a man-made sanctuary that spread out beneath Los Angeles, turning night into day with harsh artificial lighting, and day into night by nothing more astounding than barring the treacherous rays of the sun.

The light here was false, beating back the inherent darkness of a subterranean world.

The light within him was dangerous, as well. Too fragile. Too ephemeral. Too weak to withstand the constant taunting of the dark. It beat at him, calling for him to break free. To let go and become that which his nature demanded. A fiend. A monster. A killer.

Vampire.

Sergius pressed his hands against the cool tile walls, his head down, his forehead touching the ceramic as he tried to back it off, to once again control the daemon that had burst forth and demanded it be in charge.

Most nights, he failed.

He continued to try, though. Fighting so hard to push it back, to destroy the daemon before it destroyed him. Before they found him, and bound him, and thrust a stake through his heart.

He deserved it. By the gods, he deserved it.

He'd killed. He'd reveled in the blood, lost himself in the taking.

And, yes, he would kill again.

No.

He lifted his hand, fisted it, then slammed it back, the force of the impact smashing a hole through the pale blue tiles. Pieces fell to the ground, clattering on the cement floor, their edges sharp as glass. He reached down and picked one up, closing his palm tight around it.

Glass.

He had used glass in the ceremony to call the *Numen,* the spirit that could help a vampire bind his daemon and shove that vile, murderous part of him down and lock it away forever.

He'd offered blood to the *Numen.* Blood. Life. Whatever the spirit guide demanded, he'd given, and he'd still failed. Still killed.

Still, the daemon rose.

And in the deepest, darkest part of himself, he was glad of it. He was *nosferatu,* and those who had sipped of the dark lady's blood were not meant to be shackled and gelded.

That's the daemon talking.

It was. He knew that it was.

And yet he did not care.

No.

He closed his hand again over the shard, wanting now to hurl it at his enemy. He couldn't, though. His enemy was himself.

Breathe.

It's okay. You're coherent. The daemon is bound.

For the moment, at least, the daemon is bound.

For how long, though, he didn't know.

Frustrated, he paced the length of the platform. The

Hollywood station was technically closed this late at night, but that was hardly a barrier to someone like him gaining access.

Or to someone like the son of a bitch who'd slipped into the tunnels and stolen three of Serge's flock away, not using wiles and mind tricks to seduce and entice the humans, as Sergius did before he took their blood, but a hypodermic needle and a length of rope.

The humans had not returned.

Serge told himself he did not mourn the fate of human tunnel rats, that he sought only restitution for those that were taken from him.

It wasn't true. And in his moments of lucidity, he celebrated the truth beneath the lie, because it meant that a spark of compassion could still root within him.

The daemon had not entirely won.

Now he waited. Night after night, day after day, he waited for the killer's return.

And while he waited, he fought the daemon. Fought the temptation of the blood, of the flesh.

Fought it. Failed. And fed.

Even now, he could smell them. *His humans.* They didn't know what he was; he took care to shield his true nature from them and to alter their minds when he fed. None had a will strong enough to fight a vampire's mind tricks; if they did, they would not be living with him in the ground like worms.

They smelled of sweat and sex and human waste. And of blood.

It would be so easy to leave the platform, to ease into the pitch-black tunnels and make his way through the maze to where the humans slept.

Within, the daemon writhed. He'd not fed on a human in days, living instead on vermin. But that didn't satisfy, and inside the hunger built. The desperate urge to take and taste. To feed.

To kill.

No.

He fought the urge, willing the hunger to back down. To hide within. The blood would give him the strength to fight the daemon, yes, but the temptation to keep sucking, keep drinking, was too strong.

He shuddered as the daemon inside trembled with pleasure. The feel of his lips on flesh and of his teeth sinking deep into the vein. Of drinking deep. Of drinking *life*.

That was the prize, wasn't it? That was what made living in this hellhole worth it.

No.

He clenched his fists, focusing on *him*. On Sergius. He had to fight to stay clear. Had to fight back the daemon.

Don't give in. Don't back down.

He wouldn't.

He fought to push it away, to ignore the way it gnawed at him, sharp teeth begging for release. Fought to focus only on why he was here, again, this night.

He would come tonight, surely. The killer. The taker of the sheep.

He would come, and Serge would kill, quickly and smoothly. He would spill the taker's blood on the platform tiles, and he would watch as it trickled away, some puddling, some draining off the platform.

He would watch, but he wouldn't feed, and he would

know two victories that night. One against the taker. The other against his daemon.

If only the man would show himself.

The hours ticked on and on, and Serge had nothing to show for it except a hunger that burned, deeper and deeper.

Leave. Feed.

He shifted, the allure of the hunger almost overwhelming, but he clenched his fists at his sides, determined not to go. Not to move.

Serge would wait him out, then take him deeper. And while the earliest commuters arrived in polished shoes and dry-cleaned clothes, blissfully ignorant of what else was beneath the ground with them, Serge would make clear to the killer exactly how big a mistake he'd made.

It was that promise that kept him focused and in position despite the long nights without a whisper from the killer. *He's moved on. He's hunting in another tunnel.*

Possible, Serge knew, but he didn't want to believe it. Serge was dug in here, and until he was stronger—until he'd mastered control—it was too dangerous for him to go aboveground or even to search out another lair. He wanted to avoid the stake even more than he wanted to teach the killer a lesson. So he stayed and waited and hoped that the man would return.

He heard footsteps and slid silently into the dark, his face and body concealed as he looked out over the Hollywood platform. At first he saw nothing, and the echo in the silent, tiled area made it difficult to discern the direction of the footfalls.

It didn't matter, though. That much he realized soon enough. Because it wasn't a man approaching. It was a woman. Tall and skinny, balancing on nail-point heels that pushed her feet up at an unnatural angle. She wore a green silk dress that made her sallow skin seem even sicklier. Her hair hung lank and dull, and her eyes were cloudy.

One more addict wandering into the tunnels looking for a fix.

She took a step in his direction, then stumbled. She turned, as if to face someone who'd pushed her, and Serge saw the long run up the back of her stocking.

There was nothing alluring about the woman. Nothing appealing. Nothing sensual or sexy or the least bit enticing. On the contrary, she was pathetic.

Serge wanted her desperately.

He'd fought so hard, but now, faced with the reality of this female—of the blood in her veins, of the vulnerability of her movements—he had to have her.

Within, the daemon preened. One more victory; one more kill.

And once again, mighty Sergius slipped deeper into the shadows, surrendering to the promise of blood.

♦

Across the platform, in the shadows of the tunnel, four figures moved in silence, armed with a net manufactured of hematite filament and ready to be charged with ten thousand volts. Their faces were covered, their footing sure, their scent masked by an industrial spray that didn't quite blend with the musty, oily smell of the subway tunnels.

One man peeled off to stop in front of a breaker box,

then snapped the lock, gaining access to the controls. The leader gave the signal. The man flipped a switch, the lights died, and the team burst forward, their night-optic devices in place and the lights on their helmets set for infrared.

The bloodsucker ripped his head up, snarling, his nostrils flaring and fangs bared. The woman hung limp in his arms, moaning softly. Through the NODs, the bloody wound in her neck appeared as a dark gray-green blotch against the greenish tint of her skin. The vampire dropped her, staring now into the dark at the tall figure of Delta Leader, who stepped forward. He wore no goggles, but stood, face set, confident in the knowledge that although he was blind in the dark, the team behind him was well trained and ready.

"You," the vampire snarled.

The leader lifted his eyes, seeing nothing, but certain that the creature could see his own look of defiance.

A rush of air, a signal to move, and he was diving for the ground, rolling out of the way of the forward-rushing team.

They'd banked on the fact that the vampire wouldn't expect an ambush. Would have believed that Delta Leader had come alone. And they'd been right.

The net whipped through the air to meet the creature as he sped toward them, then suddenly the team looked away, protecting their eyes from temporary blindness as the net snapped and popped from the electricity arcing through it. It was over in an instant, and the vampire stood as if in shock, his body entwined in the filaments.

He gasped, still twitching from the shock to his muscles.

His mouth opened, and he reached for something unseen.

Then he collapsed in a heap on the tiled floor of the Hollywood station subway platform.

The leader gave the signal, and the man beside the breaker flipped a switch. Once again, light filled the area. A second man rushed in, then put the hematite binders on the captive's wrists and ankles. Another man bent down to pick up the limp form, hauling him over his shoulder in a fireman's carry.

The last man hurried in from the shadows and collected the woman.

Then the leader made a circular motion with his fingers, and the team slipped silently back into the tunnel, letting the darkness swallow them as they returned the way they'd come.

CHAPTER 19

Rand pressed the heels of his hands to his temples, wishing he could squeeze out the thoughts of Alicia. He didn't want her in his head. Not then. Not when he'd just been with Lissa.

Not when he'd enjoyed it so damn much.

Of course, there was still the overarching question of what she was doing at the Goat in the first place. Van Nuys was a hell of a long way from her club on Pico.

"I wanted to see you," she said when he asked her.

"Why?"

She grinned, then pulled off his shirt and switched it for her own. She handed him his with a sly grin. "Maybe I like you."

"And Priam?"

She frowned. "Him, I don't like at all."

"I meant why was he here? He followed you, but why?"

She shrugged, not looking at him as she finished dressing.

"No, Lissa. Why?" He pulled on the shirt. "I overheard you in Orlando's. What did he mean by 'trickery'?"

"It doesn't have anything to do with you."

"I just killed the man. Trust me. It has something to do with me."

From the sour expression that crossed her face, he

could tell that she didn't want to tell him. He could also tell that she was going to. He pulled on his jeans, grabbed a fresh beer, and waited.

"Do you know about the cortegery?"

"Enlighten me."

"It's where most succubi live. We're bought as infants. Taken as slaves. And we're owned by traders who use us to pull souls." She licked her lips, and he noticed how tall she stood, her chin lifted just a little and her hands fisted at her sides. "They brand us. Sometimes on the breast. Sometimes the hip. My brand was on the back of my neck. The worst of the traders abuse us. Beatings. Starvation. Rape. They have a deed, you see. It's allowed."

"The PEC is okay with that?"

She swallowed visibly, then shrugged. "Not the abuse. But who's going to tell them? And as for the ownership, yeah. That's the way it's always been, back to the beginning of time." Her smile was ironic. "Very traditional organization, the PEC."

"Okay. But what about you?"

"I got free." There was a fire in her eyes now. "I worked and I saved and I bought my way to freedom. And the first thing I did—even before I opened Orlando's—was get rid of that goddamned brand."

She turned, then lifted her hair. He saw the scar—the raised patch of mangled skin at her hairline. He'd felt it, but he hadn't known what it was.

"It's barely noticeable," he said, because he knew that was what a woman would want to hear.

"Really? That's a shame. Because it's one of the things I'm most proud of. That, and the girls."

"The girls?"

She met his eyes. "I rescue them. Buy them back, fair and square, and then assign their deeds over to them. Every succubus who works at Orlando's works there because she wants to."

"I'm guessing Priam didn't want to sell one of his girls, but that you had something on him."

"You're very astute."

"So are you." He looked her up and down, this woman who'd been so soft in his arms. It was an illusion. Really, she was steel, and the exact opposite of him. He killed—coldly, emotionlessly, tactically. She saved, and with a passion and intensity that awed him. He wanted to tell her, but couldn't find the words. "I'm impressed," he said, though that didn't cover the half of it.

"You should be. I've worked my ass off."

"I know. You're the only succubus in California who owns a trading club."

"You checked up on me?" She looked extremely pleased.

"I asked around."

Her smile was soft and inviting, like silk on steel, and he moved to kiss her. A sharp pounding at the door interrupted him.

"Busy!"

"I know—I mean, I saw her." Mia's words were fast. Rand shot a glance toward Lissa, amused. "It's just that there's someone dead, and—"

Fuck.

"My problem," he said, moving to the door.

"What?" Mia said.

"I said I'll deal with it." He tugged open the door. Mia stood there, looking rattled.

"It's just that I—I mean, I was taking out the trash, and—"

"I know." She was a nice enough girl, a human/elf halfling, and although the Slaughtered Goat brought in a colorful clientele, most kept their disputes outside, and farther away than the alley or sidewalks.

Rand had broken that unspoken rule—or Priam had—and now Mia was paying the price.

"He attacked the girl," Rand explained, nodding toward Lissa, who came over and put her arm around Mia. Almost immediately, the girl brightened, then leaned against Lissa, accepting the support without hesitation.

"Are you okay?"

"I'm fine," Lissa said. "Rand took care of it."

"And I'll take care of this, too," he said.

"I called the PEC," Mia said, speaking to Lissa. "Was that okay?"

"It's fine," Rand said, before Lissa could speak. It wasn't, of course. He didn't want Division on his back. At the same time, though, he was a high-level therian in vampire territory who'd just killed a local, albeit in self-defense. Maybe it was best to play it by the book. He just hoped that none of Division's shit would blow back on Lissa. The bastard had come for her, after all.

Lissa's teeth dragged across her lower lip, her brows knitting as she looked at him. Then her face cleared and she smiled, her attention turning back to Mia. "Don't worry. Just go and take care of the front. When the agent arrives, send him back here."

Mia nodded, then smiled at Lissa before heading out the door. She didn't look back at Rand.

"Earlier, she couldn't keep her hands off me," Rand said once the door closed, "much less her eyes. Two minutes with you and she's off men for good. Trust me when I say there are a lot of guys in the front who hate you now."

"I only cranked it up to make her feel better."

"Yeah, well, I think you managed."

Lissa laughed, the sound rising like carbonated bubbles, lifting his mood and at the same time making him wonder if he wasn't under Lissa's spell, too. Of course he was. She was a succubus, and he was sucked in. It didn't get much simpler than that.

"I don't think she's the type to forgo men, but I'm flattered you think so highly of my appeal. And I did get her mind off the body."

"The dead body, anyway," Rand said dryly. He pulled open the door. "Do you want to go before the agents get here? No one saw us in the alley. I don't have to mention that Priam grabbed you. Why he came, why he was angry—none of that has anything to do with me, and since I'm the reason he's dead, I figure it's just noise."

Her face lit with pleasure. "You're protecting me."

"No, I'm—"

She stepped over the threshold into the hallway. "I'm staying."

He shook his head, frustrated, but followed her the short distance down the hall, then stepped in front of her. He went outside first, stopping by the body and the detached head. He stared dispassionately at it, seeing it for the first time without the haze of either fury or sex. "I really don't need this shit," he murmured.

Beside him, Lissa cringed, and he felt like an ass for saying that out loud, especially since he wasn't even certain why he'd said it. He'd been thinking about Division—about the bureaucratic bullshit of cleaning up a body, and how all of that would get in the way of doing his job and getting away from Los Angeles.

But he'd been thinking about her, too. And now he had to admit that he didn't need the shit she represented, either. Didn't need her buzzing around in his head. Didn't need this lingering feeling that he wanted to hold her and comfort her.

He'd fucked her, and that was all he'd wanted. All he'd needed.

And you are a goddamned liar.

He closed his eyes and fisted his hands at his sides. Yeah, he was a liar. A damned good one, too.

She was also looking at the body. "I should thank you."

He let his gaze drift over her. "I think you already did."

The corner of her mouth twitched, but otherwise her face remained stony and businesslike. "I'm serious. You didn't just save me tonight, you saved my girls, too. That's not something I'll forget."

He didn't know her well, but he understood what those words cost her. She was a woman who could take care of herself—who took pride in taking care of herself, and her business, and her girls.

But she hadn't managed this one on her own.

She'd needed help, and it had to tweak her pride to

voice her gratitude. Maybe that's why he saw something hesitant in her eyes, something that suggested she wasn't entirely thankful or that she was holding something back.

He almost asked about it, but didn't. "You're welcome," he said instead.

Her mouth stretched briefly into a smile, and he realized that she'd heard the understanding in his tone. Time to get out of there. This wasn't the moment for gratitude any more than it was the time to pull her close, strip her bare, and sink himself deep inside her once again.

Not the time, he repeated. *Definitely not the time.*

Too bad his body wasn't listening.

"Lissa," he said, then realized he had no words. It didn't matter. The door from the pub slammed open, and a wiry man strode through, eyes going immediately to the body.

Lissa looked at Rand and nodded, and he realized she understood. *Division.*

Everything else between them could wait.

CHAPTER 20

Rand leaned against the side of the building, watching the skinny PEC officer through narrowed eyes. Not that there was much to watch. Officer Peck had introduced himself, asked a few questions, taken some pictures, then made a call back to headquarters. Now his attention was focused on Lissa, his face soft and dreamy as he watched her stand with her arms wrapped around herself in the doorway. Twice now, Rand had forced himself not to tell the officer to keep his mind on his job and his eyes off Lissa. It hadn't been easy keeping silent. The officer clearly needed the reminder.

"I'm right here," he said, and Peck's head swiveled from Lissa to him. "Don't you have any more questions? Some sort of formal procedure?"

"Absolutely, sir." The eyes darted back to Lissa. "Ma'am."

She stood up a little straighter, then let a slow smile drift onto her face. "Well, since we're here and you're here, why don't you get started?" She took one step toward him. "You can start with me if you want. I'd like to get the interview out of the way."

If the officer had been wearing a tie, he'd be tugging hard on it. Instead, he just turned a dozen shades of purple. "Oh. Sure. Okay." He blinked. "I mean, no. I can't do that. My orders are to wait."

"Oh." She let a world of disappointment slide into her voice, and Rand couldn't decide if he should laugh or rescue the poor guy. He didn't think Lissa was playing him simply for her amusement, but he also didn't think that her attempts to get the process to move faster were going to be successful. They were in an alley with a body and a gangly, ineffective officer, and they might as well get used to it.

The officer smelled human, which surprised Rand, as not too many humans worked for the PEC. Maybe he had some hidden shadow traits. Or maybe the human was more exceptional than he looked. Right then, he looked like a twelve-year-old with a crush on a cheerleader.

"What orders?" he said, and once again Officer Peck turned his head reluctantly from Lissa to Rand.

"After I arrived and took your names, I called in the initial information. Standard procedure to run a check on all witnesses."

"And?"

"And I was told to stand down. That the investigator assigned to the case would be conducting the interview." He took a step toward Rand. "I'm guessing it's because . . . well, you know." He cocked his head toward Lissa, then shrugged, apparently assuming his meaning was clear.

It was.

Peck was obviously affected by Lissa's nature, but that didn't mean every male at the PEC would be. Rand was hardly an expert on the nature of succubi, but he did know that different males reacted in different ways. A very rare few weren't affected at all by the sheen of a succubus. The vast majority, though, reacted at varying levels, and even men who were significantly affected by a succubus the first time they met could build up a resistance to the sheen. They wouldn't cease to be affected, but they wouldn't fall into a puppy-love trance or turn into a hardened, desperate animal simply because she was in the same room.

Probably for the best, then, if they were sending in an investigator with a bit of resistance. Peck obviously didn't qualify. And for that matter, neither did Rand.

He was about to ask if he and Lissa could go wait inside while Peck guarded the body when the back door opened, sending light arcing across the alley, illuminating the body and then sliding away again as the door swung shut.

Two men stood just over the threshold. One, a lanky para-daemon with a three-day beard and hard expression that suggested he'd seen it all. The other, a vampire male in a tailored suit with a pretty-boy face. He was familiar. That face, the way he held himself.

Somewhere, Rand had seen him before. And then he remembered: *The vampire was* kyne.

And from the look in his eye, the vampire recognized Rand, too.

"Why are you here?" Rand asked, because there was no reason in hell for the *kyne* to be called in for something like the death of a para-daemon trader, and Rand wasn't in the mood for games. Vampiric *kyne* reported to Tiberius alone, and at the moment, anything associated with Tiberius was bad news for Gunnolf. And for Rand.

The lanky para-daemon looked at the two of them. "You two know each other?"

"Apparently we do," the vampire said. "I didn't recognize your name when dispatch notified me." He held out a hand. "Nicholas Montegue. Nick."

Rand kept his hands in his pockets. "M," he said, pronouncing the letter clearly and noting Nick's slow nod.

"R," he said in response.

Rand nodded. He remembered the face now. Years before, when Gunnolf and Tiberius had been sliding through one of their brief periods of détente, the Alliance heads had organized a joint weren/vamp mission. Rand and his buddy Alex Courtland had been on point for the weren, and Nick and another vampire, tall and dark with a scar across his right cheek, had run the op for the vampires.

Since joint missions were rare, they hadn't bothered to introduce themselves, instead referring to each other by letters only. M and D and R and C. They'd done the job, reported back to their respective leaders, and that had been the end of it.

He'd never expected to see the man again. "Why are you here?"

"For Lissa," Nick said, turning to where she still stood, leaning against the wall by the door, hugging herself. His face was hard, calculating, but Rand saw a softness there, too, and he realized it was for the girl. An unwelcome ribbon of jealousy unfurled in his gut, and he forced himself to stand still and ignore it.

Lissa herself looked rattled, confused, overwhelmed, and Rand wanted to take her into his arms and hold her.

He wanted to be the one to comfort her, not Nick. This night had to be weighing on her. He knew she understood the way their world worked, and she was hardly naive, but he also doubted that she'd seen too many men beheaded. Thanks to him, she now had one fresh in her memory.

"I'm her advocate," Nick continued, before Rand could press him.

At his words, Lissa looked up, but she didn't meet Nick's eyes. Instead, her gaze sought Rand's, and he couldn't help the flush of victory that swelled through him.

"Orlando's advocate, actually," Nick continued. "I represent the interests of a number of clients, some extremely powerful, some more local in character, but still important to me."

The lanky para-daemon looked up from where he'd been squatting over the body. "The frat party over yet? 'Cause I thought maybe we'd try to get in a minute or so of work. If it's all right with you two."

Nick spread his hands at his sides. "It's your show, Doyle. We're at your mercy."

"Don't I fucking wish?" Doyle said, his voice low. He didn't bother looking at Nick, but turned his attention directly to Rand. "So how long's it been since you whacked the guy?"

"Excuse me?"

"That's not at issue, right?" He turned to Officer Peck, who was dutifully taking notes. "You told dispatch that Mr. Rand here acknowledged that he and the victim fought and that Rand cut our body's throat."

"Yes, I—" Peck cut himself off, shooting an accusing

look toward Rand, as if Rand had suddenly backed off from that story.

"And that's right," Rand said. "You asked how long?"

"Simple question."

Except it wasn't. By both protocol and common sense, they should have called Division first thing. They hadn't. Far from it. And Rand couldn't help but wonder how that would play in light of the fact that Lissa was a succubus, and Priam had come to the pub seeking her out.

As if she understood his hesitation, Lissa edged forward. "We didn't call right away," she said, drawing Doyle's attention away from Rand and to her. Nick didn't look at her. Instead, he'd stepped forward and was peering down at Priam's face, and Rand saw the recognition in his eyes. He waited for the advocate to say something about it, but Nick remained silent.

If Lissa noticed her advocate's reaction to the body, she didn't say anything. She was still talking to Doyle. "It was probably half an hour. Maybe more. It's my fault, I'm sorry. I was rattled." She flashed Rand a wan smile. "He . . . comforted me. We didn't think."

Doyle rocked back on his heels, his hand pressed lightly to Priam's head. "That explains why I'm not getting shit."

"Percipient daemon," Nick said in explanation.

"You don't need to get in his head," Rand said. "I already told Peck I killed him. What more do you need to know?"

Doyle's smile was thin. "Good question. What more

do I need to know?" He started in then with a machine-gun-fire series of questions. Why had Rand been in the alley? Why had Lissa? What started the altercation? Were there any witnesses?

All standard questions, and Rand answered them honestly, more or less. Yet he couldn't shake the feeling that neither Doyle nor Nick really gave a shit about the dead para-daemon, but instead were just going through the motions, as if the investigation was a necessary nuisance, but was keeping them from some bigger purpose.

But that just didn't make sense.

Doyle shifted his questions to Lissa, and she followed Rand's lead, but there were fewer questions, and she ran through them easily. Nick didn't look at Lissa, and he didn't once step in as her advocate to interrupt Doyle's interrogation.

The whole thing felt off. Hell, the whole night felt off.

The forensic team arrived, along with a rep from the medical examiner's office. Officer Peck took over then, and Doyle ushered Rand, Lissa, and Nick back inside.

"You've had a rough night," Doyle said, taking Lissa's arm as they paused at the end of the hallway in front of the door that led into the pub. "I'll give you a ride back to Orlando's."

Lissa looked at Rand, her blue eyes pale.

Was she waiting for him to suggest that she stay? He wanted to say the words, but that was the sheen talking, and he knew it. And while he would be happy for her to continue warming his bed, the truth was he had other priorities. The detour with Priam had taken up enough of his time.

He needed to get back to work.

CHAPTER 21

Melissa Jo Keeling was very drunk. But not so drunk that she was stupid. No way. Her mother didn't raise a stupid girl, and even though it was only two blocks from Andy's apartment to her place, she had her pepper spray out and tight in her hand.

Andy—damn his ugly, two-timing hide—had told her not to go. Too late, he'd said. Too dark.

Like he even cared.

Angrily, Melissa Jo brushed tears away. She'd promised herself when she moved to Los Angeles from Arkansas that she'd start acting like a woman of the world and not a little twit from Payton, population 618. So much for that. A woman of the world did not get bent out of shape when she learned her boyfriend was seeing another girl. A woman of the world turned up the charm and convinced said boyfriend that he was an idiot for even looking at any woman but her.

Apparently Melissa Jo wasn't a woman of the world, because all she'd done was run.

Bastard. Scum puppy. *Fucking prick.*

She looked up to heaven and said a quick apology, but she was ticked off, darn it, and could she help it if he really was a fucking prick?

She was so lost in her anger and her contrition that she wasn't paying attention to the ground, and she stumbled on the sidewalk, where the combination of a tree root and earthquakes had cracked the concrete and pushed it up at odd angles into a mini obstacle course. Her ankle twisted painfully, and the tears started again. Not because of the pain, but because Andy wasn't there to lean on.

Maybe she should turn back. Maybe they could work it out.

The thought propelled her to twist around, and as she did, she saw the tiniest hint of movement behind her. Something almost imperceptible that was gone so quickly it could have been her imagination.

It wasn't, of course. It was Andy. He was following and making sure she got home okay.

She turned back, facing forward, and smiled. He *did* love her. He did, and when she got home, he was going to follow her upstairs and knock on her door and beg her to forgive him.

And she would. She'd make him pay first—make him promise to dump that tramp, and make sure he understood that he was on boyfriend probation—but in the end she'd take him back.

She loved him, after all.

Limping slightly, she continued down the street, the neatly tended Brentwood houses lined up beside her. The neighborhood was awesome—and a long damn way from the drafty little farmhouse she'd grown up in. Right now, she lived in a garage apartment and worked as a nanny for the Harrelson twins. One day, though, one of these houses would be hers. Or maybe a house in Beverly Hills or on the beach.

Andy was in law school, after all. She'd be Mrs.

Andrew Cohen, and she'd host fabulous dinner parties and do all her shopping on Rodeo Drive.

Despite her sore ankle, she added a little wiggle to her hips. She wondered how long he'd wait after she got into her apartment. Not long, she hoped. She'd been mad—really mad—but now she was warming up, and there was something sweet and sexy about him following her home.

An eight-foot-tall privacy fence surrounded the Harrelson property, but she had a key to the side gate. The family wasn't home—they'd gone to Ojai for a few days—so she didn't feel weird about letting Andy in. Carefully, she pushed the gate until it was almost closed, but not quite latched. She didn't want Andy to have to call her and ruin her surprise.

She headed toward the stairs to her apartment, but stopped at the base when she heard the gate hinge creak.

She stood for a moment, trying to decide if she should play coy and quickly ruling it out. She didn't want coy. She wanted Andy. Wanted to hear his apologies and his assurances that he wanted only her.

She turned, expecting the gentle face of the man she'd been dating for the last two years.

He wasn't there.

Instead, she stared into the face of evil. Black eyes. Fanged teeth. And dry, cracked skin.

"Thirsty," it croaked, and though Melissa Jo tried to run, she didn't get far. The thing grabbed her, tumbling her to the ground, a calloused hand closing over her mouth as she tried futilely to scream.

"Thirsty," it repeated, and in a flash it was at her neck, the fangs seeping deep into her flesh.

It drank and drank, contentment settling over it. The harsh, painful thirst was dissipating. Power flowing through its veins. It could go anywhere. Do anything.

It had been a man once—the memory was fuzzy, but there. A man who had foraged for food in trash cans. Who'd held out a hand begging money from humans.

No more.

The humans were his now. And he was a god.

The girl was drained, every drop consumed. He released his hold and stood up, knowing ecstasy for the first time in his life.

He took a step toward the future and barely felt the heat as it flared inside him.

He was gone before his foot hit the ground, his body burned up from within.

And all that was left of the creature was a pile of ash dusting the ground beside the desiccated body of Melissa Jo Keeling.

♦

Lissa slid into the passenger seat of Doyle's car, an ancient Pontiac Catalina with a bench seat and doors that weighed as much as her Mini Cooper. Tucker was already in the backseat—he'd been inside the pub interviewing Mia—and he leaned forward as soon as Lissa got in, his arms hooked to the back of the front seat.

"Well, hello there."

"Down, boy," Doyle said.

Tucker made a growling noise that was obviously supposed to be sexy, then leaned back in his seat, his eyes staying on her.

"Dammit, Tucker." He looked at Lissa. "Tone it down, will you?"

She bit back a laugh. "Sorry. I can only turn it up. I can't turn it off. Will he be okay?"

"Probably die of blue balls," Doyle muttered. "But yeah. He'll deal."

He started the car, but didn't pull out. After a few seconds, Nick opened the back door and got in beside Tucker without a word, turning the backseat frosty.

Lissa didn't know what had changed his mood to ice, and she didn't care. All she wanted was to go home. Unfortunately, she wasn't going to get her wish right away. Because now it was time for the real questioning to start.

"Guess you owe old Priam a thank-you," Doyle said, once they were on the road.

She turned sharply to face him. "Excuse me?"

"Made your job easier, didn't it? How did you put it? He 'comforted' you?"

"You really are a son of a bitch, you know that? The bastard tried to kill me. It wasn't some setup so I could get close to Rand and do your damned investigation."

"Down, girl."

"Don't even—"

"You're right," he said, and she closed her mouth, crossed her arms over her chest, and waited for him to go on. "You're right. I'm an ass and you've had one hell of a night." He took his eyes off the road long enough to glance at her. "Better?"

"At least you're self-aware. Not many sons of bitches are."

"That's me," he said. "Just oozing with self-awareness."

In the backseat, Nick stayed silent.

"So what did you learn?"

"Nothing."

Doyle snorted. "So his head's completely empty? Hell, that doesn't surprise me. Never met a werewolf or a human with a useful thought, and since he was both, he's probably got a vacuum where his brain should be."

"There you go," she said. "Nothing up there for me to get. My job's done. Cut me loose."

"Not so fast, sweetheart. You got snuggly with the dude, right?"

She didn't answer.

"All right, then. You and Rand do the horizontal rumba, but you don't have shit to report? How does that work?"

"I'm not psychic," she snapped. "I can't just take a peek. You want someone with an easier path into his head, then great. Bring 'em in and I'll go happily home." Inside, her heart was breaking. It had never seemed easy, the deal she'd cut. But now it seemed both impossible and unfair. Because in order to explain why she hadn't been able to get what they'd asked for, she was going to have to reveal things about Rand. Personal things.

She was going to have to tell them about the state of his soul.

"I like you, Lissa," Doyle said. "But this isn't just friendly chatter. You made a deal with Division. Not me—*Division*. And you need to live up to that deal."

His words hit her like blows, and she remembered the tattooed line of X's on Rand's wrist and the pain in his voice when he talked about his wife's murder, his past. He'd lost his love, he'd killed for revenge, and it had ripped him up inside. And that wasn't anyone's business but his own.

But now she was going to share it. Not because she wanted to, but because she had to. Because in the end, her first priority was to protect herself so that she could protect her girls.

"It only works if I have something to attach to—something to take." She closed her eyes against the words. "And there wasn't enough."

In the backseat, Nick shifted, and Lissa stiffened, knowing damn well that if the vampire made some crack about therians and their souls, she would turn around in her seat and punch him. Fortunately, he kept silent.

Beside her, Doyle shrugged. "So grab on to what there is."

"It doesn't work that way."

"What?" He turned long enough to squint at her, and she realized she'd been whispering.

"I said it doesn't work like that."

"That a fact?"

"How does it work?" Tucker asked. She glanced over the backseat to see him leaning back, watching her now with more interest than longing. He was human, she remembered. He probably thought this whole thing was fascinating, never mind that the threads of a man's soul hung in the balance.

"It's hard to explain," she said, wanting to avoid a detailed discussion of how deep his soul was buried, how thin the strands now were, and how the only way to get ahold of it was to take it when he came—and doing that would surely rip his entire soul free. "The bottom line is I can't take any without risking taking it all. And I can't get into his head without taking at least a little bit of soul."

"So take," Tucker said, his casual words making her stomach revolt as she thought of Claude. Of what Rand could become if she did.

She shuddered.

In the backseat, Tucker frowned, his eyes meeting Doyle's in the rearview mirror. "I don't get it. It grows back. You've told me it grows back."

"We're not talking toenails here, Einstein," Doyle said.

"Think of it as a plant," Lissa said. "You prune a plant, and as long as you keep watering it and taking care of it, it's going to keep on growing. But what happens if you pull it out by its roots?"

"Oh," Tucker said. "Gotcha." He shifted his attention to Doyle. "That's why you never take it all."

"We're not talking about me," Doyle growled, his hands gripping the wooden steering wheel so tight his knuckles turned white. "This is about the werewolf, and about a deal you cut."

"You can't be asking me to take his entire soul. You, who know what will happen. Hell, you're the one who showed me those damn photographs."

"Son of a bitch is already a killer. How much more harm can you do?"

Lissa started to snap out a reply, but Nick got there first. "Try and push her on this, Doyle, and I take the particulars of this plea agreement before a judge." Lissa swiveled in her seat to face him. He'd been so silent, she'd almost forgotten he was there. Now he was watching Doyle, and although she'd turned to face him, he didn't once glance her way.

Confused and irritated, she shifted her attention back to Doyle. "So that's it, right? I made a deal, and I stuck to it, and unless you're going to insist I break the law, we can't go any further. So are we square?"

She held her breath waiting for his answer, then realized it was too long coming. The car roared down the 405, the lights of the oncoming cars hitting the windshield and bursting like fireworks. He didn't speak again until he pulled up in front of her club. In the meantime, she sat, and she breathed.

"Go on in," he said.

"Answer the question. Are we square?" She closed her hand over the door handle, her heart pounding.

"We'll talk later."

Her temper flared. "We'll talk now, dammit. You've got my ass in a sling, and you can't just leave me hanging."

His laconic expression shifted, taking on a hard edge, a visible reminder of what he was: a para-daemon, and a powerful one. "You'll hang until we tell you it's over," he said.

"Doyle." Nick spoke only the one word, but it worked. The investigator closed his mouth, the only hint of his temper the orange tinge rising in his skin.

"Out," Nick said, opening his door as well.

She hesitated when she realized he was coming with her, but not for long. Her only other option was to stay in the car, and that was unacceptable. But she didn't wait for him. He'd been a shit from the moment he arrived in the alley, and the situation was horrific enough without her own advocate being a bastard.

He caught up with her just before she slipped her key into the lock.

"It's late," she said, stating the obvious. "And I've had a hard day. So unless you're going to tell me you have a surefire way of getting Division off my back right here, right now, then I'd really like to just call this day done."

He said nothing, but his eyes never left her face. A finger of worry snaked up her spine. Since he'd volunteered as her counsel, she'd assumed he knew how to deflect the sheen, but what if she was wrong?

She took a step back, trying to change her angle to get a better look at his face and eyes, but she didn't see any sign that he was under her sheen. Just the opposite. He looked perfectly in control—and perfectly pissed.

"I want an explanation, Lissa," he said, moving fast and pinning her back to the door. "What the hell kind of scam are you pulling?"

CHAPTER 22

Lissa cringed, the force of his words and the anger in his face catching her completely off guard. "I don't know what you're talking about," she said, working hard to keep her voice level. "So back off. Right now."

He stayed there, his body hard against hers, so taut she was certain he would snap from the slightest movement. She stood perfectly still, waiting. Waiting for him to back off. Waiting for him to tell her what the hell had come over him.

He didn't back away. Instead, he moved in closer, his mouth only inches from her ear. "Priam," he said. "Of course, I knew him as Baron de Villefort. I like the spin that he was blackmailing you. Very original. What I can't figure out is if you'd planned for Rand to kill Priam, or if that was merely an added bonus. Or maybe an inconvenience? Was he the brains behind your operation, or just the brawn?"

She shook her head. Nothing in her mind connected with what he was saying, yet there was truth in his rage, and her spotty memory hid a thousand secrets.

"What did I do?" she whispered.

"Don't play naive."

"I'm not. I swear. My memories aren't back yet." She closed her eyes. "Please. Tell me what I did."

"You hurt people," he said. "You stole their secrets

and he hurt them. You and Priam, you were quite a team."

She believed him. How could she not when it explained so much? She shivered, hating the possibility that she had ever been so weak, hating even more the thought that she'd once willingly stood arm in arm with a monster like Priam.

Sometime in the past, though, she'd changed. She wasn't the Elizabeth who ran scams with Priam. She wasn't Priam's slave or his concubine. She was Lissa, and she had her own agenda.

She lifted her chin and met his eyes. "If that was me," she said, "it isn't anymore."

"I wish I could believe that."

Longing filled his voice, and she trembled. Not with desire, but with the weight of lost possibilities. The sudden sounds of birds filled the night air, so vivid that it took her a moment to realize that what she was hearing wasn't real but in her head. Birds and laughter and—

"*Nicholas,*" she said, the memory like a cloud around her.

He leaned back, taking his arm off her neck and replacing his palm on the wall, leaving her pinned inside his arms.

"We used to take walks. In an aviary." She could hear the wonder in her voice, and she struggled not to grab too tight to the memory for fear that it would slip through her fingers.

He said nothing, but she felt the subtle shift in his stance, as if he, too, were looking back on that day.

"That can't be right," she said, her words barely a whisper. "We were alone, and Priam would never—"

She closed her eyes against the sudden realization: Priam would never let a female from his cortegery walk the grounds without an escort. Which meant that either her memory was wrong . . . or Nick was right and she was more than simply one of his girls.

Another memory brushed her, and she gasped. "You gave me this name. You're the one who first called me Lissa," she said, awed by the realization. "Before you, I was only Elizabeth."

"Yes."

Her chest tightened with the sudden memory of the way she'd felt around him, light and happy and cherished. She'd thrown that all away. She didn't remember how, but she knew it with absolute certainty.

"I hurt you," she said.

"Yes."

"I'm sorry."

Sorry.

The word washed over Nick. One simple word that he'd wanted for so long to hear, and now that she finally said it, the word was little more than meaningless. "Sorry?" he repeated.

She nodded, but he could see the wariness in her eyes. He wanted to grab her by the shoulders and shake her. Wanted to demand that she explain how "sorry" was supposed to make everything right again. She'd gotten into his head—stolen his thoughts as easily as plucking fruit from a tree, and with about as much regret, too.

Inside him, the daemon flared. For so long, he'd kept such tight control, and now the edges were fraying, his grasp on sanity weakening in the face of his past laid out in front of him. His biggest mistake, Tiberius had once said. But had his mentor meant loving her . . . or not killing her when he had the chance.

Now she stood perfectly still, her back rigid and pressed up against the wall. She was afraid of him—he could smell it—yet she was holding her own, watching instead of reacting. Planning instead of fighting back.

Or maybe she was just scared.

He didn't know. He was mixing up the past and the present, he knew that. Intellectually, he understood that Lissa didn't remember her life in the court of Baron de Villafort. Emotionally, he wanted to lash out at her for betraying him. He'd been on a mission, his head full of details and plans, and she'd taken them. Had traded them to the very para-daemon he'd been hunting. And when Nick and his team had arrived on site, his target had been waiting for him.

The other two vamps on his assault team had been killed. Only blind luck had spared Nick his life—that, and the para-daemon's desire to play with his head.

His quarry had told him who had betrayed him. Had whispered it into his ear after hours of torture, strapped down on a hematite table with a sadist for a watchdog. Once he knew the truth, Nick hadn't minded. He'd longed for either the release of death or the rising of his daemon. Anything to take him away from the male he was—a male who'd been bested and betrayed by beauty. Who'd been foolish enough to profess love only to get burned by the heat of desire.

She'd used him. She'd betrayed him. She'd violated him in the most unforgivable of ways, and the thing that made his blood curdle the most was not anything that she had done or any of the torture that had been inflicted on him.

It was the simple fact that after his release—when he'd stood face-to-face with her and told her that he knew of her betrayal—he had walked away instead of killing her, then lost himself to the lure of his daemon.

Even after all that she'd done, he loved her.

He tried to tell himself it wasn't truly love. She was a succubus and she had caught him in her sheen. But that wasn't true. Perhaps when they first met, he'd been attracted to her nature, but by the time she betrayed him, he was immune to all but the woman herself. She'd become his Lissa.

She was his, and he'd believed that she loved him.

But that was more than two centuries ago, and there was no love in her eyes now.

She'd kept the name though. *Lissa.* Not Elizabeth. *Lissa.*

So what did he want from her? A touch? An apology? He'd already gotten that. Did he want to tell her everything? To force her to remember the way she'd once whispered tender thoughts to him?

Did he want her to relive her betrayal so that he could see her face? So that he could see for himself if it had been easy for her?

Was he that fucking selfish?

He closed his eyes and dropped his arms. *Yes. He was.*

And, dammit, even now—even after all he'd done—the truth was that what he really wanted was her.

"Nick?" She'd been silent for so long that his name seemed to fill the night. "Are you okay?"

He opened his eyes and saw the Lissa he wanted to see. Her blond hair now dark in the night. Her blue eyes peering at him with affection. Her lips, parted as if for a kiss.

But it was only an illusion, and as much as he wanted to thrust his fingers into her hair and draw her against him, as much as he wanted to taste her lips and feel the press of her breasts against his chest—he knew he couldn't.

The daemon within growled low, mourning the loss, reluctantly accepting the inevitable fact that he would never kiss her again, yet at the same time hoping that he was wrong.

"I'm fine," he finally said, then stepped away from her, letting one more lie slide neatly into the space between them.

◆

Her hands were shaking as she opened the door to her apartment. It was late—technically early—and she needed to sleep. But she couldn't get Nick's words out of her head.

Sleep now, and she knew what would happen. The memories would come. Nightmares.

She'd see snatches of what happened between her and Nick. Bits and pieces of her previous life with Priam.

If she could grab hold of the dream and bring it into the waking, she would remember. She'd understand. She'd *know*.

But she didn't want to. Not anymore.

Not now that she knew it was horrible.

She tossed her purse onto the couch and went into the

kitchen to pour a glass of wine, and managed instead to spill it all over the counter. Her hands were shaking too damn much.

Frustrated, she grabbed her phone and dialed Rhiana. One ring, then another, then she slammed the phone down, realizing with sudden clarity that it wasn't her friend she wanted to talk to. Realizing more that she didn't want to talk at all. She wanted to be held, to be stroked and touched and soothed, and there was only one person who could do that for her.

Rand.

Just the thought of him made her feel steadier, and she hurried to her computer to look up his cellphone number, hoping he'd come to her, knowing she'd be devastated if he didn't. Every Orlando's client was assigned a unique number for accounting purposes—drinks, takings, and the like. Not only did that make it easier on her staff, but Lissa had learned a long time ago that clients spent more money when they weren't opening their wallets.

She'd always been proud of the decision to implement that system, especially the decision to use cellphone numbers rather than randomly generated codes. Now she considered herself a genius as she logged in, found Rand's name, and immediately pulled up his number.

She hesitated only long enough to scold herself for acting like a nervous human teenager, then dialed.

The call connected on the third ring, and she didn't wait for him to answer. "Rand?"

A pause, then, "Who is this?"

But it wasn't Rand's voice. It was a woman.

It was Mia.

She slammed the phone down, realizing she was breathing hard, her skin flushed and her chest tight. *Dammit.*

Her reaction was bullshit, and so was the idea that she needed someone. She'd taken care of herself all of this life. Herself, and dozens of other women. She didn't need a man to coddle her, least of all a man who would share a bed with another woman only hours after he'd left her side.

They'd made no promises, no commitments; they hadn't even formally exchanged phone numbers. But still, there were certain rules, and Rand had just stomped all over them.

Well, fine. Chalk that up to an object lesson in what she ought to already know. That she couldn't rely on anyone, much less a man. And the only one in the world who was truly going to watch out for her was herself.

CHAPTER 23

"We're in the middle of the goddamned devil's asshole out here," Xeres said, slowing his black Land Rover as he took the first exit off the 15 into Victorville.

"Desert," Rand said, looking around at the dry landscape, the ground baking in the afternoon sun. They'd been in the car for hours now, following up a lead Xeres had on a local Outcast.

"I've found one," Xeres had said back at the Slaughtered Goat.

Xeres had arrived in the late afternoon and found Rand at his desk. He'd spent the morning playing the Sergius angle, trying to find any indication—in shadow gossip, in the *Los Angeles Times,* in Internet rumors—that the rogue vampire might still be in Los Angeles.

A call to a friend in New York had given him some insight into the vampire—brilliant, reclusive, ancient, and tormented—and had confirmed that there was no indication that he'd returned to Manhattan. The vampire's high-rise condo remained abandoned, and although Rand's source didn't know the location of Sergius's second, underground lair, New York's Division 12 had officially reported that the haven had been located in an abandoned subway tunnel and was also uninhabited.

Rand had taken that information and applied it to a

map of the victims' locations, looking for a pattern that suggested a subterranean refuge with access points near the various murders. He was cursing the lack of any such pattern when Xeres had come in with news that he'd located an Outcast male.

Now, in the car, Rand continued the conversation. "Give me the rundown on the other Outcasts in the area."

"Slow going," Xeres said, frowning. "Not too easy finding someone the system's told to get lost, you know?"

"You found this one."

"And two others so far," Xeres said.

Rand turned to face him. "And?"

"One moved to South America three months ago—that's confirmed, by the way. I called a buddy at Division in Brazil, and this Outcast actually landed on their radar."

"And the other?"

"San Diego," Xeres said. "Hell of a long way to travel just to fuck with Gunnolf, but I'm going to drive down tomorrow and check it out."

"Good," Rand said. "And this one?"

"My source says he's living in a trailer," Xeres said. "Couldn't give me any more specifics than that."

"So we check the RV parks." He pointed to a small sign advertising the chamber of commerce. "There. They'll have a list."

Xeres hung a hard right, and they wheeled in, the sharp ring of Xeres's phone punctuating his slide into a parking space.

"Yo." A pause, then, "Yeah, he's here. Hold on." He passed the phone to Rand. "Caris. You talk. I'll get our list."

Caris sounded both excited and irritated. "I tried your phone. Mia answered. Said you left it on your desk."

Rand cursed. "Tell her to give it to Joe and let him keep it behind the bar. What the fuck does she think she is, my secretary? That's why God invented voice mail."

"You tell her. I'm about to crash until sundown."

He glanced up at the blazing sun. "So why are you calling me?"

"Because I just got a damn good lead. A rumor that Sergius may be living wild in the Angeles National Forest."

"That doesn't sound like the Sergius I've heard about. He lived in a Manhattan high-rise, and before that in an apartment in Vienna. You really think he's roughing it?"

"I think he's rogue," Caris said, her voice tight. "And I think that changes everything."

"Fair enough. I'll go with you."

"Where are you?"

"According to Xeres, it's the devil's asshole. The locals call it Victorville."

"Tracking down an Outcast?"

"Any other reason I'd be out here?"

"You'll never be back by sundown. I'll take it."

"Dammit, Caris—"

"I'm on this team because of my vampire connections, right? Let me do my goddamned job. Besides, if you go, we'll have to wait until tomorrow. Tonight's a full moon."

"Shit." She was right. Moonrise was several hours after sundown, but he couldn't risk being so far away from his house when the change came on him. "Fine. Go," he said. "But don't do anything stupid."

"Wouldn't dream of it. You'll hear from me tomorrow night. I'll call right after I wake up," she said, and then the line went dead.

"Our pretty little bloodsucker making any progress?" Xeres asked, climbing back into the truck.

"Maybe. She has a lead on Sergius. She's holed up until sunset."

Xeres's smile grew wide and he showed just enough teeth to seem feral. "Just a few hours. Damn, I can feel it already." He threw back his head and howled, drawing the attention of two women coming out of the chamber of commerce. He just flashed them that smile, the big, bad wolf looking for a tasty morsel.

The women hurried their pace.

Xeres laughed. "God, I love this. That's what would suck most, you know? About being Outcast, I mean. Those sons of bitches have to lock themselves in tonight, otherwise—" He made a slicing motion across his throat. "Fuck, I can't even remember when I had to be locked inside. Musta been nine, ten years old. Didn't know what I was missing. But those Outcasts. They know. Oh, yeah. They know. And damn, it must suck."

"It's part of the punishment," Rand said, thinking of his own wolven body in a windowless room tonight, the locks controlled by a voice recognition system that didn't accept an entry until one hour after moonset.

Tonight, most of the local weren would run wild

through the mountain forests, their bodies looking like wolves, only with preternatural strength and endurance. And as for their minds, the weren would retain some rationality and control. Enough that they could stave off the hunger and control the kill. Enough that the PEC required that only noncognizant therians be restrained during a full moon. The weren who could run wild and attack humans. The newly changed. Or those, like Rand, who were already such rote killers that there was no control to be found. He couldn't find humanity during a full moon any more than he could bring about the change at will. For other weren—especially those a dozen years past the change—both were no-brainers.

For Rand, both were constant sore points. Reminders that his nature never truly changed. He always was what he always was.

As a human, he'd learned to rein it in. He'd channeled the kill, controlling it by killing tactically. Emotionlessly.

Not the wolf. The beast killed indiscriminately. Wildly.

He couldn't control the wolf because he *was* the wolf, and always had been. A wild and violent man who'd hidden behind the control of a soldier. Drop the soldier, though, and all that remained was blood.

One by one, they checked the RV parks on the chamber of commerce list, but they didn't find their man, an Outcast who'd once been called Freyling.

"We're running out of time," Rand said, looking at the sky. The moon wouldn't rise until two hours after sunset, and that was still several hours away. But the drive back was long, and Rand had no desire to tell Xeres the truth and have him lock Rand up somewhere for the night. "Where else does someone keep an RV?"

"Someplace secluded," Xeres said.

"Parking lot. Construction site. Vacant lot." Rand was running out of ideas.

"Construction site," Xeres said. "But abandoned."

With the economy in the toilet, their Outcast had his choice of abandoned sites to choose from, and after driving through three they were about to pack it in and head for home. There was one more on the road back to the highway, though, and with that one, they hit pay dirt. They found Freyling's RV shaded by the roof of the partially constructed parking garage for what was advertised as a new business complex. The paint on the sign was peeling, and the site itself had been thoroughly looted. Rand didn't expect any new business anytime soon.

They got out, both treading carefully. The werewolf once known as Freyling had been shunned by Gunnolf more than two decades prior, after Freyling had been discovered infecting teenage boys, then keeping them in cages in the basement of his London home.

During the change, he would put the boys together in a ring, then invite other shadow creatures to watch the bloodletting and bet on which boy would be the victor. The Outcast was so well versed at controlling his change that he was able to oversee his gladiatorial escapades even though the moon shone high and full.

Once discovered, Gunnolf had come down hard and fast on Freyling, exiling him from Europe and prohibiting all other therians from speaking to him, interacting with him, or giving him aid or comfort, on penalty of becoming Outcast themselves. The parameters of shunning did not extend to other shadow creatures, but by tradition, the vampires and daemons and the rest would honor Freyling's Outcast status.

As far as Rand could tell by looking around the perimeter of the RV, that tradition remained. The place was filthy. The stench of rotting food permeated the air, along with the acrid smell of decomposing excrement. Rand expected someone just as vile as the surroundings, and wasn't disappointed. The weren male who appeared at the door with a shotgun in his hand and a bandanna tied around his head was angry, unstable, and a first-class son of a bitch, but in the end, Rand couldn't point to anything that suggested he was involved with the murders in Los Angeles.

After they'd persuaded him not to blow their heads off, Freyling had begrudgingly invited them into the cramped RV, which smelled of sardines and beer. He'd hunkered down in a battered armchair, the shotgun tight between his knees, then told them bluntly that they were "damn fools to come out here, and serve you both right if that damn Scottish prick of a wolf-beast shuns the both of you."

They'd tried to steer the talk, but it was no use. He bounced from topic to topic, his mind so frazzled that he could barely hold on to a conversation. When he wasn't speaking, he clutched the shotgun tight and growled low in his throat. Unless he was putting on one hell of a show, he didn't have the clarity of mind or the energy to travel to Los Angeles and murder the girls, much less cover his tracks so well. And while he could theoretically be controlling a group of underlings, Rand couldn't imagine him masterminding lunch, much less such a nefarious plot.

They returned to L.A. as the sun was setting, and once Xeres dropped Rand at the small house he'd rented in Silver Lake, Rand headed inside and double-checked the clock against the lunar chart he'd tacked to the wall. Not that he needed to look at a chart. He could feel the wolf rising in him, the hunger taking over, the thrumming in his blood that signaled only one thing—the desire to hunt. To kill.

Methodically, he went through his routine, going first to the kitchen. He took out a pound of steak and tossed it into a frying pan, heating it only to warm. He ate the meat out of the skillet, the blade of the knife grating against the iron of the pan as he cut bites, forcing himself to go through the motions of civility even though every fiber within him wanted to grab the meat with both hands and sink his teeth into it.

He had to eat. Had to stuff himself with nearly raw meat, still oozing blood, because if he didn't, it would be worse when he was locked inside. He'd come out of it tomorrow with fingernails ripped off from clawing at the door, and his throat raw from howling.

Better to be sated.

The steak gone, he tossed in a pound of ground beef, stirred it around only enough for the odor of cooking meat to fill the kitchen, then dug in, shoveling chunks of hamburger with a large steel spoon. He chugged a gallon of milk, then another. His stomach was tight, his body stuffed, but he knew the wolf would burn through it in mere minutes, and he'd wake from the stupor of the change ravenous.

Ten minutes gone.

He glanced toward the back of the house. He still had time before he had to lock himself in and admit, as he did every month, that he truly was more beast than man. Xeres, he knew, would roam free tonight, running wild in the hills around Malibu, or possibly in the parkland beneath the Hollywood sign. He would satisfy the urge to kill by stalking and killing game, but he would keep enough of himself to prevent him from harming a human. Xeres would remember this night.

Rand would not.

He paced the spartan room, around the couch. From the window to the coffee table. Near the small metal desk and fold-up chair. The minutes moved slowly now that there was nowhere to go and nothing to do except wait and let the wolf build until he had no choice but to go to the back and close the steel door, locking himself in like the goddamned animal he was.

Without thinking, he lashed out, putting his fist through the drywall. That didn't do the trick, though, so he kicked over the coffee table. That made him feel a little better, but only because the shoebox that tumbled to the ground off the lower shelf distracted him.

The contents spilled out. His dog tags. The key from his very first car, now suspended in a Lucite block. A snapshot of his mother, another of his aunt.

And a small portrait of Alicia taken the day before their wedding. He remembered the sitting. She'd been happy, but nervous, hating having her picture taken. But the photographer had told her to look just over the lens and imagine the thing she loved most in the world. She'd asked Rand to stand there, so that she was looking at him, and he'd done it, standing there under the weight of her gaze, heavy with the promises they'd make the following day to love and honor and cherish.

And protect.

With sudden fury, he tossed the portrait across the room. He hadn't honored those vows, not one, but the void had never eaten away at him before. It was simply something there—something accepted. So what the fuck was wrong with him tonight?

He clenched his jaw and sucked in air.

Then he opened his eyes and saw Alicia looking at him from across the room, her eyes reproachful behind a spiderweb of shattered glass.

♦

Tiberius's Los Angeles residence sat on six acres that overlooked the West Side, with access from Mulholland Drive for those who weren't able to get there by flight or mist or in the form of one of the animals that roamed the wild hills nestled in the heart of the city.

Nick and Luke had arrived as mist, rolling low over the moonlit foothills, then twining up the stilts that supported the hillside mansion. They manifested on the balcony, the city lights spread out beneath them like a map of stars, and found that Tiberius was already outside, waiting for them.

"Tell me about the latest human."

"Discovered too late for Doyle to get anything out

of her head," Nick said. "He's hitting the pavement, though. Doing plain, old-fashioned detective work. She was in a backyard in Brentwood. Only discovered because a maid was out trying to catch a terrier that got off his leash. He found his way through the gate, and there she was, completely drained of blood, that same god-damned ash on the ground beside her."

"This is Gunnolf's work," Tiberius said, his voice as dark as his expression.

Nick glanced sideways at Luke, who stepped forward. Nick counted the governor among his friends, but his history with Tiberius was nothing compared to Luke's.

"Sir," Luke said, then stopped himself. "Tiber," he began again, his voice less formal. "Gunnolf swore to you he'd abandoned that idiotic scheme. He gave Paris as collateral should he not keep his word. You know he wouldn't risk losing Paris. He's a werewolf, but he's not an idiot."

"He *is* weren," Tiberius said, "and they are not to be trusted. If you believe he's too cowardly to risk his own position to gain mine, then we must assume it is another weren who would do me harm, most likely in an attempt to seek personal favor from Gunnolf."

"Possible," Luke said, and Nick knew he was mollifying Tiberius both because what he said was true and because there was no arguing with Tiberius about the weren when his ire was up.

The therian/vampire animosity had existed since the very dawn of the shadow world, and had been only slightly toned down following the Great Schism. But a feud mentality wasn't the only thing driving Tiberius's loathing. His hatred of the weren ran deep and personal. Nick didn't know why, and he wasn't going to ask, but to Tiberius's mind, Gunnolf would remain guilty until proven innocent, and that was just the way it was.

Not a legal theory to which Nick subscribed, but it had the side benefit of temporarily keeping Serge off Tiber's radar. And at the moment, to Nick's mind, Serge was as likely a culprit as Gunnolf.

Tiberius turned, giving both Luke and Nick his back. On many things, the master vampire would speak his mind to them and invite their input. About this, though, he was lost in his own political twists and turns, and he neither wanted nor sought the advice of his friends.

"I am running out of time," Tiberius said, as if speaking to the city spread out below. "The Alliance is being convened in three days. They will argue and debate, and in the end, they will oust me from my position, citing an inability to maintain control in my territory. Dirque and Trylag will be particularly vocal in their arguments against me," he added, referring to the jinn and para-daemon liaisons. "I imagine they are even now planning the celebration of my removal."

He turned, then looked at each of them. "Bring me a killer and perhaps I can keep my position. Fail, and I am no longer an Alliance member. And you, my friends, will no longer be *kyne*."

◆

Doyle's face hurt from smiling. So far, they'd talked to a half dozen friends of Melissa Jo Keeling's, and he was pretty sure that he was going to rip the face off the next human who offered him coffee with one breath then sobbed in the next.

Humans . . .

Damn, but there was a reason he didn't live in that world.

The last visit—the boyfriend—had been the worst. Pain so thick you could cut it, and the guy was all the more ripped up because the two had fought only hours before she'd been killed. If he'd been a human detective, Doyle might have put the kid on his suspect list. As it was, Doyle chalked him up to a two-timing prick who now had something to feel guilty about.

And the worst of it was they hadn't come up with a goddamned thing. Not one link between Melissa Jo and the seven previous victims. It was a goddamned fucking nightmare, made all the worse because he had to wade in among humans and didn't even get a solid lead for his troubles.

"Give it a rest, Doyle," Tucker said as they stepped off the elevator and into the apartment building's lobby. "You survived."

"That obvious?"

"You're not exactly a paragon of subtlety. Don't worry," he added, tapping his temple. "They'll remember you only as gruff and curmudgeonly, which is a far cry from asshole."

Doyle exhaled. "You're human. I put up with you."

"How can you not? I'm so damn charming."

As Doyle barked out a laugh, Tucker stopped at the reception desk to give the manager his card—the one that identified Homeland Security, not the PEC. A long shot, but maybe someone on staff would remember something. Someone following Melissa Jo. A delivery boy giving her the eye. At this point, anything would help.

"That poor guy," Tucker said as he returned.

"Yeah," Doyle said. Considering how tough the human had it, he felt a little bad about wanting to rip his face off. But damn, he was tired. And frustrated. "If we don't catch a break soon, we should send the succubus back in."

"You really want her ripping out his soul?" Tucker asked.

"Fuck, I don't know. You want more humans to die?"

Tucker swallowed. "Bad mojo all the way around."

Doyle didn't disagree, but the problem was soon forgotten when he got a look at his car. More specifically, at its new hood ornament.

"Well, if it isn't Jekyll and Hyde," Petra said. She smiled brightly at Doyle. "You really think you can pass for a human cop? Or is your partner tagging along to make sure no one asks hard questions?" She tapped her forehead as she cocked her head toward Tucker.

Tucker was squinting at Doyle. "You don't think he looks human? He's half, right? Aren't you half?"

Doyle ignored his partner. "You wanna get your ass off my car?"

The truth was, he liked the girl. She was odd, but she worked hard and she was sharp. On the few occasions he'd needed help from outside Division for one of his investigations, he'd called her.

But that didn't mean he wanted her scratching his paint.

Petra slid off, her silent mountain of a brother moving to stand between the girl and Doyle.

"Hey. You wanna give me a little space here?" He moved to the driver's side, pulled open the door, and got in.

"Oh, come on," she said. "You're not leaving so soon? We're obviously working the same gig. You get anything from the boyfriend? You share with me, I'll share with you."

"What have you got to share?"

"Why should I tell you if you're not going to reciprocate?"

"Did I say that?" Doyle asked. "Did I tell her I was going to leave her pretty feet dangling?"

"No, sir, you did not," Tucker said.

"I take it back," Petra said. "You're not Jekyll and Hyde. You're Abbott and Costello. Now come on, this thing's getting time sensitive and you boys know it."

She was right. Luke had called less than an hour ago with the latest. If they didn't come up with an answer soon, Tiberius would be out on his ass. And while as a general rule the problems of high-powered vampires didn't keep Doyle awake at night, the fact remained that Tiberius was the current Los Angeles governor, which meant that he also was the ultimate authority over Division 6.

If Tiberius was out, no one's job at Division was secure.

"So give us a sneak peek of what you've got," Doyle said. "Maybe we can work something out."

"Show me a little good faith, boys." She gave the

frame of his car a solid pat. "You want to make a deal, you call me with some decent intel and we'll play the reciprocation game. Until then . . ." She trailed off with a shrug and a glance toward her behemoth of a brother. "You know where to find me."

CHAPTER 24

Caris pressed against the rough bark of a pine tree, watching as the tall, dark figure slipped among the trees and rocks of the Angeles National Forest. The area was untamed, wicked, with rampant fires, wild animals, and beasts that humans feared.

Like the Outcast she followed.

She'd told Rand she had a lead on Sergius, but that was a bald-faced lie. She wasn't interested in rogue vampires but in Outcast male weren. And not because of the human murders.

No, she was here on her own agenda.

Of all the ancient weren that she'd tracked down over the years, he'd been the hardest to find, but it had been worth the search. Anticipation swelled in her. This one had to be the one. Had to be the weren son of a bitch who'd so cavalierly destroyed the life she'd built—who'd ripped her out of the arms of the man she'd loved—simply for his own whim.

She would find him—the one who did that to her.

And then she would kill him.

The weren turned and picked his way up a hill, an old man with a hard face and salt-and-pepper hair. She followed at a discreet distance, his scent leading her, her tread silent despite the layer of dead leaves and loose gravel. The excitement of the hunt—of the night—was building within her. She had no idea where they were going, but she was well fed and strong, and could certainly outlast him.

She'd get what she came for, even if it took all night. Even if the goddamned moon rose before she finished.

She tilted her head, catching the scent of sweat and refuse, of wood and food. *His lair was near.* She peered into the dark, saw the little cabin, so well camouflaged she almost missed it.

She pricked up her ears, wary of the slightest sound that would suggest they weren't alone.

Nothing.

He stood at the door, opened it.

It was time.

Moving so fast she was nothing more than a blur, she tackled him, knocking him inside. Their bodies tumbled onto the rough-hewn floor. He might be old, but she'd been wrong about feeble. His muscles tightened, and he fought back hard, the rising moon undoubtedly giving him strength. But she had the advantage—dual advantages, actually—and she pinned him down, her fangs bared, getting her face right in close to his.

"Are you the one, old man?" she demanded. "Are you the one who did this to me?"

"Get off me, you little bitch."

She lashed out, punching him hard in the cheek, snapping his head to the side and exposing his neck.

"Going to rip my throat out? Going to kill me? That's just like a vampire, nasty creatures the lot of you. Deserve whatever you get."

"Right back at you, buddy. And no. That's not exactly what I had in mind."

She pulled a syringe from her back pocket, jabbed the needle into the bulging vein in his neck, and then slowly lifted the plunger. Crimson blood flowed in, and when the vial was full, she yanked the needle out and stood up, keeping one foot pressed to his chest.

She tucked the vial into her pocket. She'd sleep through the day tomorrow—no avoiding that after a full moon, unfortunately. But as soon as the sun set, she'd deliver it to Orion. With any luck, within twenty-four hours, she'd finally have an answer.

"You're going to want to put pressure on that. Sorry that I'm all out of smiley-face bandages."

The moon was approaching the horizon. She could see it in his eyes and feel it in her blood. Time to leave, but she wasn't having him chase her.

She used her belt to restrain his hands as she looked for something more secure. She didn't find a thing, though. Frustrated, she had no choice but to accept that the leather would have to do—coupled with a nice hard blow to the head that should keep him out even through the change. That, she rendered with great gusto.

He groaned, then his eyes rolled back in his head. The son of a bitch. She looked at him in disgust, looked at the whole cabin in disgust.

And that was when she saw it, so small she almost missed it. A tiny photograph in a tarnished silver frame tucked up among wood carvings of bears and wolves and snakes. She crossed the room in two steps and grabbed it up, her chest tightening as she looked into the familiar eyes.

Oh, fuck. Oh, *shit*.

Rand.
She needed to tell Rand.

◆

"Goddamn you! You motherfuckers, you let me out of here!"

The sharp clatter of metal against metal underscored the female's words, the sound digging into Serge's head like nails dipped in acid. He wanted to ask what the hell she was doing alive—why he hadn't fucking drained her when the daemon had come out—because he could remember the daemon bursting free, the power surging through his limbs, the need for the kill.

For the blood.

And then . . . *nothing.*

No, he amended. Not nothing. There'd been pain.

Pain so intense his body felt white-hot. A pain that shot through his veins, threatening to burn him up from the inside.

He'd been on the subway platform, waiting for the killer. The beast who'd moved in the night, taking the sheep from his flock.

There'd been a girl. Ripe and delicious and smelling of temptation, and he'd felt the daemon rising. Rising fast and hard and—

Those motherfuckers, he thought, echoing the girl. Because damned if she wasn't right. Damned if those goddamned motherfucking bastards hadn't done something to him. Some serious shit, and—

"You get over here! You get the fuck over here and let

me out! This wasn't the deal. This wasn't the arrangement!"

"Shut up," he snarled, for the first time opening his eyes.

He could barely see through the thick gunk that coated his eyes, casting the room in a haze, as if someone had smeared Vaseline over the world. He could smell, though, and the scent that came to him was fear. Her fear, so pungent it filled the room. So thick, he wondered that she could still stand despite it. For a moment, he even admired her, fighting through the fear, through the pain.

He turned his head and saw her in a cage like his, metal cuffs on her arms, each with a loop of metal, as if at any minute someone would come and attach a long link of chain. She wasn't a human anymore. To whoever put her in that cage, she wasn't even an animal.

She was simply property, to do with what he wanted.

Considering the intensity of her fear, he guessed that what he wanted was to kill.

He gave the hematite bands that circled his arms and ankles a hard tug. *Let them try that on him. Just let the bastards try . . .*

He cursed. The threat would be a lot more serious if he wasn't bound in that damned metal.

"Oh, God. You're awake, you're awake. Please. Please, help me."

Her words, high and shrill, cut through the mist in his head.

He remembered.

They'd come from behind, the scent of their humanity reaching him before they had. He'd spun to fight, but he hadn't anticipated their weapon. A net. A fucking electrified hematite net. It had touched him and burned through him, and the daemon that was Sergius had burst free, but there'd been no way out—no way to get to them through the threads of power that bound and pierced him, the electricity that had his muscles failing and his mind going blank.

They'd caught him. They'd caught the girl. And now they held him as a fucking prisoner in a place where the stench of death seared the air.

He gave a violent yank against his bindings. Ironic that only a few months ago he'd wanted the blackness of death. Now the thought of death sickened him. He couldn't die. *Wouldn't.* At least not before he'd bled the life from every last human who'd attacked him. Every human who'd trussed him up and brought him here.

"Hey!" the girl screamed again. "Get us out of here! Please! Please, help me!"

"I would have killed you."

She made a low sound, like the groan of a dying animal. "Are you going to kill me now?"

He felt his lips curve in response and he lifted one shackled arm. "No."

"Then do something. Please. They're coming."

He looked at her thoughtfully. "The *arrangement,*" he said, repeating her earlier words. "What arrangement? And with whom?"

She shook her head, eyes scared. "I don't—I don't know what you mean."

"Who are these people? What type of deal did you have with them, and why the fuck am I here?"

"I don't know. I swear I don't know."

He could still smell the fear on her. Fear, but also the stink of the truth. He believed her. "What did they tell you?"

"They paid me. Told me to go down. To stand there. They said that was it. That I was bait, and they were trying to catch someone. They said it would be safe. They said they'd take care of me." A sob rattled her words. "They said they'd let me go."

"They lied."

"Oh, God. No. Please, please, no."

"You set me up."

"I didn't. I didn't know. I—"

He turned away, tuning out her whimpering.

His vision was clearing, and he looked out at the room, empty except for him and the girl in the cages. There were two doors at his two o'clock and ten o'clock. Both metal. Both undoubtedly locked.

A console stood in the middle of the room. He couldn't see the monitor, but he could hear the hum of the computer and occasionally saw a flash of colored light as something on the panel lit up with some unknown meaning.

Whatever purpose he'd been taken for, it didn't lie in this room. This was a holding area. A waiting room.

But what the hell was he waiting for?

The sharp scrape of metal against metal sang out across the room as the bar bolting one of the doors shifted, apparently operated by someone on the far side.

Serge tensed, wary, as the door swung open and a single man stepped in, the door clicking shut behind him. He was tall—well over six feet—and dressed in gray fatigues. Except for a shock of gray at each temple, his hair was completely black. He held a small device in his hand as he walked toward the girl, never once even looking at Sergius.

"Good afternoon, my dear."

"Please," she whimpered, her voice like a little girl's. "Please let me go."

"You're a very lucky girl," the man said. "If things go as well as we anticipate, you'll soon be an exceptional girl."

"No, I—" She screamed, her words drowned out in terror and pain as her body shook from the voltage shooting through her chains.

"She's not dead," the man said to Serge, as casually as if they were making dinner conversation. He slipped the device—some sort of remote control—into his pocket. "An exceptionally low dose, actually. Just enough to knock her out for a few moments."

"Who the fuck are you?"

"My name is Grayson Meer."

"I'm going to rip your heart out, Grayson Meer."

"I'm sure you'll try," Meer said, his voice and tone making clear that he knew the threat was idle. At the moment, damn him, he was right. Serge could do nothing. He was as helpless as the girl now passed out on the floor of her cage.

"What am I doing here?" Serge asked. He wasn't the girl; he wasn't going to scream or beg. He was simply going to gather information. And then he was going to wait for the chance to kill.

"My team brought you in."

"Why?"

But Meer didn't answer. Instead he turned and walked back toward the door.

"Goddamn it," Serge said, his voice harsh, rising more than he wanted it to, giving away more than he wanted revealed. "Why?"

The door slammed open and a second man entered, this one round and soft, with white hair and intelligent eyes. He wore a lab coat along with his frustrated expression. "The latest one's been found. A girl. Killed in Brentwood."

"Brentwood," Meer said. "Wasn't our—"

"Yes," the one in the lab coat said. "He used to panhandle near the Whole Foods on San Vicente."

"After everything, he was heading home," Meer said thoughtfully. "Interesting."

"It's dangerous to continue to release them," the lab coat said, as Serge wondered who the hell "they" were. "We have the facilities to terminate the failures on site. Release is reckless and—"

"Necessary," Meer said. "We're not having this conversation again. Their release was Santiago's price for participation."

"We don't need the weren anymore. His blood doesn't have the properties I'd anticipated, and you know damn well he's not really interested in what we're trying to accomplish."

Meer laughed, low and harsh. "This is why you're the doctor and I'm the tactical leader. You know as well as I do that double-crossing his kind would be the last mistake we'd make."

The doctor said nothing, but didn't look happy.

"Tell me about the blood. I thought you told me that weren blood would stabilize the transition."

"I expected it would," the doctor said. "But as you know, I haven't been able to achieve the results we need."

"This is unacceptable, Kessler."

"If you can find another scientist capable of working with both human and shadow genetics, feel free to offer him my job. Until then, you're going to have to trust me when I say that we are playing on a new field, and that every failure brings us closer to success."

"How much closer?"

"I have a potential solution."

"Anything you need," Meer said.

Kessler shook his head, a small smile tugging at his mouth. "Not anything. Any*one*. A unique subject who recently came to my attention. I've already sent a retrieval team."

Meer's brows lifted. "I'm intrigued."

"I thought you would be. Come with me, and I'll explain my hypothesis." He nodded toward the girl on the floor of her cage. "And have someone take her to the lab. I've made some tweaks to the current formula. If my theory is correct, she'll be an improvement over the last test subject, but not quite where we want to be."

Meer followed Kessler, but paused in front of the door. He turned back and cocked his head toward Serge. "What about that one?"

"Have Bukowski hook him up. We should start the extraction. I want to get started on a new serum as soon as the team returns."

Serge growled low in his throat. "Lay one hand on me and I'll fucking rip your throat out."

The two men exchanged amused glances. "No," Meer said, pulling a small remote from his pocket. "You won't."

He pressed a button, and electricity filled the cage. Serge screamed, his body wracked with pain, the daemon within howling, trying to burst free, but this wasn't something he could fight, and in the end, he fell, his body still twitching from the electricity that hummed through his veins.

CHAPTER 25

The beep of Rand's computer pulled him back to himself moments later, and a damn good thing it had. The clock was ticking down, and moonrise was coming.

He groped for the computer, shifted it on the coffee table so that he could see the screen and the instant message from Petra demanding to know if he was there.

<<Here.>>
<<Been trying to call. Need to meet.>>

He glanced over his shoulder at the lunar chart.

<<Not a good night.>>
<<An hour left until moonrise. I'll come to you.>>

Shit. He should have known she would have pulled his address. Damn private investigators. He hated being on the grid.

<<At the park, two blocks over. Be there in five minutes, or I'm gone.>>

She confirmed the address and said she'd be there, and Rand cursed himself for not telling her to wait until morning. He glanced once again at the clock. There was time. He was okay. And he had to admit he was curious.

The city never seemed to manage to replace the broken bulbs in the streetlamps, so he walked the two blocks to the park in the dark, with only the occasional passing car lighting a path. This was a family neighborhood, after all, and most folks were inside, snug in their beds.

Not everyone was inside, though.

There were eyes in the dark. The soldier in him sensed it the moment he entered the park, even before the wolf. He lifted his chin, nostrils flaring, trying to pick up the scent, but it was no use. The air was wrong, something hinky blanketing the freshly cut grass. Pesticides or some such shit. But he was certain nonetheless. He'd trusted his gut before he'd had his weren senses, and that gut had kept him alive. Something was out there. Watching. Waiting.

Not Petra; she wouldn't remain concealed. Not when they were meeting so close to moonrise. She might be human, but she understood the danger. She'd show herself. He was certain of it.

Someone else, then. But who?

He had no enemies in Los Angeles, but Gunnolf did. And it didn't take much in the way of brains for whoever was behind the human murders to assume that Gunnolf had sent Rand to investigate. Which meant the perp couldn't be happy to learn that Rand was poking around.

Rand had known from the moment he stepped off the plane at LAX that he had an invisible target painted on his back. This was the first time he'd felt anyone taking aim at it.

Fuck.

He growled low in his throat as he advanced toward his destination, surveying the perimeter as he did, his muscles primed, his eyes taking in every detail. The possibility of aborting didn't occur to him. Instead, he wanted to hunt down the thing that hid in the shadows.

He could feel the shifting deep inside himself. Muscles stretching, bones elongating. He was on edge, wanting to run, wanting to kill.

Without thinking, he snarled, his upper lip lifting to reveal his canines. *Not damn likely.*

He wanted it. Fuck, yeah, he wanted to get down and dirty with the cowardly son of a bitch hiding in the shadows.

No.

He pulled it back, forcing himself to let go of the blood lust, to push it back behind reason.

No.

Fight, and he might lose track of time.

He needed to pay attention to the moon.

Watch, but don't draw them out. Meet Petra. Do what needs to be done. Then go lock yourself inside.

He took a dozen more steps, moving silently toward the empty swing set, and saw nothing to give him pause. The tension in his body began to ease along with the sensation of being watched. Perhaps they'd gone. Perhaps he'd been wrong.

But that smell . . . that smell still bothered him. His nose twitched, and he snarled, frustrated.

Unnecessarily, he glanced at his watch. He knew

what time it was; he could feel the movement of the earth in his bones and the position of the moon in his blood.

Where the hell was Petra? They were right on five minutes, and he needed to be gone soon, and if he didn't get safe inside before—

A whirlwind of leaves and grass and park debris cut off his thoughts, the funnel dissolving to reveal the petite private investigator towered over by her lanky brother.

He took a step back, not wanting any of that magic shit to brush up against him.

"Sorry! Sorry!" She bounced toward him, her body seeming too small for the energy it contained. "I tried to come under my own power, but I just ain't got the mojo that Kiril does." She shook her head, as if trying to settle something that was rattling around up there. Kiril, however, stood perfectly still, his arms crossed over his chest, his eyes narrowed in Rand's direction.

"What have you got? I'm in a little bit of a hurry . . ." He trailed off, looking pointedly at the sky.

"Werewolves are always so touchy before the moon comes up."

He snarled.

She rolled her eyes. "Oh, get over yourself. You know you like me. And I think you even like working with me because I get you. What with me being human and all."

She was right, of course, but Rand wasn't about to admit it any more than he would admit that she amused him, and lately that wasn't easy to do. "So why am I here?"

"Walk with me," she said, the bouncy energy shifting

to something more focused, more professional. She eased them away from the swing set, Kiril following silently, never more than five steps from her.

"I've got a lot of nothing, and then two things I think you'll want to hear."

"What?"

"Eight bodies, right?"

"Eight?"

"They found one more just a few hours ago. You hadn't heard?"

Rand ground out a curse, frustrated that he was working on the outside. "Go on."

"The official word is that there's no physical evidence. They got Ryan Doyle at every crime scene—"

"The percipient daemon?"

"Right, but he's come up with shit. And they've tested the wounds for DNA—that's confidential by the way, but you hired the right girl, so I've got the scoop for you."

"And the scoop is?"

"Not a damn thing."

"So glad I hired the right girl," he said dryly.

She grinned, then dropped to the grass near the foot of a slide shaped like Barney and patted the space beside her. He remained standing. After a moment, she shrugged. "It's not that there's no DNA, it's that there's corrupt DNA."

"Corrupt," he repeated. "Chemically?"

"Not the way you mean. Nobody poured bleach over it or soaked the evidence in acid."

"Then what?"

"My source in Orion's office says they're seeing weird

genetic shit. Like nothing they've seen before. That's why they don't think a vamp really is the perp, despite the ripped-out throats."

"And what else does Barnaby say?" he asked, referring to Division's assistant medical tech.

"I didn't name names," she said, bristling.

He shrugged it off. "Educated guess."

"Yeah? Well, I'm cultivating a second source, too. So don't think you know all my secrets."

"Petra . . ."

"Fine. Whatever." She shot him an irritated glance. "My *source*," she said deliberately, "says that all therian DNA is genetically wonky. It has to be to let you guys, you know, change like that."

"Vampires change," Rand said. "They can transform into animals, into mist. Seems like they'd be wonky, too."

"Got me there," Petra said. "Too bad you hired a PI and not a biologist. Point is, the DNA's wonky in a way that's not vampire. At least, they're pretty sure it's not a vampire, although it might be a rogue. The chemistry's a mess, apparently, but the bottom line is that wonky DNA means they can't be certain of anything."

"No matches with anyone in the system?" he asked.

"Nope. My source says it's a big mystery. And that it's going to be hard to make a match. When the DNA is corrupt like this is, the markers don't show up the way they do with regular DNA. Or something like that."

"You said you had something that's going to help me out."

"Oh, this is good." She shifted to her knees, then stumbled as she started to rise. He reached down, offering a hand to help her up, but she scooted backward as fast as if his hand had been pure flame, her head shaking as Kiril pushed his way toward Rand, his expression menacing.

Rand matched him step for step.

"Stop, stop, stop," she said, waving Kiril off. The male stepped away, his muscles relaxing. "Sorry about that," she said to Rand. "It's just—you don't want to touch me."

His eyes narrowed. "Only trying to help."

She tilted her head, apparently fascinated with her shoes. "Don't touch me," she said. "It's better that way."

"Why?"

She climbed to her feet. "Do you want to hear the lead I do have? Well, the sort-of lead?"

He nodded. She could keep her secrets. Right now, he was out of time. "Tell me."

She held out her hand, then nodded to Kiril, who waved his hand over her palm. A tiny whirlwind appeared, then danced over the surface of her skin. When it dissipated, all that remained was a small metal box.

"Cup your hands," she said. He hesitated, and when he finally complied she dropped the box into his grasp. "Open it."

He did, and found himself staring at a small box full of ash. Wary, he leaned in, sniffed it, and caught the scent of nothing familiar but the tin of the box. "What is this shit?"

She rolled her eyes. "That, my friend, is the best lead Division has, and they are keeping it under serious wraps."

"How is it a clue?"

"It's been beside every one of the bodies."

He sniffed again. "It's organic." He shook his head, unable to identify it more specifically.

"Looks that way. It has some of the properties of vampire ash. You know, after they're staked. But not entirely. Honestly, Division's stumped, so my friend feels no guilt whatsoever leaking this to me. I mean, maybe you'll figure it out, and that's good for everybody."

"I need to go." He closed his hand around the box.

She glanced up toward the sky. "One more thing," she said, falling in step as he walked back toward his house. "I've heard rumors that the PEC thinks you might know what's going on with the dead humans."

"Blind leading the fucking blind."

"Just figured you ought to know. I'm hearing buzz that they're putting a CI on you."

Shit. He didn't give a flip if the PEC wasted its time, but he didn't want a goddamned confidential informant shadowing him. "Can you find out for sure?"

"I can ask around."

He opened his palm to reveal the little box. "Can't you do more than ask?"

She rolled her eyes. "Come on, Rand. I'm not Samantha on *Bewitched,* and I don't have a crystal ball. Hell, I don't even carry a tarot deck with me. From your perspective, I'm human, okay? I'm clever, and I'm good, but I'm human."

"And him?" Rand nodded toward her brother.

Petra lifted a shoulder. "He's better than me with the magic. Lots better. But we're not talking Harry Potter here. If magic were all that, we'd be the ones running the Alliance, now, wouldn't we?"

He stopped walking. "Why are you here, Petra?"

Her forehead creased and she glanced down toward her shoes. "To see you." She looked up, smiled brightly, and tapped her watch. "Better get moving."

He stayed put. "I mean, why are you in the shadow world?"

She licked her lips. "What can I say? You folks pay well. Most of you have been around for a couple of centuries. Built up some nice solid bank accounts. And my hourly rate doesn't even faze you. I'm overcharging the shit out of you, you know."

He didn't buy it in the least, but he reminded himself that her secrets weren't his problem. "We'll talk again tomorrow."

"You keep paying, and we can talk whenever you want." She signaled to Kiril. "We're out of here," she said, and as she spoke, Rand caught a new scent—sweat and adrenaline, the mixture pungent enough to rise over the chemical scent that blanketed the park.

"Petra!" he called, lunging to push her out of the way of the three men in black who barreled forward, their faces covered in knit hoods. She yelped, shifting to avoid his touch, and stumbling backward in the process. She grappled for balance, clinging to the only thing nearby that offered support—the bare wrist of one of the attacking men, a hulking creature with wide shoulders and thick thighs.

The hulk bellowed, long and loud, like a wild animal caught in a trap. Even more, like an animal reduced to such a feral state that it would claw its own limb off in order to be free of that which contained it.

That thing, apparently, was Petra.

Both Rand and one of the attackers rushed toward her, but the third one ambushed him from behind and Rand whipped around, barely avoiding a Taser to the shoulder as his elbow slammed into his attacker's neck, slowing—but not stopping—the son of a bitch. He'd gained a moment, though, and it was enough to confirm that Petra was safe. Kiril had reached her at the same time as the second reached the hulk, and with a swift kick to the hulk's arm and a sharp yank on the back of Petra's shirt, Kiril had broken her hold and pulled her away from the creature.

Around them, a swirling windstorm kicked up, a tornado moving fast out of the park. The hulk tried to follow, but didn't move quickly enough. Petra and Kiril were gone, and with a loud snort of disappointment, the monster turned, shaking his head like a dog caught in a collar.

It took only an instant for Rand to confirm that the girl was safe, and then he was back on his attacker, teeth bared as he kicked out, taking the offensive as the son of a bitch was still pushing himself up off the ground where he'd fallen onto his hands and knees.

Rand's foot intersected his chin, snapping the bastard's head back and slamming his mouth shut. Instantly, Rand smelled blood. The guy must have bitten off a piece of his tongue.

He reached down, using one arm to pin the guy's arms behind him, then sliding his other arm around the human's neck. One shift—one simple change of position—

and the human's neck would snap. "Who are you?" he snarled, the wolf rising inside. "What the fuck do you want?"

The man stayed resolutely quiet, and Rand was about to apply a little more persuasion when a horrific scream rent the night. With his arm still tight, Rand looked back and saw that the hulk had his teammate over his shoulders, like an exhausted soldier might carry his rifle, his arms hooked over the firm, straight metal. Only the second man wasn't straight. The hulk had squeezed his body, pressuring the spine until it had snapped.

Now the hulk tossed the dead weight aside and lunged toward his new targets.

Rand rolled to the side, out of the hulk's path. The human wasn't so lucky. The creature—and Rand was certain that only moments ago it had been human—plucked up his companion like so much lint and slammed him back down on a stone. The human's eyes dulled, and he reached blindly for a thigh holster, his mouth moving in what was probably a silent prayer as he brought a Glock up in a shaky hand.

Rand watched. The man in him wanted to rush in. To battle the hulk off and save the human. Not for his own sake, but because Rand still wanted to interrogate him and find out why the fuck the bastard had ambushed him.

The wolf simply wanted to kill.

Neither moved, though. Instead they waited. Watching. Assessing.

The human fired, the report momentarily deafening Rand. He caught the unique scent of the bullet—silver—and felt curiosity rise more than rage: These humans had come tonight knowing he was a werewolf and carrying weapons that would kill him, yet they'd burst onto the scene with Tasers, forgoing a sniper's assault. Why?

The hulk lurched backward, then righted himself, and when he did, Rand could see a patch of bloody skin on his back from where the exit wound had blown away tissue, bone, and the black fabric of his T-shirt.

With incredible speed, the hulk kicked the gun out of the human's hand, then reached up and ripped off his own hood. He sucked in air, his now-revealed face contorted with pure malice, eyes burning red. He clenched his fists, threw his head back, and howled, any suggestion of reason or rationality gone.

Rand had never seen a change like that. Not even in the vampiric *kyne*, who held onto control by a mere hairbreadth.

The hulk wasn't sentient any longer; he was pure rage. Pure power.

A pure daemon. Or worse.

The monster growled, and even in his haze, the injured human cowered back, still speaking, still praying, still looking to be saved. "Need . . . reinforcements. Base . . . do you copy? Fucked up. Boyd . . . all fucked up."

He said no more. Not after the hulk punched the human hard in the chest—so hard his fist went right through the sorry bastard's rib cage. The hand came out—and now it was clutching a still-beating heart.

The human in Rand wanted to look away, to say that no one deserved a death like that.

The wolf didn't think, but the coppery scent of blood flooded his senses, making him crave the hunt. Filling him with an alpha's need to prove himself. To take the spilled blood and make it his own.

He'd been holding tight to rational thought, fighting the lure of the wolf so that he could get through his meeting and get home. He kept holding on, though rationality had been reduced to tatters. He clutched the strands, desperate not to lose himself. Determined to fight.

But the decision was no longer his to make. With one careless motion, the hulk tossed the heart aside. And then he lunged toward Rand.

Rand kicked out hard, catching the hulk in the chest. His thigh muscles, already lethal from years of military training, had only become stronger once Gunnolf had pulled him into his inner circle. Now, with the wolf rising with the moon, his strength was multiplying.

The hulk should have stumbled backward. At the very least, he should have stopped in his tracks.

He didn't.

Instead he clutched Rand around the leg, pulled him off balance, and aimed his clawed hand toward Rand's heart.

No way. No fucking way.

Rand grabbed the hulk's arm, then used the beast's weight and strength against him by yanking forward, pulling the hulk even closer to him. Risky business, but the risk paid off. The beast lost his balance. He didn't fall—he recovered in an instant—but an instant was all Rand needed.

He sprang up, operating on reaction now, not reason. The pale glow of moonlight had crested the horizon, and the orb itself wasn't far off.

He wasn't thinking anymore, his body's movements guided by instinct alone. Animal. Soldier. *Kill.*

He landed a punch. A kick. Then another and another. He was motion personified and pain in action. But the goddamned beast was giving it right back, claws now extending from where there used to be fingers. *No. Those were* his *claws. Rand's.*

The change was on him, the rising moon working its power, and as the hulk beat and battered him—as his own body bent and twisted and grew and changed—he let go with a low, guttural scream. Not in pain, but in anticipation. As a human—even one with the wolf rising—he was at a disadvantage against whatever this creature was.

As fully weren, though . . .

That significantly evened the odds.

Too bad he wouldn't remember a moment of it in the morning.

CHAPTER 26

Lissa stood at the window of her office, watching her staff go through the familiar closing routine. She couldn't remember the last time she slept, but she didn't care. The memories were flooding back even without sleep. If she let the dreams come, she feared it would be too horrible to bear.

She'd been his partner. She'd been Priam's god-damned partner.

Maybe not in every life, but in at least one. And right then, that one was the only life that mattered. She'd been working hand in hand with Priam when she'd screwed Nick in the most horrible, awful way possible. She didn't yet remember the details, but the feelings had come rushing back. Everything, a huge muddle of emotion, but at the heart of it, there'd been love and pain and betrayal.

And she hated herself for it.

Even knowing what she did—about how the girls in the cortegery were trapped, about how anything was fair where survival was concerned—she still hated herself for what she'd done to him. Whatever her reasons back then, she should have tossed them in the gutter. Hell, she'd managed to avoid destroying anyone in *this* life, hadn't she? And she'd freed other girls, too.

But you're still using. You're still looking in their

heads. You're still nothing more than a thief and a blackmailer.

She threaded her fingers into her hair and squeezed her scalp. What she did now she did to save the girls. That was a real difference, right? What she did now, she did for good.

She drew in a breath, because there was no way she was going to let herself second-guess that choice, not for one minute more. She was Lissa now, not Elizabeth, and she was going to damn well remember it.

Below her, the floor was mostly empty, only the custodial crew left. She turned, intending to leave her office through her private back entrance and take the interior stairs up to her apartment. She was halted, however, by a soft knock simultaneous with the door sliding open.

"Is it true?" Rhiana asked, acting as spokeswoman for the girls who stood behind her.

Lissa knew what they'd come to ask. The only surprise was that they'd waited until the wee hours, when the club shut down at 3 A.M. "Is what true?"

"Priam," Rhiana said. She stepped inside, then gestured at the other girls, who followed suit. Anya stood in a corner, looking cautiously ecstatic. Jayla and Cadence and eight more girls took seats on the sofa and floor, all looking up at her expectantly, their eyes filled with a hero worship that made Lissa look away, ashamed.

Maybe she was their hero, but it had taken her lifetimes to get there, and before that she'd been vile and horrible, and she'd hurt people badly. The kind of hurt that lasted a lifetime. She thought of Nick, and cringed. A lifetime was a long damn time if you were a vampire.

"Come on, Lissa," Rhiana urged. "Is he really dead?"

"He's dead."

Anya let out a soft "oh" of relief, then sank down the wall and hugged her knees to her chest. The other girls looked at one another and the low buzz of excited whispers filled the room. Priam's cruelty had been legendary.

What would those chattering girls think if they knew Lissa had played the game with him, and she'd played it with open eyes. She'd taken souls, she'd stolen information, she'd used it willingly and calculatingly, and she'd hurt people. For every Nick, there were probably dozens of others.

And now she was racing toward redemption. She'd helped Priam shift the world off-kilter, and now she was trying to tilt it back.

What did that make her? Good? Honest?

Or was she simply scared? Terrified that if she didn't correct her past, it would come back to haunt her?

Hadn't it already?

"Out," Rhiana said, her words pulling Lissa back. She glanced at her friend, who had stood and was shooing the other girls. "The rumor's true, that's all we need to know. So go on. Scoot."

She kept waving hands toward the door until all the girls were gone. Then she shut it, locked it, and turned to Lissa. "Well? How'd he die?"

Despite her foul mood, Lissa laughed. "I thought you said you only needed to know that the rumor was true."

"*They* only needed to know. Me, you need to tell the whole story."

She settled herself in one of the guest chairs opposite Lissa, tucked a foot under her rear, and waited.

"Rhee . . ."

"Don't even," her friend said. And that was the trouble. They *were* friends. They'd both been in the same cortegery in New York before Lissa had bought her freedom. And once Lissa opened Orlando's, Rhiana was the first girl whose deed she'd purchased using money provided by a vampire whose thoughts had revealed that he was draining his own blood and selling it to humans looking for a different kind of high.

Of all the girls she'd bought, Rhee was the only one who hadn't been abused while in the cortegery. Lissa hadn't, either—for that matter, as traders went, Quimby had been the perfect owner. But that had been the problem. She'd been *owned*, and though she'd stomached that for God knows how many lifetimes, with *this* life, she couldn't take it anymore.

He'd agreed to let her buy her freedom for the same price he'd paid to acquire her. An extremely fair trade considering that infant succubi were useless to a trader until puberty.

Now, though Lissa was technically Rhiana's employer, they'd come into the arrangement because of a shared lifetime of friendship. And, what the hell, she really wanted to talk about it.

"He was harassing me," she began. "You know, about Anya." She'd never told Rhee—or anybody—about how she got into heads, and she wasn't starting now.

"I thought so," Rhiana said. "The other night when he came in here. God, he looked so harsh. I thought he was going to eat you alive and spit out the bones."

"He tried," Lissa said. "But I got rid of him."

"You're so smooth," Rhee said. "Next life, I want to come back as you."

Since Rhee expected it, Lissa forced a smile, trying to look both flattered and amused. "Anyway, I went to this pub in Van Nuys a couple of nights later—"

"Van Nuys? Why?" From the way Rhee's nose wrinkled, Lissa might as well have said she'd deliberately stomped through dog poo.

"I had my reasons. Do you want to hear what happened or not?"

Rhee made a rolling motion with her hand.

"I was in an alley behind the pub, and Priam found me." She shuddered, remembering the terror that had ripped through her.

"Oh, Lis," Rhee whispered, her voice low and full of genuine emotion now, not just prurient interest. "Lis, are you okay?"

"I am now." She tried a smile, failed, and tried again. "There was a guy and he jumped in and saved me. They fought, and he killed Priam." She shrugged, as if the story couldn't be any simpler, when really, it couldn't be more complicated.

"So what about the guy?"

"Who knows," Lissa said, feigning nonchalance. Tonight was a full moon. Was Rand out there now, prowling in the foothills? Loping along Mulholland Drive?

Was his head filled with her, too, or had he moved on the moment Doyle had pulled her away from the Slaughtered Goat?

Rhee was watching her through narrowed, knowing eyes.

"What?"

"You slept with him," Rhee said, and Lissa realized her nonchalance thing needed some work. Rhee's brow furrowed. "Are you meeting clients off premises?"

"He's not a client, he's—"

"Ha!" Rhee's expression was triumphant. "Oh, my God. What's it like?"

"What's *what* like?"

"Being with a man. Outside of business." Her eyes narrowed. "I'm right, aren't I? That you *wanted* to sleep with him? Was it better? Getting soul from someone you actually desire, I mean? I've never—never even wanted a man that way, I mean—but I've thought about it and—"

"Yes," Lissa said, stifling a smile. "It was nice. And no, I didn't take his soul."

"And it was still nice?"

She remembered the way her body had burned against his. "Very."

"Wow." Rhee breathed in deep, her eyes closed. "This is just like one of our Wednesday nights." Mid-week, on the one night Orlando's was closed, Lissa and Rhee would hole up in Lissa's apartment with wine and popcorn and watch movies, usually classic romances with Cary Grant or Humphrey Bogart. "You're probably going to fall in love with him now."

Lissa shot her friend a sideways glance. "We don't love. We're not wired that way."

"Desperately attracted to him, then."

Lissa laughed. On that point, she had to concede. Even now her skin was tingling merely from the thought of him. And she'd barely gone ten minutes without thinking of him since the moment she'd left his side.

"Some of us can, you know," Rhee said.

"Can what?"

"Love."

Lissa turned away, not wanting to admit that she knew what Rhee said was true. Some succubi were wired for love, and Lissa was one of those rare succubi who could even feel it. *Had* felt it, in fact, something she'd been slowly recalling, but the memory had only truly burst free after Nick had pressed her up against the door.

She'd loved him. She had really and truly loved him. She was certain of it.

But that was a lifetime ago, maybe more, and she was quite confident that Nick wouldn't think the whole love thing had turned out all that well.

"It's rare," Rhee was saying, going on in an academic tone and apparently not noticing Lissa's musings, "and that's probably a good thing. Considering what we do— I wouldn't want to be in love and then spend my days with other men's souls twining around me. But at the same time . . ." She drew in a breath and closed her eyes, looking like a woman who'd just touched perfection. "My God, how wonderful to feel like Lauren Bacall in Bogart's arms."

She sighed. And, yeah, Lissa did, too. If it worked out, maybe love really could be all wonderful and happily ever after. But Lissa knew enough about the way the world worked to know that things rarely worked out.

Rhee was standing at the window, looking down into the club. "Was the guy handsome?"

"What?" Her mind was on Rand, and she didn't actually hear the question.

"I asked if he was handsome."

She thought of the stark lines of his face, the hard angles of his muscles. He was power and he was heat. And, yes, he was handsome as hell, and she told Rhee so.

"Then I think maybe he's here."

"What?" To her utter mortification, she stood up so fast her chair fell backward. With her heart pounding in her chest, she moved to the window, pushed forward by the anticipation of seeing Rand.

But he wasn't standing there.

Nick was.

CHAPTER 27

He shouldn't have come.

Nick stood just inside Orlando's front door and watched the crew wiping down tabletops and mopping floors, and all he could think was that he shouldn't have come. He had no reason to be there. Doyle had said nothing about putting Lissa back into action as a CI, and at least for the moment, her deal was in place.

He had no role here as her attorney, and he'd made a damn fool of himself earlier. The moment he'd accused her of working with Priam, he'd known he was wrong. She'd had no clue as to what she'd done in the past. No clue about Nick, or the way she'd hurt him.

Now she did.

He'd seen the memories begin to flow back. Saw the spark of recognition and pain and self-loathing fill her eyes, and he'd heard the catch in her voice when she'd apologized.

He hated himself for making her remember—for hurting her in that way. And at the same time, he wanted her to hurt. Wanted her to remember and hurt, and return to his arms for forgiveness and comfort.

And he would forgive her. How could he not when she still pulsed through his veins? When in all his years walking this earth, she was the only woman who'd ever truly touched him? The only woman who'd stayed there despite pain and betrayal and even death?

She'd loved him once, too. As much as he still loved her. He was as certain of it as he was that night followed day. That was why he'd come, of course. Because she was his, and somehow he would have her again.

She didn't rush when she came down the steps that led from her office to the club's main floor, but he saw the way her pace quickened when his eyes met hers, and he smiled, nearly undone by the thought that she would hurry to him.

He was a man lost, and he knew it, but right then he didn't care. He saw only her. Wanted only her.

"Lissa," he said when she reached him, her smile bright with welcome, but her eyes clouded with wariness. Something in him twisted. This wasn't the greeting of a woman in love, but of a woman worried and confused. "I'm not here about the case. Doyle hasn't made a sound about sending you back in."

"Oh." The wariness remained. "Nick, why are you here?"

"To apologize."

"It's not necessary. You had every right to be angry. I was vile." She looked away, her brow furrowed as if in pain. "I'm so very sorry."

"So you do remember?"

"Not all. Not yet." She drew in a breath and looked in his eyes. "I don't remember exactly how I hurt you. Only that I'd loved you, and I betrayed you. And I did it even though I knew you loved me." She drew in a breath. "Priam didn't make me. Not in that lifetime. I think . . . I think I decided to on my own. To work with him, I mean. I think that was the only way out of it I could find."

"He was a son of a bitch. You were in a horrible position."

She shrugged. "There were other ways. I'd been in his cortegery in other lifetimes, and I hadn't partnered with him. And in this lifetime—well, the point is that I'm a different person now. I'm not Elizabeth anymore."

She looked so frail and sad he wanted to pull her close and stroke her until he'd erased every hint of sadness. He couldn't do that, though. Not yet. Not when they were still feeling their way through this. Instead, he simply reached out for her hand. "You were never Elizabeth to me."

Her wan smile almost broke his heart. "I think it's you I have to thank for this life. However I've made it better, it's because I'm Lissa now." She tilted her head slightly to the side, the gesture so familiar it made his body ache with longing.

He kissed her fingertips, then noticed the way her after-hours staff was looking at them. He nodded toward the door. "Walk with me?"

"I'm not sure . . ."

"It's a full moon, Lissa. You may not remember, but I do. Walk with me again in the moonlight. Is that too much to ask?"

"No." A smiled twitched at her lips. "Of course not."

They left through the front door, stepping out onto the sidewalk of the underdeveloped street, a rarity in Los Angeles. By day, the brown and gray buildings that lined this commercial neighborhood were gloomy. Now, with the moon illuminating each smooth surface, Nick thought it looked like heaven. Or perhaps that was only because of the woman at his side.

"Do you remember our talks?"

She shook her head, and he felt a pang of regret for her loss of something he cherished so deeply.

"We spoke of everything," he said. "Of the movement of the stars in the sky, of the nature of existence and the mythology of the daemon breed. And of immortality. That is something about which you and I know a great deal. Who but immortals could find each other after more than two hundred years?"

"Am I immortal? With each life, I come into the world different. Does that make me immortal, or simply forever changed?"

"You do remember." He pulled her aside, then leaned against a streetlight, searching her face. "You asked me that very question once before."

"And what did you say?"

"I had no good answer for you. I've searched for immortality my whole life, and thought I'd found the philosopher's stone in the dark lady's kiss. But it is as they say. To be *nosferatu* is to walk forever in the dark. It is more than the illusion of immortality, but it isn't what I sought those many years ago."

She watched him, memory bubbling, and she tried to bring it forward, those little bits and pieces that were still lost to her over the transom of time. She could catch only a few glimpses, but she clung to them, wanting the memories that supported the love she'd once felt for him.

"Alchemy," she said softly. She took a step to the side, memory guiding her as she reached up and pressed a hand flat against his shoulder blade. She could almost picture the tattoo. An odd, geometrical symbol. "I do remember," she said, her voice thick. "You searched. It was your passion."

"It was, and I did. But I never found." He lifted a shoulder, shrugging off the past. "Some quests are worth abandoning." He brushed her cheek with his thumb. "Some are not."

Her breath hitched as he leaned in, his lips brushing hers before she put her hands to his chest and gently but firmly pushed him back. "Nick, I thought you understood—I'm not the same girl that I was."

She saw him tense, saw the disappointment in his eyes erased by a flash of anger. She drew in a breath, remembering what he was and what she'd done to him. No matter what, he was still a vampire, and she knew that more than anyone, she could wake his daemon.

"I'm sorry," she said, not sure if the words would help, or only make it worse. "I—I think I should go."

She didn't wait for him to answer. Couldn't wait, because she had to get away from him and from the buzz in her head. She turned, then started swiftly down the alley toward the back entrance to Orlando's and the iron-grate staircase that led to her apartment. Her heart pounded, and she couldn't hear anything above it, so she kept her eyes ahead, not looking back, not checking to see if he was following her.

Sadness enveloped her. She knew she'd hurt Nick all over again by walking away, but though she remembered the way he'd once made her pulse burn, it no longer did.

Another man burned through her now, though she

wished he didn't. With disgust, she recalled the casual way Mia had answered Rand's phone. He'd fucked Lissa because that was what he did—he collected girls like trophies. And she couldn't even fault him because she'd gone to him because of what *she* did. They'd had a good night—hell, an explosive night—but that was the end of it, and she'd been running her own business long enough to know that sometimes wanting wasn't enough. Sometimes you just had to move on.

Too bad she wanted so badly.

At the base of the stairs, she paused, thoughts bouncing between Rand and Nick. Unable to bank her curiosity any longer, she turned to see if Nick was still at the end of the alley, then breathed a sigh of relief when she saw that he'd gone.

She was just about to head up the stairs to sleep when she saw it—something large and dark. Something with sharp teeth and death in its eyes.

Something racing straight for her.

◊

The wolf halted only inches from Lissa, its gray fur mangled and torn, blood glistening in the lamplight. Its familiar green eyes, shrouded with pain, looked at her with a dangerous hunger.

Slowly, she started to back up the stairs.

The wolf took a step toward her, limping slightly.

She swallowed, uncertain, wondering if she should scream for Nick to come back, or if that would only antagonize the beast.

It tilted its head to the side, its eyes turning soft, and

she noticed for the first time there was something held tight between its bloody jaws.

Probably an arm he ripped off somebody.

The wolf moved closer.

"Down, boy," she whispered, and it whimpered in response.

She hesitated, suddenly uncertain. She knew those eyes. She'd seen them before.

Rand.

Holy shit, the wolf was Rand.

"Rand?"

He looked at her, and she saw human desire behind the wolf's pale gaze. Then Rand moved and pain filled his eyes as he placed a single paw on the bottom step.

Dear God, it was him. And he was hurt.

She considered her options, genuinely unsure what to do. A werewolf during a full moon was a hunter, everyone knew that. They went out to prowl, to kill, and from the looks of it, Rand had gotten up close and personal with something that hadn't particularly wanted to die.

She needed to clean his wounds, but if she took him into her apartment he might—

No. He wouldn't hurt her. If he was going to do that, he would have attacked already. And weren kept their minds during the change, right? That was what she'd always understood.

Tentatively, she reached forward, gently brushing the fur at his muzzle. He turned, nuzzling her, then opened his mouth and dropped what he was holding onto the step.

She bent down and picked up a small metal box and

a plastic card with a magnetic stripe on it. Both were covered with dirt and saliva and blood.

Carefully, she held the items. He'd come a long way to bring them to her.

"Come up," she said, taking two steps up.

He didn't move.

"It's all right. Let me clean you up."

Those eyes met her, full of life and intelligence. A pause, and then he turned and moved away from the stairs.

"Rand?"

Power and hunger flared in those eyes, and he threw his head back, then howled at the full moon blazing overhead.

She got the message.

"Okay," she said. She held up the box and the card. "I'll keep these safe."

And then she stood there watching as the gray wolf loped down the alley and disappeared into the darkness.

CHAPTER 28

"Mister. Hey, mister?"

Something was poking at Rand. Something with a demanding voice and an irritating disposition. An elf?

He groaned and rolled to the side, hoping to discourage further pokes and prods on his person. He kept his eyes closed, certain that the shooting pain already in his head would increase exponentially when exposed to sunlight.

"He's alive." Another voice, another poke. Elves. Definitely elves.

"Hey, come on. Wake up." No poke this time. Instead, a hand touched his shoulder, shaking him slightly.

"We need to get out of here. Come on, Cory. We ain't supposed to be here."

Maybe not elves.

Knowing it was going to hurt, he peeled open his eyes. Knife blades of sunlight sliced into his skull, and he squinted up at two faces now peering down at him. The sun was behind them, obscuring their features but turning their hair into golden halos.

"You okay, mister?"

Teenagers. Christ, they were kids.

"*Come on.*" The shorter one tugged on the big one's sleeve. They both carried something flat and unwieldy, and it took Rand a moment to realize they were hauling skateboards. "He's alive, okay? Let's get out of here."

"But he's all cut up," Cory said, and Rand shifted his gaze from the kids to his own body. His chest was covered in gashes and welts, and his arms and hands were equally mucked up. Were it not for the thin layer of water in which he was lying, he imagined the wounds would look a lot worse.

Thank God for therian biology. In a few hours, they'd be healed.

Another look around and he recognized his refuge as a drainpipe, the kind that led to the ocean. And it was through the end of the pipe that the sun was now shining, hanging at such a low angle that it was causing the Pacific's waves behind the teens to dance like fire, and making the teens themselves look like angels loitering at the mouth of hell.

He rolled to the side, testing his muscles, then pushed himself up on his elbows. Both boys leaped backward. Cory stopped, then straightened his shoulders. About sixteen, he was a large guy, probably on his school football team, and he was trying hard not to act scared. His friend had less pride, and stood a good five feet back.

"Honest, mister, we won't call the cops. But if you need help . . ."

"Go," he said, barely able to force the word past the rawness in his throat. He pressed his fingertips to his temples and rubbed, trying to stop the knife blades. He was, he saw, entirely naked. He'd definitely attract some attention getting home.

The kids turned to leave, Cory's expression making

clear that Rand had soundly quashed his hopes for an adventure.

"Wait."

At Rand's croaked command, Cory turned.

"Give me your shorts," he demanded. They were oversized with a drawstring, and with luck, they'd fit Rand. "Your jacket, too."

"Yeah?" Considering he was about to lose his clothes for good, Cory looked remarkably pleased. His clothes, apparently, were a small price to pay for an adventure.

"Yeah," Rand said, holding out his hand. "Come on now, hurry up."

"Right. Sure." The kid peeled out of the shorts, leaving him in tight swim trunks, then out of the jacket.

"Now go," Rand growled.

They went, running hell-for-leather across the sand. Rand watched them go, then relaxed and let himself fall back into the cool, wet sludge that filled the drainpipe.

What the hell had happened last night?

His mind was Swiss cheese, but through some of the holes he could catch glimpses of what had happened before the change. *An attack. The hulk.*

They'd fought. Had Rand killed the hulk? For that matter, what the *fuck* was that thing? Human at first, and then . . . what?

He didn't know. All he knew was that the creature had changed when Petra had grabbed him. Why?

And changed into *what*?

Both were questions for Petra, and since there might be a monster storming through town, he was going to back off his whole let-her-keep-her-secrets thing. This shit, he needed to know about. He'd find her, he'd ask her, she'd tell.

Right then, though, he wanted to remember what happened, and he shook his head, trying to force his thinking to move linearly. This was what he hated most about the change—this goddamned inability to focus when he came out of the murk. Trying to force his mind to stay on track. On target.

He should keep his mind during a full moon. Hell, he should be able to change at will.

He couldn't.

He drew in a breath. *Not relevant right now.*

Right.

Obviously, the monster hadn't killed him. But had he killed the monster? He didn't know, but that shouldn't be hard to figure out. The hulk was hardly inconspicuous; he'd have the creature's status by nightfall.

Rand knew he was damn strong as the wolf, but even a preternaturally strong wolf would have worse injuries after a prolonged battle with the thing that he'd fought at the park. That meant that Rand either killed the monster fast or the thing ran off, leaving Rand alone with an entire night ahead of him.

An entire night roaming free in his weren state.

Just the wolf and the hunger and the blinding need to kill.

Who?

His guts twisted.

Who else had died last night when the wolf had roamed free?

◆

"Trust me," Joe said, squatting on the bar, his limber legs contorted so that his knees were up against his ears. The result of elf and nymph crossbreeding, Joe vaguely resembled a grasshopper, right down to the slightly green skin. "You drink this, you're not even gonna care that your head's about to explode."

Rand peered at the silver liquid, eyes narrowed in defense against the mining crew still whacking away at the inside of his head with a million picks. Tiny red flecks floated in it, and although he couldn't be certain, he thought something was alive in there.

He'd headed home after the beach, then changed clothes and downed a pharmacy's worth of aspirin. It hadn't helped.

He scowled again at the concoction. What the hell. Anything was better than the way his head felt at the moment.

He slammed it back—and a hundred white-hot nails ripped the shit out of his throat.

"What is this crap?"

Joe snorted. "Secret recipe. But it does the job. I oughta know. Been fixing it up and serving it to you fur fellows the morning after a full moon for decades. Never once had a complaint."

"I find that hard to believe."

"No complaints 'bout the way it works," Joe amended. "Burns like hell and tastes like rotten entrails. Lotta complaints about that." The corners of his mouth curved down pensively. "And one or two compliments."

Rand put the glass back on the bar.

"Another?"

"Hell, no."

A low laugh echoed across the room, and he turned to see Xeres striding toward him. "You're a damn pussy, Rand." He nodded to Joe. "Hit me."

Joe did, and Xeres slammed the drink back, then thrust his mug out. "Again."

"You're an arrogant mother," Rand said. "You know that, right?"

Xeres's smile showed off a mile of teeth. "Shit, yeah." He cocked his head to the circular corner booth, where Bixby was already dug in.

"You two have news?"

"We have the lack of news. And we have beer." At the last, he nodded to Joe, who signaled to Mia. The beer would arrive momentarily.

"Caris called twice, just after sunrise," Joe said, sliding Rand's phone across the bar. "I didn't answer, but her name popped on the caller ID."

"Maybe she made progress," Xeres said. "Bitch was the only one of the three of us working the case last night, that's for damn sure." He linked his fingers and thrust his arms up, bones cracking in his shoulders as he moved toward Bixby.

The were-cat shimmied over, and Xeres got in one side and Rand the other, boxing the little guy in. "Well?" Rand said, eyeing the creature. "What's the word among the nonlupines?"

"No word. No nothing. No talk at all." Bixby spit out those words in that strange cadence of his, his shifting eyes never settling on anything or anybody as he talked. "Didn't overhear nothing. Tried. Got nothing. I'll keep trying. Gotta be an answer. Gotta be one somewhere."

Xeres pointedly ignored the were-cat, whom he clearly thought was a useless little freak. Rand ignored both of them and dialed Caris, but instead of getting the vamp, he got her voice mail.

He checked his watch. It was coming on noon now, and most vampires were snug in their beds. It would be awhile before he heard from her.

"She leave a message?" Xeres asked.

Rand shook his head.

"Then we can assume she's got shit," Xeres said. He grabbed a beer off Mia's tray, almost upsetting her balance. "Let's get drunk and decide where we go next."

"Already got that figured out," Rand admitted. Part of his considerable hangover was due to the fact that he hated himself for losing the box of ash that Petra had so surreptitiously acquired for him. But he'd changed, and it wasn't as if the wolf would think to hang onto that shit. Unfortunately, the box wasn't at the park, either. He knew; he'd looked. Not surprising, considering all the kids who tramped through there, but he'd hoped. Too bad his hopes had been shot to hell.

A setback, but one that pushed him toward a more radical path. He looked at Xeres and Bixby in turn. "I'm going to walk straight through Division's front door and offer to work with them."

Bixby's mouth fell open. "You're not. You're what? You'd really?"

Xeres was more succinct. "Fuck me."

"At this point I don't see a downside." He didn't mention Petra's disturbing tidbit that the PEC might actually try to infiltrate his own people. Xeres and Bixby *were* his people, and his trust ran only as far as he could see. That was how you stayed alive in this world, especially in his business. "I'll share what I've learned so far, which is a lot of nothing, and see what they reciprocate with."

"And us? You bringing us in, too?" Xeres asked, not sounding happy about the prospect.

Rand shook his head. "You two report to me. Caris, too. I decide what the PEC learns from us." He looked to each of them in turn, mindful of Petra's warning. "Is that clear?"

"Shit, yeah," Xeres said. "The farther you keep Division from my ass, the more I like it."

Rand couldn't help but share the sentiment. His activities were usually of the sort that he wanted to keep off the PEC's radar. This was a new one on him. But another body had been found, and things were heating up. One of the PEC and the Alliance's most fervent mandates was to protect the human population from those who walked in shadows. Considering the rising death toll, that mandate was fast unraveling.

As a result, the Alliance was breathing down Tiberius's throat, threatening to oust him as governor. And while that might sound like a happy result for Gunnolf, Tiberius was doing everything he could to bring the weren leader down with him, including blaming the current deaths on Gunnolf and a weren plot against himself. The Alliance had taken no formal vote, but the whispers that were reaching Gunnolf suggested that the Alliance would simply wash its hands of the matter, ousting both Gunnolf and Tiberius from their respective territories.

They would act soon, Rand knew. More than that, Rand was certain that it was only a matter of time before another body was found.

"So when, when are you going?" Bixby asked.

Rand slid out of the booth and stood. "Looks like I'm going right now."

CHAPTER 29

"Gotta admit I wasn't expecting this," Ryan Doyle said from where he stood leaning against the wall of the conference room. Also present were Sara and Luke. And, of course, Vincent Rand, who'd walked into Division and demanded to see the team working on the dead humans.

Doyle had to admire the weren's gumption.

"It makes sense for us to work together," Rand continued, acknowledging Doyle's words with only the slightest glance. "Evidence is thin, and we're both trying to reach the same goal."

"Are we?" Luke asked, in a voice that managed to convey both menace and cooperation.

"We're looking for a killer. And at this point, I think I have an advantage over you."

"How do you figure?" Doyle asked.

"I know that Gunnolf has nothing to do with the murders."

"So you say."

"So I'll prove—but I can do it faster if we work together, and save this office one hell of a lot of wasted time." He shifted to look at Luke. "I imagine time is a concern to Tiberius."

Luke said nothing, but Doyle could see easily enough that Rand knew he'd struck a nerve.

He pushed back from the table and stood. "Think about it. You know where to find me."

He took a step toward the door.

"Wait," Doyle called.

Rand turned to him and waited expectantly.

"Good faith," Doyle said, fighting back a smile at the way he was mimicking Petra's words, particularly ironic since she was undoubtedly working for Rand. "Tell us something on good faith so we know you're sincere."

Rand hesitated only a moment. "Jacob Yannew didn't originate the rumors about Gunnolf," he finally said, and when he did, Doyle felt himself stand straighter, interested in the weren's words. At the table, both Sara and Luke tensed as well.

"Who did?"

"I don't know," Rand said. "But when I interviewed Yannew—"

"Interviewed?" Doyle said.

The barest hint of a smile touched the corner of Rand's mouth. "Interviewed," he repeated firmly. "He told me he was paid to spread the rumors."

"Who paid him?"

"An Outcast," Rand said, then looked to each of them in turn. "An Outcast with the scent of vampire on him."

"Have you located the Outcast?" Sara asked. "Do you have a name?"

"No on both counts, but that's the goal. Find the Outcast, and we're more than halfway home." He pulled open the door, then paused in the threshold. "Think about my offer," he said, then the door swung closed, and he was gone.

For a moment, they said nothing. Then Sara turned to Luke. "Well, that was unexpected."

"We should do it," Doyle said, and Sara shifted her attention to him.

"Do you trust him?"

"Hell, no, but you know what they say—"

"Keep your friends close," Luke began.

Doyle nodded. "And get in bed with your enemies."

◆

"You should have seen Ryan Doyle's face," Rand said, clinking his beer bottle against Xeres's. "You know him? Percipient daemon?"

"We've crossed paths, and anyone who can throw that bastard for a loop is all right by me." He took a long slug of beer. "So you're in?"

"Absolutely," Rand said. Neither Doyle nor the prosecutor, Constantine, had said so specifically, but Rand knew the offer was too good for them to pass up. He was in. The only question was how far. But that wasn't a question that worried him. Not with his team still in place and Petra and her sources lining up. He'd continue to do his own legwork, and when it suited, he'd compare notes with his new friends at Division.

"So where are we on the Outcast issue? You went down to San Diego?"

"Dead," Xeres said. "Hanged himself two days ago."

Rand whistled through his teeth. "Shit."

"Could still be our guy," Xeres said. "Remorse. Fear of getting caught."

"Or he could have just been a fucked-up Outcast who couldn't take it anymore. We keep looking."

"Have been," Xeres said, then took a long pull on his beer. "You know I haven't found too many. Most Outcasts settle in Europe or South America. Someplace where Division is less stringent and palms are greased more frequently. Someplace where the governor isn't a damn vampire."

"Maybe," Rand said, "but enough settle here, including the one we're looking for."

"You don't believe it was San Diego?"

"No," Rand said. "Too far away. Shit, Xeres, we've got so much wild land around here. The Angeles National Forest. Topanga State Park. There are thousands of acres an Outcast can hide in, and you've only found three?"

"The key is *hide*," Xeres said, bristling.

"Then we look harder," Rand said, not in the mood to stroke sore egos. He was about to say that he'd contact Gunnolf and request the pre-Outcast files on any weren who had ties to Los Angeles. Might not help, but might turn up a new lead.

He never got the chance, though, because Xeres's low whistle cut him off before he could even begin. "Now *that*," Xeres said, "is a fuckable woman."

Even before he turned, Rand caught Lissa's scent. He shifted, his face revealing nothing as she glided toward the bar, looking at him only long enough to flash a sultry, promise-filled smile. She wore a wraparound dress in a material that clung, and with each step, it accentuated a different curve. By the time she reached the bar, every eye in the place was on her, and most of the males were drooling.

Rand didn't know what twist of fate had brought her through those doors, but he was ready to take her to his office, strip off that dress, and show her exactly how happy he was that she'd come back—because he was certain she'd come back for him.

Xeres knew it, too, and he shifted his gaze between Rand and Lissa, his nose twitching. "Your scent," he said, the word almost an accusation. "It's on her."

Rand didn't admit, didn't deny.

"She's a succubus."

Again, Rand stayed silent.

Xeres chuckled. "Damn. Look at you, trading a little soul for a poke at a succubus. I don't know. I may have to get me some of that, too."

Beneath the table, Rand clenched his fists. Under the circumstances, he didn't think the typically human "She's not that kind of a girl" would fly.

Instead, he slid out of the booth. "Trust me, buddy, you don't want to go there." He clapped his hand on Xeres's shoulder. "She's way too much woman for you."

♦

Lissa stifled a shiver as she looked at him, tall and dark and so very human in appearance. He'd come to her, seeking her out even when he was an animal, and that simple truth meant the world to her. Whatever doubts had lingered, she knew now that there was something between them. Something more than sheen. Something *real*.

She'd paused in the middle of the pub, completely un-self-conscious even though everyone in the place was looking at her. She wasn't turning it on, but she knew her sheen was heightened.

Maybe that's why succubi weren't wired for love, because when they did find a man they wanted, they radiated desire and caught the world up in it.

Stop stalling.

Deliberately, she moved across the pub to where he stood at a booth beside another weren male. Her steps were slow, her movements fluid, and with every inch closer she got, she could see the heat rising in him. She wanted to touch him, to kiss him, and so much more. She wanted to undress him and slide her hands over his body. She wanted to feel his desire under her skin and know that it was her he was reacting to.

In other words, she was wishing she'd picked a much less public place to meet him.

She stopped inches away from him. "I brought your things."

His brow creased in what looked like confusion, but she didn't have a chance to ask him what was wrong because the burly male beside him stepped closer. "Hi, beautiful." He held out his hand. "Xeres."

She let her gaze slide over the man, taking satisfaction in the musky scent of desire that rose off of him. She allowed him a nod of greeting, but she didn't take his hand. She wasn't there for him.

She turned her attention back to Rand. "Can we go to your office?"

He fell in step beside her, and she headed toward the back, then through the No Admittance door, and then down the hall to his office. Without a word, he ushered her inside, then closed and locked the door. He turned to face her, his back to the door.

She left the small purse she carried on his desk, then smiled at him, her body tingling with so much anticipation she felt as though she would burst without his touch.

She waited for him to say something, but he only stood there, looking at her. Finally, when she was afraid she'd explode from waiting, he spoke.

"Lissa." Just the one word, her name, and he said it as he moved to her, said it as he brushed his lips over hers, murmured it as he reached back and tugged at the simple bow that held her dress closed.

It fell away, pooling around her ankles. She stepped out of it, naked now, since she hadn't bothered with bra or panties.

A muscle twitched in his cheek, and she knew he was fighting for control.

Don't. She wanted to scream the word. She didn't want him controlled. She wanted him wild again. She wanted him to take her hard and fast, to let her know that last night wasn't a fluke and that he'd come to her as the wolf because he truly wanted her.

"Touch me." As she spoke, she took his hands, then pressed them to her breasts. She closed her eyes, savoring the way his rough palms felt against her tender skin, but not before seeing the desire on his face. He did want her, and that knowledge shot through her, making her feel warm and powerful and confident.

This wasn't about her usual boldness. With most men, she knew she had the power that stemmed from the sheen. That wasn't the case with Rand, and although she'd suspected it that first night in the club when he'd so easily turned away, she knew for certain now.

The sheen didn't affect weren males when they were in full transition, yet Rand had come to her as the wolf—sought her out, needed and wanted her.

And that was heady stuff.

Without warning, he reached down and scooped her up, then carried her, naked and laughing. He lightly tossed her onto the couch, then leaned over her. "This isn't going to be gentle, and it isn't going to be slow. I can't. Not this time. I've been waiting too damn long."

"Too damn long," she repeated as she hooked her arm around his neck, her body arching up to meet his as he thrust inside her, pounding into her in a way that left no question but that he was claiming her once again, making her his.

They moved together, gasping, his soul starting to peek out, starting to flow like tattered ribbons around her. She let herself enjoy the feel of soul against flesh for only an instant—there wasn't time for more. Once again, he was too hot, too ready, and if he went over while he was inside her . . .

Dear God, she wanted the feel of him coming inside her, but she couldn't let that happen. She'd seen up close the animal he could become. Without a soul, she knew damn well what would be unleashed.

Reaching up, she took his face in her hands and kissed him, hard, then bit his lower lip. "Off," she said, then gave him her sultriest smile when he looked at her with curious horror. "I have something else in mind," she whispered as she shifted, trying to get out from under him. "Trust me."

He didn't look like he wanted to, but he complied, moving with a protesting groan onto his side, his body slipping from hers. She didn't even give the protest time to die on his lips. She slid down his body, lower and lower, until she could take him in her mouth, drawing him in, tasting and sucking. She moved her tongue around his shaft, her body warming and tightening when she felt him getting hotter and harder.

Reaching down, she cupped his balls, stroking the velvet sac.

He shifted, his movements quick and urgent, and she kept up the sweet torment. It was building inside him— an explosion of desire—and though she was no stranger to a man's satisfaction, right then the power of knowing that she was so sweetly manipulating his body sent her own excitement into a frenzy.

Hot desire flowed through her, the feeling familiar and yet unlike anything she had ever known. And she clung to it, wanting both to savor it and to feel the full force of its power.

When he finally came, she almost exploded herself.

He moaned, the noise soft, and she stayed where she was, her fingers dancing on his skin, a small smile playing at her lips, a reflection of her power as a woman. Her power over him.

Of all the men she'd lorded sensual power over, he was the first to make her feel so satisfied simply from the act of making *him* satisfied.

At least, he was the first that she remembered.

Sated, she let him pull her toward him, then tug her

down to snuggle against him on the couch. She closed her eyes, listening to the beating of his heart, the soft sound of contentment in his breath. She listened, and she felt it, too.

And that meant she also felt when it stopped.

He sat up slowly, his brow furrowed, then stood and moved to the far side of the room. At his sides, his hands clenched and unclenched.

He was fighting something—fighting hard—and she didn't understand what it was. Could only watch and wait, her chest tight and small prickles of fear dotting her skin.

"Rand?"

"Why did you come here?"

His words stung. "Because I wanted to see you. Because I needed to bring you your things."

His eyes narrowed. "What things?"

It hit her, then, and she felt like an idiot for not making the connection earlier when he'd looked so blank inside the pub. *He didn't remember.*

"Last night," she said. "The stuff you brought and left with me. When you were the wolf, I mean."

It wasn't the right thing to say. His back straightened, and the unreadable expression on his face came into sharp focus. *Fear.*

"What the fuck are you talking about? Last night was a full moon."

"I know. And you came to me. A wolf. You were injured—bloody and mangled—but you left me a card and a box. God, you really don't remember any of it?" She knew what that was like. The holes. The questions. "But I thought werewolves could—"

"Some can," he said briskly. "Not me. When the moon is full, the wolf takes over. After, I don't remember a thing. There's no control for me. I can't bring the change on during the month, and on the night of a full moon, I can't fight my way up to the surface."

"But you did. You were the wolf, but you were Rand, too. I could see you in the wolf's eyes. You came to me on purpose and for a reason."

He lashed out, snatching a paperweight off the desk and smashing it in the corner. She cringed, realizing his control was as fragile as that shattered glass.

"*Goddammit!*" he roared. "I could have killed you. I could have ripped you to shreds."

She spoke softly. Evenly. "But you didn't."

"That's not the point."

"I think it's exactly the point."

"Do you have any idea how lucky you are?"

Anger flared, but she tamped it down. "I really don't think it was luck. It was you. Are you saying that you'd hurt me?"

"Yes! As the wolf, I don't know what the fuck I'd do."

"Well, I do," she snapped.

He ran his palm over his scalp, obviously frustrated. Yeah, well, so was she.

"You said you came to bring me something."

She glanced at the desk and her purse, but didn't get up. She'd heard the note of dismissal in his voice, but there was no way she was leaving. Not yet. "I could have sent a messenger. I came for you. Rand, I wanted to see you again."

A muscle twitched in his jaw, but otherwise, his body

was as unmoving as steel. "And if I said I didn't want to see you?"

She stiffened, too. Whatever game he was playing, she was determined not to lose. "I'd say I don't believe you."

"I don't need you. I can't need you."

"Like I said, I don't believe you."

Temper sparked. "Dammit, Lissa, I'm not a man who has anything to give to a woman."

"And yet here I am."

He bent down and tossed her the dress. Then he stalked to the door, his hand on the knob. "It's time for you to go."

No way. No way was she leaving.

She stayed on the couch, the dress in her hands.

"Lissa . . ." Warning rang through his voice.

"You're strong. Toss me out."

For a moment, she thought he just might do that. Then he let go of the knob and stepped away. Inside her, victory blossomed.

"Why?" he asked. "Why me?"

The question twisted through her, and she tried to find the words, knowing that it was important. "I don't know. You touch me. Inside. You make me feel like more than I am."

"And what are you?"

She shook her head. "I don't like to think about it."

"Why not? You're good," he said. "Your club. Those girls. What you do for them."

"You don't have any idea what I do for them." He didn't know about the blackmail she used to get cash for the girls, and he sure as hell didn't know what she'd done in the past.

"You do what it takes to rescue them," he said firmly. He crossed the room and stood in front of her, then tilted her chin and forced her to look at him. "You give those girls new lives."

She looked down at the floor. "It's only an illusion."

"No," he said. "No, it's not." He twined her hair around his finger. "I know all about illusions. Hell, even this," he said, gesturing between the two of them. "That's an illusion, right? You, succubus. Me, male. It's not like I can't do the math, and it's not like I'm saying that's a bad thing," he added. "I've been there. I've had a lot of women in my bed."

The corner of her mouth twitched. "You say the sweetest things."

"I'm trying to say that you're the only one who's stuck. In here, I mean," he said, tapping his temple.

"Except your wife."

"No other woman," he repeated, and she fought a tremble, feeling the same way he'd described her—special.

His next words ripped that feeling to shreds. "But the truth is, I don't really want you. It's just juiced-up preternatural hormones, and—why are you smiling?"

"It may be hormones, but not the preternatural kind," she said. "Trust me, Rand, if this was just about me being a succubus, you wouldn't have come to my apartment last night."

"What are you talking about?"

"I suspected it at first because you walked away from me so easily at Orlando's. Pissed me off a bit, actually," she added, with a teasing smile. "I'm not used to men turning their backs on me."

"I bet you're not."

"But you're different. You're immune."

He held up a hand. "Whoa. No way. That's impossible."

"It's true. Some men are, and all animals are. And last night you were . . . well, an animal, but you sought me out and—"

He held up his hand, then turned away from her.

"Rand?"

"An animal," he said, still not looking at her, and she started to panic as understanding dawned. He didn't want to desire her, and now she'd gone and pulled the whole succubus crutch out from under him, and—

Shit. Slowly, she pressed a hand to his shoulder. "Should I go?"

"It's what I am," he said. "A goddamned animal."

She drew in a breath, hearing his pain and understanding what he really meant. "No." She pressed against him, her bare skin hot against his back. "You're not."

"You don't know me."

"Maybe not. But I know I want to." She drew in a shaky breath. "This is new for you. It's new for me, too."

Her lips brushed his shoulder, and he stiffened, his back as straight as a soldier standing at attention. Slowly, she took her hand off his shoulder.

"I didn't love Alicia."

Something trembled inside her, but she said nothing.

"I didn't love her, but I kept her on a string, because

I'd knocked her up and that meant she was mine. I could fuck her, but I didn't love her."

He pressed his fingers to his temples. "I told you I fit into the army?"

"Yes."

"I knew how to do that. How to follow orders. How to kill. I'd lived that shit. Hell, I *was* that shit. As fierce as any animal out there. But how to be a man—how to truly be a man with my wife?—I didn't have a fucking clue."

"It's not your fault you didn't love her," Lissa said. "Love doesn't work that way."

He turned and looked at her. "You're an expert?"

"No," she said, her cheeks blooming. "Succubi don't love. Not as a rule. But I don't think love is something you turn on with a switch."

"Maybe not, but I didn't let her go, did I? Didn't tell her to go find someone whose switch flipped the right way."

"She was your wife."

"Yeah," he said, his voice harsh. "And I kept her, because she was mine, dammit. And she was killed because she was mine, and I hunted down her killer and put a bullet through his head."

"Justice," she said, repeating what she'd told him before.

"Bullshit. I didn't ice him because he'd killed an innocent girl. I put a bullet through his brain because he'd taken what was mine."

She licked her lips, wanting to hold him and make all the pain go away, but knowing better than to touch him right then.

"I didn't love her, but everything I did stole the chance of love from her. And I didn't even give a fuck."

He turned and looked at her, hard. "*That's* what I am."

"You do, though," she said after a moment. "You do give a fuck. I hear it in your voice."

He stayed silent.

"And I've seen it, too. You're ripped up inside, Rand. Your soul is in tatters, but you're not the monster you think you are. I've seen real monsters—I've been owned by them—and that isn't you."

He didn't say a word.

"Rand," she pressed. "What do you want me to do?"

"Stay," he said simply. "Stay with me."

CHAPTER 30

"That's twice now. You're sure the voltage isn't going to kill him?"

"Not much would kill this one, and we only blasted him with enough to knock him out. Don't worry. He's fine."

"Good. Keep him alive. I don't want to have to send out another team to catch more vampires."

The words slid over Serge, the voices rising and falling like waves on an ocean. He thought he recognized them as belonging to Meer and the doctor, but he wasn't certain. He wanted to open his eyes, but he couldn't do that, either. All he could do was lie there, and float.

He felt a sharp stab in his arm, and realized they'd stuck a needle into his vein.

"How long?"

"Fifteen minutes in the centrifuge. Another twenty after that. Not long."

"She's prepped?"

"Everything's ready. It will go faster if you get out of my lab and let me do my work."

"What about Boyd?"

A sigh. "I've done an autopsy. I'm still waiting for the results of a few tests, but so far I have to say it's very interesting."

"No shit."

"It's him, but it's not. He changed, obviously, and yet on a cellular level, he's still Boyd."

"That doesn't make any sense."

"No, it doesn't. Do you know any more about what happened last night?"

"Some. During the op we lost the feed from Boyd and Seacrest's combat cameras, and the signal we were receiving from Hertz didn't show a damn thing. But after we retrieved their bodies, we went in and analyzed the digital footage. Hang on. I've got it on the system. It's easier to just show you."

Serge tried to open his eyes—it was important that he see, that he wake up—but it wasn't happening. He was a rock. An awake rock. And he wasn't going anywhere or doing anything.

Some tapping, and then, "This is the early shot. Before they moved in. There's the target, and he's talking to this woman."

"Who's the third? This one, off to the side."

"Haven't made an ID yet. But hold on, let me switch the input and you can see what's really interesting."

More tapping and clicking of keys, and then, "See, right there. We have the motion from Seacrest turning, and then when he looks down for just a second you can see it—hang on, I'll pause the frame."

"She touches him. The girl grabs Boyd's hand."

"And look at his reaction. Frame by frame now—it's instantaneous."

"He's changed." Awe filled the voice. "That's astounding. And look at him—he's essentially unaffected."

"I wouldn't say unaffected."

"By the change. There was no transitional period. His body simply adjusted. I wonder..." His voice drifted off, and then surged back, his words hungry. "The girl. Who is she?"

"A private investigator. Rand hired her."

"I'll rephrase. *What* is she?"

"Technically, she's human. But she dabbles in magic. Family calls themselves witches."

"Get her."

"I thought you'd find this interesting. Do you still want Rand?"

"Of course. I can manipulate genes. Magic is unpredictable, and definitely not my speciality. But we'll take them both. If one method doesn't work, we'll have the other as a backup."

A pause, then. "All right. What about this one? His fingers are twitching. Is he waking up?"

Another jab to his arm.

"Not anymore."

◆

They were gone when he woke, the world coming into hazy focus.

He was in a lab now, strapped to a table that was tilted at so sharp an angle he'd be standing if it weren't for the bindings. His skin was raw from being stabbed, and when he looked at his arms, he saw that small squares of flesh had been cut neatly away.

He examined the wounds dispassionately. Now wasn't the time for anger or fury or black, hard rage.

Now was the time for cold calculation.

He looked around, getting his bearings, and saw that he wasn't alone.

The girl lay naked on a table, the steady rise and fall of her chest the only indication that she was alive.

There were others on tables, too, and they were not so lucky. Two men. A woman. All dead.

He pressed his head back into the table, his nostrils flaring as he tried to catch a scent. *Human.* And yet somehow not.

Another scent caught his attention. *Vampire.*

And death.

Frowning, he turned his head sharply to the left, searching for the source.

He found it.

The prone shape of a beheaded vampire stretched out on plastic on the floor. The head was nowhere to be found.

Vampires died in two ways—by a stake to the heart, which turned them to ash, and by beheading, which left the body intact.

Serge could see why they'd wanted the body—dozens of probes and needles were buried in the flesh, each connected to wires or tubes that crisscrossed the ground away from the body with the opposite ends plugged into some sort of machine.

What the fuck?

He'd landed in some sort of Dr. Frankenstein laboratory, and he had a feeling that his fate wasn't far behind that of the vampire on the floor.

Shit.

Deep within him, the daemon unfurled, fighting to

break free, but Serge shoved it back. He needed awareness. Needed to figure out where he was and why. Not
to mention what he could do to get out of there.

Footsteps echoed through the room, getting louder as
they approached the door. Serge tensed, but forced himself to stay still. Calm. It wasn't as if he was going to be
ripping heads off, no matter how much he might want
to. The hematite bindings took care of that.

The door opened, and Grayson Meer stepped inside,
followed by the doctor and another man in fatigues.

The one in fatigues approached him, his manner calm
and professional. His scent, however, told a different
story.

"I'm going to rip your heart out and cram it up your
ass," Serge whispered while the guy checked his bindings. "Remember that."

The guy said nothing, but his already bulbous eyes
seemed to pop a little, and the scent of fear in the air
thickened.

Not much of a victory, but right then, Serge would
take what he could get.

"Bukowski," Meer called, "if that one's set, get over
here and help Dr. Kessler."

"He's conscious," the guy in fatigues said. "Do we
care?"

"Let him watch." Meer smiled thinly, his eyes on
Serge. "Let him bear witness to our achievements. After
all, he's playing no small part."

Serge growled low. He didn't know what the fuck
Meer was talking about, but a growl seemed a perfectly
appropriate response.

The doctor—Kessler—held a test tube under a glass

spigot as thick drops of liquid splashed into the tube, filling it slowly. "Get the collar on her," Kessler said. "We're almost ready."

Serge still had no clear idea what these men were up to, but he understood the basics. They were experimenting. Genetic experiments on vampires if his beheaded friend—and the squares of flesh missing from his own body—were any indication. To what end, though, Serge didn't know.

But he did know now for certain where Meer had gotten the victims on whom he'd tested his products: the train tunnels. Serge's private domain had been these bastards' stocking pool.

"It's on." Bukowski stepped back from the girl, who now had a black metal collar tight around her neck.

"You know the drill," Meer said, as Bukowski stepped away, a remote control in his hand. "She comes at any one of us, you fry her ass."

"That will not be a problem, sir."

Kessler moved toward the girl, filling a syringe with the contents of the test tube as he moved. "This new batch is potent. Shouldn't take long for her to wake up." He nodded at the straps holding the girl down. "Loosen them."

As Bukowski moved in to do that, Kessler injected something into the girl, then they all stepped back, making a perimeter around her bed. Bukowski held the remote in front of him like a gun.

At first nothing happened. Then the girl started to moan. Her muscles twitched as if of their own accord, the motions becoming bigger and bigger and her screams along with it. Finally, with one great burst of force, she sat up, her eyes wild and bloodshot, her hands trembling, and her teeth chattering.

He got a look at her teeth. She had fangs.

She sat there, hunched over, head slightly tilted down even as she looked up at them. She snarled, breathing hard, and Serge could see the hunger on her face. Hunger, and nothing else. No reason. No daemon. And not the slightest hint of human remaining.

She lunged—one blinding leap from the table onto Meer. He was on his back, her mouth at his throat, and the room was in chaos, the men rushing for her, screaming at her to stop, and Bukowski hanging back, his hands fumbling with the remote.

The girl screamed, grabbing her neck as her body vibrated with the shock the collar sent through her.

"The bindings!" Kessler yelled. "Quick. She won't be out for long."

They'd barely got them on her when she woke and began thrashing. Serge watched her in morbid fascination, not only because of the spectacle, but because of the one scent he'd caught when she'd lunged toward Meer. *Himself.*

He glanced down at the needle marks and missing hunks of flesh with new understanding.

He would kill them. One way or another, he would see every last one of them dead.

"Hold her steady," Kessler said, as Meer and Bukowski each grabbed an arm. The doctor moved in to draw blood. He put a drop into a centrifuge, then slowed as lines and numbers appeared on a monitor.

"Well?" Meer asked.

Kessler seated himself on a stool and started typing. The images on the monitor changed, shifting as he went through various programs and protocols. "As I thought. Progress." He pushed back, his stool rolling away. "But not enough."

"Bottom line?"

"We've controlled the light sensitivity. She could be a beach bunny in Cancún with no harm done."

"That's a big deal?" Bukowski asked. "Young vamps can go out in the light. It's not an issue for them."

"Actually, it is," Kessler said. "They're sensitive to light from the moment of the change, but early on it's not at a level that would overly bother them. Most don't even notice until the sensitivity increases. Our young lady here isn't sensitive at all, as either vampire or human. In other words, not only will she not turn to ash in the sun, she also won't need to wear her Coppertone. No burning for this one. Or for your new breed of soldier," he said, looking meaningfully at Meer.

"Then we really are that far?" The excitement in Meer's voice was unmistakable. And no wonder, thought Serge, seeing the endgame clearly now for the first time. A new race of fighter made by genetically engineering humans to have all the benefits of vampirism without any of the downsides.

Not a bad deal, actually. Maybe if he played nice, they could fix him up, too.

Too bad he was going to cut their sorry throats. They probably wouldn't consider that playing nice.

"What about transformation? A vampire's ability to transform into mist could be one of our greatest assets.

The potential applications for tactical maneuvers is unlimited."

"We'd have to take the hematite off to test it—not to mention getting her cooperation—but at a cellular level it looks like we've finally crossed that hurdle as well."

Meer nodded slowly. "This is excellent news."

Kessler cleared his throat. "Yes, well, we're close, but as I told you before, close isn't good enough."

"No," Meer said. "It's not."

Kessler stroked his chin thoughtfully as he moved around the girl. "She has no daemon," he said, obviously thinking aloud. "A benefit for your soldiers, since the daemon can't be controlled. But she also has no mind."

"So she's just a killing machine," Bukowski said. "Not a soldier."

"In a word, yes."

"I don't get it," Bukowski said. "The vamps out there keep their minds. So why's she hollow up there?"

Kessler ran his fingers through his hair, making the ends stand up, making him look even more harried than he undoubtedly felt. For a moment, Serge almost felt sorry for him. Then the moment passed, and all he could think about was sinking his teeth into the fat fuck's neck.

"The transformation at the cellular level is horrific. Vampires survive it—for lack of a better word—because they undergo it while dead. Our girl here transformed while alive, and her cells couldn't handle it."

"I don't think killing her is going to solve our problem," Meer said.

"No. We need to control the transition. I thought

drawing cellular material from a werewolf would solve the problem, considering it's their nature to change monthly, but as you know, that theory didn't pan out." He looked up at Meer. "I need Mr. Rand."

"In case you forgot, our efforts to get the son of a bitch cost us Boyd and the team."

"Try again," Kessler said.

"I intend to."

"What's so special about Rand, anyway?" Bukowski asked.

Kessler frowned, clearly put out, but Serge was glad to see that he continued. At this point, he was pretty damn interested, too. "He's a former soldier turned werewolf. That's pretty rare. Not many former U.S. military among the weren ranks."

"Tell me something I don't know," Bukowski said.

"His initial transition was almost instantanous," Kessler said. "Did you know that?"

Bukowski frowned, suggesting he didn't. "How'd you learn that? It wouldn't be in his service record."

"No," Kessler said, "but once I learned who Gunnolf sent here, I made some inquiries. That particular tidbit intrigued me."

"Why?"

"For most weren, the initial transition after the weren virus enters the bloodstream is extremely painful," Kessler said. "Some accounts describe it as fire in the brain. Others as hollowing the body out with a red-hot knife. And the pain lasts for a full month, until the next full moon when their body actually undertakes the change instead of simply craving it."

"And you're saying Rand didn't suffer like that? Why?"

"That's the sixty-four-thousand-dollar question, isn't it? And I think the answer lies in his genes. Rand is a carrier for sickle cell."

"So what?"

"The heterozygote advantage worked to his favor."

"Huh?"

"His cells are resistant to malaria," Meer clarified.

Bukowski snorted. "I'm sure that will come in useful when he travels to the wilds of Pasadena."

"I think it was his status as a carrier that worked to his advantage during the change," Kessler said. "Remember, we're combining human and shadow biology here. Now that he's been through the change, if I can pull some of his genetic material, I should be able to give the same benefit to our subjects."

"Because that's our problem, right?" Bukowski said. "Like this girl. Her body can't withstand the transformation."

"Exactly. Our subjects are transforming," Kessler said. "But the transformation is destroying everything we're working toward—and then when they feed they become even more unstable." He shrugged. "Well, you don't want your soldiers dissolving into ash."

"So we try again."

"We should never have attempted the capture so close to the full moon," Kessler said.

"I'd hoped the disorientation associated with the transformation would work to our advantage," Meer said.

"He'll be easier to capture as a man."

"What werewolf is truly a man?" Meer asked. "They have to change during a full moon, but they can change into the damned wolfman whenever they want. The team will need to be overloaded with op-tech."

"Cover your bases however you want," Kessler said, "but Rand doesn't transition without the moon."

Meer looked at him, interested. "Is that a fact?"

"It may have something to do with his genetic makeup. At any rate, Mr. Rand is going to be a very interesting subject to have on my table. I'd like him here soon."

Meer shot a look toward Bukowski. "We'll brief the team today." He turned his attention back to Kessler. "And what about the girl?"

"Her?" Kessler nodded toward the bound girl.

"No, the witch."

"You're bringing her in for me as well, correct?"

"We'll get her," Bukowski said. "She's constantly with a male—her brother—but our initial surveillance suggests that he acts like a bodyguard. We're running through scenarios, and should have her for you soon."

"Very good.

"Remind the team not to touch her," Meer said. "We've seen what happens." He motioned between Kessler and the girl, still prone on the floor. "Let her go."

A muscle twitched in Kessler's cheek. "Meer—"

Meer held up a hand. "I promised Santiago we'd release the failures. When I give my word, I keep it." He shifted his attention to Bukowski. "Transport her to a drop point," he said. "And then let the little bitch go."

"Dammit, Meer. We're playing with fire to satisfy the whim of a werewolf we don't even need anymore."

"So ungrateful, Doctor. I'm ashamed of you. Without Santiago, we never would have conceived of the possibilities, and now we're on the verge of creating a whole new race."

"We don't need him," Kessler said, his voice tight.

"We do. Santiago still has his uses," Meer said. "And his demands aren't unreasonable. She'll feed, she'll turn to ash. Our disposal problem solved, my promise kept." Meer aimed a thin smile at Kessler. "And not one goddamned thing to lead anyone back to us."

CHAPTER 31

She was beautiful, Rand thought, staring down at the woman who lay beneath him on the sofa, soft and warm and ready for him. He bent over, the need to touch overwhelming his desire to look, and he traced his lips down from her breasts, to her navel, and then down lower still, making her body arch up to meet his touch. With soft kisses, he teased her flesh, letting the wonder of her drive the storm from his head. He breathed in deep, her scent arousing him even more, their scents mingling together, as entwined as their bodies.

He explored her curves with fingers and lips and tongue, memorizing every intimate inch of her, but ultimately ending up back at the prize, cupping his mouth over her sex, his tongue and lips tasting and exploring. He had her rear in his hands, and he lifted her gently, feeling her body respond to him, knowing that soon she'd melt in his hands.

Melt for me, Lissa. Come for me.

More and more, he urged her on. Touching and sucking, until her body started to tremble. First, just a little shiver. Then she moaned, soft and needy—for him. Her hips bucked up, no longer hers to control, but his to play, and all she could do was ride it out.

He kept his mouth on her, riding with her, until the bucking stopped and she lay, soft and spent from his touch. Then he eased up beside her, sighing as she curled up next to him, her chin finding a soft spot in his neck where she fit perfectly.

It was nice. More than nice. Fucking perfect.

"I could stay here all day," she murmured as he was about to drift into sleep.

Stay? He waited for the automatic excuses to form in his head, expected panic to rise. But nothing happened.

Stay, he thought.

And then he remembered the monster and the missing box of ash and Petra's damn freaky touch.

Reluctantly, he sat up, then stretched. "I have things to do that I can't put off. Stay here. Wait for me."

She followed his lead and levered herself upright. "I'll get out of your hair."

"No," he said, pressing his hand on her thigh. "If you can, stay. I need to go see someone, but I won't be long."

"Work?"

He grinned. "I'm not heading out with a sniper rifle, if that's what you're asking."

She cocked a brow. "Then I won't have to remind you to be a good little soldier."

He laughed, then realized it was the first time he could remember ever laughing about what he did. "Actually, I'm going to see a PI."

"Why? Sorry. None of my business."

"Not a big deal."

"All right. Then I'm curious."

"I came to L.A. to look into the murder of those humans."

"And the PI? Has he learned anything?" She stood at

an angle to him, concentrating on wrapping the dress around her slim body rather than looking at him.

"She," Rand corrected. "And that's a good question. She gave me some sort of ash yesterday that I wanted to try and get analyzed this morning." Despite his semi-arrangement with the PEC, he still wanted to do his own analysis. Assuming Petra could get her hands on any more ash. "But what with turning into a wolf and all, I managed to lose it."

Her eyes went wide. "Ash! Oh, hell, I forgot. The thing you lost—I think I might have it." She'd pulled her purse off the desk and rummaged through it, then handed him the box with the ash and a plastic card-key. "That's what you brought me. It helps?"

He kissed her. Hard. "Shit, yes. This is good. This is very good."

He held up the card-key. "I had this, too?"

She nodded.

It was white with no markings other than a magnetic stripe on the back and raised letters on the front: Boyd.

Base . . . do you copy? Fucked up. Boyd . . . all fucked up.

The dying man's words hung in Rand's memory. So this card was Boyd's . . . and Boyd had become the hulk.

He must have taken it from the hulk during the fight. Closing his eyes, he tried to remember. No luck. But maybe there was information hidden in the magnetic strip. It was another lead, at any rate, but not one he intended to immediatly share with the PEC. Boyd and his buddies had been coming after him—after Rand. Most likely, the attack had to do with the dead humans, but until Rand confirmed that, Boyd was his, and his alone.

"So what's in the box?" Lissa asked.

"That's the question of the hour," Rand said.

"Oh. Right." She slipped into her shoes. "I'll let you get to work, then. I mean, I should probably go check the supply lists. My newest office assistant is still a little iffy on detail work."

He reached for her. "Why don't you come with me? Your assistant will figure it out."

She cocked her head. "With you?" The idea was tempting, and her staff really was competent enough to handle the preopening routines at Orlando's. Still . . . "You're working. Do you really want me around?"

"Yes," he said, without any hesitation. "It's not as if I'm undercover. I may not be advertising why I'm in town, but I haven't made a secret of it, either." He paused. "Stay with me."

His words made her smile even as fear for him built in her gut. "Last night," she said. "You were all beat up. Was that just a wolf thing? Or were you attacked by someone who's afraid you're going to figure out what's going on?"

"Attacked."

She ran her fingers through her hair. "Shit." One little word, and it encompassed so much. Her fear for him. Her certainty that Doyle would want her to go with him, to report back what she learned. But she wasn't his CI anymore—or was she? Nick had told Doyle that she was done, but Doyle hadn't ever agreed, and if her ass was still on the line . . .

She rubbed her temples, warding off a massive headache, and again craving a damn cigarette. A habit from another life that only proved there really were no other lives. In the end, it was all just Lissa.

His hand pressed against her back. "Are you okay?"

"Sorry. Just hungry." She smiled at him. "I'd love to spend the morning with you." At least that was the absolute truth. What she'd do if she learned anything about the murders from him . . . well, she'd worry about that if Doyle came calling again.

◆

Petra passed the card-key back to Rand. "Yeah, I can try to get some info off it, but you can do it faster and cheaper."

"Can I?" He feigned innocence.

They were in her bright and shiny outer office, and Rand took a seat on the floral-print sofa next to Lissa, who was watching the girl with interest.

"Come on, dude," Petra said. "I thought you were above playing games. Those guys were military, probably former, and that means their names are in some system somewhere. You're former military, too, and now you're a head honcho for Gunnolf, and he's not stupid enough to let you cut all your ties, even if you wanted to. Which means you've got some contacts still working for Uncle Sam, and I bet you use them for this exact kind of shit. Tracking people down." She eased herself up onto her desk and started swinging her legs. "How am I doing so far?"

"Not bad. I think you've just demonstrated to Lissa why I hired you."

"She's sharp," Lissa said. "And quick."

"She is," he agreed. "Of course she has her raw edges."

"You didn't really come about the card-key, did you?"

"No," Rand admitted. "I've got that one covered. I want to know what happened to that son of a bitch you grabbed."

"It's not your damn business."

"If that thing's still out there," Rand countered, "I'm making it my business."

"Dammit, Rand, just drop it."

"Why?"

She groaned, low and exasperated. "I can't . . . if people know what I am . . ."

He eyed her, wary. "What are you?"

She turned away. "It doesn't matter. The monster's not still out there." She took a deep breath, then shifted back to face him. "You know it's not. You would have heard. So please, just let it go."

"How do you know it's not?"

"Shit, Rand. A monster like that? Everybody would have heard. The whole city would be on high alert." She shivered, then pressed her lips tight together as she blinked furiously. "Believe me, that thing would have killed a dozen people by now. No, fuck, that's way too low. A dozen would mean the entire city's charmed. Try a hundred. Maybe more. And that number would just keep on growing. They start out weak, you know. Then they get stronger."

He considered her words, thinking what it would take to bring the monster down. "How much stronger?"

She shrugged. "Exponentially. If it were still alive, I doubt you'd be able to kill it."

Lissa leaned forward. "Are you saying Rand killed it while it was weak?"

"Yeah, he's dead," she said flatly. "Kiril saw the body. He couldn't get to it, though. Boyd's friends had come in to clean up the mess."

Rand sat up straighter. "Tell me he followed them."

"Shit, Rand, you think we're idiots over here? My brother may not be a PI, but he works with me. Yeah, he followed." She glanced toward the door that led to her inner offices. And where, Rand was certain, Kiril stood, ready to come to his sister's aid if Rand or Lissa looked at her funny.

"Where did they go?" he asked, because wherever it was, that was where he was going next.

"A goddamned heliport."

"Shit," Rand said. "He lost them."

"Sorry."

"I saw the guy turn into a damn whirlwind. He couldn't follow a helicopter?"

"It doesn't work that way. But at least we got new information. Now we know they have money and other resources."

"Pull the log for the heliport."

"Already did," she said. "It doesn't show any arrivals or departures last night."

"They're under the radar," Rand said.

"Shadow?" Lissa asked.

"Maybe," Rand said, "but they smelled human."

"I'm human," Petra said. "Well, more or less."

Rand stood. He'd accomplished everything here that

he needed to. "You're really not going to tell me what happened to that guy."

She looked at the floor. "I'm really not."

Lissa stood up, her fingers brushing Rand as she stepped past him toward Petra. "Is it a curse?"

Petra's chin jerked up, her eyes both defiant and scared. "Why do you say that?"

"I—" Lissa cut herself off, her brow furrowing. "I'm sorry, I don't know why. Something in my memory—in my past—but I can't get to it."

"You know about curses? About this kind of curse?" Petra leaned forward, her expression animated.

"When you touch someone," Lissa said. "Or when they touch you. That's when it happens."

"Yes," Petra said, excited. "Yes, that's it. What do you know?"

Lissa squeezed her eyes shut in concentration, then opened them and glanced helplessly at Rand. "I'm sorry. I can't remember, but—"

"You'll keep trying?"

There was pity in Lissa's smile, and she nodded. "Of course. Of course, I will."

Petra drew in a breath. "Thank you." After a second, she shook herself and returned her attention to Rand. "So, you've got the card handled. What do you want me doing?"

"Doyle," he said.

"What about him?"

"I made a deal with him—with Division, actually. We're sharing information now."

Petra's brows lifted, and beside him, Lissa's eyes were wide. Not surprising. Rand knew damn well he wasn't the type that played well with others. Obviously, it showed.

"Gotta admit I wasn't expecting that," Petra said.

Lissa licked her lips. "And you trust them? To share evidence with you?"

He grinned. "You've zeroed in on my problem," he said, shifting his attention back to Petra. "I don't think they will. Not completely."

"Why not?" Lissa asked.

"Because I wouldn't."

"You want me to keep tabs," Petra said.

"Especially on Doyle. He's point on the investigation. What he knows, I want to know."

"I'm on it."

"Good."

Lissa tucked her hand in his, and his fingers folded around hers. Joined together. He didn't pull away. Didn't even think of pulling away.

Petra watched, her eyes on their intertwined fingers, her expression achingly sad until the weakness stopped and she met his eyes, all business. "I'll have a report for you by tomorrow. You know the way out."

She left them standing there as she crossed the room toward the doorway leading to the hall and her private office. She slipped inside, closed the door, and leaned against it. Then she clenched her hands into fists and squeezed her eyes tight.

"Petra," Kiril said, his voice full of understanding.

"Don't." She drew in a breath, then let it out slowly. "I'm going to grab my bag, and then let's go find Doyle."

By the time she and Kiril left her home office, Rand and Lissa were no longer in sight.

They walked down the block in silence, then turned the corner on autopilot, with Petra's mind going somewhere close to a million miles an hour as she mentally sorted through contacts, wondering whom she could call at PEC who'd be willing to do her a favor and shoot her Doyle's current location. Barnaby wouldn't know, but maybe he had a friend in dispatch?

It was worth a shot, and it wasn't until she was digging in her bag for her cellphone that she realized Kiril was no longer beside her. She turned sharply, and caught the last second of his fall, when his large body collapsed to the ground, a huge dart protruding from his throat.

She didn't scream—there was no time for that.

All she could do was run.

Except there was nowhere to go.

CHAPTER 32

The day was going by fast—too fast, considering that Rand had a shitload of work to do. But not fast enough, considering he was seeing Lissa later.

After they visited Petra, Lissa had called in to work and discovered that her new girl really did need help with the inventory. Rand had detoured to Orlando's, and his cheek still tingled from the kiss she'd given him before slipping out of the car. "Will you come tonight?" she'd asked. "I can promise you a seat at the owner's table."

He'd hesitated only an instant, but she'd seen it, and she'd given him a firm shake of her head. "No. Don't think about it. Don't second-guess it. Just come."

Yeah, he'd see her tonight. No doubt about it.

But first, he had to make some serious headway.

He'd called in Bixby, wanting the little cat's tech-spertise, and now the wiry were-cat was cross-legged on the floor, three laptops forming a circle around him, the peripherals he'd brought with him wired to the machines, stretched out like a spiderweb. Bixby would say that was accurate; he was hunting, after all.

While Bixby tried to hack into the information contained on the card-key's magnetic strip, Rand worked the Boyd angle. Petra was right that he'd kept connections, but for this he didn't need to use them. He'd kept

318 ♦ J. K. Beck

passwords, too, and made sure that his sources regularly updated his information.

Now he was poking around in payroll files, looking for anyone named Boyd who was drawing a military pension in the area. It was only a guess, but in Rand's experience, most of the private Black Ops soldiers did their time in the legit military, learning the toys, seeing the world, and building their connections. They'd retire when they'd done their mandatory twenty, go private, and watch the money roll in. With any luck, Boyd was cut from that mold.

It was slow business, but he found half a dozen Boyds in the L.A. basin. That only got him partway to his goal. Another hour of searching led him to an Arnold Boyd, an employee with Meer Consulting, a firm owned by Grayson Meer. Rand followed that thread, learned that Meer was a former Delta Team leader, and figured he'd crossed the line from long shot to damn solid lead. He still didn't have answers, but with any luck, he was closing rank on the bastards who jumped him.

He picked up the phone and dialed the number listed on Meer Consulting's Franchise Tax Board filings. He got voice mail, a perky young woman asking him to please leave a message and someone on staff would return his call as soon as possible. He glanced at the clock. Already after five, so it wasn't unusual that he wasn't getting through. But he didn't want to wait until tomorrow to find Boyd or Meer Consulting.

Which left him only one thing to do.

Time to take a little drive.

♦

Rand's trip to Montclair and the offices of Meer Consulting accomplished two things. First, it told him that Meer Consulting was nothing more than a damn paper shell, as evidenced by the fact that its supposed office was located inside a private postal mailbox. Second, it proved that Boyd's buddies were still interested in Rand—*that* he knew not because of the mailbox but because of the sedan that had tailed him all the way from Van Nuys.

He even considered slamming on the brakes, startling the tail in the silver Toyota Camry, and offering to exchange phone numbers. That way Rand could just call them if he actually started to make serious progress toward the bad guys, and they wouldn't have to waste valuable time on useless surveillance.

In the end, he decided he wasn't that magnanimous. More entertaining to have a little fun with them, and as soon as he hit West Covina, he kicked it up to ninety, cut over three lanes of traffic, and exited the freeway. He kept his eye on the rearview and saw the Camry sideswipe an orange barrel, splashing water everywhere as the car fishtailed, the driver trying to gain control while making a hard right onto the exit ramp.

They made it down to the surface streets, and Rand almost applauded. Messy, but they made it.

He'd see how they did with a few more obstacles.

As soon as the light turned green, he raced down the road, turning at every light, making his way north toward the toll road. His tail was sticking like glue, all effort at nonchalance abandoned after the fiasco at the exit ramp. Just to make sure they were on their toes, Rand pulled a hard U-turn in the middle of traffic, headed in the opposite direction, and waved politely at the startled face of the Camry's driver, who was already slamming on his brakes and spinning to follow.

He kept the chase up through West Covina, but by the time he reached the city's edge he was bored with the game. He dropped back down to the speed limit, then slammed on his brakes and turned. Around him, cars veered into other lanes, trying not to crash into their neighbors. Rand wasn't concerned about them, though. All he wanted was to get his hands on the son of a bitch who was following him, and he jammed the accelerator down and headed straight for the Camry.

He hit it head-on, his Range Rover barely even feeling the crunch. He got out of the car and headed toward the now-steaming Camry and the bug-eyed little human in the front seat.

"Just sit tight, little dude," he said. "Ain't nowhere for you to go."

About that, though, Rand was wrong. His quarry shoved his door open and burst into the street, pulled a gun, and fired three shots directly at Rand.

Rand dove for the pavement. Silver bullets would kill him, and regular bullets were no picnic. Either way, he was avoiding them.

He was down for only a few seconds, but it was enough. His quarry yanked open the door of a nearby car, shoved his gun into the driver's face, and ripped the hapless woman out of the vehicle. Then he sped off, with Rand spitting and cursing behind him.

He was still cursing when he got back to the Goat. And the fact that he'd gotten a good look at the ratty little driver's face didn't lessen his overall foul mood one bit. He shoved open the car door, then slammed it shut once he was on the pavement. He smacked his palm against the door so hard he left a dent. Dammit. *Goddammit!*

He stood, breathing deep, trying to get a handle on both anger and frustration, and as he did, his phone rang, and the frustration evaporated when he saw Lissa's name on the display.

"Hey," she said, her voice soft. "I miss you."

Dear God, he missed her, too.

"How's the new girl doing? Inventory taken care of?"

"It took two hours, but we got it worked out. Hang on, okay?" There was a shuffle, then her voice lowered, as if she'd put her hand over the mouthpiece. "Can't you see I'm on the phone? No, tomorrow does me no good. Well, I don't know. Reroute power from the upper levels. Something. But I need electricity to run this business." She came back on the line, the frustration erased from her voice. "Sorry. It's been one of those days. I didn't want to bother you, I just wanted—oh, hell. I just wanted to hear your voice."

He looked at the dent he'd made in the body of the car. "I'm glad you called," he said. And the miracle was, he meant it. "What's the trouble?"

"Wish I knew. For some reason, there's no power in any of my subterranean rooms. I've got electricians here, and—well, it's a mess. Doesn't matter. I'll get it worked out. What about you? Anything solid? Any new leads?"

"Maybe, but I won't bore you with it right now. Sounds like you've got your hands full."

"Unfortunately that's true. Sorry."

"No," he said. "Don't be."

"Rand?"

"Yes?"

"I'll see you later?"

"Hell, yes." He clicked off, the anticipation of seeing her rising within him, and he forced himself to beat it back even as something she'd said tugged at him and wouldn't let go.

Subterranean.

He frowned, thinking about the New York subway tunnels in which Sergius had lived.

Sergius was still out there, and still one hell of a likely suspect.

Time to go vampire hunting.

◊

Nick had come back to the Red Line tunnel, as much because he wanted to continue the search for Serge as because he wanted to be alone. Underground. Doing something so that he wasn't thinking about Lissa.

So far, that plan wasn't working very well. Lissa was filling his thoughts, and he'd made no progress in the hunt for his friend.

He was under Hollywood now, and about to give up. There were rats along this stretch of track. Rats and humans, too. At least a dozen, their faces grimy and their bodies reeking.

Their eyes peered at him from the shadows, and they held no fear.

If Serge had been here, they would have been afraid.

Hell, if Serge had been here, they would have left.

Nick sighed. He might as well get out of there, too.

He turned to head back the way he came, and one of the faces materialized from the shadows. A face he knew.

Vincent Rand.

"We have to stop meeting like this," Rand said.

Nick frowned. Luke had told him that Rand had suggested he work directly with the PEC, a suggestion Nick applauded as it put Lissa even more in the clear. But Rand's presence down in the tunnels was disturbing. Rand himself had told the team that an Outcast was behind the rumor, and yet very few weren were comfortable living belowground, especially when there were acres of forestland in the area.

No, Nick's best guess was that Rand was searching for a rogue vampire. And that meant he was searching for Sergius.

He took a step toward Rand. "I understand you've teamed up on the investigation about the dead humans."

If Rand was surprised that Nick knew that, he didn't show it.

"I made the suggestion. You're involved with that?"

"I play a small role," Nick said, thinking of Lissa. And thinking also of this man's hands on her. That wasn't something he wanted to think about, so he forced himself to keep his mind on his goal of getting Rand the hell out of the tunnels. He glanced up toward the surface. "Want to grab a beer and compare notes?"

Rand narrowed his eyes, studying Nick's shadowed face. "You're not an investigator."

"No."

Rand considered the answer, along with the question

of what the hell a vampiric *kyne* was doing slumming in the subway tunnels. There were a number of possible explanations, but only one felt right to Rand. "You're searching for the rogue. For Sergius."

A pause, then, "I am."

"By yourself. Without Doyle or a RAC team or any sort of backup."

Nick met his eyes, and Rand could read nothing on the vampire's face.

"He's your friend," Rand said, and again the vampire remained silent. "And what will you do if we find him?"

Nick sighed, the sound hollow and full of pain. "Right now, I only hope that I do find him."

"Is he behind the murders?"

"I don't know," Nick said, and there was truth in his words, but also fear.

"Where have you looked?"

"You made your deal with Division," Nick said. "Not with me." He glanced back down the tunnel. "I think it's time I leave."

"Wait."

Nick halted, looking at Rand expectantly, and Rand realized he had nothing to say. He hadn't called the vampire back to discuss the rogue. He'd called him back because this ancient vampire knew Lissa. He represented her club. And, considering the expression on Nick's face the night when Priam had died, he cared for her.

And what about Lissa? Did she care for him, too? This vampire who searched the night for his friend?

He wondered how she could not, and he waited for jealousy to spark within him.

It didn't.

She cared for him. *For Rand.* As unbelievable as that was, he'd won.

He looked again at Nick. "I'll buy you that beer if you want."

Nick studied him, then nodded. "Let's go."

They were heading back down the tunnel, scouring the shadows for signs of Serge as they moved toward the service entrance, when a small voice interrupted them.

"Are you looking for someone?" The boy couldn't be more than twelve.

"Maybe," Rand said. "Seen anyone unusual?"

The boy shook his head, and Rand saw something just below his collar. Nick saw it, too, and he reached out and grabbed the boy's filthy chin.

"Hey!"

Nick ignored him, then tugged the collar down. *Punctures.*

"Who did that to you?" Rand asked.

The boy frowned. "Did what?"

Rand opened his mouth to explain, but Nick held up a hand to stop him, and Rand understood. Sergius had been feeding down here, but taking the trouble to tweak the memories of his walking, talking Happy Meals.

"Never mind," Nick said. "Tell me this. Is there someone who lives down here that keeps to himself?"

"Just the strange man. But he left."

"How is he strange?"

The boy shrugged.

"All right then, when did he leave?"

"When they brought their nets and took him," the boy said, and Nick's eyes turned cold as ice.

"Who?"

But the boy just shook his head, then ran off into the dark.

"They have him," Rand said. "They managed to take Sergius."

Nick's expression turned dangerous. "But who are they?"

"That's what we need to find out." He thought of Boyd and Meer and realized it was time to share what he knew. "Let's go find Doyle and I'll tell you what else I've learned."

Nick's cellphone rang, and he glanced at the display. "Luke," he said, then answered the call. A moment later, he snapped the phone shut. "Come on," he said. "I found Doyle."

"Where?"

"With the latest victim."

CHAPTER 33

The sun had only recently dipped beneath the horizon, and the world was painted in shades of gray as Nick watched as Doyle laid one hand on the body's chest and the other on his forehead. A young man this time, probably no more than twenty. His throat had been ripped open quite recently—two violent, messy punctures. A vampire wound, yes, but not one made with any sort of finesse. And that same disturbing ash was piled up right next to the body.

A scent lingered in the air, familiar. Too familiar, thought Nick as he pushed down a rising sense of dread. Luke and Sara were standing a few feet away, Rand right beside them, talking to the Division agent who'd discovered the body. Nick caught Luke's eye, and knew that his friend had caught the scent, too.

Serge.

He clenched his fists, digging his nails into the flesh of his palms, forcing himself to stay calm. Forcing his daemon back down. *Goddammit all to hell.*

"Any particular reason you're here?" Tucker asked, sidling up next to Nick.

"Get the fuck out of my face," he snapped.

Tucker's eyes went wide, and he took a step back, his hands up to ward off the lunatic vampire. "Shit, man, take a fucking pill."

"Luke called me."

"We don't usually let defense attorneys wander the crime scenes," Tucker commented. "Bad enough you brought that one along," he added, with a nod toward Rand.

Nick regarded the human. "And here I thought you all were playing nice together."

"As nice as we know how," Tucker countered. "But that doesn't extend to defense attorneys wandering the crime scene."

"My client isn't a suspect in this investigation," he said shortly. "She's cooperated fully with you people, and yet you still haven't officially cut her loose. Consider me your official pain in the ass."

Tucker snorted. "You got that right."

On the ground in front of them, Doyle gasped, then fell back. Tucker rushed forward, helping to steady his partner.

"What did you see?" Nick asked.

Doyle squinted up at him, his face pale and pasty, his eyes burning orange. Nick had the impression that Doyle wanted to toss a few choice insults his way, but didn't have the energy.

Above, a black falcon circled. Nick glanced up at it. *Tiberius.*

"We may have gotten lucky," Doyle said, then sucked in air. "Damn, that one wiped me out."

"I'll take care of you," Tucker said. "Just tell us what you saw."

Sara and Luke came up to stand beside Nick, Rand with them. "He saw something?" Rand asked.

"Apparently."

"A female," Doyle said, and Nick let out a breath in relief. Maybe Serge's scent was there, but he hadn't killed the victim.

"Our vic saw her across the park." Doyle's voice was flat, as if it was all he could do to push the words out. "She was running. He was . . . worried. His head was full of wolves and moons and black capes and fangs. But the bitch jumped him from behind, and that's all we got."

"Could be a lead," Nick said. "More likely it's just a human worrying about the bogeyman behind him in the night."

"You think I don't know that?" Doyle retorted. "But the thoughts were there, and we have to follow up. Werewolves," he added, looking hard at Rand.

"And capes and fangs," Rand retorted. "Sounds like Hollywood-inspired fears to me. Not reality."

"Maybe," Doyle said, as Nick frowned, considering the possibility that Serge had been taken by a group of werewolves. It wasn't completely out of the realm of possibility.

Tucker hooked his arms under Doyle's and hoisted his partner to his feet. "He went deep. I need to take care of him."

"Go," Sara said.

"Hold on," Doyle said, his attention turning to Rand. "Promised your little PI I'd share information. Guess I don't need to bother, huh?"

Rand's mouth pulled into a tight smile. "No," he said. "I guess you don't."

♦

"Did I not tell you a weren was behind this?" Tiberius said. He stalked from one side of the conference room to the other as Luke, Sara, and her boss, Nostramo Bosch, the head of the violent crimes division, stood in the doorway, their eyes on the master vampire.

Doyle sat in one of the chairs, leaning back, his body drained of energy and his temper sharp. Tiberius had convened this little confab, and Doyle had come as ordered, even though he needed to get to Orlando's. Needed to get some soul.

But Tiberius was calling the shots, and he'd dragged Doyle's sorry ass back to Division. Doyle knew why, too, and he didn't like it. The fanged bastard was going to start poking his bony fingers into the details of Doyle's investigation.

It rankled whenever anyone fucked with the way he ran a case. It rankled more when the one doing the fucking was a bloodsucker.

"The victim saw fangs along with the weren images," Sara said. "We still can't be certain a weren is key."

"*I'm* certain," Tiberius growled, and Doyle almost laughed at the way Sara stepped back, pressing her body against Luke. She wasn't that far from being human, and Tiberius was intimidating even to the most seasoned shadow world citizen.

"The weren who was at the scene," Tiberius continued. "He is Gunnolf's man?"

"Rand," Luke said.

"And his thoughts? The succubus was not able to retrieve them?"

"She tried," Doyle said. "There wasn't enough soul."

"A soulless weren. Why does that not surprise me?"

"He has a soul," Sara explained. "But it's tattered. She would have had to take all of it in order to access his thoughts."

"Then that is what she will have to do."

"No," Sara said. "You can't—"

"He killed Jacob Yannew? The weren who named Gunnolf for these crimes?" The question hung in the air, obviously rhetorical. "How very odd that Mr. Rand hasn't been charged with that crime."

"We decided it made more sense to see what he knew," Sara said, but her voice had lost its punch. She knew where Tiberius was going with this as much as Doyle did.

"And yet the succubus is no longer enticing him. Interesting."

"You really want to send her back in?" Doyle asked. "Let her rip out his entire soul?" He'd raised that very possibility to Tucker not that long ago. Faced with the possibility of actually doing it, though, Doyle thought that the plan seemed reprehensible. He knew better than anyone what kind of shit could happen when you took an entire soul.

"He is a weren," Tiberius said dismissively. "Apparently only a hairsbreadth away from being soulless." He looked at each of them in turn. "And I don't trust him."

"No," Sara said, turning to Bosch. "The PEC cannot possibly condone this." There was a plea in her voice. "Taking his soul is bad enough, but we just agreed to work with him. Luke?" she added, turning to her husband.

But Luke merely shook his head.

Bosch stepped forward. "On this matter, Tiberius's

decision is final." He turned to Doyle. "Go see her," he said. "Tell her that we're still open to her plea. But if she wants to stay out of prison, we'll need her full cooperation. Tell her the mandate comes from Tiberius himself."

♦

Doyle lay back on the couch in the feeding room at Orlando's as the girl fixed the mask over his face and hooked the bottle up to the release valve.

"You're all set," she said. She ran a finger down his arm. "Do you want me to stay?"

He shook his head. Some soul-eaters liked the feel of flesh beside them as they took nourishment through the feeding machine. Doyle didn't. This wasn't real, and a woman beside him wasn't going to trick his brain into thinking that his mouth was on hers rather than on the tube, that he was breathing in her soul rather than one extracted last week or last month or last year.

He did this only because he had to. Because the law wouldn't let him take a stranger on the street except under certain dire circumstances. And without a diet of souls he would lose his gift. For that matter, he'd lose his life.

He closed his eyes and breathed deep, drawing it in, relishing the tang of it.

It wasn't real, but it also wasn't terrible.

The setup at Orlando's was nice compared to some feeding rooms. Soft music. A soft bed. A comfortable feeding mask.

He drew in the last wisps of soul, then just lay there for a while, feeling strength returning. He hated what he was—what he had to do—but he'd learned to live with it. And in moments like this—in the actual feeding—he had to admit that he liked it a little. He sincerely doubted a human ever felt so good.

His mother sure as hell never had. Or if she had, she'd kept it to herself. Right up to the day she'd impaled herself on his father's sword.

Sitting up, he pushed thoughts of his mother out of his mind. He didn't like to think of her, and right now he had plenty of other fucked-up things to focus on. Like finding Lissa.

Like telling her she was going to have to take Rand's soul.

♦

"No," Lissa said into the phone. "I'm not interested in receiving a credit to my account. I'm interested in service. If I don't have power to all parts of my business, I lose profits. Yes, I appreciate the speed with which you got three of the rooms back up and running, but I need a permanent, complete solution. I need a tech here now, and I need him to stay around the clock until this is resolved. Well, then I'll find another company to deal with. Good. Thank you. I knew I could count on you."

She put the phone down feeling the satisfaction of fixing something broken. But Orlando's was easy. Rand, she thought, was harder.

His soul was so ripped up, and he knew it. Hell, he thought he deserved it.

She didn't.

She'd seen firsthand the way he'd stepped in to help

her, even before he knew her. She'd seen his fear at the possibility a monster still roamed L.A. His life had been hell, she'd grant him that, and he'd stayed in a marriage he shouldn't have. He wasn't perfect, not by a long shot, but he felt perfect to her. He felt like he fit, as if when she cast a shadow, it was shaped like Rand.

He was dangerous—she could see that easily enough. And there was a wild rage lurking just beneath the surface. But he held the leash. She'd seen the control in the eyes of the wolf. But in the eyes of the man, she'd seen only the blanket of ice that he believed he had to wrap tight around him in order to keep from exploding.

He needed to explode, she thought. Needed to lose it, if only so he'd realize that he could control it.

She sighed. In so many ways he was like her, climbing his way out of a life spent in hell. And she'd be damned if she'd feel guilty about the way she'd been in the past. Maybe she wasn't a saint, but she'd told Nick the truth—she wasn't Elizabeth anymore.

And Rand wasn't the beast he thought he was, either. If he'd only realize that, his soul could start to heal.

Stop it.

She'd come into her office to work, not brood, and since she'd spent the afternoon dealing with a multitude of crises, she was still buried in paperwork. She needed to get busy.

She was frowning at a tax bill, and cursing the fact that she paid taxes to both the state and the Alliance, when someone rapped sharply at her door. "In," she called, almost too eagerly. But really, anything to avoid thinking about taxes.

She was expecting Marco or Rhiana. Instead, she saw Doyle.

"Oh. You." She looked him over. His skin was flushed, and he wasn't as slouched as the last time she'd seen him. "I'm assuming this is a professional call? You've been downstairs?"

"Yup. Nice place you've got here."

"I know."

He took a seat in one of her guest chairs, then stretched his legs out. "And this is a professional call. Just not your profession."

"I see." She picked up the letter opener and twirled it between her fingers. When she realized what she was doing, she stopped, fumbling as she put it back down on the desk. She didn't want him to realize she was rattled, but she had a feeling it was too late for that. "What do you want?"

"I need you back with Rand. I need you in his head."

A chill swept over her.

"I thought he was working with you now."

"You thought right."

"But—"

"Orders come straight from Tiberius. Not my call to make." He stood up, then pointed at the window that overlooked Orlando's main floor. "Nice operation. Would be a shame to have to turn it over to someone else. But you can't run a place like this from prison. Nope. Don't think that would go over at all."

Her entire body shook. Not from fear, but from anger, and she clenched her fists at her side, because if she didn't, she'd surely claw his eyes out. "Get out of my office."

"Tomorrow," he said. "You get inside that wolf's head by sundown tomorrow, or this deal is off the table." His shoulders sagged, and for a moment his face seemed weary. "That's the way it is, kid."

He didn't wait for an answer, which was a damn good thing, as she couldn't breathe.

Prison. Holy shit, she was going to end up in prison.

The door clicked behind Doyle, and Lissa stood, then started pacing, her movements fueled by anger and fear. Her girls, her club. What the hell was going to happen to them?

She pressed her hands against the glass and looked down at Orlando's, letting its rhythm wash over her. She wanted to curse Priam for starting this shit, but it wasn't him—it was her. She'd stolen and she'd blackmailed and she'd walked that line, and all the while she'd thought she was oh-so-righteous for doing it. But she wasn't righteous. She was a criminal, the same as any other, and the fact that she'd pulled a few girls out of a few shit holes didn't change that.

She'd do it all over again, though. About that, she was absolutely certain.

Looking up, she caught her own reflection in the glass, and promised herself she wouldn't cry. She could wallow later. Right now, she needed to make a phone call.

Nick answered on the first ring, then cursed when she told him about Doyle's visit.

"Goddamn Tiberius," he said.

"So you think it's really true? Tiberius insisted?"

"Yeah," Nick said. "I think it's true." She heard him

draw in a breath and imagined him pacing. He did that, she remembered, when he needed to think.

"What are you going to do?" Nick finally asked.

For a moment, she was so startled she couldn't answer. "What the hell do you think I'm going to do? I can't do what Doyle asks. Do you really think I could do that to Rand?"

"I've seen you do worse."

"Goddamn it, Nicholas. You either be my advocate, or you don't. But we are not playing that game."

There was silence on the other end, then a brief "I'm sorry."

"You ought to be."

"Have you considered what's going to happen to your girls?"

"Of course I have. And I've considered what would happen to him if I took his soul. You know what Claude did. You saw those pictures."

"Rand's practically there, though, isn't he? You said yourself he has no soul."

"He's not hopeless."

"Well, that's great news for him, but it puts a bit of a damper on the entire rest of your life."

"What if he just tells me what he knows? He's already told me about the investigation. What if I just ask him?"

"You've been seeing him?"

"Yes," she snapped. "Will Doyle go for that?"

"It's a shot, but I'm guessing no. He's not going to believe you have everything unless you pull it straight from his head."

"That's not going to happen," she said. "I couldn't.

Not on purpose. Not to anybody, and certainly not to a man I—" She cut herself off, realizing what she was about to say.

"A man you love," Nick said, the words slow. "No, you're not a woman who could ever betray the man she loves."

She closed her eyes, stung as much by his words as by her own realization. She hung up the phone. "Good-bye, Nick," she said, but the words came after the handset was already down, and Lissa's thoughts were across town, with Rand. With the man she loved.

CHAPTER 34

Rand pulled into the Slaughtered Goat parking lot only a few seconds before Caris brought her Porsche squealing in behind him.

"About time," he said, glancing up at the darkened sky. "I've been waiting to hear back from you."

"I had a rough night. Crashed all day."

"I'm assuming you didn't make any progress. Serge isn't in the forest. He's been living in the subway tunnels."

"Oh, I've made progress," she said, looking hard at him. "But not about Serge. About Xeres."

Rand tensed. "What about him?"

"His father is a goddamned Outcast."

"Bullshit. Xeres is an orphan. Gunnolf found him at age four."

"Gunnolf took him at age four," she corrected. "Right after he shunned Xeres's father. Apparently Santiago started getting up close and personal with some humans. Got all buddy-buddy with some military dude."

She had Rand's full attention. "Military?"

"Apparently."

"Who?"

"I don't know. It's probably in his file. Word is Santiago started cluing in his human buddies about the shadow world. Bad mojo, you know. Not to mention a violation of the Covenant."

"If you're wrong—"

She held up her phone. "I've already called Gunnolf. He thought Carlos Santiago died years ago. But it looks like the lupine bastard was just covering his tracks. Turns out he's been living in the Angeles National Forest for a decade. Moved here about the time Xeres did."

"And Xeres knows all this?"

At the question, she deflated a little. "I don't know, but it fits, Rand. You know damn well it fits."

He couldn't argue. It did fit. A weren male raised by a man who tells him that he's an orphan, then he finds out that not only was that a lie, but that his foster father was actually the one who sent Daddy Dearest packing. Yeah, he could see how that might be a sore point for a werewolf in Xeres's shoes. Revenge was strong motivation, and the dead humans had the potential to seriously screw with Gunnolf. And if the ploy ended up taking Tiberius down, too, that was hardly going to overly bother a werewolf.

Santiago earned a spot high on Rand's suspect list, but Xeres was only tagged if he knew about his father. Not an easy thing to find out without asking all sorts of pesky, revealing questions.

Rand frowned, remembering how Xeres had brushed off Rand's suggestions that he hadn't pursued the Outcast angle hard enough and that he hadn't focused his attention deeply enough on the nearby national forest lands. "How did you learn this?"

"I saw a picture."

He waited for her to say more. She didn't.

"Where, Caris?"

He watched as the debate raged over her features.

"Where?" he repeated.

"In Santiago's cabin," she said.

"Coordinates," Rand said. "Give them to me."

She pulled out her phone and shot him the GPS information. He checked to make sure his phone registered the location, then nodded. Carlos Santiago would soon have a houseguest.

He turned his attention back to the question at hand. "And you were there why? And don't tell me you were looking for Sergius. If you're going to feed me bullshit, at least try to come up with a better story."

"I was looking for him," she said. "Santiago, I mean."

"I assigned Xeres the Outcast search." Quite possibly a mistake, if Caris's intel was correct, but at the moment that wasn't the point.

"I had my reasons," she said. "And they have nothing to do with the dead humans."

"Caris—"

"*No.*" she lifted her chin and squared her shoulders. "Gunnolf's ass is on the line here, and you should know that I wouldn't do anything—*anything*—to risk that. Why the hell do you think I'm coming to you now? I could have just kept my mouth shut and pretended like I'd never seen the guy. You wouldn't have known the difference."

About that, he believed her.

"And Santiago? Is he aware you made the connection?"

She shook her head. "No. I don't think Papa Wolf

realized it clicked for me. He was, ah, distracted as I was looking around the cabin."

Rand nodded. If that was true, the elder weren wouldn't have contacted Xeres to give him a heads-up.

"The information's solid, Rand," Caris continued. "Xeres is dirty, and this is the biggest lead we've had. Say 'thank you, Caris,' and do with it what you will."

"Thank you, Caris," he said. And then, as she headed back to her car, he pulled out his phone and called Xeres.

Maybe Caris was wrong. Or maybe Xeres knew the truth about his father, but hated the Outcast.

Or maybe the weren was dirty as shit.

Possibilities stacked on possibilities, but he needed facts, and the fastest way was to go to the source himself.

"Yo," he said when Xeres answered his phone. "What have you got going on tonight?"

"Hanging. Working. Same old shit. I've got a list of Outcasts known to live in Ventura County. One of them might have decided to put on his dancing shoes and haul his ass down to L.A. But I gotta tell you, I don't think we're ever going to catch a fish with this line."

"You may be right. I'm coming by," Rand said. "Got a lead I want to bounce off you. See if you can make anything of it."

"I'll be here."

Rand hung up, frowning. There'd been nothing suspicious in Xeres's voice, but nothing to confirm he was squeaky clean, either. He glanced down the road in the direction Caris had traveled, an Outcast named Carlos Santiago filling his mind.

A black Hummer careened toward him, stopping only inches from Rand's feet. The door opened, and Murray stepped out, shaking his head. "Nerves of steel, dude. You didn't even flinch."

"Figured you're too much a pussy to run me over."

"Play nice, soldier boy. I'm the man with intel you want."

Immediately, Rand dropped the bullshit. "Spill."

Murray looked around, confirming that they were alone in the dark. "They've got a CI on you. Have for a while, actually."

Rand's shoulders dropped. Petra had warned him about the possibility of a confidential informant. "I thought they might."

"Shit, man. You've got me risking my neck to get you intelligence and you already have a source inside?"

"A source outside, but it's effective. Not relevant anymore, though. Haven't you heard? I signed up to play nice with the devil."

"Yeah? Well, the devil is playing you, my friend. Division's keeping the CI active."

"No shit?"

Murray smiled thinly. "Forget playing with the devil. You need to play with the little bitch."

Bitch? "My source?"

Murray gave him a look that suggested Rand had lost it. "No, asshole. The CI."

"A woman?" He thought of Caris and tensed. Goddamn the bloodsucker. This whole song and dance about Xeres was just—

"Well, look at that," Murray said, watching Rand's face. "I'm not a fifth fucking wheel after all. Yeah, a woman. Not only that, a succubus. She's supposed to pull her crazy-ass mojo on you and—"

But Rand couldn't hear the rest over the howl of betrayal inside his head.

◆

"You fucking *lied* to me."

Lissa looked up from her desk, saw the fury on Rand's face, and started to go to him.

"No," he said, stalking toward her. "Stay."

She clenched her hands on the arms of her desk chair, her heart pounding. "What's going on? What happened?"

"This was all part of some fucking plan, wasn't it? You and me? You came to the Goat that first night with your sheen all nice and bright so that you could learn all about my investigation. Well, I guess it worked. I told you what I'm up to, introduced you to my PI. Anything else you need? Anything I've missed? Have you relayed all of that to your handler? Who is it? Doyle? Nick?"

Anger pushed her to her feet. "Don't you *dare* accuse me of betraying you—"

"*Goddammit.*" He picked up one of her guest chairs and tossed it across the room. It crumpled and buckled, the legs splintering. She cringed, and suddenly he was right there, one hand gripping her arm and holding her in place as he got right in her face. "Don't I *dare*?"

The crack of her palm against his cheek silenced him, and she stood there facing him, shaking with rage and hurt and the horrible unfairness of it all.

Numb, she jerked her arm free, her entire body raw. "Get out."

"Tell me the truth," he said, his voice low and slow and dangerous.

Anger boiled within her. He actually thought she could do that—thought she was still the kind of person she used to be. A woman who could betray a man she loved.

He didn't know her at all.

And she'd sure as hell been wrong about him.

"Talk," he said, his voice like fire.

Pain swelled up inside her, and she wanted to lash out. Wanted to hurt him like he'd hurt her.

She swallowed, and then she straightened her shoulders and looked him in the eye. "Yeah," she said, "it's true. But I wasn't supposed to just walk around like a puppy hoping you'd throw me scraps of information. No, I'm much better than that." She stood up and paced, knowing she should stop, should pull it back and tell him the truth, but she didn't care. Right then she was too numb to care.

"I get into heads, Rand. I take a piece of soul, and I take thoughts, too. I've been doing it for years, for lifetimes. And the PEC signed me up to do it on you."

He stared at her, not saying a word.

She held his gaze, forcing herself not to blink. Not to cry.

"Bitch," he whispered, and she cringed.

"Just get out," she said, listless.

"Screw that," he said. "You're coming with me."

"The hell I am."

"The hell you are." He looked at her, a hard, cold,

calculating look. "If the PEC wants to use you so bad, then that's exactly what we're going to do."

"What are you talking about?"

"Xeres," he said. "I need to get into the son of a bitch's head."

CHAPTER 35

Lissa sat in the back of the cargo van outside of Xeres's house in Venice Beach, hardly able to believe her life had gotten so twisted around. *Xeres.* Rand was actually sending her in to lie with another man. To take his soul, and his thoughts.

Before Rand, she hadn't considered sex particularly intimate. It was what she did, who she was.

That had changed with Rand, but now he was taking that intimacy and shoving it in her face, telling her without speaking that it didn't mean a thing to him. Or that it meant too much, and that she'd cut him too deep.

Either way, there was no going back, and the thought of Xeres's hands on her made her stomach roil.

"He likes her," Rand was saying. He was in the passenger seat, talking to Doyle, who was driving. Lissa was in the back with her advocate and Tucker. The plan was that she'd go in and do her thing, and all the while the van would be right outside, just in case Xeres had gotten wind of Rand's suspicions and tried to harm her. They'd all agreed that was doubtful, though. If he knew he'd been made, he would have bolted.

"She shouldn't have any problem getting in," Rand continued. "Doubt she'll even have to turn on the charm."

She caught Nick's eyes, saw the flare of anger in

them, and looked down at the ground. "Can I go now?" she asked. "I'd like to get this over with." Once she walked out of Xeres's house and told them what she knew, she was done. Charges dropped, game over. She wouldn't have Rand, but she'd have her life back, her club, her girls. It wasn't enough, but it was going to have to do.

Nick followed her out of the back of the van, and although she waited for Rand to open the passenger door and come around to them, he never did.

"You get in, you get out, and you're done," Nick said. He cupped her cheek in his hand. "Lissa? It's going to be all over soon."

She swallowed. "Yeah," she said. "Over."

Heat flashed in Nick's eyes. "Dammit, Lissa, he's not worth it."

She flinched at his words.

"Vincent Rand is one sorry son of a bitch. You're better than him. You know that, right?"

Her smile was thin. "You of all people should know that isn't true."

She didn't wait for his response, just turned and headed across the street, giving her back to the van and the men inside it.

Outside Xeres's door, she took a deep breath. An hour at the most. One hour out of all her lives, and then this would be over.

Her finger lingered over the buzzer, then pressed it firmly. She held her breath, waiting, half hoping he wasn't home, but that would just drag this out, and she really wanted it done.

Less than a minute later, she heard the locks turning.

"Well, hello beautiful."

As men went, he wasn't bad to look at. His hair was unkempt, and his smile was a little crooked, like he was constantly grinning at a secret he wouldn't share. He smelled good, too. Soap and cologne and a little bit of tobacco. Maybe this wouldn't be as horrible as she expected.

It would be, though. Because once his soul started to come out, she knew only too well that she would enjoy it. She'd revel in it, and his soul would build her up, caressing her, filling her, letting her touch ecstasy.

She'd enjoy it, all right, and she'd hate herself all the more for it.

"Rand sent me," she said, forcing a smile as she spoke her lines. "He said he was going to be later than expected, but that he remembered the way you looked at me." She tilted her head and gave him her most sultry smile. "He said you should consider me your reward for working so hard."

"Did he?" He held the door open for her. "In that case, it would be rude of me to say no."

♦

Inside the van, Rand flinched as Xeres's front door swung shut. She was in there, with him, and soon he'd be touching her. Soon, another man would be filling her.

Rand shouldn't care, he knew that.

But he did.

Frustrated, he climbed out of the passenger seat and into the back of the van, then jerked open the sliding door, stepping outside and leaning against the cool metal, his body blocked from Xeres's view by the bulk of the cargo van. He closed his eyes, took long deep breaths, and told himself to get the fuck over it.

He wasn't listening to himself.

Another door opened, then slammed shut, sending a tremor through the van. Footsteps, and then Nick was standing right in front of him, his now-familiar scent laced with both anger and frustration. *Yeah, well, welcome to the club, buddy.*

Rand kept his eyes closed. Nick might be *kyne,* and he might be Lissa's advocate, but right then he wasn't anything but a pain in Rand's ass.

"You're a complete asshole, you know that?"

A complete pain in the ass. Rand peeled open his eyes and faced the man who'd so succinctly spoken the truth. "What's your point?"

"Whatever you think she did to you, you're wrong."

"Am I?"

"Arrogant prick," Nick snarled. "Yes. You are. She was heading to prison because of you. Or didn't you know that?"

"Because she didn't get anything out of my head," Rand said. "Not for lack of trying."

"No," Nick said. "Because she refused to go back in and take whatever she could. You think the PEC gives a rat's ass about the state of your soul? They know what you are, Vincent Rand, and so do I."

"And what is that?"

"Someone unworthy of a woman like Lissa. She turned the deal down. The PEC has a list of charges on her as long as your arm—charges that will get her life in prison—but she still turned down the deal, because she wasn't willing to betray you. Personally, I think she made a mistake."

Nick's words hit Rand like a series of punches, but the last words struck the final blow. Not even the words so much, but the tone of Nick's voice.

"What did she do to you?"

Slowly, Nick looked up at him. "I know what betrayal looks like, Rand. And I know an idiot when I see one, too."

He turned, then headed back into the van, leaving Rand to stand there thinking about how he'd fucked up, and what he'd lost.

◆

This male was definitely susceptible, Lissa thought, and she was glad for it. She didn't want anything about this encounter to be real. She'd leave her own body if she could, but that wasn't one of her gifts. She had to stand there, and pretend, and be the object of this male's desire.

He was sweating slightly, his face flush with need as his fingers fumbled at the buttons of her shirt. Normally, she would take care of that herself, throwing a few teasing moves into the mix just to spice things up. But nothing about tonight was normal, and as much as she wanted this over, she couldn't actually bring herself to do anything to speed it up.

When the shirt was unbuttoned to her navel, he used his hands to push it open, exposing the curve of her breasts and the lace of her bra.

Lissa closed her eyes, feigning ecstasy, but really trying to hide.

And then the world exploded.

She opened her eyes to see a blurred fist smash into Xeres's nose, knocking the weren backward. Another second, and she identified the owner of the fist—*Rand*.

"What the fuck?" Xeres spat, back on his feet and rushing toward Rand, who stopped him with a punch to the jaw.

"Sorry, Xeres," Rand said in a low, firm growl. "Change of plans."

"Fuck that," Xeres said, circling Rand, looking for a punch.

"She's mine."

"Not tonight she's not."

"Now," Rand said. "Always."

"She came to me. You fucking sent her."

"I changed my mind."

"Not the kind of mistake you walk away from, my friend." Xeres leaped, knocking Rand backward over a coffee table. He kicked out and up, catching Xeres in the gut and landing him on his ass. Lissa ran forward, grabbed Rand's arm, and pulled him up.

"Don't!" she said. "He's under the sheen. He won't stop. Not while I'm here. He's too far under."

As if to prove her words, Xeres came once again. His fighting was sloppy, his reactions affected by the sheen, but he was still strong, and she didn't want to see Rand hurt.

Not something she needed to worry about, though. He met Xeres midflight and hauled the other male backward to the far wall. And then, in a quick, practiced move, Rand slammed the other weren's head hard against the brick of Xeres's small fireplace.

Xeres collapsed, out cold.

"Doyle's outside. They're going to haul him in for questioning."

"But—"

He didn't let her finish the question. Instead, he took her hand and tugged her toward a set of French doors that opened onto the bike path and then out to the beach. He stepped outside, the sky above them like a blanket of stars. She almost didn't follow. It would be easier to simply leave. Easier, but so much harder, too.

They walked in silence across the hard-packed sand. "I fucked up, Lissa," he said as they approached the surf. "I'm sorry."

"You did," she said. "But I shouldn't have lost my temper like that."

"I deserved it."

"Yeah. You did."

"I've never felt like this. You make me a little crazy."

She shot him a wry grin. "Trust me when I say the feeling is mutual."

He stopped walking, then held out a hand, just held it out there, but this wasn't about holding hands on the beach. He was extending an invitation to start over.

She wanted to take it. Dear God, she wanted so desperately to put her hand in his and have him pull her close.

But it wasn't that simple. Nothing was that simple, and when he'd cut her, the wound had gone deep.

He'd believed her capable of betraying him, and then he'd pushed her toward another man. And although his hand now urged her back to him, although she wanted to twine her fingers with his and tell him that everything was all right between them—she couldn't. It wasn't.

"I'm sorry, Rand," she said, and slowly he dropped his hand. "I'm sorry, but I need to go."

She turned. Then she walked away and didn't look back.

CHAPTER 36

The void that had been Lissa seemed to rise up and swallow him, and Rand reeled, punched in the gut by the knowledge that he'd screwed up. Bad. Possibly beyond repair.

Holy fuck, what had he done?

She'd been the brightest thing that had ever shined in his life, and he'd tossed it all away, telling her he didn't trust her. Getting in her face and accusing her of intentionally betraying him.

And the goddamned worst of it?

He'd actually fucking believed it.

Not now—not with hindsight being what it was.

Now he could look back and see her clearly, along with the truth.

Along with what he'd thrown away.

Goddammit.

He lashed out, bringing his fist down hard on the wooden stair rail, splintering the thing.

"Feel better?"

Rand whipped around to face Ryan Doyle, who stood in Xeres's back doorway.

"No." He turned back, then started walking toward the beach. He didn't know where he was going, and right then he didn't much care.

"Hold up there, lover boy," Doyle said. "We need to get back to Division."

"You don't need me to interrogate Xeres."

"Fuck Xeres," Doyle said. "It's about Petra."

Concern flared, cutting through the regret. "What about her?"

"She's missing," Doyle said. "But her brother's not. He's in the infirmary, out cold, with a few gallons of supercharged tranq coursing through him."

◊

"When was he brought in?" Rand asked, looking down at Kiril's lifeless form.

The doctor, a short female with graying hair and the no-nonsense attitude typical of female jinns, adjusted the IV leading into Kiril's arm. "A few hours ago. Transferred from Cedars."

"Cedars-Sinai?" The hospital was decidedly human. Technically, of course, Kiril was, too, but years of magic had changed him. Even now, unconscious, his body was sorting through its power, making a comfortable breeze fill the small room.

"We have a few medics working shifts there for exactly this reason. They monitor admissions and notify us if anyone from the shadow world comes through the system."

"How's he doing?"

"Stable. That's all I can say right now."

"Doyle said he was tranqued." The agent had parted ways with Rand as soon as they'd arrived at Division, sending Rand on to see the sorcerer first.

She pursed her lips in obvious disapproval. "Military-grade hardware—human military. I'm afraid his biology is unique, even to the shadow world. He didn't react well to the tranq. He's stable, and he's not in a coma, but I have no way to predict when he'll come to."

"But he will come to?"

She nodded firmly. "I believe so, yes."

He gave her his card. "Whoever did this to him has his sister. He may know something. The second he recovers, you call me."

"Don't worry."

But Rand was worrying. He'd hired Petra, and now she'd been taken, and by someone with military skills. That was no coincidence, and his attention was focused on Grayson Meer and Carlos Santiago. He'd intended to go after Santiago himself, but he'd detoured that plan when he'd decided to destroy his fucking life by believing the worst of Lissa.

Luke had gone instead, along with a RAC team, and so far Rand hadn't heard anything about the result of the raid.

In the meantime, he had Bixby in one of Division's many computer rooms, combing through old PEC records, trying to find proof that Santiago and Meer were in fact connected. To hear Bixby tell it, the task was near impossible. The older records weren't data-based, and he was having to blow through hundreds of pages of poorly scanned and awkwardly indexed documents. The only saving grace was that they'd been able to pull U.S. military records and knew where Meer had been stationed approximately thirty years prior.

"Not that knowing helps," Bixby had said when he'd

first dug into the records. "No, not much at all. Moved all over Asia, he did. Europe, too. Africa, even. And," he added, sounding unusually morose, "if we're wrong about Meer, this work may take twice as long."

Rand understood what he meant. They were narrowing Bixby's search based on the assumption—which was little more than wishful thinking—that Grayson Meer was in fact one of the men Santiago had cozied up to. But if they were wrong and those men weren't even in Meer's detachment, then they were wasting precious time.

He'd just finished listening to a fresh slew of Bixby's moans when he stepped off the elevator at the medical examiner's floor. As long as he was there, he wanted to discuss the mysterious ash with Orion himself.

The antechamber of the ME's area looked like any other reception area except that it was completely empty. He heard voices coming from the back, though, so he headed that direction, stopping when he got close and realized who was talking.

Caris.

"Are you certain?" she asked. "Because I'm running out of possibilities."

"He's not the guy. I'm sorry, but the blood work is clear. The werewolf you took this sample from is not the same one who made you."

Rand froze, trying to make sense out of the conversation. *Werewolf? Made her?*

Caris was a vampire. A powerful one at that. So what the fuck were they talking about?

"Dammit, Orion, this is not good news."

"I'm sorry, Car. I can't change what the sample says."

The sound of breaking glass echoed through the room.

"Well, fuck. Now I'm going to have to explain that in this month's requisition report."

"Sorry."

"Why not just embrace it? Do you know how rare you are? There used to be rumors about were-vamps, but that was centuries ago. You've got the strength and skill of both groups. You're stronger. You're—I don't know. You're special."

"Lucky me."

"I really am sorry."

"This isn't over. I'm going to find the weren who did this to me."

"I know you will. I just don't think you should."

Her footsteps clattered on the concrete floor, and when she slammed the door open, Rand stepped behind it, temporarily blocked from view before it swung shut again. If it closed, she'd see him, but she didn't turn around, and only when he was alone again did he breathe.

A vampire who'd been turned into a werewolf.

A vampire with one hell of a chip on her shoulder.

Were Santiago and Xeres nothing but a smokescreen she'd manufactured? It was a real possibility. A vampire like Caris might very well have an agenda of her own. Might even point the finger at an Outcast and his missing son if she thought it would deflect attention from her.

And what were a few dead humans if in the end they served her purpose?

He caught up to her in the parking garage, though he

wouldn't have if she hadn't paused to lean against a concrete post, eyes shut tight, her hands in fists.

"Caris."

The eyes flew open, first with shock, then with dismissal. "Not in the mood, Rand." She tossed her dark hair and started walking away.

"I heard."

She stopped.

"Pretty big secret," he said, trying to sound casual. "Interesting that you shared it with Orion. Or did you just need him for the lab work?"

For a moment, she didn't say anything, as if debating whether or not she could wriggle her way out of this. Eventually, she shrugged. "Lab work, sure. That and the fact that he's family."

Rand couldn't help the laugh. "Is he?"

"Yeah. He is. I'm his great-aunt. Or cousin. Or some such relative. Who can keep up? Only about a hundred times removed." She shrugged. "He's descended from my sister's family tree. I paid attention, even after I changed. Once I beat my damned daemon back, I didn't want to let go." She lifted her chin, her expression challenging. "You got a problem with that?"

"No."

She nodded, then focused on something over his shoulder rather than meet his eyes. "Are you going to keep my secret?"

"How long have you been this way?"

"It feels like forever." She squared her shoulders, then looked him dead in the eye. "I've been looking for the weren who did this to me for years."

"Does Gunnolf know?"

She nodded. "He's been helping me."

Rand thought about his suspicions. About the possibility that she'd been jerking his chain about Santiago and Xeres. He thought about it, but he didn't believe it.

"I'm leaving tonight," she added. "Going back to Paris."

"Are you?" He waited for the burn of envy—she was going home, and he was staying in hell.

Except L.A. didn't feel so much like hell anymore. Even after his royal fuckup, he didn't want to run the way he had after Alicia had died. He wanted to stay.

He wanted to try and make things right.

"Gunnolf has another lead for me," Caris said. "Looks like he and I are heading to Moscow."

"And when you find the one?"

She didn't answer, but her cold-blooded smile told him everything he needed to know. He couldn't fault her. If he ever ran across the weren male he'd met in that cold Balkan cave, Rand knew damn well he'd slit the bastard's throat. "Good luck," he said simply.

She hesitated, then nodded. "You, too, Rand. You're not the shit I thought you'd be."

From Caris, that was high praise indeed.

CHAPTER 37

Lissa had been standing in her office staring down at the floor of Orlando's for over an hour, yet for the first time in her life she didn't have a clue what was going on in her club. All she could think about was Rand. A particularly disturbing situation since right then she wanted nothing more than to forget him and ease the hollow, aching place inside her.

She pressed her forehead against the cool glass and forced herself to actually see the girls below. Anya, dancing playfully on the stage. Jayla, enticing the nearby men with her smile and her laugh and her sheen cranked up high. Rhiana, working the floor with practiced skill even though her worried eyes kept darting up toward Lissa's office.

Lissa wished she could reassure her friend, but what would she say? That everything would be okay? It wouldn't. That things would get back to normal? How?

Even if the PEC ignored the terms of her plea agreement and let her stay out of prison, the simple truth was that she needed soul to live. Needed to draw it in, let it twine around her. Let it fill her and nourish her and make her strong. She needed to be Lissa, the coveted owner of Orlando's, with the pick of any client who walked through that door.

But she didn't want to be. She couldn't imagine any man's touch except Rand's, and the thought of enjoying another man's soul . . .

Her mind drifted to Nick. She'd loved him once, and she was certain that he loved her still. He would have her—would hold her close and let her take her fill of soul. She knew it. And yet the thought only made her cringe.

She would rather fade away than lie with any man other than Rand.

She shivered, thinking of what Rhiana had said about why succubi weren't wired for love, because how could they love one man and be with another?

How, indeed?

She felt a tear trickle down her cheek, and she brushed it away. Oh, God, she did love him.

She loved him, and the hurt of losing him just about killed her.

Except she hadn't really lost him. She'd walked away.

In another life, she'd tossed love aside and hurt Nick. Now she was tossing it aside and hurting Rand. Did it matter that she was justified? That he'd hurt her first?

Did it matter that she was protecting her heart even while she was breaking it?

She heard someone at her door and turned sharply, prepared to tell Marco that she'd given specific instructions not to be disturbed.

Rand.

Her throat was so thick she almost couldn't speak. "How did you get up here? Marco wasn't supposed to let anyone—"

"I can be very persuasive." He stood still in the door-way, his posture and manner punctuating his words.

"Oh." She forced herself not to walk toward him.

He took a step backward. "Should I go?"

"No!"

"Good."

"Rand—"

"I love you, dammit," he said, and she wanted to pull the words around her like a blanket, then hide both of them away inside. "I love you," he repeated, stalking across the room until he was standing right in front of her, and she was having trouble breathing simply because of his proximity. "And I was a complete ass."

"You were," she said. "You really were."

"I've made a lot of mistakes in my life," he said. "This was the biggest."

She tilted her head back. "I know something about mistakes."

"How about forgiveness?"

A smile tugged at her lips. "I'm still feeling my way with that one."

"Can I help?"

Her heart twisted. He hadn't touched her yet, and all she could think about was closing the distance between them and sliding into the comfort of his arms. She wanted it so desperately she could taste it—but there was so much still looming between them.

She loved him, but would it be enough? Because this wasn't just about the way she felt—he had to match her. He had to grow his soul back. Because she couldn't lie with another man. Not even if it meant staying alive to be with Rand one more day.

And yet she couldn't walk away from him now, either.

She had to have faith. Faith in him, and in both of them together.

He was watching her face. "Please," he finally said. "Please come home with me."

Once again, he stretched his hand out to her, then simply stood there, the need on his face palpable, his self-recriminations still echoing in the room.

She tried to breathe, but her throat was so damn tight. He'd hurt her, more deeply than she would have thought possible, yet she couldn't imagine any other man filling her the way he did. She felt whole when she was with him, and being apart had hurt even more than the wound he'd inflicted.

She didn't know if she was being smart, and she didn't care. This wasn't business, it was love. And right then, she was going to trust her heart. The truth was, she couldn't do anything else.

She took a step forward, filling the void that loomed between them. Then she reached out, and closed her hand in his.

◆

"This is it," Rand said, opening the door and letting her move past him into the basic, boring living room. They'd said little on the ride over, mostly because he'd brought her here on the back of his bike, a method of transportation that he considered a blessing at the moment, because he'd been able to soak up the feel of her without having to talk.

Now that words were required, he felt awkward. As if they'd pulled off a bandage and the skin beneath, though healed, was still tender.

"It's nice," she said, and he winced. Very tender.

Not that he was complaining, but he wanted her back in his arms. Wanted to know by the feel of her skin against his that the desire—and the forgiveness—in her eyes was real.

"How's Kiril?" she asked.

"Stable. Unconscious, though."

"Is Xeres talking?"

"Swears he doesn't know a thing, and challenged us to prove otherwise."

"What about Santiago?" She'd learned all about the Outcast on the ride to Xeres's.

"No luck. By the time Luke got to his cabin, he'd split. Either he realized the heat was on, or Caris's stunt freaked him out enough to leave."

"I'm sorry." She was still standing, as if she wasn't quite sure what to do with herself.

"It's okay," he said. "I'll find him." He took a step toward her, relieved when she didn't move a reciprocal step back. "Right now, though," he said, grabbing the hem of her T-shirt and tugging her closer, "there's something else I have to do."

He caught her mouth in a kiss, and sparks of victory and relief shot through him as she pressed against him with a low, deep moan of satisfaction.

"Thank God," she said, breaking the kiss only long enough to speak. "I was afraid you weren't going to touch me."

He remedied that fear immediately, capturing her mouth once again, his tongue stroking and tasting, his teeth biting. They locked together, making wild love with their mouths until Rand was certain he would explode from the pleasure of it.

With his hands, he stroked her, fingers sliding over cloth, then inching beneath to trace delicate skin. She shivered under his touch, her own hands cupped behind his neck, pulling him closer as she rose up on tiptoe as if she wanted to crawl inside of him. Dear God, he knew the feeling.

"Rand," she whispered, then brushed her lips over his mouth. "God, Rand."

He melted under her words, silencing her with his mouth, capturing her and drinking in her taste like a dying man in the desert.

In his arms, Lissa melted against him, reveling in his touch and wishing she never, ever had to be parted from him.

"Lissa," he breathed, his hands under her shirt, cupping her waist, his thumbs stroking tender skin. He slid them up, until his rough skin brushed the curve of her breasts and she gasped, almost unable to bear the pleasure.

"Please," she whispered, and he complied with the demand, pushing the shirt up and tugging it over her head to let it fall to the floor.

His hands cupped her breasts. "So beautiful . . ."

"Please," she repeated, her body tingling with need. "Don't wait."

He picked her up and carried her to a room with

nothing in it but a bed and an unpacked duffel bag, soon buried under their discarded clothes.

The mattress was hard against her back, and he pressed his body over hers, capturing her completely. She closed her eyes, soaking in the pleasure of it, for the first time completely comfortable being beneath a man, his body holding hers in place.

His mouth dropped to her breast, and she arched up, wanting him to take more, to increase the violent heat of pleasure that was ripping through her. Wanting not just his mouth, but all of him. "Rand, please. Inside me."

"God, yes."

He stroked her first, his fingers sliding in, making her even slicker. Then he thrust inside, and she lifted her hips, meeting him, drawing him in, wanting him deeper and deeper until they were only one person, moving together in a frenzy of heat and rising passion.

He was getting closer, strands of his soul starting to slip out, tattered bits twining around her, brushing her skin, making her feel even more exquisite.

There was more.

She gasped, trying to tell if the fresh soul was real or only an illusion. She thought it was real, but she couldn't be certain. It was too fresh, too new, and there still wasn't enough to risk letting him come inside her.

Time to get off.

She shifted beneath him. "Rand, be careful."

He moaned in protest, and she shifted, urging him off, stroking his body with her hands, sliding down to finish what they started with her mouth, tasting and taking him, but at the same time wanting more.

Wanting so much more.

Later, sated, they lay together, Rand's fingers idly stroking her skin. "I don't want it to always be this way between us," he said.

She nuzzled close, pretending not to understand. "I think it's pretty good between us."

"I want to lose myself inside of you," he said. "And I think you want it, too."

Her back was to him, and she allowed herself one long breath, before schooling her features into a soft smile and turning in his arms to face him. "I do," she said. "But that's not everything, Rand. Don't make it be everything."

He sat up, his expression grave. "It may not be everything, but it's more than you're letting on. Come on, Lissa, do you think I don't see the big picture here? I might have been human twelve years ago, but I live in this world now. I know what questions to ask when I'm trying to find out about someone."

She swallowed. "So what did you find out about me?"

"If you don't take in soul regularly—hell, frequently—you start to fade. You get weak. You get sick. You lose your allure."

"Afraid you won't be attracted to me anymore?" she teased.

"I'm not joking, Lissa."

She took his hand. "I know you're not. I'm sorry."

"You need souls, Lissa. And you can't get any from me."

"I can."

He looked at her warily. "I thought you said there wasn't enough to take."

"Not yet." She brushed a kiss over his cheek.

"Lissa." His voice was low, raw. "Dammit, Lissa, you can't do that."

"Do what?"

"You can't wish me into something I'm not. You. Me. Soul. It's something we're going to have to deal with."

"I know," she said. "And I'm not wishing you into anything."

He sat up roughly, edging away from her, but she wasn't about to let him get away with that. She pressed her body to his back, her hands clutching his shoulders. "You're an idiot, Rand, do you know that?"

"I'm glad we're having this little talk."

"You look at your past, and you think you're cold and horrible because your cousin made you kill for him and you didn't love your wife. But you're not. You weren't then, and you certainly aren't now." She drew in a breath. "And you know what? Even if you were some vile beast back a dozen, two dozen years ago, you've changed."

"Lissa."

"No, listen to me. You say you don't have control during a full moon, but you do. If you didn't, you wouldn't have come to me. I think you forget because you've got this image of yourself in your thick skull. You're so certain there's nothing human inside you that you refuse to acknowledge when the human is actually stronger than the wolf."

He tried to get a word in, but she was on a roll. "And this bullshit about not being able to change at will—you say you're an animal, and you always have been and you accept that. But you don't, Rand. You don't accept it. And that's why you can't change. Because you think it would be like giving in to what you don't want to be."

"No," he said.

"Yes," she argued. "You're a good man, Rand, wolf and all. You just need to learn to accept it. Do that, and your soul will grow back just fine."

She stopped, afraid he was going to kick her out of bed or out of the house, or out of Los Angeles for that matter. But she'd said her piece, and she felt better for it. And if he'd just take it to heart . . .

He was staring at her.

"What?"

"It's been a long time since I've received so thorough a dressing-down."

She leaned back against the wall and hugged the sheet to her chest. "You deserved it."

"Maybe." He leaned in and kissed her. "Thank you."

"For chewing you out?"

"For believing in me."

She pressed her lips together, afraid she might cry. "I do," she said. "Now shut up and kiss me."

◆

Rand woke up with the sun streaming through the window and Lissa spooned against his side. The morning felt different. Strange. And he lay there until he put a finger on it: *He was content.*

It was enough of a smack-you-in-the-face revelation that he stayed in bed, listening to the gentle rise and fall of her breathing beside him, as he stared at the ceiling and soaked it in.

Content. The emotion felt new and exotic. It had been one hell of a long time since he'd felt like this.

He rolled sideways and looked at Lissa, now sleeping on her stomach, the sheet gathered somewhere around her knees. She was naked, and he trailed his fingers over her bare back, then over the curve of her perfect rear.

No, he corrected. Not a long time. He'd *never* felt this way before. Not this. Not the way he felt around Lissa.

She made him laugh, she made him think. And she didn't take any shit.

Most of all, she believed in him, which was something he couldn't quite wrap his head around. It was a heady blend, and he was afraid he couldn't live up to the man she saw. He'd try, though. For her, it was worth trying.

Beside him, she stirred. He bent over and pressed a kiss to that perfect ass, then heard her laugh, muffled by the pillow.

"Good morning," he whispered.

She started to sit up, but he pressed a hand to her shoulder.

"No," he said. "Stay there."

Contentment wasn't the only thing he'd awakened with. He was already hard, and right then he had to have her. Had to claim her. This woman, this amazing woman—she was his. Only his. "You're mine," he whispered, bending so that his lips were near her ear. He straddled her, almost coming undone from the way her soft ass rubbed his steel cock.

She exhaled, her body trembling, and spread her legs in answer. His balls tightened, and he knew this would be fast. He couldn't wait. And when he slipped his hand down, touching her, and found her slick and ready, he almost came on the spot.

"Wider," he said, and when she complied, he held on to her waist and thrust himself into heaven.

Right away, her muscles tightened around him, drawing him in, milking him as he moved in a sensual rhythm above her. "Lissa," he moaned, his body tightening, needing. "Oh, God, Lissa."

She lifted her rear, meeting his thrusts, but as he was almost ready to come, she shifted, pulling free from him.

His body screamed from the betrayal, but she leaned forward, taking his mouth hard with her own, as her clever hands slid down his body, finding him hard and ready and so close. She stroked him, her tongue teasing his, her hands taking him higher and higher until his body couldn't take it anymore and his body went supernova.

He cried out against her mouth, his head rocking back, as he breathed, trying to prolong the pleasure even as he tried to bring himself back.

In one quick move, she straddled him, her hands stroking his chest, their bodies as close as if he'd finished inside her.

He locked his arms around her, pulling her close, letting their heartbeats mingle as one. He didn't know how long they stayed like that. He only knew that after some small eternity she nipped his earlobe. "I'm going to take a shower." She slid gracefully off of him, then took his hand. "Join me."

She liked her showers hot, and the water beat down on them, drenching them as they stood together, bodies pressed close, slippery with soap. He ran his hands over her skin, helping the water that sluiced over her wash the soap away, using the excuse of bathing to explore her, wanting to touch and feel every inch that he might have missed before.

Without a word, he pressed her back to the tiled shower stall, then dropped to his knees. She had no hair at her crotch—none on her body except for eyelashes and eyebrows and the blond curls that framed her face. She'd said that was the nature of succubi, and right then he fully approved. His hand slipped over her so easily, his fingers sliding in, feeling a wetness that had nothing to do with the shower.

He brought his tongue to her, tasting her clit, sliding over her warm, slick flesh, making her tremble and gasp. With his hands, he held onto her hips, holding her steady. He wanted to hold her as she lost herself, wanted to know that he was the one who took her there.

She tasted like sin and sex and summer rains, and he kept his tongue on her, stroking and teasing, his body tightening again with the taste of her. He could feel her tremble, could hear her breath catch, and he wanted to tell her not to hold back, but to let go and melt in his hands.

He wanted to tell her he'd catch her.

But he couldn't say anything right then; he couldn't have stopped even if he wanted to, so instead he told her with his touch, his tongue.

Then it came—that final tremor, building higher and higher until she screamed and grabbed his shoulders and pressed hard against him as if he wanted to extract the last tiny bit of pleasure.

She slid down the walls and into his arms, and they lay there, wrapped together, until the hot water started to turn cool.

He hung his towel back up, then stood there naked, simply looking at her. She smiled at him, so sure and confident he thought he would burst. She was right.

Hell, she had to be right.

With one hand, he urged her closer. Then he kissed her forehead and ran his hand over her silky hair. "I'm going to go make breakfast."

She raised an eyebrow. "I looked in your refrigerator last night," she said. "How exactly are you going to manage that?"

He had to acknowledge that she had a point, then changed his strategy to include pulling on jeans and a shirt. "I'm going to run out for breakfast tacos," he said. "We'll eat in the dining room. Formal dress is not required."

"Glad to hear it."

As he was leaving the room, he saw that she'd pulled on her jeans, which was a shame, and his T-shirt, which made him happy. He was still thinking about that— about being happy—when he went through the kitchen door and stepped into the backyard where he'd left the Ducati.

He was pulling the key out of his pocket when he heard the back door open. "Let me guess," he said, turning. "You miss me alrea—"

The words died in his throat, cut off by the image of the black-clad man firing the tranq gun. Rand dove to the side, the dart barely missing him. Behind the gunman, he saw another figure rush into the house.

Lissa.

In him, the wolf rose.

And then, when the gunman lifted the weapon to fire again, the wolf sprang, and the man knew nothing more.

CHAPTER 38

If she moved, Lissa's head would explode. She was certain of it, so she stayed very still and tried to open her eyes. One at a time, and very, very slowly.

Little by little, the world came into focus, and she realized that the face above her belonged to Nick.

"Rand?" she asked.

His face hardened. "In the hall. He didn't think you'd want to see him."

"What are you talking about?" she asked, but as she did, the room shifted into focus. Not Rand's house. A hospital room. Complete with beeping machines and antiseptic smell. "*Rand.*" She tossed the sheet off and tried to sit up, but her head was having none of that and her body was sore and stiff and covered in bandages, and Nick's gentle hands pressed her back down against the pillow.

"It's not a concussion. Just a nasty headache, and some of those scrapes and bites are pretty intense. You were out for a while, so you're going to want to move slow."

"What the hell happened?"

"That fucking animal almost ripped you to pieces."

She shook her head slowly, not believing. "No. No, that can't be right."

"It's my goddamned fault," he said sharply. "You

were all set to walk away, and he was all set to let you go, and I had to stick my damn head in and tell him what an idiot he was."

"About what?"

"About you not betraying him. About you being willing to go to prison to protect the precious soul of a fucked-up bastard who'd do something like this to you."

"He didn't."

"He did, Lissa." He gestured to her bandaged arms and legs. "These are werewolf wounds. You think the doctors here don't know what they look like?"

"Rand would never hurt me."

"Not on purpose. I believe that. But when he changes . . ."

She shook her head. "It's not a full moon. He can't change whenever he wants. He's never been able—"

"He did," Nick said. "He was attacked. He saw them go in the house. He was worried about you. He changed."

"See? He didn't hurt me. He was saving me."

"They're dead. Two attackers, right in the middle of his floor. And all Rand knows is that he changed and they're dead, and you're in the hospital. You do the math."

"You're wrong."

"You're naive," he countered, then immediately softened. "Lissa, I'm sorry."

"Just go." She turned her head to the side, then felt his fingers caress her hair. "Go."

"Denying it isn't going to help," he said. "Rand's dangerous. Always has been, always will be. And thinking you've fallen in love with him isn't going to change a thing."

She closed her eyes, not wanting to hear his words. Not wanting to believe he could be right.

She didn't know how much time had passed before a sharp tap at the door startled her awake, and Rand stepped in, his expression filled with pain.

"You didn't do this to me," she said firmly.

"You're wrong." He traced a finger down a bandaged arm.

"No," she said. "I'm not."

"I lost control. I was in the kill zone, and so were you, and I *fucking* did this to you." His hand came down hard on her mattress, accentuating his speech.

"No."

"Dammit, Lissa, open your eyes. You're hooked up to a damn IV. You're covered with bites and scratches. And they fucking cleaned weren fur out of your wounds."

Her chest tightened with each of his words, but she wasn't going to give up. Not on him. Not on them.

"No," she repeated.

"You really believe that?"

She met his eyes. "I believe in you."

He drew in a breath. "I don't."

♦

Petra closed her eyes, trying to hear better as the one called Meer chewed out his team.

"Unacceptable!" he said. "Two more of the team are

dead, and we don't have a goddamned thing to show for it. You say there was a woman with Rand?"

"There was." A low voice, and Petra opened her eyes, saw that the speaker was older, grizzled, with salt-and-pepper hair.

"If you'd brought her back with you, we'd have him by now. Catch the girl, and we have the wolf."

"She's in the hospital," one of the men reported.

"Then I suggest you go get her."

◆

Rand sat at the bar in the Slaughtered Goat, his laptop open in front of him, waiting for the PEC identification database to return the identity of the two dead shit-fucks in his house.

Once he knew that, he was going to see where they led, and he had a feeling they'd lead to Grayson Meer.

He'd follow those leads, find Meer, and rip his fucking head off.

Until then, he was getting drunk.

Damn drunk.

And his glass was currently dry, which was completely unacceptable.

"Another," he said to Joe, who raised an eyebrow but poured the whiskey.

"You wanna talk about it?"

"About what?"

"About whatever's put the bug up your ass."

He opened his mouth, then shook his head. "No. I don't want to talk about it."

He'd hurt her. And not just once. No, he'd hurt her

twice. Mind and body. Wouldn't want to leave anything out, after all.

Goddammit all to hell. The first woman he'd truly cared about—the first woman he'd ever loved—and he'd hurt her.

Love. The word twisted and twined through his head with Rand trying to grab hold of it, trying to decide if it was real or an illusion and how the hell he'd fallen in love without any warning.

Except there'd been warnings and signals and even a bunch of damn signposts. It wasn't an illusion. He loved her. Truly loved her. And he was certain that she loved him.

And that made hurting her all the harder to bear.

He banged at the keys, trying to get the computer to work faster. No use, and his head wandered back to painful, wonderful subjects.

"You ever been in love, Joe?"

Joe hopped onto the bar, his knobby knees up around his ears. "Once. Long time ago."

"She love you back?"

"Yup."

Rand finished off his whiskey. "Nice, huh?"

"You have a fight with your woman?"

He snorted. "You could say that."

"She kicked you out, huh?"

Rand shook his head. "No. Actually, she wants me to stay."

"Well, that's nice, too, right? When they want you, I mean. It doesn't get much better than that."

Rand thought about the way Lissa had clung to him after he'd gone to her at Orlando's. The way she'd tugged at his fingers, trying to draw him back when he'd left her hospital bed. About the hurt in her eyes when he'd said he was leaving. She'd been hurting for him, and now he was aching for her.

He closed his eyes and sighed. "No," he said simply. "It doesn't get much better than that."

CHAPTER 39

Lissa took the steps to her apartment very slowly, her body still stiff and sore. But she'd been given a clean bill of health, and her various cuts, bites, and scrapes had been thoroughly disinfected. The staff had assured her that since she wasn't bitten on a full moon, she wouldn't succumb to the weren virus.

Now she was just glad to be home. She wanted to be in her own place. With her own stuff.

And she wanted Rand.

She'd called and left him a message. With any luck, he'd call or come by soon.

As if on cue, her phone rang, but it wasn't Rand. "Lissa? This is Barnaby down in Orion's office. Is this a good time?"

"Great," she said, leaning against the railing. "What's up?"

"I wanted you to know I ran the DNA on the were-wolf bites like you asked."

"And?" Her stomach fluttered. She told herself she wasn't nervous. *She* knew what the result would be. She had faith. This was only for Rand.

But she still couldn't help the nerves.

"You were right. The DNA isn't Rand's."

"Were you able to identify it?"

"It's Santiago's," Barnaby said, and Lissa's blood ran cold.

"Have you told Rand?"

"He's next on my list."

"Good. If you talk to him before I do, tell him to come to me when he's done."

"You got it."

She hung up, a smile on her face. Rand hadn't hurt her, and soon he'd know it. Not only that, but he was going to get his hands on the bastard who did. That, in Lissa's mind, deserved a full-fledged cheer.

She slid her key into her lock and pushed open the door, then stepped inside and tossed her bag onto the table.

Then she froze.

Someone was standing in her apartment. Someone with a craggy face and salt-and-pepper hair, and the look of the wolf about him.

She turned, racing back toward the stairs.

He was on her in an instant, his mouth right beside her ear. "Hello, Lissa," he whispered. "I'm Carlos Santiago. And you're coming with me."

◆

"Former military, yes," Bixby said, peering at the information scrolling across his screen. "No ties to Meer. No ties that I see."

"That's bullshit," Rand said. The computer had kicked back two names and very little data on the bodies in his house. Rand had hauled his ass and his laptop to Bixby, who was in tech heaven on sublevel five of the

PEC, hidden in a concrete room alive with the hum of computers. "You have to get me something."

"Will keep looking, I will, I will. But nothing on the surface pops. Got something else, though." His grin was wide and feline. "Got the connection, I do."

"Meer and Santiago?" Rand could almost kiss the little were-cat. "You made a connection?"

"I did. Yes, I did." He tapped keys and pulled up another screen. "Was about to call when you came. About to tell you, I was."

"Tell me now."

"Show you," he said, pointing at the image that opened onto the screen, a fuzzy scan of a legal document charging Carlos Santiago with fraternizing with human military personnel in Honduras almost twenty-five years ago. Specifically, troops from 3rd Operational Detachment Delta, Bravo Team.

"The personnel, Bixby," Rand said. "Tell me you pulled the names of the men on Bravo Team."

"Oh, yes," he said. "Got the list right here."

A few more taps as Bixby flipped the pages of the charge until he reached a document that listed the four soldiers with whom Santiago had consorted. Ian Kessler, Jonas Brick, Scott Ailey, and Grayson Meer.

"Brick and Ailey died," Bixby said. "Dead in the nineties. Kessler's alive. Doctor, he is. In Los Angeles. Got out early. Got out soon."

"But Meer stayed in longer," Rand said. "And he and Santiago stayed in touch."

He gave Bixby a pat on the back. "Good work," he said. There were still holes—Rand couldn't picture Meer and Santiago's endgame—but the noose was tightening.

Once they found them, they could interrogate them, and the rest of the details would fall into place.

It was the finding that was key.

"Real property," Rand said. "Purchased, leased, I don't care. Trace by their names, by company names, run a damned anagram of their names mixed together. But find me something. Santiago's skipped out of his cabin, but I don't believe he's left the area. He started Jacob on the rumors—he'll stick around to see how it all plays out."

Rand was thinking aloud as much as giving Bixby his marching orders, but the little were-cat was writing it all down, his head bobbing and his fingers tapping the keyboard. "On it. I'm on it," he said.

The phone on the desk buzzed and a female voice filled the room. "Is Mr. Rand there?"

He picked up the handset. "Here."

"The medical examiner's office is trying to locate you. Apparently your cellphone isn't working."

Rand pulled it out of his pocket. No signal.

"Tell them I'll be right there."

The trouble with Rand's phone wasn't caused by being underground, because as soon as he was away from all those damned computers, the thing rang. He flipped it open, impatient. "I'm on my way."

"That's very good to hear." The voice was harsh, cold, and unfamiliar.

"Who is this?"

"I think it's time for us to talk."

"Is it?" Rand's fingers tightened around the phone.

"One hour. On Sunset," the voice added, giving the specific address.

"And if I say no?"

"Then your female will die."

♦

Nick ran his fingers through his hair, forcing his thoughts to focus. Somebody had taken Lissa. And if Serge was still alive, that same somebody probably also had Serge in a cell. Or worse. "It's a trap," he said, referring to Rand's phone call. "It has to be a trap."

"No shit," Rand countered. "Which is why I'm not meeting them. Not on Sunset, anyway."

Nick looked over and saw that Rand was holding up Boyd's card-key. "If I don't have Lissa out of there by the rendezvous time, then they'll kill her, and you damn well know it."

"Where exactly are you planning on using that key?" Nick asked. If the weren had been holding back investigation results after supposedly teaming with the PEC—

"I need to talk to Xeres. Now."

Nick's eyes narrowed. "What are you suggesting?"

"All I need is for you to get me into his cell and turn off surveillance. I'll come out with an address."

Nick nodded, his fingers itching to beat the information out of Xeres himself. But Rand was right about the surveillance, and Nick already had resources in place who would do him a favor.

"Meet me at Detention Block A. You'll have ten minutes. I can't risk longer than that."

"It'll be enough," Rand said. "I'll make it be enough."

As Nick slipped off to work his magic in the security

section, Rand moved to the detention block, meeting up with Nick outside the corridor leading to Xeres's cell.

"Ten minutes," Nick repeated, then spoke to the guard, a troll who escorted Rand to the cell.

The door opened, Rand stepped in, and the troll shut him in tight.

Xeres stood up, his expression full of hate.

"Hello, Xeres," Rand said, walking over to lean against the far wall. "I was thinking that you and I should have a good, long talk."

"I don't have shit to say to you."

Rand shrugged. "Okay."

He started to walk past Xeres, then sucker punched him in the gut, grabbing the back of his head and slamming his face down against the edge of the stainless steel sink.

His fingers tightened in Xeres's hair, and he pulled the weren's head up. "You were saying?"

"Fuck you."

"Wrong answer."

Another slam against the metal, and he heard Xeres's nose break.

"Where is he? Where's Santiago? Where's your father?"

"I don't know," Xeres growled. Beneath Rand's hand, the weren's body tensed, the flesh heating as Xeres summoned the change.

"Won't help," Rand said, his voice low and hard. "I can hurt you even when you're half wolf." To prove the point, he smashed Xeres's head down again, then thrust his knee up, catching the bastard in the ribs. "Talk."

Xeres collapsed to the ground, but stayed quiet. Rand

kicked him hard in the small of the back, refusing to let the weren concentrate on bringing on the change. Refusing to let him do anything except think about the world of hurt he'd be in if he didn't cooperate. And soon.

"Tell me, dammit," he said, crouching over Xeres's prone form, his fingers twined in the bastard's hair. The weren was facedown on the concrete, and Rand jerked his head up, then smashed it down hard, leaving a bloody imprint where his face shattered against the concrete.

"Nothing . . . to . . . say."

"Bullshit."

Xeres held up a hand, and Rand loosened his hold, but not too much. They had Lissa—those fuckers Meer and Santiago had her—and if Rand had to pull Xeres's fingernails out one by one to get the information he needed, he'd do it. And with pleasure.

"I'm not . . . with him."

"But you know something."

"I . . . I don't."

Rand tightened his grip and lifted Xeres's head again.

"Okay, okay. He's . . . doing something."

"No shit," Rand said. "Where's he doing it?"

"I don't know. I swear . . . I . . . I'd meet him in the forest. But I'm not . . . I'm not tied in with him."

"Not liking the answer," Rand said. He rolled the weren over, and pulled out his knife and pushed the tip of it into the soft flesh under Xeres's chin.

"I don't know," Xeres said, his voice utterly defeated. "I don't know."

"Not good enough." He pushed harder, and a drop of blood trickled down from the point of the blade.

Rand shifted his knee, crushing the weren's balls. Pain shot through Xeres's eyes. "Goddamn it, give me something."

"There's nothing," Xeres moaned. "Nothing to give. I never saw him go anywhere. I never saw him with anybody."

Rand tensed. "Never *saw*? But he talked about someone?"

The weren closed his eyes and nodded, looking absolutely miserable.

"Who? Dammit, *who*?"

"I don't know. Friends, he said. From the old days."

"Names, dammit. I need names. I need addresses."

"I swear . . . I don't know."

"Meer?"

Xeres's eyes were blank. "No," he whispered. "No."

"*Who?*"

He was trembling now, his skin mottled, his face contorted with pain. "I don't know," he repeated, "I don't know, I don't know, I don't know."

A tap sounded at the door, and Nick stepped in. He looked dispassionately at the broken form of Xeres on the floor. "Time," he said. "You need to leave."

Rand stood, looking down on Xeres with disgust. "You just better pray I find her in time."

He followed Nick out, Xeres's moans trailing them down the hall.

"You believe him?" Nick asked, after Rand ran through what he'd learned.

"Yeah. *Fuck*." He lashed out, slamming his fist into the wall beside the elevator. "All he knew was that Santiago had friends."

The elevator door opened, and Nick started to step on. Rand reached out, pulling the vampire back. "He said friends. Plural. Meer and somebody else."

"Yeah. We knew that. We didn't think Meer was a solo op."

"From the old days," Rand said, his mind whirring. "There were four of them. Two died in the nineties. But Meer and Kessler are still alive. A doctor, Bixby said. Kessler's a doctor."

Nick nodded. "That fits."

"Shit, yeah. The ash is organic. And we know they took Serge." He met Nick's eyes. "They're doing some sort of experiments. Medical experiments. Come on."

They rushed through Division to Bixby's office, but when they arrived, the little were-cat was out.

"Dammit."

Nick slid in front of the keyboard. "What are we looking for?"

"Ian Kessler. A doctor. We're looking for real-property records."

Nick was typing fast, pulling up property-tax records and deeds and all sorts of shit. Unfortunately, he wasn't finding much. "Hang on," he said, shifting to a different site. "This is where working with an advocate comes in handy."

Rand watched as Nick waded through lists of corporate registrations, his hands clenched tightly at his sides so he wouldn't lash out in frustration. Time was running out, and Lissa—

"Ha," Nick said. "Will you look at that?"

"What?"

"A warehouse. Leased one year ago to MK Enterprises, a subsidiary of Kessler Medical Research."

"That's it," Rand said, looking over Nick's shoulder and noting the address. "That has to be it." He clapped Nick on the shoulder. "Not bad work for a guy with fangs," he said, then he raced to the parking garage, his mind full of Lissa.

Nick got there first, and when Rand arrived he found the vampire standing next to the Ducati, Nick's Porsche parked beside the bike. The passenger and driver's doors hung open. "We're going together."

Rand nodded, then slid behind the wheel of the Porsche. "I'm driving."

CHAPTER 40

Santiago paced in front of Lissa, looking smug. She'd tried to fight him off, but even if her wounds had been completely healed, she was no match for a werewolf. Maybe if she had the strength that came from a steady diet of soul, but the last soul she'd taken in had been Claude's, and she was as weak as a human.

He'd knocked her out, and she'd come to here, tied to a post in some sort of medical facility, looking out at Petra strapped to a gurney and a vampire alongside her. Petra looked as miserable as Lissa felt, and more than a little woozy, but at least the PI was still alive. The vampire looked ready to rip off limbs.

She hoped he had the chance.

Across the room, a door opened and a tall man with dark hair graying at the temples stepped inside. "Carlos! I see you brought us the prize."

"You didn't think I'd fail?" the werewolf said, and the tall man laughed.

"Never." He turned to Lissa. "I suppose introductions are in order. You've already met Mr. Santiago. I'm Grayson Meer."

She said nothing.

"Lissa, Lissa . . ." He clucked his tongue. "I'm surprised at you. Such terrible manners. But then, perhaps you don't believe you'll be staying with us very long? Let me assure you that your prince isn't riding to your rescue," he said. "Oh, he *thinks* he is, but it's a wild-goose chase. He thinks he's going to save you, but I promise you, he can't."

She forced her mind to slow and her body to relax, and from the depths she managed to dredge up a smile. She kept it there, bright and shiny and falsely cheerful as she tried to ignore his words and focus only on raising her sheen.

It wasn't working.

"Oh, dear, now there's a frustrated female. What's the matter? Sheen not working?"

"Fuck you."

He tilted his head to the side. "Nope. Must not be working. No desire at all to take you up on that rather sweet offer."

Lissa seethed. Meer might be immune, but what about Santiago? If she could just affect him enough to make him loosen her bindings . . .

"It's not you, you know," Meer said. He reached into his pocket and pulled out a syringe. "Our medical team is very resourceful. Don't worry, though. It wears off. Of course, you'll probably be dead when it does."

"Rand is going to kick your ass."

"No. He won't. He's walking into a trap, and I promise you there's no wriggling out of it. We're prepared, I assure you. After all, look." He pointed at the vampire. "We captured the mighty Sergius. We'll capture your Rand."

Sergius? She blinked, suddenly thrown back in time. She knew that name. *Nick's friend.* The vampire was Nick's friend, or had been centuries ago.

"It's not even me you want," she said, her stomach wrenching so violently she was certain she'd vomit. "I'm bait."

"Clever girl."

"What do you want with Rand?"

"His blood, actually. That's really a question for the doctor, but it's going to help us with our project. Although it might be unnecessary. Ms. Lang here was kind enough to give us some of her blood, and we're hopeful the magical properties can be isolated." He patted Petra, who hawked back and spat in his face as Lissa silently cheered.

The man wiped it away, completely unperturbed. "Until we accomplish that, though, our experiments with her blood cells are rather hit or miss. Your Rand is by far the better option." He checked his watch. "Hopefully he'll arrive soon."

Lissa tensed, wanting desperately to see Rand, and at the same time terrified he'd show up and get caught in this madman's net.

"Let's get on with it," Santiago said.

"Of course." Meer smiled at Lissa. "Since you're here, we decided that we might as well test the most recent serum on you. I hope this distillation of Ms. Lang's blood works. Our earlier test subject died on the table."

A door on the far side of the room opened, and a man in a lab coat stepped in.

"Doctor! Right on time."

"I think I've made some progress with this batch, although I'm still dubious. Magic isn't housed in a cellular structure, and I can't be sure I've captured whatever fundamental element controls the transformation."

"We won't know until we try," Meer said.

"I need Rand. Until I have him, our progress is severely stymied."

"We'll have him soon," Santiago said.

"And in the meantime, we can see if the progress you've made is tangible."

"Very well." The doctor moved to a nearby table and plucked up a syringe. "The collar?"

"Right," Meer said. He picked up a black collar that sat on a tray next to the Petra's gurney, then he brought it toward Lissa. "I apologize if the color's not to your liking. We only have it in black."

She squirmed, trying to avoid his hands, but there was nowhere to go, and soon the collar was tight around her neck.

"It keeps you under control after the change," he said. "Wouldn't want you to kill us all."

"No," she said dryly. "Wouldn't want that."

"Doctor?"

The doctor moved forward, the syringe outstretched. Lissa tried to shrink into herself. She wanted to disappear, evaporate, turn back into the mist she'd come from.

Most of all, she wanted Rand.

She could even imagine him. Could hear him. And she took comfort in the fantasy of his voice.

Except it wasn't a fantasy.

It was real.

He was standing on the far side of the room, Nick right beside him, and both of them were holding guns.

"Let the girl go," he said, as Lissa cried with relief. "Or die."

"All right," Meer said. "You win. The girl goes free."

Lissa held her breath as Meer came to her, then reached up to where her wrists were bound above her head, fastened to a hook embedded in the pole. Except he didn't touch the ropes or the hook. Instead, he pressed a button, and as he did, a giant net fell from the ceiling above Nick and Rand, sparking and hissing as the electrified webbing sent volts coursing through their bodies, knocking the only two men she'd ever loved onto the hard concrete floor, completely unconscious.

CHAPTER 41

Rand tested the bindings, but he couldn't break free. He was strapped down on a gurney next to Petra, who looked at him with an ironic smile as soon as Meer and Santiago and the other male—presumably Kessler—left the room. "Glad you could join us."

He grimaced. "Lissa?" he called.

"Here!" Her voice came from behind him, and although he tried to shift, he couldn't see her.

"Are you okay?" He looked at the needles and tubes sticking out of his arms. "Did they hurt you?"

"I'm fine. I swear."

"I'm getting you out of here," he promised, despite the rather obvious setback. "Where's Nick?"

"Here," came the answer from the far side of the room. "These bindings are hematite. Serge? Are you—"

"I'm fighting it," Serge said, and Rand could see him straining against the bindings. "If I let the daemon take me, I'll never get back."

Nick snapped out a curse, then groaned as he struggled against the bindings.

"Give it up, Montegue," Serge said. "I've been trying for days."

"Where's Kiril?" Petra asked. "Did he bring you here?"

Rand turned to face her. "What? No."

Her forehead creased. "But he's okay, right?"

"They got him pretty hard, but he was coming out of it last I heard. What do you mean? How could he bring us here?"

"When we were kids, he was charged with protecting me. And that means I'm a walking Lo-Jack and he's my damn receiver."

Rand frowned. Too bad Kiril had been out cold all this time. "We had another source."

"Thank God for that," Petra said. "Not that me and my friend Serge here weren't having the time of our lives, but the more the merrier, right?"

"I've seen Meer, Santiago, and a human in a lab coat," Rand said. "That's Kessler, I assume?"

"You got it," Petra said.

"How many more are we dealing with?" If he could get free, he'd happily kill all three with his bare hands, then move on to the rest.

"Those three are all I can confirm," Serge said. "There were more, but their team's been dwindling."

"Good," Rand said, thinking about the unidentified humans he'd killed in his living room.

"It's a military-style operation, though," Serge said. "Wouldn't surprise me if there were men we haven't seen. This room's for the doctor and the shit he's developing."

"He's experimenting with vamps," Rand said. "That much I've figured out. But what's the endgame?"

"Supersoldiers," Lissa said. "I was listening to them earlier. Meer was going on and on about how they were going to change the world. Megalomaniacal bullshit, but since we're the ones trapped, I'm not sure we have room to criticize . . ."

"And the dead humans?" Rand asked. "Their super-soldier prototypes are killing them?"

"Pretty much," Petra said.

"Explain."

"See where your blood's going?" Serge said. "Through the tube and into that contraption? It's cooking a formula. They're trying to shoot up soldiers with all the perks of being a vampire, but without pesky things like the daemon and light sensitivity and the need for blood."

"Impossible."

"Tell that to Kessler," Serge said. "He's almost managed it."

"So these soldiers are killing the humans," Nick said. "But where are the soldiers?"

"They're the ash," Petra said. "They're doing experiments on people, and then they're letting them go. These pseudovamps, I mean. They attack, take blood, but their bodies can't process it and—*poof*—they turn to ash."

Rand let out a low whistle. "Shit."

"Still a few flaws in their system if all their subjects turn to ash," Nick said.

"Not anymore," Petra said. "At least they don't think so. Not now that Rand is here."

Rand went cold. "What are you talking about?"

"They think your blood is some sort of wonder drug," Petra said. "They're trying again, with you."

"They're not trying anything," Rand said. "We're getting the fuck out of here."

His words, however, would have had more force if

the door hadn't slammed open right then, ushering in Meer, Santiago, and the bug-eyed little human who'd tailed him to Montclair. At Meer's order to check Rand's IV, Bugs grabbed a tranq gun from a weapons rack on the wall, then hustled over to adjust the flow rate on the tubes.

"I'm going to rip your head off," Rand said, low and slow. "You know that, right? How does it feel knowing you're looking at the man who's going to end you?"

Bugs didn't answer, but he worked faster, then scooted back toward Meer.

Kessler hurried in, lab coat flying, and stopped a spinning centrifuge. He opened it, pulled out a syringe, then let a single drop of liquid fall onto a slide. He slid it under a microscope, peered into the eyepiece, and nodded with satisfaction.

"This is looking very promising. Ten minutes."

"And this will work?"

"I believe Mr. Rand's blood has solved our problem."

Meer turned to Rand, a frat-boy smile on his cold, cocky face. "I guess I should thank you for stopping by. Terribly kind of you."

"Fuck you."

"And such a charming guest to have around." He turned away, his attention returning to Bugs. "We need to evacuate and get to Beta Facility. These two found us. It's a good bet someone else will, too."

Kessler pressed a button, and one panel in the wall slid open. Beyond it was the interior of a transport truck, obviously reinforced with steel, hematite, and who knew what else. The kind of truck that could keep even shadow creatures locked up tight. "We can leave as soon as the formula's ready, then test it at the new location."

They headed out of the room again, leaving Rand and the rest still trapped.

"They'll be back soon to put us on that truck," Lissa said.

"More likely they'll just kill most of us," Nick said.

"I'm guessing we've got five minutes max before they come back." Rand gave his bindings a hard jerk. "That's five minutes to get out of these straps and get ready to overpower them. Nick?"

"Not possible. Even if I wanted to let my daemon out—and at the moment, that sounds pretty damn sweet—the hematite won't let me. I'm not going anywhere."

"Your straps are leather, Rand," Lissa said. "You can break through."

He struggled, trying to do that. "No use."

"The wolf," she said. "You can bring out the wolf."

Frustration cut through him. She knew he couldn't change on command, and now that failure was going to get them all killed.

"You *can*," she said, even before he'd spoken. "You changed at the house."

"I didn't control it. It happened—"

"Because you needed to," she put in. "You changed to protect me and you kept control. It wasn't you who hurt me, Rand. I heard back from Barnaby. It was Santiago."

He swallowed, her words giving him hope . . . and strengthening his already intense desire to rip Santiago's fucking head off.

"You can do this," she said. "You have control, Rand, you just need to use it."

He didn't know if he could. But Lissa believed in him, and he could try.

He closed his eyes, tensing as he concentrated. He tried to picture the moon, tried to feel the lunar tug in his blood and the wolf snapping and snarling inside.

It was there, the wolf. So close to the surface.

It was right there wanting to sink its teeth into Meer's neck, wanting to get into it with Santiago and see the other weren fall.

Everything, right there, right under the surface, but he couldn't bring it up. He'd been fighting it so damn long he didn't know how.

He let his body go slack.

"No use."

Maybe with time, but time was running out.

"Can you get your gurney to roll over?" he asked Petra. "The straps are probably tightened with mechanisms on the side. If we roll, maybe they'll loosen." He tried to throw his weight, but he had no motion at all; he was strapped too tight, and it was futile.

Petra, a human, was less tightly bound. "They drugged me to suppress the magic," she said. "But these straps aren't very tight." She shifted violently and the gurney teetered. It didn't fall over, though. Just inched a bit closer to Serge.

"Serge?"

"No luck here, either. I'm in the same boat as Rand."

"Maybe if I keep ooching sideways I'll hit Serge's gurney and knock him over."

"Or hit Serge himself," Rand said. "All things considered, probably not a good idea."

"Definitely not."

"What?" Serge asked. "What are you talking about?"

"Petra's touch," Rand says. "It's a curse. It changes whoever she touches."

"Boyd," Serge said, his voice thoughtful. "Of course. I remember them talking about him. About the way he changed. That's how they found out about her. Why they wanted her. He was a bad motherfucker."

"Shit, Serge," Nick said. "Don't go there."

Serge laughed. "You always could tell what I was thinking."

"No."

"It could work."

"Oh, dear God," Lissa said.

"Whoa, whoa, whoa!" Petra said. "No way, Serge. Are you insane?"

"Sometimes, yes."

She shook her head. "No. There's no going back. Once you're changed, that's it."

"It wouldn't even work," Rand said, fighting a tug of disappointment at the lost possibility. He didn't want to sacrifice anyone to a monster, but he did want to see their captors dead and Lissa safe. "He'd still be in the hematite."

"That right, Petra?"

Her eyes were wide and frightened. "I don't think so. He won't be a vampire anymore. He'll be something . . . different."

"And you really think I could break out of these bonds?"

"Yes," Petra said, sounding absolutely terrified. "But you won't be yourself. You could destroy all of us."

"Or I could destroy them."

From across the room, Nick shouted protests at Serge. "Don't you do it, Serge. Don't you fucking do it."

"Why not?" Serge asked, letting his friend's protests slide off of him. "If they don't stake me, I'm killing the bastards, and that means my daemon is coming out hard and fast—and you know as well as I do that this time it's staying out for good." He'd been lost in the daemon before—he knew what it was like to be a monster.

He thought of the subterranean humans, his tunnel rats. The ones that Meer had come down into the dark to take. Serge should have protected them. Should have kept them safe from all the monsters except himself.

He hadn't.

"Petra's curse or my daemon or a stake through the heart—no matter how you deal it, I still land in hell. Don't you think I should try to do one good thing before I go?"

"*Dammit, no.*"

"Sorry, Nick. This one, we're playing my way."

◆

Serge focused on Petra's words, knowing it might be the last time speech made sense to him.

"No one's ever changed on purpose," she was saying. "So I don't know if you can hold onto reason long enough to do this. I mean, you could be the one who ends up killing us. But, you know, let's hope not."

"If he doesn't do this," Lissa said, "we're dead anyway. They're not going to let any of us out of here alive."

"At least this way there's a chance to stop these bastards," Rand added. "And there's a possibility he won't rip our heads off."

"A slim one," Petra said under her breath.

"If you keep any presence of mind, go for our gurneys," Rand continued. "Knock us over. If we're lucky, the latches on the straps will pop."

"And then?"

"Kill them all."

Serge smiled. "I like the way you think, man."

"What about after?" Petra asked. "If he hasn't killed us, I mean."

"Tranq me," Serge said, nodding to the wall lined with tranquilizer guns. "Then put me in that truck and lock it up. That should hold me." He met Petra's eyes. "Ready, girl?"

"I guess."

"Nick?" Nick hadn't said a word since his last protest. "Dammit, man, don't let me go out like this."

"You shouldn't be going out at all," his friend said. "But since you're determined to be a goddamned idiot, then you have my good wishes, too."

"You're the best. You and Luke. You tell him I said so."

"Dammit, Serge," Nick said, with a crack in his voice. "It shouldn't end like this."

Serge closed his eyes, silently agreeing. But at least

this way he was going out on his own terms, and not the daemon's.

"Ready," he said to Petra.

"Right." Her voice was shaky, too. "Okay."

It took a few tries, and with each attempt, Serge could hear the gasps from Lissa and catch the scent of quiet determination from Rand. They said nothing, though, and finally Petra managed to scoot herself up beside him. "Okay."

"Go."

She touched him, and at first he felt nothing, just the brush of her hand over his skin.

Then it hit him. A wall of power, consuming him. Taking him. Filling him up with fury and rage and energy colored black as coal. Things swam away from him. His name. What he was doing. What he was.

He grappled for reality, forcing himself to hold on. He couldn't hold forever, but he had to hold on for a bit, though he couldn't remember why.

Bound.

He realized suddenly that he was bound. With a roar and a violent burst of fury, he sat up, throwing his bindings off, seeing the way the two people beside him looked at him, eyes open wide, fear in their eyes.

Kill.

No.

No.

Save them. Turn them. Save them.

He leaped from the table, then lashed out, knocking the girl's table over. He stomped on the side, snapping a latch, then watching with curious satisfaction as she scrambled free of the straps, then reached up to loosen the bindings of a male.

The male burst off the table, pulling her behind him, pushing them both back toward a pillar where another girl was strapped.

Kill.

Serge cocked his head, looking at them, then took a step forward, ready to squash them.

Serge.

That was his name. He'd done this for a reason.

He'd changed for a reason.

He heard a noise behind him, and he turned. Men were racing into the room. Men he recognized. Men who'd hurt him.

He forgot about the two who'd been on the tables.

And with a sweet, sublime satisfaction, he let the monster rise up in him—and then he set it free on the men he'd sworn to kill.

CHAPTER 42

Lissa watched in horror as Serge ripped the head off a soldier, then let the body sag to the floor as he turned his sights on the bug-eyed human and the half-dozen men in fatigues who'd raced in after Meer and the gang.

"Get Lissa down," Rand shouted to Petra, ripping off his shirt as he spoke. "Cover your hands with this. And get Nick free. I have to stop him before he can't be stopped."

Petra nodded, her eyes wide, then turned to work on Lissa's binds, the going slow because of the shirt on her fingers. "Tell me what's going on."

"Serge," Lissa said, her voice tight. "He just—well, two of the soldiers are now in four pieces."

"Jesus," Petra whispered, and Lissa echoed the curse. Rand was going into that melee. Rand was facing down the monster.

"He'll be fine. He's a badass, right?" Petra spoke with a smile, teasing, but the words actually helped. Petra got that right. Lissa just hoped that the badass man would be enough. What she wanted right then was the wolf.

"Okay," Petra said, and Lissa realized her arms were free.

"Go do Nick. I can get my legs free."

As Petra ran off, Lissa bent to take care of the ties at

her ankles, the work slow because she kept looking up to check on Rand.

Everything around him was chaos, but it was chaos that was operating in their favor, so she considered that a good thing. For now.

Most of that was Serge's doing. He was tossing anything that wasn't nailed down, including soldiers, and had weeded the bad guys down to the four she knew.

He caught the bug-eyed man's arm, pulled, and sent the arm flying.

Lissa swallowed bile.

Make that three . . .

On the far side of the room, Kessler and Santiago raced toward a door, only to be tackled by Nick.

And as the vampire whaled on the two, his body moving with incredible speed and power, Lissa saw Serge's attention turn toward the wall of weapons. And Rand.

"Rand!"

He didn't turn, but she knew he heard her, because he quickened his pace, then turned, a gun in each hand, and Serge snarling and poised for attack.

"Throw!" Nick shouted, reaching to catch a gun. Kessler lay on the floor, bloody and still. Santiago, too.

Nick's attention was on Rand, but Lissa could see what was happening. Santiago wasn't down—he was calling up the change. And now he sprang up—half wolf, half man—and launched himself at Nick.

Lissa didn't realize she'd screamed until she heard the sound of her cry suspended in the air.

It did the trick, though. Instead of tossing the tranq gun to Nick, Rand fired it, and the dart sank deep into

Santiago's neck at the same instant the creature tackled Nick.

They fell to the ground in a heap, and Lissa held her breath, releasing it only when Nick stood, extricating himself from the beast now truly passed out at his feet.

"Here!" Rand tossed him a fresh gun, and not a moment too soon. They each emptied the weapons into the rushing Serge. Then Rand grabbed two more guns and they did it all over again. On the third volley, Serge fell.

"The truck," Rand said. "Quick."

They each took an arm and hauled him that direction, shooting him with another dose of tranq before closing and locking the door.

All the while, Lissa scanned the room for Meer.

"Where is he? Where's Meer?"

"I don't know," Petra said. She'd returned to Lissa's side, and was working on the stubborn knot at Lissa's left ankle.

Lissa cursed. If that prick had gotten free . . .

"There!" Petra said, pointing toward something moving on the ground by the console.

"Rand! Meer!"

He turned that direction, Nick following. But Kessler was stumbling to his feet, and as Nick passed in front of the farthest doorway, Kessler slammed his hand against a button in the wall, and another hematite net fell, buzzing with electrical charge.

"Nick!" Petra called.

"Go," Lissa said, as Petra raced toward Nick. "A gun. Rand, toss her a gun."

Rand grabbed a fresh weapon and tossed it to Petra, who snatched it out of the air, then fired a dart into

Kessler, knocking him once again on his ass. Petra kept running, finally skidding to a stop beside Nick. She hesitated only a moment, then skirted the charged net as she headed toward the wall panel.

She cut the current, then returned to Nick and tried to peel the net off the semiconscious vampire.

On the far side of the room, Meer had climbed to his feet, and even from across the room, Lissa could see there was something very wrong with him.

Then he opened his hand, and the syringe fell to the floor.

He'd used his formula on himself.

She didn't know what he was now, but whatever it was, he wasn't human.

◆

Rand grabbed the last tranquilizer gun from the rack, then stood facing Grayson Meer. Or the thing that had once been Meer. Grayson Meer was no longer a man. He wasn't exactly a vampire, either. He was something else entirely. Something that, unlike Serge, had retained reason and awareness.

Something that was supremely pissed off.

"Do you think you're going to walk out of here?" Meer asked. "Years of work, completely destroyed. *My* research. *My* project."

"Gee, I'm sorry," Rand said, the gun aimed at Meer's chest. What he meant was *Die now, you bastard.*

Considering the rage that crossed Meer's face, he heard Rand's real words, too.

Before Rand could fire, Meer was on him. He

knocked Rand aside, sending the gun skittering across the warehouse, then bounded across the room to Lissa.

Rand had never seen such speed, and as he followed, he calculated. Lissa was still bound. Nick was out of commission. And if Petra got into the fight, this thing that was Meer might turn even more badass, and they were all out of tranquilizer darts.

It was all on Rand.

That was okay. He worked best when he worked alone.

Beside Lissa, Meer smiled cruelly. "You take from me," he said. "I take from you."

Lissa's chin lifted, her eyes defiant. "You're not going to do anything but die," she said, filling Rand with pride.

Meer ignored her. "Pretty little thing, isn't she? Do you know she tried her tricks on me?" He nuzzled his nose against Lissa's ear. "I think she must like me. What do you think?"

Rand wasn't thinking. He was simply acting.

He wanted to snap and snarl and take Meer down. Wanted to rip his throat out and then claim what was his—the woman. *Lissa.*

He felt the power surge through him. The power of the wolf. His muscles stretching. His canines sharpening, his body shifting into something neither man nor beast, but stronger than either and as clever as both.

He wanted it—he accepted it.

He embraced it.

For a split second, he saw Meer's face as he knocked him backward, loosening his hold on Lissa, whose eyes were blazing with love and approval.

He wanted to tell her she'd been right all along. Right then, he was in complete control. The wolf was doing just fine. And so was the man inside.

They fought, rough and bloody, and painful. Fists smashing against bones. Powerful kicks breaking ribs. Claws slicing through skin. And the scent of blood everywhere.

Rand was slippery with it, his body aching from blows and cuts, his lungs heaving as he launched punch after punch, each one more powerful than the last.

Meer fought hard, giving as good as he got, but in the end, a newly turned creature was no match for the practiced skills of the wolf.

Rand took him down, laying him flat, then breaking his neck.

He left Meer crumpled there like yesterday's garbage, then hurried to Lissa, his elongated fingers no match for the tiny knot of cording.

"Just rip it," she said urgently. He did, and she fell against him, soft flesh brushing against coarse fur. He held her close, his eyes closed, pulling it back in, finding himself again in her arms.

He was Rand, and he was the wolf. And Lissa was right there, holding him tight.

"You're okay," she murmured, her hands roaming over him, as if she couldn't believe he was safe and whole again.

"I'm okay," he said, then kissed her hard. "We're both okay."

A rush of footsteps echoed into the room, and he tensed, ready for a new battle, but this time, it was just the cavalry. Luke and Kiril rushed in, with Doyle, Tucker, and a fully armed RAC team on their heels.

Petra squealed, then raced to her brother. There was no hug, but he held out a gloved hand, and she bumped fists with him, hers still wrapped tight in Rand's shirt.

As Doyle and Tucker took Kessler and Santiago into custody, Luke went to Nick, his face going hard as he listened to Nick's words, and then walked to the truck.

Luke stood there for a moment, then met Nick's eyes. Something unspoken passed between them, and then Luke slipped around the cargo box of the truck, and a moment later Rand heard the engine fire and saw the truck pull out of the bay.

Nick hesitated in the doorway, his gaze searching the room until he found Rand. For a second, his eyes flickered to Lissa, her face pressed against Rand's shoulder.

Nick nodded, a silent salute of acceptance, then he turned away, leaving Rand and Lissa alone in each other's arms.

CHAPTER 43

Tiny white tea candles littered every flat surface in Rand's kitchen—the floor, the counters, the top of the refrigerator. The only surface not covered with candles was the shabby pine table, and that had been transformed into a monument to fine dining. Draped with a silk tablecloth and covered with delicate china, the table could have been the centerpiece of a five-star Parisian restaurant.

Instead, it was the center of a celebration.

"Open your eyes," Lissa said. She'd tugged Rand gently from the living room to the kitchen, which she'd made him promise to avoid throughout the day. Now he opened his eyes and she watched his face, her hard work rewarded when she saw the smile bloom in his eyes. He pulled her close, his arm around her making her feel safe and warm and loved.

"Amazing," he said, then kissed her. "You're amazing."

"You might want to withhold judgment until after you've tasted the food. Before today, my cooking résumé was of the defrost and microwave variety. I've never attempted French cooking."

He laughed. "I told you I would handle the food. You turned me down flat."

She crossed her arms and looked down her nose in an

expression of mock sternness. "This is our celebration. Which means we do the work. Which means you driving to get takeout is out of the question."

"What can I say? My cooking skills are even more meager than yours."

She laughed—today she'd been doing a lot of laughing. That morning they'd received word that the PEC would not seek to prosecute Vincent Rand in the death of Jacob Yannew. The official reason was that the evidence was purely circumstantial. The real reason was that Division would seem utterly disingenuous locking Rand up after the role he'd played in eliminating Meer and capturing his cohorts. Even Tiberius had publicly congratulated the team—including Rand—for wrapping the case . . . and for saving his seat on the Alliance. Although he didn't mention the latter in his official statement.

And since Kessler and Santiago were both in high-security cells with very little chance of ever seeing the light of day again, today was pretty close to perfect.

"We've got almost an hour until the appetizers are ready," she said, moving to the counter where an open bottle of wine was breathing among the candles. She handed him a glass. "Care to join me on the couch?"

"I'll do better than that," he said, setting his glass down beside the one she'd poured for herself. Without warning, he swept her up into his arms. "I think the wine needs to breathe a bit longer."

She nodded, her heart pounding and her skin on fire. He did that to her. With just a touch, a glance, and she didn't think the wonder of that would ever get old.

"An hour?" he asked, settling them both on the

couch, then brushing his lips over hers before skimming his hands up the thin silk of her blouse, her nipples hardening under his hands.

Her breath stuttered in her throat, but she managed a nod. "And, you know. What the hell. If they burn, they burn."

She hooked her arms around his neck and pulled him close, losing herself in the kiss, wanting nothing more than to stay like this forever.

He stroked her arms, deft fingers untucking her blouse, hands trailing over sensitive skin. Before she knew it, she was naked, and he was over her, equally bare, and just as turned on. "Amazing," he said, stroking her cheek.

"What?"

"That you're mine." He slid into her, the words making her gasp with pleasure as much as the joining. She *was* his. And the truly amazing thing was that he was hers.

They made love slowly, lazily, and she never wanted it to end. He was close—threads of soul starting to peek out and twine around them, vibrant in the dim glow of candlelight cast through the open door.

When he pulled out, she wanted to cry, so badly did she want that ultimate connection. Not just sex, but her lover's soul. She craved it . . . and yet still hadn't tasted it.

He shifted, looking down at her face. "Lissa."

She didn't meet his eyes. "It's nothing. I'm just thinking. About everything." That wasn't a lie. The events of the past few weeks were almost constantly on her mind. "It's ironic, don't you think? Meer didn't give a damn about the feud between the weren and the vamps. And Santiago couldn't care less about building supersoldiers with vampiric traits. And yet they each fueled the other."

"With Kessler in it for the science. Or so he says."

She shivered, finding the idea of mucking with shadow biology particularly disturbing. At least the doctor was locked up tight.

"Have you heard any more about Petra?" she asked. As far as the PEC knew, Serge had gone missing in the confusion at the warehouse, and now the PEC was circling Petra, making noises about how she should have come forward and identified herself as a dangerous entity, something that worried Lissa a great deal.

"Last I heard there's going to be a formal inquiry."

"That doesn't sound good."

"If it comes to it," he said, "we'll speak for her."

She kissed him lightly. "I love you," she said, simply because it made her feel good to say it.

"That's good," he said. "Because I'm here to stay."

"You damn sure better be," she said, teasing, then realized what he'd actually said. She shifted so that she had a better look at his face. "Here?" she repeated.

"You don't want to leave Orlando's, do you?"

Her breath hitched. "You know I don't."

"And I don't want to leave you."

"So . . . " she prompted.

"So I spoke with Gunnolf this morning. How do you feel about a quick trip to Paris? See the sights, pack up my things?"

"Pack up?" She threw her arms around him and hugged him exuberantly. "You're staying here? Truly?

In Los Angeles?" He was right—she wouldn't leave Orlando's, but that didn't mean she couldn't move it, and relocating had been on her mind. She didn't want to, but if that was the only way to stay with Rand . . .

"Are you sure? It's Los Angeles," she said, knowing how he felt about the town he'd grown up in.

"I'm sure." He stretched out on the couch and pulled her close, so that her side and cheek rested against his chest. Slowly, he stroked her hair. "Do you remember me telling you about my Aunt Estelle?"

"Of course."

"I drove by her house," he said. "Not long after I got into town. Just drove by and looked at it, and thought how much I wanted to go in and see her."

"Did you?"

"No." He said nothing else, but Lissa understood.

"Do you want to go see her now?"

"No," he said again, and she opened her mouth to argue. To make him see once and for all that he wasn't the beast that for so long he'd imagined he saw staring back from the mirror.

"Wait," he said, before she could speak. "Let me finish." He drew in a breath. "I don't want to go because that's not my world anymore. But I've been thinking about her, and, well, maybe after all these years I did turn out okay. Maybe I am a man she'd be proud of."

"You are," Lissa said, sliding up his body to seal her words with a soft, sweet kiss that didn't stay sweet for long. A low growl rolled in his throat, and she opened her mouth to him, closing her eyes as his hands skimmed down, caressing her back, her rear.

Gentle caresses that built into frantic touches until

they couldn't wait any longer and she straddled him, lowering herself and letting him fill her, the rhythm of their movements making her wild, making her want more and more.

Making her want everything. The man, the soul, as much as she could get, if not today, then soon. Oh, please, please soon . . .

His hand slid down, stroking her where their bodies were joined, and she tossed back her head, letting the heady sensations fill her, then gasping when she opened her eyes and saw the colored strands of his soul twining around them. Almost afraid this was a fantasy, she reached out, letting a shimmer of soul trail up her arm, gliding over her skin, brushing her with ecstasy, making her feel flush and alive.

"Rand," she whispered. "Oh, God, Rand—*there's more.*"

She felt him shift beneath her, alert.

"I wish you could see it. The new parts are so vibrant they glow."

"Is there enough to take?" His voice was rough. Needy.

She hesitated, wanting it so badly, and yet . . . "Just barely."

"Take some," he said.

She wanted to—oh, how she wanted that final connection between them—but she was afraid of moving too fast.

"Take," he said, and she heard an almost sensual plea in his voice. "There's enough. You know I'm right, and I can't wait any longer."

His words crashed over her. *He* couldn't wait any longer?

"I want this, Lissa. I want to know that part of me is inside you. I want to fill you up every way that I can."

Her heart beat faster, and she nodded, then closed her eyes and let the soul flow around her, this time not just playing with it but actually taking it in, soaking it in through her pores, letting it color her and fill her.

Letting *Rand* fill her.

Dear God, it felt like heaven.

With increasing urgency, they rocked together, getting closer and closer, sensation building. She watched his face, felt his body, and when he came, it was like a rainbow showering down upon her, an ecstasy of color and pleasure like nothing she'd ever experienced before, even in all her lives—all her years.

And with the soul came the inevitable thoughts—a peek inside Rand's head.

Right then, only one thought filled his mind: *Lissa*. And how much he loved her.

She bent forward and pressed a kiss to his lips. "I love you, too," she whispered. "For always."

PROLOGUE

The vampires moved through the night, their unconscious cargo even more deadly than they—who had seen much throughout the centuries—could imagine.

"We need a secure location," Nicholas said. He had an angel's face and a scientist's mind. But nothing in his studies had prepared him for the transformation he had just witnessed in his friend.

"I know a place." Lucius, practical and methodical, steered the truck through the Los Angeles night. They had escaped a fierce battle, but this wasn't over. Both of them knew that for their friend Sergius—tranqued in the cargo bay—it might never be over. Once a tormented vampire whose daemon had fought for release, he was now so much worse, his reality shifted by nothing more substantial than a touch.

The girl's curse had transformed him into something unnatural and terrifying. Something monstrous even by the broad standards of a world that lived in shadows and hovered on the fringes of human nightmares.

"They will look for him," Nicholas said. "If we want to have any chance of reversing this thing, I need time to investigate. Time to think."

"The girl said there was no way to reverse the transformation."

"The girl is human. She may well be wrong."

Lucius nodded. "We don't have time, especially once word of what happened spreads. The Alliance will search for Sergius. And eventually they will find him."

"Not if they believe there is no reason to look."

Lucius took his eyes off the road long enough to glance briefly at Nicholas. "You have a plan."

"A pound of flesh," Nicholas said, his voice heavy with purpose. "Not taken in the service of justice, but instead as the price for time."

CHAPTER 1

Petra Lang did not want to die.

Too bad she didn't have even the slightest say in the matter.

A specially convened Alliance Tribunal had indicted her, an Alliance prosecutor had outlined the evidence against her, and the high examiner had sentenced her. Now she awaited her punishment from within a coffin-size portable holding cell, her hands bound tight in front of her despite the fact that the space was so tiny, there was no way she could have even shot someone the finger, were she so inclined.

And, frankly, she was definitely so inclined. As far as she was concerned, the preternatural assholes who'd sentenced her to die deserved one hell of a lot more than a rude gesture.

Never mind that she was willing to submit to whatever restrictive and oppressive rules the Alliance wanted to subject her to. Because of her curse, she'd been deemed a danger to both the human and shadow communities, and in less than an hour she would be dead.

She closed her eyes, trying not to think about it. Trying not to wonder if it would hurt or if she would slip softly away into the black. Trying not to wish she'd had the chance to lift the curse, to touch a man, to see the friggin' Eiffel Tower or the Great Wall of China. Hell, she'd never even made it up to San Francisco to see the Golden Gate Bridge. She was only twenty-six. She wasn't supposed to die.

She hoped she wouldn't cry; if she could make it without tears, at least then she could take some small victory with her to the grave.

Mostly, she thought about Kiril. Worried about him. Her brother who'd dedicated his life to protecting her. The boy who wrote such beautiful poems and could spend hours searching for the proper word for one of his short stories. The sorcerer who'd exploded in a frenzy of wind and thunder when the elite Covert Alliance Apprehension Squad had burst through the door of their house in Studio City.

The squad members had gone for Kiril first, with such swiftness that Petra had assumed they'd come for her brother and had no interest in her. She'd tried to help him, but though the family's magic flowed in her veins, too, the curse had always interfered, and summoning her meager power during a crisis had never been easy for her.

Instead, she'd watched, horrified, as the officers fired tranquilizer darts at him, the magic fading as Kiril collapsed unconscious onto the floor. She'd raced to him, but hadn't made it to his side. Instead, a burly officer had lassoed her—*lassoed!*—then dragged her back toward the door.

She'd fought, digging in her heels, tugging on the rope, screaming for her brother. But she had never once run toward her captor. Never tried to rip the cloth that covered his body from nose to toes. Never yanked her own glove off or tried to touch skin upon skin.

She hadn't used the curse to fight back—she hadn't even tried.

And yet it was for that very curse that she would die tonight. She'd intentionally pushed the curse once. Only once. And it had been Serge's decision as much as her own. The vampire knew what would happen—what he would become. But they'd had no choice. They'd been trapped, and time had been running out.

It had been a total Hail Mary ploy, but it had paid off. She'd touched, he'd transformed, and the monster he became had wreaked havoc on their captors.

Serge had sacrificed his sanity, his soul, and even his life to save countless more, but did the Alliance care? Not one damn bit. They didn't look at the reason or the result, they looked only at the curse, at what she could wreak with nothing more substantial than the slightest brush of skin against skin.

She closed her eyes, clenched her fists at her sides, and wished she had the power to turn back time. If she had, she wouldn't hesitate. She would touch them all and take her chances with the vicious monsters she unleashed. She would do that very thing for which they were now executing her. She would turn them all, torture them all, and, dammit, she would fight to live.

She didn't deserve this.

Tears pricked her eyes, spilling out over her lashes, and she tried to lift a hand to wipe them away, then reacted in fear and fury when her arm wouldn't move. She couldn't even dry her own damn tears! Dear God, she hadn't asked for this. Didn't want it. Would walk away if she could, so how was it fair that she died tonight, when she'd spent her whole life apart and alone, protecting the entire world from what she was?

Stop it! Stop thinking!

She almost wished the guards would hurry up and come. Right then, locked in the small concrete cell, she had no company other than her thoughts. And those thoughts were tormenting her.

"Prisoner!"

A tremor ran up her spine, and she took back the earlier wish. She wasn't ready, not at all.

"Prisoner!"

"Yes." Her voice was soft, but she took a small bit of pride from the fact that it didn't shake.

"It is time."

"What about my brother? My advocate? Can't I see them?" Didn't the condemned have the right to say good-bye to their family? To speak one last time to their legal representative?

"Your brother's request for visitation has been denied."

"Oh." She squeezed her eyes shut, not quite able to believe she wouldn't get the chance to say good-bye to Kiril, that she'd never again hold his hand when a blue moon filled the sky, or read one of his stories, or harass him about kicking up a whirlwind inside the house. Her chest tightened. There were too many things left undone. Too many things she still wanted to say. Now she'd never be able to.

She swallowed, forcing thoughts of her brother out of her mind. "What about Montegue?" she asked, referring to Nicholas Montegue, the vampire advocate who had represented her during the proceedings. Following the verdict and sentencing, he'd filed an appeal with the Alliance, specifically addressing it to Tiberius, the governor of the Shadow Alliance's Los Angeles territory.

Petra still hadn't heard the outcome, but Nicholas had been hopeful. Tiberius, he'd said, owed her one.

"The appeal was denied," the voice said. "The Tribunal has ordered that your execution proceed with all due speed. And Montegue filed no request to visit or be present at the execution."

She tried to draw a breath as the walls of the already tiny cell seemed to crowd even closer against her while she processed what the voice was saying. He'd fought for her—spent hours researching centuries of shadow law and drafting brief after brief, his intensity and determination so thick that she'd actually dared to hope.

He'd been her courage during the weeks leading up to the hearing, and she'd relied on his quiet strength and sharp reputation. He was Nicholas Montegue, after all, the advocate who represented all vampiric interests on behalf of the Alliance. Who had a hand in the affairs of Tiberius himself.

If anyone could see her safely out of this mess, it was Nicholas. And each day she'd anticipated his visit, eagerly working beside him, poring over the cases he'd copied and the statutes he'd dug up from faraway jurisdictions, so desperately grateful that he'd given her the gift of hope.

But that hope had died with the sentencing, and now he couldn't even face her?

How completely pathetic.

"Prisoner!" The sharp voice brought her back to the

present, to the small cell and the reality in front of her. "Do you willingly accept your fate?"

"No!" The word seemed to burst from her mouth without any forethought.

There was nothing but silence around her, and she took some small satisfaction in having apparently mucked up their formality, even if only a little.

"You may proceed," the voice said, only this time he wasn't speaking to her. Within moments, the air in the cell grew thicker, as if it were pressing in against her head; after a few seconds, the air seemed to be actually drilling into her. She wanted to reach up and clasp her skull in her palms—wanted to press her hands hard against her cranium and hold her head together before it exploded—but her shoulders were jammed against the concrete walls and there was no moving; she could only scream, and scream, and scream.

Something creeping.

Something looking.

Something moving like a worm through her mind. Digging and twisting and turning. Searching.

Searching . . .

It hurt. Oh dear God, it hurt, and as the pain spread out through her body—as bile rose in her throat and her chest heaved in acid-filled gags—she realized what it was. A Truth Teller, a rare creature in the shadow world. Although she'd spent years poking around in the shadows trying to find the truth for her clients, she'd never once met anyone who'd experienced the mindmeld of a Truth Teller. It was horrible, and the more the creature poked around, the worse it became.

What the hell was it looking for?

The claws of the Teller's grasp scraped through the dark spots of her mind, riffling through long-forgotten memories, stirring up lost scents and fears and small joys along with the raw, red pain of the search.

And then, as fast as it had entered, the intruder withdrew. Her head felt strange, as if there was cotton inside it, and she had to struggle not to sink into herself but to instead listen to the low voices outside her small concrete prison.

"Clean," announced the baritone voice. "There are no plots. No plans for escape. She will take no secrets to her grave. Her mind is prepared to die."

No, she wanted to shout. *No, it wasn't.* Her mind wasn't any more prepared than she was. But it didn't matter. They didn't care.

This wasn't about her; it was about the ceremony.

It was about the result.

With a jolt, the concrete cell into which she was locked started to rise. She was being lifted to the execution chamber. This was it. Time's up. *Arrivederci, au revoir,* and *auld lang syne.*

Petra tried to swallow, but her throat was too thick. She couldn't do anything anymore.

All she could do now was die.

CHAPTER 2

The small cell rose through the floor, then came to a stop with a sudden jolt, shaking Petra and kicking her pulse back up, her body primed for flight even though there was nowhere to flee. Without warning, the front and side walls of her tiny cell fell away, crashing to the ground with a thud that reverberated through the chamber. She was on the stage of a very small theater, her back still strapped to the standing concrete block, on display for the three Tribunal members who sat in the plush chairs and stared at her, their faces impassive.

She'd witnessed executions in the Preternatural Enforcement Coalition's theater before, but those were always following a criminal conviction and took place in a cavernous room with dozens upon dozens of witnesses. Her termination might be taking place within the walls of the PEC, but this was an Alliance execution, not punishment rendered following a crime.

She was not being executed because of what she'd done to the vampire but because they were afraid of what she might do in the future. She scared them, and because of that they were going to kill her.

She forced her chin high. It was their shame, not her actions, that had her dying in this dingy little room; the shame of knowing that what they did was unjust. Vile. And as she looked out upon the three of them, she hoped her expression telegraphed what she didn't have the guts to voice: *Screw you all.*

She recognized the three, of course. Dirque, Trylag, and Narid. A jinn, a para-daemon, and a wraith, and all three members of the Alliance.

She'd seen them every day during the charade they'd called a hearing. She'd hated them during the trial, and she didn't feel any more charitable to them now. They were the last people she wanted to watch her die. She wanted Kiril. Hell, she wanted Nicholas. But the guard was right—neither her brother nor her own advocate would be with her at the end. She'd been isolated her entire life, and she'd learned to accept that. This, however . . . this bruised her heart.

A door in the center of the back wall opened, and since the theater had only two rows of seats, she could easily see the face of the person who stepped in. Or she could have seen him had he not been covered head to toe in black, swathed just as she was. Her they'd covered so that an accidental brush against her skin could bring no harm. He was covered, not for safety, but for anonymity.

The executioner.

Dirque, acting as the high examiner, stood, a brooding jinn who ruled the territories he governed with an iron hand. The executioner lifted a bow, then notched an arrow into it. Petra tried to breathe and realized she couldn't.

"Petra Lang!" the executioner called in a low, harsh voice that seemed almost familiar. "This Tribunal has determined you to be a Dangerous Entity and subject to termination pursuant to the Fifth International Covenant and the Common Law of the shadow world. I ask the high examiner: Is this so?"

Dirque's eyes glowed yellow in the dimly lit room, and his mouth stretched into a thin, smug smile. "The punishment is just and good."

"Petra Lang, do you have any last words?"

Did she? She wanted to talk and talk. To babble her way back to life. But she didn't. What was the point? All the talk in the world would change nothing, and in the end she'd be six feet under.

"Then let us proceed."

In the audience, the high examiner returned to his seat. In the back of the room, the executioner positioned the bow, the tip of an arrow aimed straight for her heart. Slowly, he pulled the string back. In front of her, not one spectator moved. No one in the room even breathed.